NON SANZ DROICT.

The Tragedy of
CORIOLANUS

Edited by Reuben Brower

The Signet Classic Shakespeare
GENERAL EDITOR: SYLVAN BARNET

*Revised and Updated
Bibliography*

A SIGNET CLASSIC
NEW AMERICAN LIBRARY
TIMES MIRROR
NEW YORK AND SCARBOROUGH, ONTARIO

SIGNET, SIGNET CLASSICS, MENTOR, PLUME, MERIDIAN AND NAL
BOOKS are published *in the United States* by
The New American Library, Inc.,
1633 Broadway, New York, New York 10019,
in Canada by the New American Library of Canada Limited,
81 Mack Avenue, Scarborough, Ontario M1L 1M8

First Printing, January, 1966

8   9   10   11   12   13   14   15   16

PRINTED IN THE UNITED STATES OF AMERICA

Contents

Contents

Shakespeare: Prefatory Remarks

Between the record of his baptism in Stratford on 26 April 1564 and the record of his burial in Stratford on 25 April 1616, some forty documents name Shakespeare, and many others name his parents, his children, and his grandchildren. More facts are known about William Shakespeare than about any other playwright of the period except Ben Jonson. The facts should, however, be distinguished from the legends. The latter, inevitably more engaging and better known, tell us that the Stratford boy killed a calf in high style, poached deer and rabbits, and was forced to flee to London, where he held horses outside a playhouse. These traditions are only traditions; they may be true, but no evidence supports them, and it is well to stick to the facts.

Mary Arden, the dramatist's mother, was the daughter of a substantial landowner; about 1557 she married John Shakespeare, who was a glove-maker and trader in various farm commodities. In 1557 John Shakespeare was a member of the Council (the governing body of Stratford), in 1558 a constable of the borough, in 1561 one of the two town chamberlains, in 1565 an alderman (entitling him to the appellation "Mr."), in 1568 high bailiff—the town's highest political office, equivalent to mayor. After 1577, for an unknown reason he drops out of local politics. The birthday of William Shakespeare, the eldest son of this locally prominent man, is unrecorded; but the Stratford parish register records that the infant was baptized on 26 April 1564. (It is quite possible that he was born on 23 April, but this date has probably been assigned by tradition because it is the date on which, fifty-two years later, he died.) The attendance records of the Stratford grammar school of the period are not extant, but it is reasonable to assume that the son of a local official attended the school and received substantial training in Latin. The masters of the school from Shakespeare's seventh to fifteenth years held Oxford degrees; the Elizabethan curriculum excluded mathematics and the natural sciences but taught a good deal of Latin rhetoric, logic, and literature. On 27 November 1582 a marriage license was issued to Shakespeare and Anne Hathaway, eight years his senior. The couple had a child in May, 1583. Perhaps the marriage was necessary, but perhaps the couple had earlier engaged in a formal "troth plight" which would render their children legitimate even if no further ceremony were performed. In 1585 Anne Hathaway bore Shakespeare twins.

That Shakespeare was born is excellent; that he married and had children is pleasant; but that we know nothing about his departure from Stratford to London, or about the beginning of his theatrical career, is lamentable and must be admitted. We would gladly sacrifice details about his children's baptism for details about his earliest days on the stage. Perhaps the poaching episode is true (but it is first reported almost a century after Shakespeare's death), or perhaps he first left Stratford to be a schoolteacher, as another tradition holds; perhaps he was moved by

> Such wind as scatters young men through the world,
> To seek their fortunes further than at home
> Where small experience grows.

In 1592, thanks to the cantankerousness of Robert Greene, a rival playwright and a pamphleteer, we have our first reference, a snarling one, to Shakespeare as an actor and playwright. Greene warns those of his own educated friends who wrote for the theater against an actor who has presumed to turn playwright:

> There is an upstart crow, beautified with our feathers,
> that with his *tiger's heart wrapped in a player's hide* sup-
> poses he is as well able to bombast out a blank verse as
> the best of you, and being an absolute Johannes-factotum
> is in his own conceit the only Shake-scene in a country.

The reference to the player, as well as the allusion to
Aesop's crow (who strutted in borrowed plumage, as an
actor struts in fine words not his own), makes it clear
that by this date Shakespeare had both acted and written. That Shakespeare is meant is indicated not only by
"Shake-scene" but by the parody of a line from one of
Shakespeare's plays, *3 Henry VI:* "O, tiger's heart wrapped
in a woman's hide." If Shakespeare in 1592 was prominent enough to be attacked by an envious dramatist, he
probably had served an apprenticeship in the theater for
at least a few years.

In any case, by 1592 Shakespeare had acted and
written, and there are a number of subsequent references
to him as an actor: documents indicate that in 1598 he
is a "principal comedian," in 1603 a "principal tragedian,"
in 1608 he is one of the "men players." The profession
of actor was not for a gentleman, and it occasionally drew
the scorn of university men who resented writing speeches
for persons less educated than themselves, but it was
respectable enough: players, if prosperous, were in effect
members of the bourgeoisie, and there is nothing to suggest that Stratford considered William Shakespeare less
than a solid citizen. When, in 1596, the Shakespeares
were granted a coat of arms, the grant was made to Shakespeare's father, but probably William Shakespeare (who
the next year bought the second-largest house in town)
had arranged the matter on his own behalf. In subsequent
transactions he is occasionally styled a gentleman.

Although in 1593 and 1594 Shakespeare published two
narrative poems dedicated to the Earl of Southampton,
Venus and Adonis and *The Rape of Lucrece,* and may
well have written most or all of his sonnets in the middle nineties, Shakespeare's literary activity seems to have
been almost entirely devoted to the theater. (It may be

significant that the two narrative poems were written in years when the plague closed the theaters for several months.) In 1594 he was a charter member of a theatrical company called the Chamberlain's Men (which in 1603 changed its name to the King's Men); until he retired to Stratford (about 1611, apparently), he was with this remarkably stable company. From 1599 the company acted primarily at the Globe Theatre, in which Shakespeare held a one-tenth interest. Other Elizabethan dramatists are known to have acted, but no other is known also to have been entitled to a share in the profits of the playhouse.

Shakespeare's first eight published plays did not have his name on them, but this is not remarkable; the most popular play of the sixteenth century, Thomas Kyd's *The Spanish Tragedy,* went through many editions without naming Kyd, and Kyd's authorship is known only because a book on the profession of acting happens to quote (and attribute to Kyd) some lines on the interest of Roman emperors in the drama. What is remarkable is that after 1598 Shakespeare's name commonly appears on printed plays—some of which are not his. Another indication of his popularity comes from. Francis Meres, author of *Palladis Tamia: Wit's Treasury* (1598): in this anthology of snippets accompanied by an essay on literature, many playwrights are mentioned, but Shakespeare's name occurs more often than any other, and Shakespeare is the only playwright whose plays are listed.

From his acting, playwriting, and share in a theater, Shakespeare seems to have made considerable money. He put it to work, making substantial investments in Stratford real estate. When he made his will (less than a month before he died), he sought to leave his property intact to his descendants. Of small bequests to relatives and to friends (including three actors, Richard Burbage, John Heminges, and Henry Condell), that to his wife of the second-best bed has provoked the most comment; perhaps it was the bed the couple had slept in, the best being reserved for visitors. In any case, had Shakespeare not excepted it, the bed would have gone (with the rest of his household possessions) to his daughter and her husband. On 25 April 1616 he was buried within the chancel of the church at Stratford. An unattractive monument to his memory, placed on a wall near the grave, says he died on 23 April. Over the grave itself are the lines, perhaps by Shakespeare, that (more than his literary fame) have kept his bones undisturbed in the crowded burial ground where old bones were often dislodged to make way for new:

> Good friend, for Jesus' sake forbear
> To dig the dust enclosèd here.
> Blessed be the man that spares these stones
> And cursed be he that moves my bones.

Thirty-seven plays, as well as some nondramatic poems, are held to constitute the Shakespeare canon. The dates of composition of most of the works are highly uncertain, but there is often evidence of a *terminus a quo* (starting point) and/or a *terminus ad quem* (terminal point) that provides a framework for intelligent guessing. For example, *Richard II* cannot be earlier than 1595, the publication date of some material to which it is indebted; *The Merchant of Venice* cannot be later than 1598, the year Francis Meres mentioned it. Sometimes arguments for a date hang on an alleged topical allusion, such as the lines about the unseasonable weather in *A Midsummer Night's Dream*, II.i.81–117, but such an allusion (if indeed it is an allusion) can be variously interpreted, and in any case there is always the possibility that a topical allusion was inserted during a revision, years after the composition of a play. Dates are often attributed on the basis of style, and although conjectures about style usually rest on other conjectures, sooner or later one must rely on one's literary sense. There is no real proof, for example, that *Othello* is not as early as *Romeo and Juliet*, but one feels *Othello* is later, and because the first record of its performance is 1604, one is glad enough to set its composition at that date and not push it back into Shakespeare's early years. The following chronology, then, is as much indebted to informed guesswork and sensitivity as it is to fact. The dates, necessarily imprecise, indicate something like a scholarly consensus.

PLAYS

1588–93	*The Comedy of Errors*
1588–94	*Love's Labor's Lost*
1590–91	*2 Henry VI*
1590–91	*3 Henry VI*
1591–92	*1 Henry VI*
1592–93	*Richard III*
1592–94	*Titus Andronicus*
1593–94	*The Taming of the Shrew*
1593–95	*The Two Gentlemen of Verona*
1594–96	*Romeo and Juliet*
1595	*Richard II*
1594–96	*A Midsummer Night's Dream*
1596–97	*King John*
1596–97	*The Merchant of Venice*
1597	*1 Henry IV*
1597–98	*2 Henry IV*
1598–1600	*Much Ado About Nothing*
1598–99	*Henry V*
1599	*Julius Caesar*
1599–1600	*As You Like It*
1599–1600	*Twelfth Night*
1600–01	*Hamlet*
1597–1601	*The Merry Wives of Windsor*
1601–02	*Troilus and Cressida*
1602–04	*All's Well That Ends Well*
1603–04	*Othello*
1604	*Measure for Measure*
1605–06	*King Lear*
1605–06	*Macbeth*
1606–07	*Antony and Cleopatra*
1605–08	*Timon of Athens*

Shakespeare's Theater

In Shakespeare's infancy, Elizabethan actors performed wherever they could—in great halls, at court, in the courtyards of inns. The innyards must have made rather unsatisfactory theaters: on some days they were unavailable because carters bringing goods to London used them as depots; when available, they had to be rented from the innkeeper; perhaps most important, London inns were subject to the Common Council of London, which was not well disposed toward theatricals. In 1574 the Common Council required that plays and playing places in London be licensed. It asserted that

> sundry great disorders and inconveniences have been found to ensure to this city by the inordinate haunting of great multitudes of people, specially youth, to plays, interludes, and shows, namely occasion of frays and quarrels, evil practices of incontinency in great inns having chambers and secret places adjoining to their open stages and galleries,

and ordered that innkeepers who wished licenses to hold performances put up a bond and make contributions to the poor.

The requirement that plays and innyard theaters be licensed, along with the other drawbacks of playing at inns, probably drove James Burbage (a carpenter-turned-actor) to rent in 1576 a plot of land northeast of the city walls and to build here—on property outside the jurisdiction of the city—England's first permanent construction designed for plays. He called it simply the Theatre. About all that is known of its construction is that it was wood. It soon had imitators, the most famous being the Globe (1599), built across the Thames (again outside the city's jurisdiction), out of timbers of the Theatre, which had been dismantled when Burbage's lease ran out.

There are three important sources of information about the structure of Elizabethan playhouses — drawings, a contract, and stage directions in plays. Of drawings, only the so-called De Witt drawing (c. 1596) of the Swan— really a friend's copy of De Witt's drawing—is of much significance. It shows a building of three tiers, with a stage jutting from a wall into the yard or center of the building. The tiers are roofed, and part of the stage is covered by a roof that projects from the rear and is supported at its front on two posts, but the groundlings, who paid a penny to stand in front of the stage, were exposed to the sky. (Performances in such a playhouse were held only in the daytime; artificial illumination was not used.) At the rear of the stage are two doors; above the stage is a gallery. The second major source of information, the contract for the Fortune, specifies that although the Globe is to be the model, the Fortune is to be square, eighty feet outside and fifty-five inside. The stage is to be forty-three feet broad, and is to extend into the middle of the yard (i.e., it is twenty-seven and a half feet deep). For patrons willing to pay more than the general admission charged of the groundlings, there were to be three galleries provided with seats. From the third chief source, stage directions, one learns that entrance to the stage was by doors, presumably spaced widely apart at the rear ("Enter one citizen at one door, and another at the other"), and that in addition to the platform stage there was occasionally some sort of curtained booth or alcove allowing for "discovery" scenes, and some sort of playing space "aloft" or "above" to represent (for example) the top of a city's walls or a room above the street. Doubtless each theater had its own peculiarities, but perhaps we can talk about a "typical" Elizabethan theater if we realize that no theater need exactly have fitted the description, just as no father is the typical father with 3.7 children. This hypothetical theater is wooden, round or polygonal (in *Henry V* Shakespeare calls it a "wooden *O*"), capable of holding some eight hundred spectators standing in the yard around the projecting elevated stage and some fifteen hundred additional spectators seated in the three roofed galleries. The stage, protected by a "shadow" or "heavens" or roof, is entered by two doors; behind the doors is the "tiring house" (attiring house, i.e., dressing room), and above the doors is some sort of gallery that may sometimes hold spectators but that can be used (for example) as the bedroom from which Romeo—according to a stage direction in one text—"goeth down." Some evidence suggests that a throne can be lowered onto the platform stage, perhaps from the "shadow"; certainly characters can descend from the stage through a trap or traps into the cellar or "hell." Sometimes this space beneath the platform accommodates a sound-effects man or musician (in *Antony and Cleopatra* "music of the hautboys is under the stage") or an actor (in *Hamlet* the "Ghost cries under the stage"). Most characters simply walk on and off, but because there is no curtain in front of the platform, corpses will have to be carried off (Hamlet must lug Polonius' guts into the neighbor room), or will have to fall at the rear, where the curtain on the alcove or booth can be drawn to conceal them.

Such may have been the so-called "public theater." Another kind of theater, called the "private theater" because its much greater admission charge limited its audience to the wealthy or the prodigal, must be briefly mentioned. The private theater was basically a large room, entirely roofed and therefore artificially illuminated, with a stage at one end. In 1576 one such theater was established in Blackfriars, a Dominican priory in London that had been suppressed in 1538 and confiscated by the Crown and thus was not under the city's jurisdiction. All the actors in the Blackfriars theater were boys about eight to thirteen years old (in the public theaters similar boys played female parts; a boy Lady Macbeth played to a man Macbeth). This private theater had a precarious existence, and ceased operations in 1584. In 1596 James Burbage, who had already made theatrical history by building the Theatre, began to construct a second Blackfriars theater. He died in 1597, and for several years this second Blackfriars theater was used by a troupe of boys, but in 1608 two of Burbage's sons and five other actors (including Shakespeare) became joint operators of the theater, using it in the winter when the open-air Globe was unsuitable. Perhaps such a smaller theater, roofed, artificially illuminated, and with a tradition of a courtly audience, exerted an influence on Shakespeare's late plays.

Performances in the private theaters may well have had intermissions during which music was played, but in the public theaters the action was probably uninterrupted, flowing from scene to scene almost without a break. Actors would enter, speak, exit, and others would immediately enter and establish (if necessary) the new locale by a few properties and by words and gestures. Here are some samples of Shakespeare's scene painting:

> This is Illyria, lady.

> Well, this is the Forest of Arden.

> This castle hath a pleasant seat; the air
> Nimbly and sweetly recommends itself
> Unto our gentle senses.

On the other hand, it is a mistake to conceive of the Elizabethan stage as bare. Although Shakespeare's Chorus in *Henry V* calls the stage an "unworthy scaffold" and urges the spectators to "eke out our performance with your mind," there was considerable spectacle. The last act of *Macbeth*, for example, has five stage directions calling for "drum and colors," and another sort of appeal to the eye is indicated by the stage direction "Enter Macduff, with Macbeth's head." Some scenery and properties may have been substantial; doubtless a throne was used, and in one play of the period we encounter this direction: "Hector takes up a great piece of rock and casts at Ajax, who tears up a young tree by the roots and assails Hector." The matter is of some importance, and will be glanced at again in the next section.

The Texts of Shakespeare

Though eighteen of his plays were published during his lifetime, Shakespeare seems never to have supervised their publication. There is nothing unusual here; when a playwright sold a play to a theatrical company he surrendered his ownership of it. Normally a company would not publish the play, because to publish it meant to allow competitors to acquire the piece. Some plays, however, did get published: apparently treacherous actors sometimes pieced together a play for a publisher, sometimes a company in need of money sold a play, and sometimes a company allowed a play to be published that no longer drew audiences. That Shakespeare did not concern himself with publication, then, is scarcely remarkable; of his contemporaries only Ben Jonson carefully supervised the publication of his own plays. In 1623, seven years after Shakespeare's death, John Heminges and Henry Condell (two senior members of Shakespeare's company, who had performed with him for about twenty years) collected his plays—published and unpublished—into a large volume, commonly called the First Folio. (A folio is a volume consisting of sheets that have been folded once, each sheet thus making two leaves, or four pages. The eighteen plays published during Shakespeare's lifetime had been issued one play per volume in small books called quartos. Each sheet in a quarto has been folded twice, making four leaves, or eight pages.) The First Folio contains thirty-six plays; a thirty-seventh, *Pericles,* though not in the Folio is regarded as canonical. Heminges and Condell suggest in an address "To the great variety of readers" that the republished plays are presented in better form than in the quartos: "Before you were abused with diverse stolen and surreptitious copies, maimed and deformed by the frauds and stealths of injurious impostors that exposed them; even those, are now offered to your view cured and perfect of their limbs, and all the rest absolute in their numbers, as he [i.e., Shakespeare] conceived them."

Whoever was assigned to prepare the texts for publication in the First Folio seems to have taken his job seriously and yet not to have performed it with uniform care. The sources of the texts seem to have been, in general, good unpublished copies or the best published copies. The first play in the collection, *The Tempest,* is divided into acts and scenes, has unusually full stage directions and descriptions of spectacle, and concludes with a list of the characters, but the editor was not able (or willing) to present all of the succeeding texts so fully dressed. Later texts occasionally show signs of carelessness: in one scene of *Much Ado About Nothing* the names of actors, instead of characters, appear as speech prefixes, as they had in the quarto, which the Folio reprints; proofreading throughout the Folio is spotty and apparently was done without reference to the printer's copy; the pagination of *Hamlet* jumps from 156 to 257.

A modern editor of Shakespeare must first select his copy; no problem if the play exists only in the Folio, but a considerable problem if the relationship between a quarto and the Folio—or an early quarto and a later one—is unclear. When an editor has chosen what seems to him to be the most authoritative text or texts for his copy, he has not done with making decisions. First of all, he must reckon with Elizabethan spelling. If he is not producing a facsimile, he probably modernizes it, but ought he to preserve the old form of words that apparently were pronounced quite unlike their modern forms—"lanthorn," "alablaster"? If he preserves these forms, is he really preserving Shakespeare's forms or perhaps those of a compositor in the printing house? What is one to do when one finds "lanthorn" and "lantern" in adjacent lines? (The editors of this series in general, but not invariably, assume that words should be spelled in their modern form.) Elizabethan punctuation, too, presents problems. For example in the First Folio, the only text for the play, Macbeth rejects his wife's idea that he can wash the blood from his hand:

> no: this my Hand will rather
> The multitudinous Seas incarnardine,
> Making the Greene one, Red.

Obviously an editor will remove the superfluous capitals, and he will probably alter the spelling to "incarnadine," but will he leave the comma before "red," letting Macbeth speak of the sea as "the green one," or will he (like most modern editors) remove the comma and thus have Macbeth say that his hand will make the ocean *uniformly* red?

An editor will sometimes have to change more than spelling or punctuation. Macbeth says to his wife:

> I dare do all that may become a man,
> Who dares no more, is none.

For two centuries editors have agreed that the second line is unsatisfactory, and have emended "no" to "do": "Who dares do more is none." But when in the same play Ross says that fearful persons

> floate vpon a wilde and violent Sea
> Each way, and moue,

need "move" be emended to "none," as it often is, on the hunch that the compositor misread the manuscript? The editors of the Signet Classic Shakespeare have restrained themselves from making abundant emendations. In their minds they hear Dr. Johnson on the dangers of emending: "I have adopted the Roman sentiment, that it is more honorable to save a citizen than to kill an enemy." Some departures (in addition to spelling, punctuation, and lineation) from the copy text have of course been made, but the original readings are listed in a note following the play, so that the reader can evaluate them for himself.

The editors of the Signet Classic Shakespeare, following tradition, have added line numbers and in many cases act and scene divisions as well as indications of locale at the beginning of scenes. The Folio divided most of the plays into acts and some into scenes. Early eighteenth-century editors increased the divisions. These divisions, which provide a convenient way of referring to passages in the plays, have been retained, but when not in the text chosen as the basis for the Signet Classic text they are enclosed in square brackets [ ] to indicate that they are editorial additions. Similarly, although no play of Shakespeare's published during his lifetime was equipped with indications of locale at the heads of scene divisions, locales have here been added in square brackets for the convenience of the reader, who lacks the information afforded to spectators by costumes, properties, and gestures. The spectator can tell at a glance he is in the throne room, but without an editorial indication the reader may be puzzled for a while. It should be mentioned, incidentally, that there are a few authentic stage directions —perhaps Shakespeare's, perhaps a prompter's—that suggest locales: for example, "Enter Brutus in his orchard," and "They go up into the Senate house." It is hoped that the bracketed additions provide the reader with the sort of help provided in these two authentic directions, but it is equally hoped that the reader will remember that the stage was not loaded with scenery.

No editor during the course of his work can fail to recollect some words Heminges and Condell prefixed to the Folio:

It had been a thing, we confess, worthy to have been wished, that the author himself had lived to have set forth and overseen his own writings. But since it hath been ordained otherwise, and he by death departed from that right, we pray you do not envy his friends the office of their care and pain to have collected and published them.

Nor can an editor, after he has done his best, forget Heminges and Condell's final words: "And so we leave you to other of his friends, whom if you need can be your guides. If you need them not, you can lead yourselves, and others. And such readers we wish him."

SYLVAN BARNET
Tufts University

Introduction

The closing speech of *Coriolanus* reminds us of similar speeches at the end of other plays by Shakespeare:

> Take him up.
> Help, three o' th' chiefest soldiers; I'll be one.
> Beat thou the drum, that it speak mournfully;
> Trail your steel pikes. Though in this city he
> Hath widowed and unchilded many a one,
> Which to this hour bewail the injury,
> Yet he shall have a noble memory.
> > *Exeunt, bearing the body of Marcius.*
> > *A dead march sounded.*

So *Julius Caesar:*

> According to his virtue, let us use him
> With all respect and rites of burial.
> Within my tent his bones tonight shall lie,
> Most like a soldier, ordered honorably. . . .

And *Hamlet:*

> Let four captains
> Bear Hamlet like a soldier to the stage,
> For he was likely, had he been put on,
> To have proved most royal; and for his passage
> The soldiers' music and the rite of war
> Speak loudly for him. . . .

Though we recognize in all these endings the convention by which the curtainless Elizabethan stage was cleared of its actors, yet we can easily imagine that the convention might have been expressed in different language, and without this special emphasis on the protagonist—borne from the scene "like a soldier," with "music and the rite of war" —particularly when he happened to be Hamlet. It seems certain that the gesture so expressed was more than a stage-convention, or rather that it represented another and deeper convention about the nature of the chief actor in a tragedy. The modern reader certainly feels some strain in speaking of *The* Tragedy *of Coriolanus,* particularly if he has just been reading *King Lear* or *Antony and Cleopatra,* plays that most of us regard as prime examples of that ever debatable term. George Bernard Shaw has called *Coriolanus* Shakespeare's "finest comedy"; one critic has described it as a satire; another, as a debate rather than a tragedy. Most of us will agree that when we speak of *Coriolanus* as a "tragedy," we mean something rather peculiar. But those who admire the play will rejoice in that "peculiarity." The aim of this introductory essay is to give some clue to its essence, to its rare and special value. (The editor assumes that the reader will have read the play at least once before turning to the Introduction.)

The more alert and more literate members of Shakespeare's audience—not to be identified with any one social class—would have recognized that the three processional speeches above marked the death of a hero in a more than modern conventional sense. Even if they were relatively unread, they were literate in a most relevant respect, through hearing in the theater the language of dying heroes in these and in many other plays. They would have sensed much by way of implication in "virtue," "like a soldier," and "a noble memory," just as they would have appreciated the special force of "deeds" in the great speech of Cominius:

> *Cominius.* I shall lack voice: the deeds of Coriolanus
> Should not be uttered feebly. It is held
> 85   That valor is the chiefest virtue and
>   Most dignifies the haver. If it be,

The man I speak of cannot in the world
Be singly counterpoised. At sixteen years,
When Tarquin made a head for Rome, he fought
Beyond the mark of others. Our then dictator,   *90*
Whom with all praise I point at, saw him fight,
When with his Amazonian chin he drove
The bristled lips before him. He bestrid
An o'erpressed Roman, and i' th' consul's view
Slew three opposers; Tarquin's self he met,   *95*
And struck him on his knee. In that day's feats,
When he might act the woman in the scene,
He proved best man i' th' field, and for his meed
Was brow-bound with the oak. His pupil age
Man-ent'red thus, he waxèd like a sea;   *100*
And, in the brunt of seventeen battles since,
He lurched all swords of the garland. For this last,
Before and in Corioles, let me say,
I cannot speak him home. He stopped the fliers,
And by his rare example made the coward   *105*
Turn terror into sport; as weeds before
A vessel under sail, so men obeyed
And fell below his stem. His sword, death's stamp,
Where it did mark, it took; from face to foot
He was a thing of blood, whose every motion   *110*
Was timed with dying cries. Alone he ent'red
The mortal gate of th' city, which he painted
With shunless destiny; aidless came off,
And with a sudden reinforcement struck
Corioles like a planet. Now all's his,   *115*
When by and by the din of war 'gan pierce
His ready sense, then straight his doubled spirit
Requick'ned what in flesh was fatigate,
And to the battle came he; where he did
Run reeking o'er the lives of men, as if   *120*
'Twere a perpetual spoil; and till we called
Both field and city ours, he never stood
To ease his breast with panting.

Menenius: Worthy man! . . .

Cominius: Our spoils he kicked at,   *125*
  And looked upon things precious as they were
  The common muck of the world. He covets less

Than misery itself would give, rewards
His deeds with doing them, and is content
To spend the time to end it.

130 *Menenius:*   He's right noble.
  Let him be called for.

                              (II.ii.83–123; 125–31)

Consider the growth of the picture of Coriolanus in this
speech and, in particular, certain words and phrases important for defining the special character of his tragedy.
Menenius' comment at the end, "right noble," is the key
to the speech, and also one of the more important thematic
expressions for interpreting Coriolanus' whole career. The
meaning of "noble"—like "worthy," it is often equivalent
in Shakespeare to "heroic"—is summed up in this tremendous survey of the "deeds of Coriolanus." The theme
is anticipated at the start by direct statement: "It is held/
That *valor* is the chiefest virtue. . ." (line 85), "valor"
being defined here as the ancient Roman "virtue," the
Latin *virtus*.

As Cominius' story begins, the stress falls first on Coriolanus as wonder boy ("At sixteen years," line 88), as the
beardless youth with "Amazonian chin" (line 92)—a
description that reminds us oddly of his potent mother,
Volumnia. We next see him crowned, "brow-bound with
the oak" (line 99); then we get an impression of boy-
hood swiftly thrust into manhood: "His pupil age/Man-
ent'red thus" (lines 99–100). The brusque compound
renews the physical energy of "ent'red" ("initiated into"),
especially as it is linked at once with "waxèd like a sea"
(line 100), an image that turns the "man" into a vast
natural force. Again Coriolanus is crowned: "He lurched
all swords of the garland" (line 102); but how oddly this
is put, as if men were swords and swords wore garlands,
as if the man himself now wore the ornament of "swords."
He stands a "rare example" (line 105) against the "fliers,"
who appear as mere "weeds before/A vessel" (lines 106–
07). With "below his stem" (line 108), the man becomes
the "stem," the bow, of a ship. From pointed bow, the
image glides in true Shakespearean fashion to "sword,"

to "stamp" (line 108), a die for stamping a coin or a medal. Where the "stamp" made its "mark," its cutting edge "took" (line 109): it killed. The sword is seen now as a sword-machine coming down on its victims, quite literally "impressing" them. Then Coriolanus himself is dehumanized, turned into a mere blood-thing (line 110), with "every motion . . . timed" (lines 110–11), working with mechanical regularity, yet incongruously dripping with blood.

"Alone"—once more the "rare example"—he entered the "mortal," the fatal, gate by which death comes (lines 111–12). He "painted [it]/With shunless destiny" (lines 112–13): the bloody instrument smeared it with the gore of dying men, made it one with the death of men who could not escape their fate. The abstractness of idiom fits in with the whole style of Shakespeare's vision in the speech and in the play, imparting to the hero the added impersonality of a divine power. We may recall Volumnia's awesome image:

> Death, that dark spirit, in's nervy arm doth lie,
> Which, being advanced, declines, and then men die.
>
> (II.i.166–67)

She too sees Coriolanus as the great sword-sweeping arm of Death.

He "struck/Corioles like a planet" (lines 114–15). Now Coriolanus is a more terrifying force of nature, "striking" with fatal disease as the planets were believed to do, by the death-ray of the Elizabethan cosmos. There is a final impression of swift action and "reeking" gore before Cominius' summing up (lines 125–30). Coriolanus' reward for his "deeds" lies in the pure doing, in "living it up in action." Heroic violence, it is suggested, is self-destructive: in killing time, the hero is killing himself.

Shakespeare's audience—that better part of which we have spoken—would have recognized more quickly and more certainly than a twentieth-century audience that the core of this speech was an epic, or rather, heroic, narrative in the Greco-Roman tradition. Many would have already seen other "noble Roman histories," plays on similar Roman or Greek subjects; and many would have had in grammar school some direct contact with Latin epic and with Greek epic story in Latin versions. They would have caught in "noble" and the "deeds of Coriolanus" an echo of phrases like Homer's *klea andron,* "the glorious deeds of great heroës dead," as Chapman translates it. In "The man I speak of," they would have heard Virgil's *arma virumque cano,* in which *virum* is related to *virtus,* to "valor" as described by Cominius. (Stanyhurst's translation of Virgil [1582] renders *virum* as "manhood," a word that shows the identification, frequent in Shakespeare, of "man" with "hero.") To appreciate more fully the "nobility" of Coriolanus' career and what Shakespeare made of it, we need to have some notion of the heroic ideal implied by Cominius' speech and by Coriolanus' further history in the play.

Shakespeare himself was familiar with the ancient heroic tradition in various forms. If he knew little Greek, he had access to Latin and French translations of Homer, to Virgil, Ovid, and Seneca in the original and translation, and to the early books of Chapman's *Iliad,* of which he had made use in *Troilus and Cressida* (1601–02). Although Chapman considerably revised his earlier version before publishing his complete *Iliad* in 1611, his translation may serve as a relevant example of the Renaissance remaking of the ancient heroic ideal. Back of Chapman stands the Homeric hero as he is presented in the *Iliad:* he is the man who "goes forward" in battle to display his excellence in fighting, who faces death with clear-eyed awareness and with very human fears, knowing that his lot or *moira* is unchangeable, that his every act is related to divine if only partially understood powers. The greatest of heroes, Achilles, goes well beyond the typical heroic norms, both in the excesses of his wrath and in the assertion of an absolute superheroism that aims at being "godlike" indeed, and that makes him finally a deeply tragic figure. In asserting his own will, Achilles ironically brings on himself the death of Patroclus, and in living out the violence of wrath, he comes to recognize the uselessness and the inevitability of all violence. In the scene with Priam near the close of the *Iliad,* he sees that both the hero and his victim are acting parts within a pattern controlled by the gods.

The Renaissance image of the ancient hero, though ultimately inherited from Homer, had been much affected by the two great Roman transformations of Virgil and Seneca, and by the reshaping of the Greco-Roman tradition in the medieval romances. These various traditions were complexly blended in the Renaissance theory of the Heroic Poem, an ideal pattern that attempted to strike a compromise between Romance and ancient epic. (*The Faerie Queene* is the unclassic example of what happened when traditions so opposed were combined in a single work.) But the theory itself was much more classical than romantic and much more Virgilian than Homeric. The true heroic poem was like the *Aeneid,* required to have an abstract subject, preferably Christian and explicitly moral, and a hero who equaled and surpassed Aeneas as an exemplar of virtue.

There are many signs in Chapman's *Iliad* of his response to this Renaissance theory: for example, his view that the *Iliad* is "the true image of all virtues and humane government." Homer embodies all truth, and the highest truth is "learning," learning in a very special sense:

> . . . this is learning; to have skill to throw
> Reins on your body's powers that nothing know,
> And fill the soul's powers so with act and art
> That she can curb the body's angry part,
> All perturbations; all affects that stray
> From this one object, which is to obey
> Her sovereign empire. . . .
>
> *The Tears of Peace* (1609)

In the first word of the *Iliad*—"wrath"—Homer "contracts" his "Proposition," his subject: "predominant perturbation," that is, "the body's fervor and fashion of outward fortitude, to all possible height of heroical action." The "affects," the passions when "predominant," do not obey the rule of "the soul," or "reason," as Chapman says elsewhere. We have in Chapman the translator a heroic poet who distrusts heroic passion—since it leads almost inevitably to a failure of "learning"—but who has the wisdom to admit that this same passion offers the greatest occasions for the exercise of moral control.

Consider now Chapman's version (1611) of the scene in the *Iliad,* Book I, in which Achilles is tempted to draw his sword, but on Athena's advice decides not to:

> Thetis' son at this stood vext. His heart
> Bristled his bosom and two ways drew his discursive
>   part—
> If, from his thigh his sharp sword drawn, he should make
>   room about
> Atrides' person, slaught'ring him, or sit his anger out
> And curb his spirit. While these thoughts strived in his
>   blood and mind
> And he his sword drew, down from heaven Athenia
>   stooped and shined . . .
> He, turning back his eye, amaze struck every faculty,
> Yet straight he knew her by her eyes, so terrible they
>   were
> Sparkling with ardor, and thus spoke: "Thou seed of
>   Jupiter,
> Why com'st thou? To behold his pride, that boasts our
>   empery?
> Then witness, with it, my revenge, and see that insolence
>   die
> That lives to wrong me." She replied: "I come from
>   heaven to see
> Thy anger settled, if thy soul will use her sovereignty
> In fit reflection. I am sent from Juno, whose affects
> Stand heartily inclined to both. Come, give both respects
> And cease contention. Draw no sword. Use words, and
>   such as may
> Be bitter to his pride, but just. For, trust in what I say,

A time shall come when thrice the worth of that he
    forceth now
He shall propose for recompense of these wrongs. There-
    fore throw
Reins on thy passions, and serve us."

Chapman, we see, has turned the episode into one of
"learning" in his sense. First, the inner action is given
much greater importance than in the original. This
Achilles is more of a meditator than Homer's: "his heart
. . . two ways drew his *discursive* part," that is, the part
that reasons. In Homer we have simply a very physical
heart in a "shaggy chest," whereas in Chapman we find
Hamlet's contrast of man and "beast that wants discourse
of reason." The process by which Chapman's Achilles
"curbs his spirit" is a good example of how Chapman
takes over an elementary form of thought from Homer
and gives it a new and complex interpretation. So we hear
of various powers of mind: "amaze struck every fac-
ulty. . . ." More significant is Athena's advice on the right
way to settle anger. Homer's goddess says merely, "Stop
quarreling; don't draw your sword." But Chapman's says:

"Therefore throw
Reins on thy passions, and serve us."

This Athena adds another note; like Hamlet, Achilles is
to "speak daggers," but use none: "Draw no sword. Use
words . . . but *just*" ones. The addition is important, since
Chapman is in fact eager to make Achilles' wrath moral
by substituting controlled anger for mere passion. Achilles'
reply to Athena is another example of "learning":

"Though my heart
Burn in anger, yet my soul must conquer th' angry part
And yield you conquest. Who subdues his earthly part
    for heaven,
Heaven to his prayers subdues his wish."

The basic opposition of passions and soul may be either

Platonic or Christian, but Chapman's language is so emphatically Christian that we may wonder whether we are listening to a hero or a saint. (At other points in Chapman's *Iliad,* Achilles is as bloodthirsty and cruel as Homer's hero at his worst.) Whatever Chapman's intention may have been, his true hero seems more often to be Hector, who displays the self-control, the self-knowledge, that Achilles aspires to but rarely achieves.

Although Chapman has so completely reinterpreted the ancient heroic image in Renaissance terms, we can still trace in his heroes the main outlines of the heroic role as it appears in the *Iliad.* But it is the Renaissance transformation of the ancient ideal that is most instructive if we are to understand the heroes of Shakespeare: in particular, Chapman's tendency to regard the heroic career as moral education or as a tragic failure to live up to a moral ideal. Modern readers, it should be added, are in general too prone to see the meditativeness of the Renaissance hero and to miss the complete heroic image as Shakespeare and Chapman understood it.

For a practicing dramatist, this ideal, a blend of the ancient and modern, pagan and Christian, held important possibilities. A Renaissance Achilles or Hector who faced the irony of his situation, who clearly recognized the conflict of allegiances, would be tragic in the fullest sense. He would be, for example, the Antony of *Antony and Cleopatra.* The ideal that Shakespeare had encountered in Chapman's *Iliad* and elsewhere was wonderfully renewed for him by his reading of another ancient classic, one that he read with the closest attention, Plutarch's *Lives of the Noble Grecians and Romans* in North's translation. (See pages 209–48.) It is worth noting here that twice in the *Life of Coriolanus* Plutarch illustrates his point by quoting Homer, and especially interesting that in defending Homer's allowance for "our own free will and reason" he quotes, in a fairly lax version, the lines on Achilles' "angry heart."

The concept of the true hero implied in the North-Plutarch *Life,* on which Shakespeare's play is largely based, is very close to Chapman's, as may be seen from some of the more general comments on the hero's character:

> ... this Martius' natural wit and great heart did marvelously stir up his courage to do and attempt notable acts. But on the other side, for lack of education, he was so choleric and impatient, that he would yield to no living creature: which made him churlish, uncivil, and altogether unfit for any man's conversation. Yet men marveling much at his constancy, that he was never overcome with pleasure nor money and how he would endure easily all manner of pains and travails, thereupon they well liked and commended his stoutness and temperancy. But for all that, they could not be acquainted with him, as one citizen useth to be with another in the city. His behavior was so unpleasant to them by reason of a certain insolent and stern manner he had, which, because he was too lordly, was disliked. And to say truly, the greatest benefit that learning bringeth unto men is this: that it teacheth men that be rude and rough of nature, by compass and rule of reason, to be civil and courteous, and to like better the mean state than the higher. Now in those days, valiantness was honored in Rome above all other virtues, which they call *virtus*, by the name of virtue itself, as including in that general name all other special virtues besides. So that *virtus* in the Latin was as much as valiantness.

> (Plutarch's *Life of Coriolanus*, p. 210)

Note first the high praise of Martius' "great heart" and "notable acts," and more especially what follows: *"But on the other side"*—here North sounds exactly like Chapman—"for lack of education, he was so choleric and impatient, that he would yield to no living creature . . ." North reinforces this with a remark showing clearly that "education" means "learning" in Chapman's sense of the word: "And to say truly, the greatest benefit that learning bringeth unto men is this: that it teacheth men that be rude and rough of nature, by compass and rule of reason, to be civil and courteous. . . ." But in the next sentence we are reminded that Coriolanus was the pattern of *virtus*. Yet according to North's view—and it would be Chapman's, too—Coriolanus was not fit to be "a prince" or "governor," because he "lacked the gravity and affability that is gotten with judgment of learning and reason . . ." (p. 223). He has another characteristic that is connected with his "choler" and his "self-will and opinion" (we should say, "pride") : "[he] remembered not how willfulness is the thing of the world, which a governor of a commonwealth for pleasing should shun, being that which Plato called solitariness" (p. 223). Note how Coriolanus' obstinacy and pride are described as "solitariness," the uncivil "aloneness" of men "who will never yield to others' reason. . . ."

Bearing in mind Plutarch's picture of heroic Coriolanus, and this brief sketch of the ancient hero in Renaissance guise, let us return to the "deeds of Coriolanus" in Shakespeare's play. We can now appreciate more fully certain features of Cominius' narrative: the august and at times coldly Latin style, the *nobility* of this display of *virtue*, the terrifying energy of a hero who is a lone instrument of death and destiny. We see in Coriolanus a figure like Achilles in his most vengeful phase, hurrying for slaughter, who "did/Run reeking o'er the lives of men. . . ." We recall, too, how in earlier scenes Shakespeare has stressed by imagery and stage business the "bloodiness," "aloneness," and other nonhuman qualities underlined also in Cominius' portrait. Coriolanus has been pictured as "mantled," "painted," "smeared," and "masqued" in blood; heard cannon-like with "thunder-like percussion" of sounds; seen swordlike "outdaring his senseless sword" and acting alone, apart from his plebeian followers—both impressions being vividly merged in the very scene when his men *"wave their swords"* and *"take him up in their arms"*:

O me alone! Make you a sword of me?

Whether these cries are to be read as questions or as ex-

clamations—and there is no certainty—it is clear that in
uttering them Coriolanus sees' himself in splendid isolation, like a sword swung aloft in battle.

But this very emphasis on a nonhuman aloneness is a
sign that Shakespeare was not writing an ancient heroic
tragedy, not even of the Renaissance type of *Antony and
Cleopatra.* He had seen in Plutarch's "solitariness" another subject and another possible treatment. "Suppose
we set Achilles down in the Roman forum—what then?"
There are subtle hints in Cominius' speech of this other
subject and attitude: "It is *held*/That valor is the chiefest
virtue . . . *if it be*. . . ." Then Menenius' "He's right noble./
Let him be called for" is just, but also offhand and curt
in Coriolanus' own manner. "Enough of that," Menenius
seems to say—and irony breaks in. "Say more," he implies, "and you may remind people of this hero's immense
pride," "his haughty obstinate mind," as North puts it, a
quality that Shakespeare stresses much more than Plutarch. But Shakespeare does not limit himself, as some
critics suppose, to portraying a flawed proud and angry
man. He had grasped in the *Lives* and in the Roman
historians the importance of the forum, of the Roman
state, which he viewed with his contemporaries as an
example both of "the mischiefs of discord and civil dis-
sention" and of the well-ordered society, a model of a
true commonwealth. Shakespeare sets the "deeds of Coriolanus" against the great parable of Menenius, "the body's
members" and their revolt "against the Belly" (I.i.97–
155). There are many contemporary documents that show
a familiarity with this figure and with the related metaphor
of the "disease" and "health" of the body politic. To the
Elizabethan mind, the state, in more than a modern fig-
urative sense, embodies a natural order: the parts receive
from the governing center "that natural competency/
Whereby they live. . . ." The dramatic point of the bril-
liantly comic scene in which this fable is presented does
not lie in the fable itself, but in the way it is acted out
by Menenius in cooperation with the citizens. The good-
natured insolence and sturdy candor, the tough repartee
of the exchanges, belong to a game played between patri-

cian and people. The "Belly-smile" of the patrician, and the "great toe" of the plebeian, both help to impart the feeling of healthy relatedness in a civil society. To that, *Enter Caius Marcius*—followed by Menenius' greeting:

> Hail, noble Marcius!

with the answer:

> Thanks. What's the matter, you dissentious rogues
> That, rubbing the poor itch of your opinion,
> Make yourselves scabs?

The "nature" of the state is henceforth counterpoised by the "nature" of Coriolanus: "What he cannot help in his nature," one citizen says to another in the beginning of this same scene, "you account a vice in him." From here to the end of the play Shakespeare keeps dramatizing this clash of natures until Coriolanus, still protesting, hears "Great Nature" cry " 'Deny not.' " and

> He bowed his nature, never known before
> But to be rough, unswayable, and free.
> (V.vi.25–26)

In North's version of the climactic scene where Coriolanus gives in to his mother's pleas (V.iii), there is considerable emphasis on the claims of "nature" and the "natural" in various senses. But there is nothing in the *Life* as a whole like Shakespeare's interweaving throughout his drama of variations on this central theme. The opposition of "natures" in *Coriolanus* produces a continuous play of irony, as every protestation of the hero, or of his friends and enemies, is heard against a suppressed negation.

Again taking a hint from Plutarch—which he develops fully and explicitly—Shakespeare introduces one further strand of ironic ambiguity into his picture of Coriolanus, the link between his heroic energy and his love of his mother. "There's no man in the world," she explains near the end of the play, "More bound to's mother." (Such is

the stuff of heroes: Achilles must have his guardian
Thetis.) "What he hath done famously . . ." a citizen
says, "though soft-conscienced men can be content to
say it was for his country, he did it to please his mother
and to be partly proud, which he is, even to the altitude
of his virtue." (I.i.36–41) More curious still, war-making,
love, and marriage are closely related and almost identified in the minds of Volumnia and her son. Coriolanus
has a way of embracing generals as if they were brides
of war:

> *Marcius.* [*To Cominius*] O, let me clip ye
> In arms as sound as when I wooed; in heart
> As merry as when our nuptial day was done,
> And tapers burned to bedward!
>
> (I.vi.29–32)

Much later—with the inevitably ironic echo—Aufidius
answers him in kind:

> that I see thee here,
> Thou noble thing, more dances my rapt heart
> Than when I first my wedded mistress saw
> Bestride my threshold.
>
> (IV.v.119–22)

If we keep in mind these many contrasts in the nature
of Coriolanus, and the heroic image that his role evokes
by similarity and by contrast, and if we remember, too,
the vision of society symbolized by Menenius' fable, we
shall appreciate better the Shakespearean complexity of
the climactic scenes of the play. We shall also reach a truer
measure of its peculiar flavor as tragedy. Consider first
the scene where Coriolanus, about to be made consul,
makes his magnificent attack on the tribunes and their
officers. To him, the advice to abolish the tribuneship is
a call to a godlike "noble life":

> Therefore, beseech you—
> You that will be less fearful than discreet;
> That love the fundamental part of state

> More than you doubt the change on't; that prefer
> A noble life before a long, and wish
> To jump a body with a dangerous physic
> That's sure of death without it—at once pluck out
> The multitudinous tongue; let them not lick
> The sweet which is their poison. Your dishonor
> Mangles true judgment, and bereaves the state
> Of that integrity which should become't;
> Not having the power to do the good it would
> For th' ill which doth control't.
>
> (III.i.149–61)

By this point in the play the noble life is not only being equated with the "deeds of Coriolanus," but with the ironic qualifications of his pride. "A 'noble' life" on his lips can be taken by the tribunes and people simply as "the life of the nobles, the senate." Coriolanus' plea for the "fundamental part of state," his concern for the "integrity" of the body-politic seemingly echoes Menenius' fable; but "to pluck out/The multitudinous tongue," to eliminate the tribunes, is effectively to deny the people any part in the government. Coriolanus does not want a "blended" voice, but only one. He alone, he half implies, is the proper voice of the state. He is making this plea, he says, in the interest of avoiding "confusion." The hero who pleads for order, who fears revolution, speaks revolutionary doctrines and nearly starts one. He of course intends a counterrevolution; but he very nearly sets a true popular revolution under way.

The metaphor that runs through Coriolanus' speech is the familiar medical one of the play (used once, but only once, by Plutarch): he offers "a dangerous physic," and in his view he is the health of the state. But to the tribune Sicinius "He's a disease that must be cut away" (III.i.293). Menenius accepts the implication, but proposes "a cure" rather than "surgery." He would proceed by "the humane way" of compromise; that is, by Chapman's (and Plutarch's) way of "humane government." But the fatality of Coriolanus' nature—his pride and "choler," his lack of temperance—carries him on to destroy what he thinks he is saving. "His nature is too noble for the world," says Menenius,

> He would not flatter Neptune for his trident,
> Or Jove for's power to thunder. His heart's his mouth:
> What his breast forges, that his tongue must vent;
> And, being angry, does forget that ever
> He heard the name of death.
>
>   (III.i.255–59)

Here is the man who will equal the gods, the forgelike machine of war and death, deafened by wrath.

Coriolanus' insistence on being true to his heroic nature is constantly to the fore from this point to the end of the play. So in the next scene with the nobles and Volumnia, a scene that has no parallel in Plutarch, he asks with boyish puzzlement,

> Why did you wish me milder? Would you have me
> False to my nature? Rather say I play
> The man I am.
>
>   (III.ii.14–16)

Her sensible advice fits—up to a point—Chapman's and North's concept of "education":

> I have a heart as little apt as yours,
> But yet a brain that leads my use of anger
> To better vantage.
>
>   (III.ii.29–31)

And Menenius comments, "Well said, noble woman!" But this is not Coriolanus' nobility; his is of the pure Homeric type, absolute and without compromise. "You are too absolute," Volumnia well says,

> Though therein you can never be too noble
> But when extremities speak.
>
>   (III.ii.40–41)

But Volumnia does not altogether understand her son:

it is exactly in "extremities" that the hero must be "too noble," that his nature clearly cries out. Coriolanus faces a dilemma similar to Antony's—how to be both noble and politic. Volumnia attempts to make him feel that the politic can be identified at one and the same time with nobility, with loyalty to the better part of the state and to the family, and most significantly, with loyalty to herself:

> I am in this
> Your wife, your son, these senators, the nobles. . . .
> (III.ii.64–65)

Her despairing

> Do as thou list.
> Thy valiantness was mine, thou suck'st it from me,
> But owe thy pride thyself.
> (III.ii.128–30)

only increases the sense of their likeness, of the physical bond between them: they are one flesh and one blood.

But the physical intensity of the appeal is persuasive for the moment, and for the first time in the scene, Coriolanus calls her "mother":

> Mother, I am going to the marketplace. . . .

What this curbing of his nature costs him comes out earlier in the same scene, when like Othello he says farewell to arms:

> Away, my disposition, and possess me
> Some harlot's spirit! My throat of war be turned,
> Which quired with my drum, into a pipe
> Small as an eunuch. . . .
> (III.ii.111–14)

And when he suddenly reverses himself:

> I will not do't,
> Lest I surcease to honor mine own truth,

> And by my body's action teach my mind
> A most inherent baseness.
>   (III.ii.120–23)

Though the words Coriolanus uses are very like Chapman's, his actions have really turned the ideal upside down. While everyone is urging him to "curb the body's angry part" by exercise of "spirit," he sees only a betrayal of spirit by flesh.

He will seek "a world elsewhere," outside state and family, out of the ordered nature he had known in Rome, and fight, now truly "alone,/Like to a lonely dragon, that his fen/Makes feared and talked of more than seen . . ." (IV.i.29–31). With splendid irony he asserts that though outside society he will still be the same noble hero: "you shall/Hear . . . never of me aught/But what is like me formerly" (IV.i.51–53). In the flattering talk of the Volscians he seems to recover his old nobility, "as if he were son and heir to Mars," but this new-found independence is an illusion, as Aufidius' ominous hints make clear. Aufidius' explanation of why Coriolanus was "hated" and "banished"—though it neglects some reasons, and though it is not Shakespeare's "last word" on his hero —does offer one important hypothesis borne out by much of the play:

> whether ['twas] *nature*,
> Not to be other than one thing, not moving
> From th' casque to th' cushion, but commanding peace
> Even with the same austerity and garb
> As he controlled the war. . . .
>   (IV.vii.41–45)

In this last phase of Coriolanus' career there is, as in Achilles' last battles, something much more frightening about his pride and his wrath. "He was," says Cominius

> a kind of nothing, titleless,
> Till he had forged himself a name o' th' fire
> Of burning Rome.
>   (V.i.13–15)

He harshly rejects his "old father," Menenius,

> Away! . . .
> Wife, mother, child, I know not. . . .
> (V.ii.81, 83)

The Second Watch gives one final impression of Coriolanus' dehumanization just before the women come to beg him to save the city: "He's the rock, the oak not to be wind-shaken" (V.ii.111–12). What then will happen to the man who supposes he is "author of himself," the absolute hero detached from humanity?

As when Menenius pleads with him earlier, he will attempt to separate personal allegiance from allegiance to country. When the women approach, his eye moves quickly from his wife to his mother, who claims and receives his attention during most of the scene. He speaks to her first in the strange impersonal style that others have used of him: "the honored mold/Wherein this trunk was framed . . ." (V.iii.22–23); but at once he is stressing the close physical bond of mother and son: "and in her hand/The grandchild to her blood." With a typical turn, he at once denies this and all similar bonds: "All bond and privilege of nature, break!" He will be deliberately unnatural; but when he sees those "doves' " eyes, he "melts" —and how wonderfully the imagery recalls the hard godlike self he has tried to be: "I melt, and am not/Of stronger earth . . ."—he is not the metallic machine man of earlier scenes. When his "mother bows," it is indeed a "perturbation" in Nature, and "Great Nature" cries out against it (V.iii.33). He denies "instinct," innate impulse, and, with consummate irony, declares that he is "author of himself," as it were, self-born!

But soon he is yielding to Nature in the sense of family affection, as he gives his wife "a kiss/Long as my exile," while still insisting that he is not yielding to Nature in the sense of allegiance to his country. When he sees his mother kneeling he comes out with great hyperbolic oaths in the best heroic vein:

> Then let the pebbles on the hungry beach

> Fillip the stars! Then let the mutinous winds
> Strike the proud cedars 'gainst the fiery sun. . . .
> (V.iii.58–60)

Like Othello and Lear, Coriolanus invokes the very disorder he fears, the disorder of which he is the unconscious instrument. Like Hector he sees his son as the reincarnation of his own heroism, his words recalling his own nobility and his lonely strength and inhumanity. He prays that the boy may prove

> To shame unvulnerable, and stick i' th' wars
> Like a great sea-mark, standing every flaw. . . .
> (V.iii.73–74)

But he is still trying to hold off the claims of wife and mother: "Tell me not," he shouts, "Wherein I seem unnatural."

Then come Volumnia's two great appeals in answer to his poignantly absurd assertion. The keynote of the first is struck in

> thy sight, which should
> Make our eyes flow with joy, hearts dance with comforts,
> Constrains them weep and shake with fear and sorrow,
> Making the mother, wife, and child, to see
> The son, the husband, and the father tearing
> His country's bowels out.
> (V.iii.98–103)

The body of the state, here realized with such physical vividness, is equated with mother, wife, and child, as if to say "tearing that body is tearing us." During the rest of the speech, Volumnia's language intensifies this identification until the climax,

> thou shalt no sooner
> March to assault thy country than to tread
> (Trust to't, thou shalt not) on thy mother's womb
> That brought thee to this world.
> (V.iii.122–25)

This violent image is Plutarch's, and the identification of the mother with the body of the state is suggested by one of his comments; but the comment shows also the relative simplicity of his analysis, and his unawareness of the emotional confusion that Volumnia is exploiting so successfully:

> yet he had no reason for the love of his mother to pardon his country, but rather he should in pardoning his country, have spared his mother, because his mother and wife were members of the body of his country and city, which he did besiege.
> (Plutarch: *The Comparison of Alcibiades with*
> *Marcius Coriolanus*)

Volumnia's second appeal falls into three distinct phases. First she urges him to reconcile the Romans and the Volsces, offering the same kind of sensible advice she had given earlier when begging him to be "mild" to the tribunes. Next she makes a masterly attack on the very nobility that stands in the way of compromise, pointing out that the only practical "benefit" of being so absolutely noble is to destroy his country and gain a "name . . ./To th' ensuing age abhorred." She enforces her argument with a satirical picture of the Jove-like role Coriolanus has aimed at, seeking "To imitate the graces of the gods . . ." as if he were to "thunder" like Jove, and yet to "charge" his lightning with a "bolt" that would only split "an oak" (V.iii.140–53). Something, yes, but hardly a cosmic catastrophe. She keeps reminding him that she speaks for wife, son, and mother; and in her final stroke she reinforces all three claims:

> This fellow had a Volscian to his mother;
> His wife is in Corioles, and his child
> Like him by chance.
>
> (V.iii.178–80)

Again she identifies personal and social bonds, as she reads him out of family, Rome, and humanity. His reply is one of the great speaking silences in Shakespeare:

> *Holds her by the hand, silent.*
>   O mother, mother!
> What have you done? Behold, the heavens do ope,
> The gods look down, and this unnatural scene
> They laugh at.
>
>   (V.iii.182–85)

"Unnatural"—just when he is responding to all these most natural claims. For a moment he seems to see his dilemma more clearly, and to understand that in giving in to his mother he is responding to the demands of his native country and state. But he soon is talking as if all can be well: he can give in to his mother, be false to the Volscians, and "frame convenient peace."

The last scene of the play begins as an ironic repetition of the scene in which he had "mildly" given in to his mother's advice. At that time he had not been able to sustain the part; but now he "bows his nature" and comes "marching" in, *"the commoners being with him."* In contrast to the usual isolation of his figure from the plebeians, Coriolanus is seen *with* the people, and we catch another ironic reflection from the past: Menenius' easy companionship with the lower orders. Coriolanus seems for once to "belong," and he cries happily, "I am returned your soldier;/No more infected with my country's love . . ." (V.vi.71–72). What was once his health is now disease, and loyalty to the enemies of Rome is his "cure." He is so terribly unaware of what he has been doing that he responds with dreamlike deafness to Aufidius' cry of "traitor"—the exact echo of the Tribunes' earlier "Has spoken like a traitor . . ." (III.i.162).

When he finally takes in Aufidius' cruel caricature of how he had given in to his mother, he can hardly speak: "Hear'st thou, Mars?" His incoherent cry, reminding us of the godlike soldier he had been, is inadequate, but dramatically concentrated in the highest degree. Shakespeare was never more successful than in this brief dialogue in focusing the rich meanings of a whole play in the slightest verbal gestures. To Aufidius' slanderous "boy of tears," he cries:

Cut me to pieces, Volsces, men and lads,
Stain all your edges on me. "Boy"! False hound!
If you have writ your annals true, 'tis there,
That, like an eagle in a dovecote, I
Fluttered your Volscians in Corioles.
Alone I did it. "Boy"?

                                        (V.vi.112–17)

"Alone" and " 'Boy'?" carry the weight of his whole
dramatic career. In "Alone" we recall his cult of independence, his integrity, his insistence on being Coriolanus. But
we hear also the opposite theme in a play in which
wholeness of the state is the public ideal, in which metaphors of the body politic keep reminding us that the great
natural order is realized in a whole of which the single
man is only a part. This is his final denial of nature's bond,
making only clearer his real dependence on Rome, his
mother, Menenius, and now on the Volscians. "Boy"?" in
its scornful tone is Coriolanus' way of saying "*man*-hero."
But the hero cannot act in this setting; he can only utter
frustrated cries. He is in part behaving like a boy, and
he had responded to his mother. The single word recalls
too a long history of boyish irresponsibility and lack of
control.

But there is another view, as always in this play: "The
man is noble," one of the Volscians says, "and his fame
folds in/This orb o' th' earth" (V.vi.125–26). The "deeds
of Coriolanus" cannot be forgotten any more than "the
impatience" that North finds so dangerous in the "governor of a state." The closing processional speech, with
which we began, marks the death of a hero: "Yet he
shall have a noble memory."

If we now compare Coriolanus with the model of all
Greek and Roman literary heroes, Achilles, and with the
Renaissance counterpart in Chapman and North, and
finally with the chief characters of other Shakespearean
tragedies, we can define more clearly the character of the
play—surely the most original of Shakespeare's heroic
dramas, whatever we choose to call it. Throughout *Coriolanus* Shakespeare is continually recalling the ancient

model in imagery associating his hero with divinities and "shunless destiny." Like Menenius, Shakespeare has "godded him indeed." Perhaps Coriolanus is most like Achilles in his passionate pride, in his "choler," in his shifting from "rage to sorrow," emotions that lie very close together, as Plutarch had noted. But he comes nearest to the essence of Homer's hero in his absoluteness, in his determination to imitate "the graces of the gods," in his will to push the heroic to the limit until he destroys his own society along with his enemy's. In reducing all virtues to *virtus,* he is the Greek hero Romanized, while in his assertion of his own nature in the face of "Great Nature," he betrays the Senecan ancestry of the Elizabethan hero. Though many read him lessons in patience, he is incapable of true "learning."

But there is no moment when, like Achilles, he sees his anger and curses it, nothing to correspond to the scene with Priam, no vision of himself and a higher order within which his action and suffering are placed and made more comprehensible. His last gesture is like his first, to "use his lawful sword." He knows little of what Chapman calls the soul's "sovereignty in fit reflection," not to mention "subduing his earthly part for heaven." He is the most Roman, the least Christian, of Shakespeare's major heroes.

This Roman-ness is felt in the austerity of a style that lends itself so well to irony, and that is the best index to the quality of the play. In *Coriolanus,* Shakespeare seems to turn his back on the richness of language in *Antony and Cleopatra,* with the deliberate intention of creating a protagonist who will deny much that is common to his own and the Renaissance heroic ideal. And yet there are in Coriolanus the makings of a tragedy in Shakespeare's more typical manner: he is a man nobly conscious of his role, a "governor" like Lear or Macbeth on whom the health of society depends, a person like Lear and Othello of immense impatience in a situation calling for utmost patience, a man like Antony whose action is godlike and connected with dimly perceived supernatural forces. Both are instruments of the mighty Roman state, for Romans a prime symbol of the directing power of fate.

But there is of course an obvious defect that makes even Macbeth tragic in a sense of the word that does not fit Coriolanus: the lack of the troubled conscience that separates Macbeth from the tyrant he seems to be to his enemies. In the final scene with his mother, Coriolanus is barely conscious that he is betraying the Volscians, just as in his last entrance he does not realize that he has been "infected by his country's love." His whole career is based on an illusion of *aloneness,* the belief that a man, a general, a statesman can act alone. Hence the bafflement and humiliation when he must bow to others—feelings he can express only in rotelike speeches. It is the spectator, not Coriolanus, who feels the poignancy of this betrayal of others and himself. Like a "dull actor," as he says, he performs dully, and when out of his part, he is completely "out."

For Coriolanus has only one way of meeting the world —assertion of simple soldierly nobility. In this he has much in common with Othello, who also lives by absolutes, whose world collapses at any suggestion that he is *not* a soldier. But there is no terrible recognition by the hero, as there is in the final scenes of *Othello,* that simple soldiery and simple justice have not been enough, that they have indeed brought chaos again. Damnation, which Othello calls on himself, and which presupposes a sense of sin, is incomprehensible to this noble Roman. He is equally incapable of "noble" Antony's "I am so lated in the world that I/Have lost my way for ever."

One last comparison with Achilles is to the point. In comparison with Shakespeare's "men," these two are great boys. Both are strangely allied with their mothers, both produce "confusion" by their overdeveloped sense of self and their disregard of the claims of society. The difference in the end result depends on the difference noted earlier: Shakespeare sets his hero in a much more complex social world. The noble voice that calls to battle may no longer sound noble in the Capitol. Though it calls for order, it becomes indistinguishable from the voice of tyrant and traitor. The man who fears innovation, who has no gift for making compromises and dealing "mildly," may prove the most violent of innovators, worse than a mere mob. Shakespeare's picture of the people is not flattering, but not unintelligent: one cannot build an orderly society by following the whims of the many-headed monster. But fixity of principle in a prince can be as dangerous to the state as the fickleness of a mob.

Shakespeare's state is necessarily not that of the Roman republic, since both society and cosmos have been translated in Elizabethan-Jacobean terms. His subject—apart from the peculiar character of Coriolanus—is implicit in the "degree" speech of *Troilus and Cressida* (I.iii.75). It should be remembered that Ulysses' speech was occasioned by Achilles' revolt and that Ulysses later tried to show Achilles the evils resulting from his loss of heroic nobility. Shakespeare returns in *Coriolanus* to the subject implied in these scenes of *Troilus and Cressida,* but with a new Achilles and a new certainty of aim, and with a resultant concentration lacking in the earlier play. In *Troilus,* Achilles was an ambiguous creature, a lover and a gangster, and the drama of disunity in the state was crossed by a drama of disunity in love. The end appropriately is sound and fury signifying nothing. But in *Coriolanus,* Shakespeare limits the social subject more severely, and though his picture of the social order is highly particularized, it does not lose a large clarity. As in *Antony and Cleopatra,* the "wide arch/Of the ranged" Roman state is never lost from view.

Against that ordered complexity the simple extremism of Coriolanus stands out in all its nobility and absurdity. The noble simplicity of the hero and the certainty with which issues are expressed and arguments are presented by Coriolanus and by his enemies, the high decorum of the rather chill oratorical style take us in the direction of French classical drama. This is, after *Julius Caesar,* Shakespeare's most *Latin* play.

It was "all in Plutarch," we may be tempted to say. (See pp. 209–48.) But when we read Plutarch we discover what Shakespeare was capable of learning—how wonderfully he selected and how skillfully he concentrated on his themes, embodying them in particular dramatic expressions. We can almost feel Shakespeare's excitement as he read; his recognition that here was a subject he had wanted to handle as early as when he was writing *Julius Caesar* and *Troilus*. What a discovery—after reading late medieval versions of the ancient heroic in which the hero is reduced to a chivalric lover or worse, to find that the hero is a man who has never ceased loving his mother, a man for whom marriage is second to war, whose true love is his own heroic image. Hints of these and other traits of Shakespeare's hero—his nobility and heroic virtue, his obstinate pride and lack of self-control—can be found in the *Life of Coriolanus*. Other basic features of Shakespeare's drama—the picture of the Roman state and society, the debate over the claims of nature, great and small—can also be traced to Plutarch's text. But though many separate elements of Shakespeare's grand design are Plutarchan, it is Shakespeare who has "put them together," and the "putting together" is a dramatic and poetic feat. The imagery of Volumnia's appeal, for example, is resonant with the sense of the state and society that Shakespeare had presented early in the play. In reporting Coriolanus' death, Plutarch merely says the conspirators "all fell upon him, and killed him in the marketplace, none of the people once offering to rescue him." There is no speech from Aufidius, and more notable, none from Coriolanus, nothing to correspond to "Alone I did it. 'Boy'?" Those few words show that Shakespeare had combined perfectly an intense and rich understanding of the hero-boy, mother's son, and noble Roman with his sharply outlined picture of the social and political world, in a total vision that makes the cry so large in reference, so poignantly absurd, so tragic in a curiously ironic sense.

REUBEN BROWER
Harvard University

The Tragedy of Coriolanus

DRAMATIS Personae

Caius Marcius, afterwards Caius Marcius Coriolanus
Titus Lartius } generals against the Volscians
Cominius
Menenius Agrippa, friend to Coriolanus
Sicinius Velutus } tribunes of the people
Junius Brutus
Young Marcius, son to Coriolanus
A Roman Herald
A Roman, named Nicanor
Tullus Aufidius, general of the Volscians
Lieutenant to Aufidius
Conspirators with Aufidius
A Volscian, named Adrian
A Citizen of Antium
Two Volscian Guards
Volumnia, mother to Coriolanus
Virgilia, wife to Coriolanus
Valeria, friend to Virgilia
Gentlewoman attending on Virgilia
Usher attending on Valeria
Roman and Volscian Senators, Patricians, Aediles,
Lictors, Soldiers, Citizens, Messengers, Servants to
Aufidius, and other Attendants

Scene: Rome and the neighborhood; Corioli and
the neighborhood, Antium

[Dramatis Personae

Caius Marcius, afterwards Caius Marcius Coriolanus
Titus Lartius }
Cominius } generals against the Volscians
Menenius Agrippa, friend to Coriolanus
Sicinius Velutus }
Junius Brutus } tribunes of the people
Young Marcius, son to Coriolanus
A Roman Herald
A Roman, named Nicanor
Tullus Aufidius, general of the Volscians *Coriolanus enemy*
Lieutenant to Aufidius
Conspirators with Aufidius
A Volscian, named Adrian
A Citizen of Antium
Two Volscian Guards
Volumnia, mother to Coriolanus
Virgilia, wife to Coriolanus
Valeria, friend to Virgilia
Gentlewoman attending on Virgilia
Usher attending on Valeria
Roman and Volscian Senators, Patricians, Aediles, Lictors, Soldiers, Citizens, Messengers, Servants to Aufidius, and other Attendants

Scene: Rome and the neighborhood; Corioli and the neighborhood; Antium]

The Tragedy of Coriolanus

ACT I

Scene I. [*Rome. A street.*]

Enter a company of mutinous Citizens, with staves,
clubs, and other weapons.

First Citizen. Before we proceed any further, hear me
    speak.

All. Speak, speak.

First Citizen. You are all resolved rather to die than
    to famish?   5

All. Resolved, resolved.

First Citizen. First you know, Caius Marcius is chief
    enemy to the people.

All. We know't, we know't.

First Citizen. Let us kill him, and we'll have corn°1 at   10
    our own price. Is't a verdict?

All. No more talking on't; let it be done. Away,
    away!

1 The degree sign (°) indicates a footnote, which is keyed to the text
by line number. Text references are printed in **boldface** type; the
annotation follows in roman type. I.i.10 **corn** grain (wheat, barley,
etc., not Indian corn)

Second Citizen. One word, good citizens.

15 *First Citizen.* We are accounted poor citizens, the patricians good.° What authority surfeits on would relieve us. If they would yield us but the superfluity while it were wholesome, we might guess° they relieved us humanely; but they think we are too 20 dear;° the leanness that afflicts us, the object° of our misery, is as an inventory to particularize their abundance;° our sufferance is a gain to them. Let us revenge this with our pikes° ere we become rakes.° For the gods know I speak this in hunger 25 for bread, not in thirst for revenge.

Second Citizen. Would you proceed especially against Caius Marcius?

First Citizen. Against him first: he's a very dog to the commonalty.°

30 *Second Citizen.* Consider you what services he has done for his country?

First Citizen. Very well, and could be content to give him good report for't, but that he pays himself with being proud.

35 *Second Citizen.* Nay, but speak not maliciously.

First Citizen. I say unto you, what he hath done famously he did it to that end; though soft-conscienced men can be content to say it was for his country, he did it to please his mother and to be 40 partly proud,° which he is, even to the altitude of his virtue.°

Second Citizen. What he cannot help in his nature you account a vice in him. You must in no way say he is covetous.

16 **good** well-off   18 **guess** think   20 **dear** expensive   20 **object** sight 21–22 **inventory to particularize their abundance** list in which to read a detailed account of their wealth as compared with our poverty 23 **pikes** pitchforks   24 **rakes** cf. "lean as a rake"   29 **commonalty** common people   39–40 **to be partly proud** in part from pride 41 **virtue** valor (Latin sense)

First Citizen. If I must not, I need not be barren of   45
    accusations. He hath faults (with surplus) to tire in
    repetition. (*Shouts within.*) What shouts are these?
    The other side o' th' city is risen. Why stay we
    prating here? To th' Capitol!°

All. Come, come.   50

First Citizen. Soft,° who comes here?

            Enter Menenius Agrippa

Second Citizen. Worthy Menenius Agrippa, one that
    hath always loved the people.

First Citizen. He's one honest enough; would all the
    rest were so!   55

Menenius. What work's, my countrymen, in hand?
        Where go you
    With bats and clubs? The matter? Speak, I pray
        you.

First Citizen. Our business is not unknown to th'
    Senate; they have had inkling this fortnight what
    we intend to do, which now we'll show 'em in   60
    deeds. They say poor suitors have strong breaths;
    they shall know we have strong arms too.

Menenius. Why, masters, my good friends, mine
        honest neighbors,
    Will you undo yourselves?

First Citizen. We cannot, sir; we are undone already.   65

Menenius. I tell you, friends, most charitable care
    Have the patricians of you. For your wants,
    Your suffering in this dearth,° you may as well
    Strike at the heaven with your staves as lift them
    Against the Roman state, whose course will on   70
    The way it takes, cracking ten thousand curbs°
    Of more strong link asunder than can ever

49 **Capitol** Capitoline Hill, on which the Temple of Jupiter stood
(here and often, for the Senate House nearby)   51 **Soft** stop (an
interjection)   68 **dearth** famine   71 **curbs** restraints

Appear in your impediment.° For the dearth,
The gods, not the patricians, make it, and
75 Your knees to them (not arms) must help. Alack,
You are transported° by calamity
Thither where more attends you; and you slander
The helms° o' th' state, who care for you like
      fathers,
When you curse them as enemies.

80 *First Citizen.* Care for us! True, indeed! They ne'er
cared for us yet. Suffer us to famish, and their store-
houses crammed with grain; make edicts for usury,
to support usurers; repeal daily any wholesome act
established against the rich, and provide more
85 piercing statutes daily to chain up and restrain the
poor. If the wars eat us not up, they will; and
there's all the love they bear us.

Menenius. Either you must
Confess yourselves wondrous malicious,
90 Or be accused of folly. I shall tell you
A pretty tale; it may be you have heard it;
But since it serves my purpose, I will venture
To stale't° a little more.

First Citizen. Well, I'll hear it, sir. Yet you must not
95 think to fob off° our disgrace° with a tale. But,
and't° please you, deliver.

Menenius. There was a time when all the body's mem-
      bers
Rebelled against the Belly; thus accused it:
That only like a gulf° it did remain
100 I' th' midst o' th' body, idle and unactive,
Still cupboarding the viand,° never bearing
Like labor with the rest; where th' other instru-
      ments°

73 **in your impediment** in any hindrance you make   76 **transported**
carried out of your minds   78 **helms** helmsmen   93 **stale't** make it
stale   95 **fob off** set aside with a trick   95 **disgrace** misfortune
96 **and't** if it   99 **gulf** whirlpool   101 **viand** food   102 **instruments**
organs

Did see and hear, devise, instruct, walk, feel,
And, mutually participate,° did minister
Unto the appetite and affection° common　　　　　*105*
Of the whole body. The Belly answered—

First Citizen. Well, sir, what answer made the Belly?

Menenius. Sir, I shall tell you. With a kind of smile,
Which ne'er came from the lungs, but even thus—
For, look you, I may make the Belly smile　　　　　*110*
As well as speak—it tauntingly replied
To th' discontented members, the mutinous parts
That envied his receipt;° even so most fitly
As you malign our senators for that
They are not such as you.

First Citizen.　　　　　Your Belly's answer—What?　*115*
The kingly crownèd head, the vigilant eye,
The counselor heart, the arm our soldier,
Our steed the leg, the tongue our trumpeter,
With other muniments° and petty helps
In this our fabric, if that they—

Menenius.　　　　　What then?　　*120*
'Fore me,° this fellow speaks! What then? What
then?

First Citizen. Should by the cormorant Belly be restrained,
Who is the sink° o' th' body—

Menenius.　　　　　Well, what then?

First Citizen. The former agents, if they did complain,
What could the Belly answer?

Menenius.　　　　　I will tell you;　　*125*
If you'll bestow a small (of what you have little)
Patience awhile, you'st° hear the Belly's answer.

First Citizen. Y'are° long about it.

104 **mutually participate** taking part in common　105 **affection** inclination　113 **his receipt** what he received　119 **muniments** furnish-
ings (fortifications)　121 **'Fore me** by my soul　123 **sink** sewer
127 **you'st** you'll (for "you shalt")　128 **Y'are** you're

Menenius. Note me this, good friend;
Your most grave Belly° was deliberate,
130 Not rash like his accusers, and thus answered:
"True is it, my incorporate friends," quoth he,
"That I receive the general food at first,
Which you do live upon; and fit it is,
Because I am the storehouse and the shop°
135 Of the whole body. But, if you do remember,
I send it through the rivers of your blood,
Even to the court, the heart, to th' seat o' th' brain;
And, through the cranks° and offices° of man,
The strongest nerves° and small inferior veins
140 From me receive that natural competency°
Whereby they live; and though that all at once"—
You, my good friends, this says the Belly, mark
me—

First Citizen. Ay, sir; well, well.

Menenius. "Though all at once cannot
See what I do deliver out to each,
145 Yet I can make my audit up, that all
From me do back receive the flour of all,
And leave me but the bran." What say you to't?

First Citizen. It was an answer. How apply you this?

Menenius. The senators of Rome are this good Belly,
150 And you the mutinous members. For examine
Their counsels and their cares, disgest° things rightly
Touching the weal o' th' common,° you shall find
No public benefit which you receive
But it proceeds or comes from them to you,
155 And no way from yourselves. What do you think,
You, the great toe of this assembly?

---

129 **Your most grave Belly** this most grave belly we speak of
134 **shop** factory   138 **cranks** winding paths   138 **offices** parts of a
house where household work is done, e.g., kitchen   139 **nerves**
tendons   140 **natural competency** supply adequate to their nature
151 **disgest** digest   152 **weal o' th' common** welfare of the people

First Citizen. I the great toe! Why the great toe?

Menenius. For that, being one o' th' lowest, basest, poorest,
Of this most wise rebellion, thou goest foremost.
Thou rascal,° that are worst in blood° to run,   160
Lead'st first to win some vantage.°
But make you ready your stiff° bats and clubs;
Rome and her rats are at the point of battle;
The one side must have bale.° *Harm*

                    Enter Caius Marcius.

                              Hail, noble Marcius!

Marcius. Thanks. What's the matter, you dissentious
    rogues   165
That, rubbing the poor itch of your opinion,
Make yourselves scabs?°

First Citizen.   We have ever your good word.

Marcius. He that will give good words to thee will
    flatter
Beneath abhorring. What would you have, you curs,
That like nor peace nor war? The one affrights you,   170
The other makes you proud. He that trusts to you,
Where he should find you lions, finds you hares;
Where foxes, geese. You are no surer, no,
Than is the coal of fire upon the ice,
Or hailstone in the sun. Your virtue is   175
To make him worthy whose offense subdues him°
And curse that justice did it.° Who deserves great-
    ness
        Passions
Deserves your hate; and your affections° are
A sick man's appetite, who desires most that
Which would increase his evil. He that depends   180
Upon your favors swims with fins of lead

---

160 **rascal** a lean deer, or a hound 160 **blood** condition 161 **vantage** advantage 162 **stiff** stout 164 **bale** harm 167 **Make yourselves scabs** make scabs for yourselves (also, "make yourselves into loathsome fellows") 176 **subdues him** lays him low 177 **that justice did it** the justice that punished him 178 **affections** desires

And hews down oaks with rushes. Hang ye! Trust
    ye?
With every minute you do change a mind,
And call him noble that was now your hate,
185 Him vile that was your garland. What's the matter
That in these several places of the city
You cry against the noble Senate, who
(Under the gods) keep you in awe, which else
Would feed on one another? What's their seeking?

Menenius. For corn at their own rates, whereof they
190   say
The city is well stored.

Marcius.   Hang 'em! They say!
They'll sit by th' fire, and presume to know
What's done i' th' Capitol: who's like to rise,
Who thrives and who declines; side factions° and
    give out
195 Conjectural marriages, making parties strong,
And feebling° such as stand not in their liking
Below their cobbled shoes. They say there's grain
    enough!
Would the nobility lay aside their ruth,°
And let me use my sword, I'd make a quarry°
200 With thousands of these quartered slaves, as high
As I could pick my lance.

Menenius. Nay, these are almost thoroughly per-
    suaded;
For though abundantly they lack discretion,
Yet are they passing° cowardly. But, I beseech you,
What says the other troop?

205 *Marcius*.   They are dissolved. Hang 'em!
They said they were an-hungry;° sighed forth
    proverbs°—

---

194 **side factions** take sides (form parties)   196 **feebling** weakening
(bringing down)   198 **ruth** compassion   199 **quarry** heap of dead
(usually of game animals)   204 **passing** exceedingly   206 **an-hungry**
hungry   206 **sighed forth proverbs** (implying that they talk like
rustics)

That hunger broke stone walls, that dogs must eat,
That meat was made for mouths, that the gods sent
not
Corn for the rich men only. With these shreds
They vented their complainings, which being an-
swered,   210
And a petition granted them, a strange one,
To break the heart of generosity°
And make bold power look pale, they threw their
caps
As they would hang them on the horns o' th' moon,
Shouting their emulation.°

Menenius.   What is granted them?   215

Marcius. Five tribunes to defend their vulgar° wisdoms,
Of their own choice. One's Junius Brutus—
Sicinius Velutus, and—I know not. 'Sdeath!
The rabble should have first unroofed the city,
Ere so prevailed with me; it will in time   220
Win upon power° and throw forth greater themes
For insurrection's arguing.°

Menenius.   This is strange.

Marcius. Go, get you home, you fragments!

                Enter a Messenger, hastily.

Messenger. Where's Caius Marcius?

Marcius.   Here: what's the matter?

Messenger. The news is, sir, the Volsces are in arms.   225

Marcius. I am glad on't: then we shall ha' means to
vent°
Our musty superfluity. See, our best elders.

---

212 **break the heart of generosity** give the deathblow to the nobility   215 **Shouting their emulation** expressing envious joy   216 **vulgar** common, plebeian   221 **Win upon power** get the better of
authority   222 **For insurrection's arguing** for rebels to debate in
action (abstract for concrete, as often in *Coriolanus*)   226 **vent**
get rid of

Enter Sicinius Velutus, Junius Brutus, Cominius,
Titus Lartius, with other Senators.

First Senator. Marcius, 'tis true that you have lately
 told us;
 The Volsces are in arms.

Marcius.   They have a leader,
230 Tullus Aufidius, that will put you to't.°
 I sin in envying his nobility;
 And were I anything but what I am,
 I would wish me only he.

Cominius.   You have fought together.

Marcius. Were half to half the world by th' ears, and
 he
235 Upon my party, I'd revolt, to make
 Only my wars with him. He is a lion
 That I am proud to hunt.

First Senator.   Then, worthy Marcius,
 Attend upon Cominius to these wars.

Cominius. It is your former promise.

Marcius.   Sir, it is,
240 And I am constant.° Titus Lartius, thou
 Shalt see me once more strike at Tullus' face.
 What, art thou stiff?° Stand'st out?°

Titus.   No, Caius Marcius;
 I'll lean upon one crutch and fight with t'other
 Ere stay behind this business.

Menenius.   O, true-bred!

First Senator. Your company to th' Capitol; where
245 I know
 Our greatest friends attend us.

Titus.   [*To Cominius*] Lead you on.

_____

230 **put you to't** test you severely 240 **constant** faithful 242 **stiff**
obstinate, set (on not fighting) 242 **Stand'st out** you're staying out
of it?

[*To Marcius*] Follow Cominius; we must follow
  you;
Right worthy you priority.°

Cominius.   Noble Marcius!

First Senator. [*To the Citizens*] Hence to your homes;
  begone!

Marcius.   Nay, let them follow.
  The Volsces have much corn; take these rats
    thither   250
  To gnaw their garners. Worshipful mutineers,
  Your valor puts well forth.° Pray, follow. *Exeunt.*

  Citizens steal away. Manet° Sicinius and Brutus.

Sicinius. Was ever man so proud as is this Marcius?

Brutus. He has no equal.

Sicinius. When we were chosen tribunes for the people—   255

Brutus. Marked you his lip and eyes?

Sicinius.   Nay, but his taunts.

Brutus. Being moved, he will not spare to gird° the
  gods.

Sicinius. Bemock the modest moon.

Brutus. The present wars devour him; he is grown
  Too proud to be so valiant.°

Sicinius.   Such a nature,   260
  Tickled with good success,° disdains the shadow
  Which he treads on at noon. But I do wonder
  His insolence can brook to be commanded
  Under Cominius.

---

248 **Right worthy you priority** you well deserve first place   252 **puts
well forth** gives fair promise (literally, buds)   252 s.d. **Manet** remains (Latin; although the subject is plural, this form, the third
person singular, commonly appears in Elizabethan stage directions)
257 **gird** taunt   259–260 **grown/Too proud to be so valiant** i.e., such
pride is not permissible in one so warlike (because dangerous)
261 **success** outcome

Brutus.   Fame, at the which he aims,
265 In whom already he's well graced, can not
     Better be held, nor more attained, than by
     A place below the first. For what miscarries
     Shall be the general's fault, though he perform
     To th' utmost of a man; and giddy censure
270 Will then cry out of Marcius "O, if he
     Had borne the business!"

Sicinius.   Besides, if things go well,
     Opinion, that so sticks on Marcius, shall
     Of his demerits° rob Cominius.

Brutus.   Come:
     Half all Cominius' honors are to Marcius,
275 Though Marcius earned them not; and all his faults
     To Marcius shall be honors, though indeed
     In aught he merit not.

Sicinius.   Let's hence, and hear
     How the dispatch° is made; and in what fashion,
     More than his singularity,° he goes
     Upon this present action.

280 *Brutus.*   Let's along.   *Exeunt.*

[Scene II. *Corioli. The Senate House.*]

Enter Tullus Aufidius, with Senators of Corioles.

First Senator. So, your opinion is, Aufidius,
     That they of Rome are ent'red in° our counsels,
     And know how we proceed.

Aufidius.   Is it not yours?

273 **demerits** deserts   278 **dispatch** execution of the business   279
More than his singularity apart from his usual peculiarity of manner
I.ii.2 **ent'red in** initiated into (familiar with)

What° ever have been thought on in this state
That could be brought to bodily act ere Rome   5
Had circumvention?° 'Tis not four days gone
Since I heard thence—these are the words—I think
I have the letter here. Yes, here it is:
"They have pressed a power,° but it is not known
Whether for east or west. The dearth is great;   10
The people mutinous; and it is rumored,
Cominius, Marcius your old enemy
(Who is of Rome worse hated than of you),
And Titus Lartius, a most valiant Roman,
These three lead on this preparation°   15
Whither 'tis bent—most likely 'tis for you.
Consider of it."

First Senator.   Our army's in the field.
We never yet made doubt but Rome was ready
To answer us.

Aufidius.   Nor did you think it folly
To keep your great pretenses° veiled till when   20
They needs must show themselves; which in the
    hatching,
It seemed, appeared to Rome. By the discovery
We shall be short'ned in our aim, which was
To take in° many towns ere almost Rome
Should know we were afoot.

Second Senator.   Noble Aufidius,   25
Take your commission; hie you to your bands:
Let us alone to guard Corioles.
If they set down before's,° for the remove°
Bring up your army; but I think you'll find
They've not prepared for us.

Aufidius.   O, doubt not that;   30
I speak from certainties. Nay, more,

---

4 **What** (plural, i.e., "counsels," line 2) 6 **circumvention** means
to circumvent 9 **pressed a power** collected troops 15 **preparation**
force that has been prepared 20 **great pretenses** main intentions
(cf. "grand design") 24 **take in** capture 28 **set down before's** lay
siege to us 28 **remove** raising of the siege

Some parcels° of their power are forth already,
And only hitherward.° I leave your honors.
If we and Caius Marcius chance to meet,
35 'Tis sworn between us we shall ever strike
Till one can do no more.

All.   The gods assist you!

Aufidius. And keep your honors safe!

First Senator.   Farewell.

Second Senator.   Farewell.

All. Farewell.   *Exeunt omnes.°*

[Scene III. *Rome. A room in Marcius' house.*]

*Enter Volumnia and Virgilia, mother and wife to
Marcius. They set them down on two low stools,
and sew.*

Volumnia. I pray you, daughter, sing, or express yourself in a more comfortable° sort. If my son were
my husband, I should freelier rejoice in that absence wherein he won honor than in the embrace-
5 ments of his bed where he would show most love.
When yet he was but tender-bodied, and the only
son of my womb; when youth with comeliness
plucked all gaze° his way; when, for a day of kings'
entreaties, a mother should not sell him an hour
10 from her beholding; I, considering how honor
would become such a person°—that it was no
better than picture-like to hang by th' wall, if renown made it not stir—was pleased to let him seek

32 **parcels** portions   33 **hitherward** i.e., to attack Rome   38 s.d.
omnes all (Latin)   I.iii.2 **comfortable** cheerful   8 **plucked all gaze**
drew the eyes of all   11 **person** handsome figure

danger where he was like to find fame. To a cruel
war I sent him, from whence he returned, his brows   *15*
bound with oak.° I tell thee, daughter, I sprang not
more in joy at first hearing he was a man-child than
now in first seeing he had proved himself a man.

Virgilia. But had he died in the business, madam,
how then?   *20*

Volumnia. Then his good report should have been my
son; I therein would have found issue. Hear me
profess° sincerely: had I a dozen sons, each in my
love alike, and none less dear than thine and my
good Marcius, I had rather had eleven die nobly   *25*
for their country than one voluptuously surfeit out
of action.

Enter a Gentlewoman.

Gentlewoman. Madam, the Lady Valeria is come to
visit you.

Virgilia. Beseech° you give me leave to retire myself.   *30*

Volumnia. Indeed, you shall not.
   Methinks I hear hither your husband's drum;
   See him pluck Aufidius down by th' hair;
   As children from a bear, the Volsces shunning him.
   Methinks I see him stamp thus, and call thus: *35*
   "Come on, you cowards, you were got° in fear,
   Though you were born in Rome." His bloody brow
   With his mailed hand then wiping, forth he goes,
   Like to a harvest-man that's tasked to mow
   Or° all or lose his hire.   *40*

Virgilia. His bloody brow? O Jupiter, no blood!

Volumnia. Away, you fool! It more becomes a man
   Than gilt his trophy.° The breasts of Hecuba,°
   When she did suckle Hector, looked not lovelier
   Then Hector's forehead when it spit forth blood   *45*

16 **oak** ("garland" of honor for saving a fellow Roman in battle)
23 **profess** declare   30 **Beseech** I beg   36 **got** begotten   40 **Or**
either   43 **trophy** monument   43 **Hecuba** (Queen of Troy and
mother of Hector, who defended the city from the Greeks)

       At Grecian sword, contemning.° Tell Valeria
       We are fit° to bid her welcome. *Exit Gentlewoman.*

Virgilia. Heavens bless° my lord from fell° Aufidius!

Volumnia. He'll beat Aufidius' head below his knee,
50   And tread upon his neck.

       Enter Valeria with an Usher° and a Gentlewoman.

Valeria. My ladies both, good day to you.

Volumnia. Sweet madam!

Virgilia. I am glad to see your ladyship.

Valeria. How do you both? You are manifest house-
55   keepers.° What are you sewing here? A fine spot,°
       in good faith. How does your little son?

Virgilia. I thank your ladyship; well, good madam.

Volumnia. He had rather see the swords and hear a
       drum than look upon his schoolmaster.

60 *Valeria.* O' my word, the father's son! I'll swear 'tis
       a very pretty boy. O' my troth, I looked upon him
       o' Wednesday half an hour together; has such a
       confirmed° countenance! I saw him run after a
       gilded butterfly; and when he caught it, he let it go
65   again; and after it again; and over and over he
       comes, and up again; catched it again; or whether
       his fall enraged him, or how 'twas, he did so set
       his teeth, and tear it. O, I warrant, how he mam-
       mocked° it!

70 *Volumnia.* One on's° father's moods.

Valeria. Indeed, la, 'tis a noble child.

Virgilia. A crack,° madam.

---

46 **contemning** in scorn   47 **fit** ready   48 **bless** guard   48 **fell**
savage   50 s.d. **Usher** servant accompanying a lady   54–55 **manifest housekeepers** clearly stay-at-homes   55 **spot** pattern in em-
broidery   63 **confirmed** determined   68–69 **mammocked** tore to
pieces   70 **on's** of his   72 **crack** rascal

Valeria. Come, lay aside your stitchery; I must have you play the idle huswife with me this afternoon.

Virgilia. No, good madam; I will not out of doors.   75

Valeria. Not out of doors!

Volumnia. She shall, she shall.

Virgilia. Indeed, no, by your patience;° I'll not over the threshold till my lord return from the wars.

Valeria. Fie, you confine yourself most unreasonably;   80
come, you must go visit the good lady that lies in.

Virgilia. I will wish her speedy strength, and visit her with my prayers; but I cannot go thither.

Volumnia. Why I pray you?

Virgilia. 'Tis not to save labor, nor that I want° love.   85

Valeria. You would be another Penelope;° yet, they say, all the yarn she spun in Ulysses' absence did but fill Ithaca° full of moths. Come; I would your cambric were sensible° as your finger, that you might leave pricking it for pity. Come, you shall go   90
with us.

Virgilia. No, good madam, pardon me; indeed, I will not forth.

Valeria. In truth, la, go with me, and I'll tell you excellent news of your husband.   95

Virgilia. O, good madam, there can be none yet.

Valeria. Verily, I do not jest with you; there came news from him last night.

Virgilia. Indeed, madam?

Valeria. In earnest, it's true; I heard a senator speak   100
it. Thus it is: the Volsces have an army forth;

---

78 patience leave   **85 want** am lacking in   **86 Penelope** (Ulysses' faithful wife, who by using her weaving as an excuse, postponed her answer to offers of marriage)   **88 Ithaca** (Ulysses' home city)
89 sensible sensitive

against whom Cominius the general is gone, with
one part of our Roman power. Your lord and Titus
Lartius are set down before their city Corioles; they
105 nothing doubt prevailing, and to make it brief wars.
This is true, on mine honor; and so, I pray, go
with us.

Virgilia. Give me excuse, good madam; I will obey
you in everything hereafter.

110 *Volumnia.* Let her alone, lady; as she is now, she will
but disease our better mirth.°

Valeria. In troth, I think she would. Fare you well,
then. Come, good sweet lady. Prithee, Virgilia, turn
thy solemnness out o' door, and go along with us.

115 *Virgilia.* No, at a word,° madam; indeed, I must not.
I wish you much mirth.

Valeria. Well then, farewell.

                                    Exeunt Ladies.

[Scene IV. *Before Corioli.*]

*Enter Marcius, Titus Lartius, with drum and colors,
with Captains and Soldiers, as before the city Corioles.
To them a Messenger.*

Marcius. Yonder comes news: a wager they have met.

Lartius. My horse to yours, no.

Marcius.   'Tis done.

Lartius.   Agreed.

Marcius. Say, has our general met the enemy?

_____

111 **disease our better mirth** spoil our fun, which would be better
(without her)   115 **at a word** to put it briefly

Messenger. They lie in view, but have not spoke° as
    yet.

Lartius. So, the good horse is mine.

Marcius.   I'll buy him of you.   *5*

Lartius. No, I'll nor sell nor give him; lend you him
    I will
For half a hundred years. Summon the town.

Marcius. How far off lie these armies?

Messenger.   Within this mile and half.

Marcius. Then shall we hear their 'larum,° and they
    ours.
Now, Mars, I prithee, make us quick in work,   *10*
That we with smoking° swords may march from
    hence
To help our fielded° friends! Come, blow thy blast.

    They sound a parley. Enter two Senators
    with others, on the walls of Corioles.

Tullus Aufidius, is he within your walls?

First Senator. No, nor a man that fears you less than
    he;
That's lesser than a little. (*Drum afar off.*) Hark,
    our drums   *15*
Are bringing forth our youth. We'll break our walls
Rather than they shall pound us up.° Our gates,
Which yet seem shut, we have but pinned with
    rushes;
They'll open of themselves. (*Alarum far off.*) Hark
    you, far off!
There is Aufidius. List what work he makes   *20*
Amongst your cloven° army.

Marcius.   O, they are at it!

I.iv.4 **spoke** engaged   9 **'larum** alarum, call to arms   11 **smoking**
reeking (with blood)   12 **fielded** in the field of battle   17 **pound**
us up shut us in (cf. "dog pound")   21 **cloven** divided

Lartius. Their noise be our instruction.° Ladders, ho!

Enter the Army of the Volsces.

Marcius. They fear us not, but issue forth their city.
Now put your shields before your hearts, and fight
With hearts more proof° than shields. Advance,
25   brave Titus.
They do disdain us much beyond our thoughts,
Which makes me sweat with wrath. Come on, my
       fellows.
He that retires, I'll take him for a Volsce,
And he shall feel mine edge.

*Alarum. The Romans are beat back
to their trenches. Enter Marcius, cursing.*

30 *Marcius.* All the contagion of the south° light on you,
You shames of Rome! You herd of—boils and
       plagues
Plaster you o'er, that you may be abhorred
Farther than seen, and one infect another
Against the wind a mile!° You souls of geese
35   That bear the shapes of men, how have you run
From slaves that apes would beat! Pluto and hell!
All hurt behind, backs red, and faces pale
With flight and agued° fear! Mend° and charge
       home,°
Or, by the fires of heaven, I'll leave the foe,
40   And make my wars on you. Look to't. Come on;
If you'll stand fast, we'll beat them to their wives,
As they us to our trenches. Follow's.°

---

22 **be our instruction** be a lesson to us   25 **proof** tested (and so
impenetrable)   30 **south** south wind (pestilential)   34 **Against the
wind a mile** i.e., the infection carrying a mile in the face of a
contrary wind   38 **agued** i.e., shaking as if from an ague-fit (*ague*
= malarial fever)   38 **Mend** do better (pun on the hygienic sense)
38 **home** i.e., into the heart of the enemy's forces   42 **Follow's** follow us, i.e., follow me (the Folio gives "trenches followes." The
adopted reading makes sense out of the Folio reading, but it is ugly
and anticlimactic. Perhaps "followes" is a misplaced stage direction)

Another alarum; and Marcius follows them to
[the] gates and is shut in.°

So, now the gates are ope. Now prove good sec-
    onds!°
'Tis for the followers° Fortune widens them,
Not for the fliers. Mark me, and do the like.   *45*
                    Enters the gates.

First Soldier. Foolhardiness; not I.

Second Soldier. Nor I.

First Soldier. See, they have shut him in.
                    Alarum continues.

All.   To th' pot,° I warrant him.

        Enter Titus Lartius.

Lartius. What is become of Marcius?

All.   Slain, sir, doubtless.

First Soldier. Following the fliers at the very heels,   *50*
With them he enters; who, upon the sudden,
Clapped to their gates. He is himself alone,
To answer all the city.

Lartius.   O noble fellow!
Who sensibly° outdares his senseless sword,
And when it bows stand'st up! Thou art left,
    Marcius!   *55*
A carbuncle° entire, as big as thou art,
Were not so rich a jewel. Thou wast a soldier
Even to Cato's° wish, not fierce and terrible
Only in strokes; but with thy grim looks and
The thunder-like percussion of thy sounds   *60*
Thou mad'st thine enemies shake, as if the world
Were feverous and did tremble.

---

42 s.d. **is shut in** i.e., at the end of this speech Marcius enters the gates
and is shut in   43 **seconds** helpers   44 **followers** pursuers   48 **To
th' pot** to destruction (cf. "gone to pot")   54 **sensibly** though subject
to feeling   56 **A carbuncle** a red precious stone   58 **Cato** (the
Censor, stern upholder of old Roman virtues; see North, below,
p. 216)

*Enter Marcius, bleeding, assaulted
by the enemy.*

First Soldier.   Look, sir.

Lartius.   O, 'tis Marcius!
Let's fetch him off, or make remain alike.°
                              They fight, and all enter the city.

[Scene V. *Within Corioli.*]

Enter certain Romans, with spoils.

First Roman. This will I carry to Rome.

Second Roman. And I this.

Third Roman. A murrain on't!° I took this for silver.
                                                        Exeunt.
                    Alarum continues still afar off.

*Enter Marcius and Titus Lartius
with a Trumpet.°*

Marcius. See here these movers° that do prize their
        hours
5   At a cracked drachma!° Cushions, leaden spoons,
        Irons of a doit,° doublets that hangmen would
        Bury with those that wore them, these base slaves,
        Ere yet the fight be done, pack up. Down with
            them!
        And hark, what noise the general makes! To him!
10   There is the man of my soul's hate, Aufidius,
        Piercing our Romans. Then, valiant Titus, take
        Convenient numbers to make good° the city;

63 **make remain alike** stay like him (*remain*, a noun, means "a
stay") I.v.3 **murrain on't** plague on it   3 s.d.**Trumpet** trumpeter
4 **movers** active fellows (ironical)   5 **drachma** Greek coin   6 **of a
doit** worth a doit (coin of little value)   12 **make good** make
sure of

Whilst I, with those that have the spirit, will haste
To help Cominius.

Lartius.   Worthy sir, thou bleed'st;
Thy exercise hath been too violent   15
For a second course° of fight.

Marcius.   Sir, praise me not;
My work hath yet not warmed me. Fare you well.
The blood I drop is rather physical°
Than dangerous to me. To Aufidius thus
I will appear, and fight.

Lartius.   Now the fair goddess, Fortune,   20
Fall deep in love with thee; and her great charms
Misguide thy opposers' swords! Bold gentleman,
Prosperity be thy page!°

Marcius.   Thy friend no less
Than those she placeth highest! So farewell.

Lartius. Thou worthiest Marcius!

                              [*Exit Marcius.*]   25
Go, sound thy trumpet in the marketplace;
Call thither all the officers o' th' town,
Where they shall know our mind. Away!   *Exeunt.*

[Scene VI. *Near the camp of Cominius.*]

Enter Cominius, as it were in retire, with soldiers.

Cominius. Breathe° you, my friends; well fought; we
    are come off°
Like Romans, neither foolish in our stands
Nor cowardly in retire.° Believe me, sirs,
We shall be charged again. Whiles we have struck,

16 **course** bout 18 **physical** beneficial 23 **page** attendant I.vi.1 **Breathe**
rest   1 **are come off** leave the field   3 **retire** retreat

5   By interims and conveying gusts° we have heard
      The charges of our friends. The Roman gods,
      Lead their successes° as we wish our own,
      That both our powers, with smiling fronts° encoun-
          t'ring,
      May give you thankful sacrifice!

                    Enter a Messenger.

                                        Thy news?

10 *Messenger.* The citizens of Corioles have issued,
      And given to Lartius and to Marcius battle.
      I saw our party to their trenches driven,
      And then I came away.

    Cominius.   Though thou speakest truth,
      Methinks thou speak'st not well. How long is't
          since?

15 *Messenger.* Above an hour, my lord.

    Cominius. 'Tis not a mile; briefly° we heard their
          drums.
      How couldst thou in a mile confound° an hour,
      And bring thy news so late?

    Messenger.   Spies of the Volsces
      Held me in chase, that I was forced to wheel
20   Three or four miles about; else had I, sir,
      Half an hour since brought my report.

                    Enter Marcius.

    Cominius.   Who's yonder
      That does appear as he were flayed? O gods!
      He has the stamp° of Marcius, and I have
      Before-time seen him thus.

    Marcius.   Come I too late?

---

5 **By interims and conveying gusts** at intervals, by gusts of wind
carrying (the sound) 7 **successes** outcomes 8 **fronts** first lines
(also, "faces") 16 **briefly** a short time ago 17 **confound** waste
23 **stamp** characteristic features (metaphor from coining)

Cominius. The shepherd knows not thunder from a
   tabor°   25
  More than I know the sound of Marcius' tongue
  From every meaner man.

Marcius.   Come I too late?

Cominius. Ay, if you come not in the blood of others,
  But mantled in your own.

Marcius.   O, let me clip° ye
  In arms as sound as when I wooed; in heart   30
  As merry as when our nuptial day was done,
  And tapers burned to bedward!°

Cominius.   Flower of warriors!
  How is't with Titus Lartius?

Marcius. As with a man busied about decrees:
  Condemning some to death and some to exile;   35
  Ransoming him, or pitying, threat'ning th' other;
  Holding Corioles in the name of Rome,
  Even like a fawning greyhound in the leash,
  To let him slip° at will.

Cominius.   Where is that slave
  Which told me they had beat you to your trenches? 40
  Where is he? Call him hither.

Marcius.   Let him alone;
  He did inform° the truth. But for our gentlemen,°
  The common file°—a plague! tribunes for them!—
  The mouse ne'er shunned the cat as they did budge
  From rascals worse than they.

Cominius.   But how prevailed you? 45

Marcius. Will the time serve to tell? I do not think.
  Where is the enemy? Are you lords o' th' field?
  If not, why cease you till you are so?

Cominius.   Marcius,

25 **tabor** small drum 29 **clip** embrace 32 **burned to bedward**
burned low, announcing the time for bed 39 **let him slip** unleash
him 42 **inform** report 42 **gentlemen** (ironically) 43 **common file**
i.e., the plebeian soldiers

We have at disadvantage fought and did
50   Retire to win our purpose.

Marcius. How lies their battle? Know you on which
        side
They have placed their men of trust?

Cominius.   As I guess, Marcius,
Their bands i' th' vaward° are the Antiates,
Of their best trust; o'er them Aufidius,
Their very heart of hope.

55 *Marcius.*   I do beseech you,
By all the battles wherein we have fought,
By th' blood we have shed together, by th' vows
We have made to endure friends, that you directly
Set me against Aufidius and his Antiates;
60   And that you not delay the present,° but,
Filling the air with swords advanced and darts,
We prove° this very hour.

Cominius.   Though I could wish
You were conducted to a gentle bath,
And balms applied to you, yet dare I never
65   Deny your asking. Take your choice of those
That best can aid your action.

Marcius.   Those are they
That most are willing. If any such be here—
As it were sin to doubt—that love this painting
Wherein you see me smeared; if any fear
70   Lesser his person° than an ill report;
If any think brave death outweighs bad life,
And that his country's dearer than himself;
Let him alone, or so many so minded,
Wave thus, to express his disposition,°
75   And follow Marcius.

        They all shout, and wave their swords; take
        him up in their arms, and cast up their caps.

---

53 **vaward** vanguard, advance troops   60 **delay the present** put off
the present occasion   62 **prove** make trial of   69–70 **fear/Lesser his
person** fear less for his body   74 **disposition** inclination

O me alone! Make you a sword of me?
If these shows be not outward, which of you
But is four Volsces? None of you but is
Able to bear against the great Aufidius
A shield as hard as his. A certain number,   80
Though thanks to all, must I select from all. The
     rest
Shall bear the business in some other fight,
As cause will be obeyed.° Please you to march;
And four shall quickly draw out my command,
Which men are best inclined.

Cominius.   March on, my fellows: 85
Make good this ostentation,° and you shall
Divide in all with us.   *Exeunt.*

[Scene VII. *The gates of Corioli.*]

*Titus Lartius, having set a guard upon Corioles, going
with drum and trumpet toward Cominius and Caius
Marcius, enters with a Lieutenant, other Soldiers, and
a Scout.*

Lartius. So, let the ports° be guarded; keep your
     duties
As I have set them down. If I do send, dispatch
Those centuries° to our aid; the rest will serve
For a short holding. If we lose the field,
We cannot keep the town.

Lieutenant.   Fear not our care, sir.   5

Lartius. Hence, and shut your gates upon's.
Our guider, come; to th' Roman camp conduct us.
                    Exit [with the rest].

83 **cause will be obeyed** occasion shall demand   86 **ostentation**
display   I.vii.1 **ports** gates   3 **centuries** companies (smallest units
of Roman legion)

[Scene VIII. *A field of battle.*]

Alarum as in battle. Enter Marcius and Aufidius,
at several doors.°

Marcius. I'll fight with none but thee, for I do hate
thee
Worse than a promise-breaker.

Aufidius.   We hate alike:
Not Afric° owns a serpent I abhor
More than thy fame and envy. Fix thy foot.

5   *Marcius.* Let the first budger° die the other's slave,
And the gods doom him after!

Aufidius.   If I fly, Marcius,
Holloa° me like a hare.

Marcius.   Within these hours, Tullus,
Alone I fought in your Corioles walls,
And made what work I pleased. 'Tis not my blood
10   Wherein thou seest me masked. For thy revenge
Wrench up thy power to th' highest.

Aufidius.   Wert thou the Hector
That was the whip of your bragged progeny,°
Thou shouldst not scape me here.
        Here they fight, and certain Volsces come in
        the aid of Aufidius. Marcius fights till they
        be driven in breathless.
Officious, and not valiant, you have shamed me
15   In your condemnèd seconds.°

I.viii.s.d. **at several doors** from different entrances   3 **Afric** Africa
5 **budger** one who moves   7 **Holloa** shout "halloo" after (in hunt-
ing)   12 **whip of your bragged progeny** the whip used by your
boasted ancestors, the Trojans, against the Greeks   15 **In your
condemnèd seconds** by your damnable help (cf. I.iv.43)

[Scene IX. *The Roman camp.*]

Flourish. Alarum. A retreat is sounded. Enter at one door, Cominius with the Romans; at another door, Marcius, with his arm in a scarf.

Cominius. If I should tell thee o'er this thy day's work,
Thou't° not believe thy deeds. But I'll report it
Where senators shall mingle tears with smiles;
Where great patricians shall attend, and shrug,°
I' th' end admire; where ladies shall be frighted,   5
And, gladly quaked,° hear more; where the dull tribunes,
That with the fusty° plebeians hate thine honors,
Shall say against their hearts "We thank the gods
Our Rome hath such a soldier."
Yet cam'st thou to a morsel of this feast,°   10
Having fully dined before.

Enter Titus [Lartius], with his power, from the pursuit.

Lartius.   O general,
Here is the steed, we the caparison!°
Hadst thou beheld—

Marcius.   Pray now, no more. My mother,
Who has a charter° to extol her blood,
When she does praise me grieves me. I have done   15
As you have done, that's what I can; induced
As you have been, that's for my country.

I.ix.2 **Thou't** thou wouldst   4 **shrug** i.e., in disbelief   6 **quaked** made to shake   7 **fusty** moldy   10 **cam'st thou to a morsel of this feast** (refers to Marcius' coming to support Cominius in the latter part of the battle just ended)   12 **caparison** the (mere) trappings   14 **charter** privilege granted her

He that has but effected his good will°
Hath overta'en° mine act.

Cominius.   You shall not be
20   The grave of your deserving; Rome must know
The value of her own. 'Twere a concealment
Worse than a theft, no less than a traducement,°
To hide your doings; and to silence that
Which, to the spire and top of praises vouched,°
25   Would seem but modest. Therefore, I beseech you,
In sign of what you are, not to reward
What you have done, before our army hear me.

Marcius. I have some wounds upon me, and they
    smart
To hear themselves rememb'red.

Cominius.   Should they not,
30   Well might they fester 'gainst° ingratitude,
And tent themselves° with death.° Of all the
    horses—
Whereof we have ta'en good, and good store°—
    of all
The treasure in this field achieved and city,
We render you the tenth; to be ta'en forth
35   Before the common distribution at
Your only choice.

Marcius.   I thank you, general;
But cannot make my heart consent to take
A bribe to pay my sword. I do refuse it,
And stand upon my common part with those
40   That have beheld the doing.
                    A long flourish. They all cry "Marcius!
                    Marcius!" cast up their caps and lances.
                    Cominius and Lartius stand bare.

---

18 **good will** firm intention   19 **overta'en** surpassed   22 **traduce-**
ment slander   24 **to the spire and top of praises vouched** though
attested in the highest terms of praise   30 **'gainst** against, in the
face of   31 **tent themselves** be cleansed (refers to cleaning a wound
with a linen roll, a "tent")   31 **death** (the "tent" being "death,"
the wounds would prove fatal)   32 **good store** plenty

Marcius. May these same instruments, which you
    profane,
    Never sound more! When drums and trumpets shall
    I' th' field prove flatterers, let courts and cities be
    Made all of false-faced soothing!°
    When steel grows soft as the parasite's silk,   45
    Let him be made a coverture° for th' wars!
    No more, I say! For that° I have not washed
    My nose that bled, or foiled° some debile° wretch,
    Which without note here's many else have done,
    You shout me forth   50
    In acclamations hyperbolical;
    As if I loved my little should be dieted
    In° praises sauced with lies.

Cominius.   Too modest are you;
    More cruel to your good report than grateful
    To us that give° you truly. By your patience,   55
    If 'gainst yourself you be incensed, we'll put you
    (Like one that means his proper° harm) in
        manacles,
    Then reason safely with you. Therefore, be it
        known,
    As to us, to all the world, that Caius Marcius
    Wears this war's garland: in token of the which,   60
    My noble steed, known to the camp, I give him,
    With all his trim belonging;° and from this time,
    For what he did before Corioles, call him,
    With all th' applause and clamor of the host,
    Caius Marcius Coriolanus.   65
    Bear th' addition° nobly ever!
                Flourish. Trumpets sound, and drums.

Omnes.° Caius Marcius Coriolanus!

Coriolanus. I will go wash:
    And when my face is fair, you shall perceive
    Whether I blush, or no. Howbeit, I thank you.   70

44 **soothing** flattery   46 **coverture** clothing   47 **For that** because
48 **foiled** defeated   48 **debile** weak   52–53 **dieted/In** fed by   55 **give**
report   57 **proper** own   62 **his trim belonging** the equipment that
goes with it   66 **addition** title   67 **Omnes** all (Latin)

I mean to stride your steed, and at all times
To undercrest your good addition°
To th' fairness° of my power.

Cominius.   So, to our tent;
Where, ere we do repose us, we will write
75 To Rome of our success. You, Titus Lartius,
Must to Corioles back; send us to Rome
The best,° with whom we may articulate°
For their own good and ours.

Lartius.   I shall, my lord.

Coriolanus. The gods begin to mock me. I, that now
80 Refused most princely gifts, am bound to beg
Of my lord general.

Cominius.   Take't; 'tis yours. What is't?

Coriolanus. I sometime lay here in Corioles
At a poor man's house; he used me kindly.
He cried to me; I saw him prisoner;
85 But then Aufidius was within my view,
And wrath o'erwhelmed my pity. I request you
To give my poor host freedom.

Cominius.   O, well begged!
Were he the butcher of my son, he should
Be free as is the wind. Deliver him, Titus.

Lartius. Marcius, his name?

90 *Coriolanus.*   By Jupiter, forgot!
I am weary; yea, my memory is tired.
Have we no wine here?

Cominius.   Go we to our tent.
The blood upon your visage dries; 'tis time
It should be looked to. Come.   *Exeunt.*

---

72 **undercrest your good addition** support the fine title you give
(a "crest" in heraldry is a figure above a shield; the suggested
image is of a shield with a man on horseback [line 71], beneath a
crest [the "addition"])   73 **To th' fairness** to the exact measure
77 **best** chief men   77 **articulate** make terms

[Scene X. *The camp of the Volsces.*]

*A flourish. Cornets. Enter Tullus Aufidius,
bloody, with two or three soldiers.*

Aufidius. The town is ta'en!

First Soldier. 'Twill be delivered back on good condition.°

Aufidius. Condition!
  I would I were a Roman; for I cannot,
  Being a Volsce, be that I am. Condition!
  What good condition° can a treaty find   5
  I' th' part that is at mercy?° Five times, Marcius,
  I have fought with thee; so often hast thou beat me;
  And wouldst do so, I think, should we encounter
  As often as we eat. By th' elements,   10
  If e'er again I meet him beard to beard,
  He's mine or I am his. Mine emulation
  Hath not that honor in't it had; for where
  I thought to crush him in an equal force,
  True sword to sword, I'll potch° at him some way, 15
  Or wrath or craft may get him.

First Soldier.   He's the devil.

Aufidius. Bolder, though not so subtle. My valor's,
    poisoned
  With only suff'ring stain° by him; for him
  Shall fly out of itself.° Nor sleep nor sanctuary,
  Being naked,° sick, nor fane° nor Capitol,   20
  The prayers of priests nor times of sacrifice,

I.x.2 **condition** terms   6 **condition** (with pun on sense of "quality")
7 **I' th' part that is at mercy** on the side that is vanquished (at the
mercy of the victor)   15 **potch** poke (thrust, in fencing)   18 **stain**
darkening   19 **fly out of itself** go out of its natural course   20 **naked**
unarmed   20 **fane** shrine

Embarquements° all of fury, shall lift up
Their rotten privilege and custom 'gainst
My hate to Marcius. Where I find him, were it
25 At home, upon my brother's guard,° even there,
Against the hospitable canon,° would I
Wash my fierce hand in's heart. Go you to th' city;
Learn how 'tis held, and what they are that must
Be hostages for Rome.

First Soldier.   Will not you go?

Aufidius. I am attended° at the cypress grove. I pray
30   you—
'Tis south the city mills—bring me word thither
How the world goes, that to the pace of it
I may spur on my journey.

First Soldier.   I shall, sir.   [*Exeunt.*]

---

22 **Embarquements** restraints   25 **upon my brother's guard** with my
brother on guard (over him)   26 **hospitable canon** law of hospi-
tality   30 **attended** awaited

ACT II

[Scene I. *Rome. A public place.*]

Enter Menenius, with the two Tribunes of the people, Sicinius, and Brutus.

Menenius. The augurer° tells me we shall have news tonight.

Brutus. Good or bad?

Menenius. Not according to the prayer of the people, for they love not Marcius.   5

Sicinius. Nature teaches beasts to know their friends.

Menenius. Pray you, who does the wolf love?

Sicinius. The lamb.

Menenius. Ay, to devour him, as the hungry plebeians   10
would the noble Marcius.

Brutus. He's a lamb indeed, that baas like a bear.

Menenius. He's a bear indeed, that lives like a lamb.
You two are old men: tell me one thing that I shall
ask you.

Both. Well, sir.   15

Menenius. In what enormity° is Marcius poor in, that
you two have not in abundance?

II.i.1 **augurer** (more correctly "augur," Roman official who fore-
told the future)   16 **enormity** fault

87

Brutus. He's poor in no one fault, but stored with all.

Sicinius. Especially in pride.

20 *Brutus.* And topping all others in boasting.

Menenius. This is strange now. Do you two know how you are censured° here in the city—I mean of us o' th' right-hand file?° Do you?

Both. Why, how are we censured?

25 *Menenius.* Because you talk of pride now—will you not be angry?

Both. Well, well, sir, well.

Menenius. Why 'tis no great matter; for a very little thief of occasion° will rob you of a great deal of
30 patience. Give your dispositions the reins, and be angry at your pleasures; at the least, if you take it as a pleasure to you in being so. You blame Marcius for being proud?

Brutus. We do it not alone, sir.

35 *Menenius.* I know you can do very little alone; for your helps are many, or else your actions would grow wondrous single:° your abilities are too infantlike for doing much alone. You talk of pride: O that you could turn your eyes toward the napes of
40 your necks, and make but an interior survey of your good selves! O that you could!

Both. What then, sir?

Menenius. Why, then you should discover a brace of unmeriting, proud, violent, testy° magistrates (alias
45 fools) as any in Rome.

Sicinius. Menenius, you are known well enough° too.

21–22 **how you are censured** the opinion held of you   23 **o' th' right-hand file** of the upper classes, patricians   28–29 **a very little thief of occasion** i.e., a very little occasion is a thief who   37 **single** weak, slight   44 **testy** snappish   46 **known well enough** i.e., notorious

Menenius. I am known to be a humorous° patrician,
and one that loves a cup of hot wine with not a
drop of allaying° Tiber in't; said to be something
imperfect in favoring the first complaint,° hasty and   50
tinderlike upon too trivial motion;° one that con-
verses° more with the buttock of the night than
with the forehead of the morning. What I think I
utter, and spend my malice in my breath. Meeting
two such wealsmen° as you are—I cannot call   55
you Lycurguses°—if the drink you give me touch
my palate adversely, I make a crooked face at it.
I cannot say your worships have delivered the
matter well, when I find the ass in compound with
the major part of your syllables;° and though I   60
must be content to bear with those that say you
are reverend grave men, yet they lie deadly that
tell you you have good faces. If you see this in the
map° of my microcosm,° follows it that I am
known well enough too? What harm can your   65
bisson conspectuities° glean out of this character,
if I be known well enough too?

Brutus. Come, sir, come, we know you well enough.

Menenius. You know neither me, yourselves, nor any
thing. You are ambitious for poor knaves' caps and   70
legs.° You wear out a good wholesome forenoon in
hearing a cause° between an orange-wife and a
forset-seller,° and then rejourn° the controversy of
'hreepence to a second day of audience. When you
are hearing a matter between party and party, if   75
you chance to be pinched with the colic, you make

---

47 **humorous** whimsical   49 **allaying** diluting   49–50 **something imperfect in favoring the first complaint** somewhat at fault in siding
with the party who first puts his case   51 **motion** impulse
51–52 **converses** associates   55 **wealsmen** statesmen   56 **Lycurgus**
(a Greek lawgiver)   59–60 **ass in compound with the major part of
your syllables** (pun on over-use of "as-es" in legal expressions, e.g.,
"whereas")   64 **map** i.e., face   64 **microcosm** little world, i.e.,
body   66 **bisson conspectuities** blind visual powers   70–71 **caps
and legs** salutes and bows   72 **cause** case   73 **forset-seller** seller of
taps for wine kegs   73 **rejourn** adjourn

faces like mummers,° set up the bloody flag°
against all patience, and, in roaring for a chamber
pot, dismiss the controversy bleeding, the more en-
80 tangled by your hearing. All the peace you make
in their cause is calling both the parties knaves.
You are a pair of strange ones.

Brutus. Come, come, you are well understood to be
a perfecter giber° for the table than a necessary
85 bencher in the Capitol.°

Menenius. Our very priests must become mockers, if
they shall encounter such ridiculous subjects as you
are. When you speak best unto the purpose, it is
not worth the wagging of your beards; and your
90 beards deserve not so honorable a grave as to stuff
a botcher's° cushion or to be entombed in an ass's
packsaddle. Yet you must be saying Marcius is
proud; who, in a cheap estimation, is worth all
your predecessors since Deucalion;° though per-
95 adventure some of the best of 'em were hereditary
hangmen. Good-e'en to your worships. More of
your conversation° would infect my brain, being
the herdsmen of the beastly plebeians. I will be
bold to take my leave of you.

Brutus and Sicinius [step] aside.

Enter Volumnia, Virgilia, and Valeria.

100 How now, my as fair as noble ladies—and the
moon, were she earthly, no nobler—whither do
you follow your eyes so fast?

Volumnia. Honorable Menenius, my boy Marcius approaches; for the love of Juno, let's go.

105 *Menenius.* Ha? Marcius coming home?

---

77 **mummers** Christmas masquers, who act impromptu plays
77 **bloody flag** war flag   84 **giber** joker   84–85 **necessary bencher
in the Capitol** indispensable judge in the Senate (cf. "the bench" for
"court")   91 **botcher** mender of old clothes   94 **Deucalion** (the
Noah of Greek myth)   97 **conversation** cf. lines 51–52

Volumnia. Ay, worthy Menenius; and with most prosperous approbation.°

Menenius. Take my cap, Jupiter,° and I thank thee.
Hoo! Marcius coming home!

Two Ladies. Nay, 'tis true.   110

Volumnia. Look, here's a letter from him; the state
hath another, his wife another; and, I think, there's
one at home for you.

Menenius. I will make my very house reel tonight.
A letter for me?   115

Virgilia. Yes, certain, there's a letter for you; I saw't.

Menenius. A letter for me? It gives me an estate° of
seven years' health; in which time I will make a
lip° at the physician. The most sovereign prescrip-
tion in Galen° is but empiricutic,° and, to this pre-   120
servative, of no better report° than a horse-drench.°
Is he not wounded? He was wont to come home
wounded.

Virgilia. O, no, no, no.

Volumnia. O, he is wounded; I thank the gods for't. 125

Menenius. So do I too, if it be not too much. Brings
'a° victory in his pocket? The wounds become him.

Volumnia. On's brows, Menenius. He comes the third
time home with the oaken garland.

Menenius. Has he disciplined Aufidius soundly?   130

Volumnia. Titus Lartius writes they fought together,
but Aufidius got off.

Menenius. And 'twas time for him too, I'll warrant
him that. And° he had stayed by him, I would

106–107 **with most prosperous approbation** with signs of the greatest
success   108 **Jupiter** (god of the sky and upper air)   117 **estate**
state (fortune?)   118–119 **make a lip** make a face   120 **Galen**
Greek physician   120 **empiricutic** quackish   121 **report** reputation
121 **horse-drench** drink of horse-medicine   127 **'a** he   134 **And** if

135   not have been so fidiused° for all the chests in
      Corioles, and the gold that's in them. Is the Senate
      possessed° of this?

Volumnia. Good ladies, let's go. Yes, yes, yes. The
      Senate has letters from the General, wherein he
140   gives my son the whole name of° the war. He hath
      in this action outdone his former deeds doubly.

Valeria. In troth, there's wondrous things spoke of
      him.

Menenius. Wondrous! Ay, I warrant you, and not
145   without his true purchasing.°

Virgilia. The gods grant them true!

Volumnia. True? Pow waw!°

Menenius. True! I'll be sworn they are true. Where
      is he wounded?——[*To the Tribunes*] God save your
150   good worships! Marcius is coming home. He has
      more cause to be proud.——Where is he wounded?

Volumnia. I' th' shoulder and i' th' left arm. There
      will be large cicatrices° to show the people, when
      he shall stand for his place.° He received in the
155   repulse of Tarquin seven hurts i' th' body.

Menenius. One i' th' neck, and two i' th' thigh——
      there's nine that I know.

Volumnia. He had before this last expedition twenty-
      five wounds upon him.

160 *Menenius.* Now it's twenty-seven: every gash was an
      enemy's grave. (*A shout and flourish.*) Hark! the
      trumpets.

Volumnia. These are the ushers of Marcius. Before

----

135 **fidiused** "Aufidius-ed" (cf. line 130 "disciplined Aufidius
soundly")   137 **possessed** duly informed   140 **name of** credit for
145 **true purchasing** really earning (the praise)   147 **Pow waw** (a
Volumnian "pooh-pooh")   153 **cicatrices** scars (Latin)   154 **place**
i.e., the consulship

him he carries noise, and behind him he leaves
tears.   165
Death, that dark spirit, in's nervy° arm doth lie,
Which, being advanced, declines, and then men die.

*A sennet.° Trumpets sound. Enter Cominius the
general and Titus Lartius; between them, Coriolanus, crowned with an oaken garland; with
Captains and Soldiers, and a Herald.*

Herald. Know, Rome, that all alone Marcius did fight
Within Corioles gates, where he hath won,
With fame, a name to Caius Marcius; these   170
In honor follows Coriolanus.
Welcome to Rome, renownèd Coriolanus!
                                        Sound. Flourish.

All. Welcome to Rome, renownèd Coriolanus!

Coriolanus. No more of this, it does offend my heart;
Pray now, no more.

Cominius.   Look, sir, your mother!

Coriolanus.   O,   175
You have, I know, petitioned all the gods
For my prosperity!   *Kneels.*

Volumnia.   Nay, my good soldier, up;
My gentle Marcius, worthy Caius, and
By deed-achieving° honor newly named—
What is it?—Coriolanus must I call thee?—   180
But, O, thy wife!

Coriolanus.   My gracious silence, hail!
Wouldst thou have laughed had I come coffined
home,
That weep'st to see me triumph? Ah, my dear,
Such eyes the widows in Corioles wear,
And mothers that lack sons.

---

166 **nervy** sinewy   167 s.d. **sennet** (set of notes for trumpet or
cornet to herald an important person, differing from a "flourish"
or "fanfare"; cf. s.d. line 161)   179 **deed-achieving** achieved by
deeds (cf. "the deeds of Coriolanus," II.ii.83)

185 *Menenius.*   Now, the gods crown thee!

Coriolanus. And live you yet? [*To Valeria*] O my
  sweet lady, pardon.

Volumnia. I know not where to turn. O, welcome
  home!
  And welcome, General: and y'are welcome all.

Menenius. A hundred thousand welcomes. I could
  weep,
  And I could laugh, I am light and heavy.° Wel-
190 come!
  A curse begin at very root on's heart
  That is not glad to see thee! You are three
  That Rome should dote on. Yet, by the faith of
  men,
  We have some old crab-trees here at home that
  will not
195 Be grafted° to your relish. Yet welcome, warriors.
  We call a nettle but a nettle, and
  The faults of fools but folly.

Cominius.   Ever right.

Coriolanus. Menenius, ever, ever.

Herald. Give way there, and go on.

Coriolanus. [*To Volumnia and Virgilia*] Your hand,
200 and yours!
  Ere in our own house I do shade my head,
  The good patricians must be visited;
  From whom I have received not only greetings,
  But with them change of honors.°

Volumnia.   I have lived
205 To see inherited° my very wishes
  And the buildings of my fancy. Only
  There's one thing wanting, which I doubt not but
  Our Rome will cast upon thee.

---

190 **light and heavy** both merry and sad   195 **grafted** i.e., improved
204 **change of honors** fresh honors   205 **inherited** in my possession

Coriolanus.   Know, good mother,
  I had rather be their servant in my way
  Than sway with them in theirs.

Cominius.   On, to the Capitol!   *210*
            Flourish. Cornets. Exeunt in state, as before.
            Brutus and Sicinius [come forward].

Brutus. All tongues speak of him, and the blearèd
        sights
  Are spectacled to see him. Your prattling nurse
  Into a rapture° lets her baby cry
  While she chats° him; the kitchen malkin° pins
  Her richest lockram° 'bout her reechy° neck,   *215*
  Clamb'ring the walls to eye him. Stalls, bulks,°
        windows,
  Are smothered up, leads° filled and ridges horsed°
  With variable complexions,° all agreeing
  In earnestness to see him. Seld-shown flamens°
  Do press among the popular throngs, and puff   *220*
  To win a vulgar station.° Our veiled dames
  Commit the war of white and damask in
  Their nicely gawded° cheeks to th' wanton spoil
  Of Phoebus'° burning kisses. Such a pother,°
  As if that whatsoever god who leads him   *225*
  Were slyly crept into his human powers,
  And gave him graceful posture.

Sicinius.   On the sudden,
  I warrant him consul.

Brutus.   Then our office may,
  During his power, go sleep.

Sicinius. He cannot temp'rately transport his honors   *230*

---

213 **rapture** fit   214 **chats** gossips about   214 **malkin** slut   215 **lock-ram** coarse linen   215 **reechy** dirty   216 **bulks** stalls (stands for goods to be sold)   217 **leads** roofs (leaded)   217 **horsed** "ridden" by viewers   218 **variable complexions** different physical types   219 **Seld-shown flamens** priests rarely seen in public (each flamen was in charge of the cult of a particular deity)   221 **vulgar station** place with the common people   223 **gawded** adorned   224 **Phoebus** sun-god   224 **pother** commotion

From where he should begin and end,° but will
Lose those he hath won.

Brutus.   In that there's comfort.

Sicinius.   Doubt not
The commoners, for whom we stand, but they
Upon° their ancient malice will forget
235 With the least cause these his new honors; which°
That he will give them make I as little question
As° he is proud to do't.

Brutus.   I heard him swear,
Were he to stand for consul, never would he
Appear i' th' marketplace, nor on him put
240 The napless° vesture of humility;
Nor, showing, as the manner is, his wounds
To th' people, beg their stinking breaths.

Sicinius.   'Tis right.

Brutus. It was his word. O, he would miss it rather
Than carry° it but by the suit of the gentry to him
And the desire of the nobles.

245 **Sicinius.**   I wish no better
Than have him hold that purpose and to put it
In execution.

Brutus.   'Tis most like he will.

Sicinius. It shall be to him then as our good wills:°
A sure destruction.

Brutus.   So it must fall out
250 To him or our authorities. For an end,°
We must suggest° the people in what hatred
He still° hath held them; that to's power he would
Have made them mules, silenced their pleaders and

---

231 **and end** i.e., to where he should end   234 **Upon** on account of
235 **which** i.e., "cause"   237 **As** as that   240 **napless** threadbare
244 **carry** win   248 **as our good wills** as we strongly desire   250
For an end to force the issue (?) finally (?)   251 **suggest** insinuate
into the minds of   252 **still** ever

Dispropertied° their freedoms; holding them,
In human action and capacity,   255
Of no more soul nor fitness for the world
Than camels in their war, who have their provand°
Only for bearing burdens, and sore blows
For sinking under them.

Sicinius.   This, as you say, suggested
At some time when his soaring insolence   260
Shall touch the people—which time shall not want,°
If he be put upon't,° and that's as easy
As to set dogs on sheep—will be his fire
To kindle their dry stubble; and their blaze
Shall darken him forever.

                    Enter a Messenger.

Brutus.   What's the matter?   265

Messenger. You are sent for to the Capitol. 'Tis
    thought
That Marcius shall be consul.
I have seen the dumb men throng to see him and
The blind to hear him speak. Matrons flung gloves,
Ladies and maids their scarfs and handkerchers,   270
Upon him as he passed; the nobles bended,
As to Jove's statue, and the commons made
A shower and thunder with their caps and shouts.
I never saw the like.

Brutus.   Let's to the Capitol,
And carry with us ears and eyes for th' time,   275
But hearts for the event.°

Sicinius.   Have with you.° *Exeunt.*

254 **Dispropertied** dispossessed them of   257 **provand** provisions
261 **want** be lacking   262 **put upon't** provoked to it   276 **event** outcome   276 **Have with you** coming with you!

[Scene II. *Rome. The Senate House.*]

Enter two Officers, to lay cushions,° as it were,
in the Capitol.

First Officer. Come, come, they are almost here. How
many stand for consulships?

Second Officer. Three, they say; but 'tis thought of
everyone Coriolanus will carry it.

5 *First Officer.* That's a brave fellow; but he's ven-
geance° proud, and loves not the common people.

Second Officer. Faith, there hath been many great
men that have flattered the people, who ne'er loved
them; and there be many that they have loved,
10 they know not wherefore; so that, if they love they
know not why, they hate upon no better a ground.
Therefore, for Coriolanus neither to care whether
they love or hate him manifests the true knowledge
he has in their disposition,° and out of his noble
15 carelessness lets them plainly see't.

First Officer. If he did not care whether he had their
love or no, he waved° indifferently 'twixt doing
them neither good nor harm. But he seeks their
hate with greater devotion than they can render it
20 him, and leaves nothing undone that may fully dis-
cover° him their opposite.° Now, to seem to affect°
the malice° and displeasure of the people is as bad
as that which he dislikes, to flatter them for their
love.

II.ii.s.d. **cushions** i.e., seats for dignitaries   5–6 **vengeance** fright-
fully (cf. "with a vengeance")   14 **in their disposition** of their mood
17 **waved** would waver   20-21 **discover** show   21 **opposite** oppo-
nent   21 **affect** aim at   22 **malice** ill will

Second Officer. He hath deserved worthily of his *25*
country; and his ascent is not by such easy degrees
as those who, having been supple and courteous
to the people, bonneted,° without any further deed
to have them at all into their estimation and report.° But he hath so planted his honors in their *30*
eyes and his actions in their hearts that for their
tongues to be silent and not confess so much were
a kind of ingrateful injury; to report otherwise were
a malice° that, giving itself the lie, would pluck
reproof and rebuke from every ear that heard it. *35*

First Officer. No more of him; he's a worthy man.
Make way, they are coming.

*A sennet. Enter the Patricians and the Tribunes of the
People, Lictors° before them; Coriolanus, Menenius,
Cominius the Consul. Sicinius and Brutus take their
places by themselves. Coriolanus stands.*

Menenius. Having determined of° the Volsces, and
To send for Titus Lartius, it remains,
As the main point of this our after-meeting, *40*
To gratify° his noble service that
Hath thus stood for° his country. Therefore, please
   you
Most reverend and grave elders, to desire
The present consul and last° general
In our well-found° successes, to report *45*
A little of that worthy work performed
By Caius Marcius Coriolanus; whom
We met here both to thank and to remember°
With honors like himself.

First Senator.   Speak, good Cominius:

28 **bonneted** took off their caps (in flattery)   29–30 **to have them
at all into their estimation and report** to get themselves at all into,
win their way into, their esteem   34 **malice** act of ill will   37 s.d.
Lictors (attendants who preceded Roman officials to announce their
approach)   38 **determined of** decided concerning   41 **gratify** reward   42 **stood for** defended   44 **last** late   45 **well-found** fortu-
nately met with   48 **remember** distinguish

50   Leave nothing out for length, and make us think
        Rather our state's defective for requital
        Than we to stretch it out.° [*To the Tribunes*] Mas-
           ters o' th' people,
        We do request your kindest ears; and, after,
        Your loving motion toward the common body,°
        To yield° what passes here.

55 *Sicinius.*   We are convented°
        Upon a pleasing treaty,° and have hearts
        Inclinable to honor and advance
        The theme of our assembly.

Brutus.   Which the rather°
        We shall be blessed° to do, if he remember
60   A kinder value° of the people than
        He hath hereto prized them at.

Menenius.   That's off,° that's off;
        I would you rather had been silent. Please you
        To hear Cominius speak?

Brutus.   Most willingly.
        But yet my caution was more pertinent
        Than the rebuke you give it.

65 *Menenius.*   He loves your people;
        But tie him not to be their bedfellow.
        Worthy Cominius, speak.
                Coriolanus rises and offers to go away.
                    Nay, keep your place.

First Senator. Sit, Coriolanus; never shame to hear
        What you have nobly done.

Coriolanus.   Your honors' pardon:
70   I had rather have my wounds to heal again
        Than hear say how I got them.

51–52 **our state's . . . out** our government (the Senate) is lacking in
the resources for reward rather than we in our effort to extend it
54 **motion toward the common body** influence with the common
people   55 **yield** approve   55 **convented** convened   56 **treaty** proposal for discussion   58 **rather** sooner   59 **blessed** happy   60 **value**
estimate   61 **off** not to the point

Brutus.   Sir, I hope
My words disbenched° you not.

Coriolanus.   No, sir. Yet oft,
When blows have made me stay, I fled from words.
You soothed° not, therefore hurt not; but your
    people,
I love them as they weigh—

Menenius.   Pray now, sit down.   73

Coriolanus. I had rather have one scratch my head
    i' th' sun
When the alarum were struck than idly sit
To hear my nothings monstered.° *Exit Coriolanus.*

Menenius.   Masters of the people,
Your multiplying spawn how can he flatter—
That's thousand to one good one—when you now
    see   80
He had rather venture all his limbs for honor
Than one on's ears° to hear it? Proceed, Cominius.

Cominius. I shall lack voice: the deeds of Coriolanus
Should not be uttered feebly. It is held
That valor is the chiefest virtue° and   85
Most dignifies the haver. If it be,
The man I speak of cannot in the world
Be singly counterpoised.° At sixteen years,
When Tarquin° made a head for° Rome, he fought
Beyond the mark of others. Our then dictator,   90
Whom with all praise I point at, saw him fight,
When with his Amazonian° chin he drove
The bristled lips before him. He bestrid
An o'erpressed Roman, and i' th' consul's view
Slew three opposers; Tarquin's self he met,   95

---

72 **disbenched** unseated   74 **soothed** flattered   78 **monstered** turned
into marvels   82 **Than one on's ears** than venture one of his ears
85 **virtue** (cf. Latin *virtus*, manly strength; on this speech, see Introduction pp. xxiv–vii)   88 **singly counterpoised** matched in value
(literally, in weight) by one man   89 **Tarquin** (early king of Rome,
expelled from the city)   89 **made a head for** raised a force against
92 **Amazonian** i.e., beardless

And struck him on his knee.° In that day's feats,
When he might act the woman in the scene,°
He proved best man i' th' field, and for his meed
Was brow-bound with the oak. His pupil age°
Man-ent'red° thus, he waxèd like a sea;
And, in the brunt of seventeen battles since,
He lurched° all swords of the garland. For this last,
Before and in Corioles, let me say,
I cannot speak him home.° He stopped the fliers,
And by his rare example made the coward
Turn terror into sport; as weeds before
A vessel under sail, so men obeyed
And fell below his stem.° His sword, death's
    stamp,°
Where it did mark, it took;° from face to foot
He was a thing of blood, whose every motion
Was timed with dying cries. Alone he ent'red
The mortal gate of th' city, which he painted
With shunless destiny;° aidless came off,
And with a sudden reinforcement struck
Corioles like a planet.° Now all's his,
When by and by the din of war 'gan° pierce
His ready° sense, then straight his doubled° spirit
Requick'ned what in flesh was fatigate,°
And to the battle came he; where he did
Run reeking o'er the lives of men, as if
'Twere a perpetual spoil;° and till we called
Both field and city ours, he never stood
To ease his breast with panting.

Menenius.   Worthy man!

96 **on his knee** to his knees   97 **in the scene** on that stage   98 **meed**
reward   99 **His pupil age** the years when he was learning (the art of
war)   100 **Man-ent'red** having been initiated into manhood   102
lurched robbed   104 **speak him home** find words to match his merit
108 **stem** bow   108 **stamp** a die for stamping a coin or medal
109 **took** made its mark; killed (perhaps also, "infected fatally," cf.
"struck," line 114)   112–13 **painted/With shunless destiny** smeared
with blood of dying men, who could not shun their fate   114–15
struck/Corioles like a planet (planets supposedly had power to
"strike," i.e., infect with disease)   116 **'gan** began to   117 **ready**
responsive   117 **doubled** renewed   118 **fatigate** fatigued   121 **spoil**
slaughter

First Senator. He cannot but with measure fit° the
 honors
 Which we devise him.

Cominius.   Our spoils he kicked at,   *125*
 And looked upon things precious as they were
 The common muck of the world. He covets less
 Than misery° itself would give, rewards
 His deeds with doing them, and is content
 To spend the time to end it.°

Menenius.   He's right noble.   *130*
 Let him be called for.

First Senator.   Call Coriolanus.

Officer. He doth appear.

     Enter Coriolanus.

Menenius. The Senate, Coriolanus, are well pleased
 To make thee consul.

Coriolanus.   I do owe them still°
 My life and services.

Menenius.   It then remains   *135*
 That you do speak to the people.

Coriolanus.   I do beseech you
 Let me o'erleap that custom, for I cannot
 Put on the gown,° stand naked,° and entreat them,
 For my wounds' sake, to give their suffrage. Please
  you
 That I may pass° this doing.

Sicinius.   Sir, the people   *140*
 Must have their voices;° neither will they bate°
 One jot of ceremony.

---

124 **with measure fit** measure up to; or, "bear with self-control" (?)
128 **misery** poverty 130 **To spend the time to end it** to kill it in
action ("to live it up in action") 134 **still** always 138 **gown**
"vesture of humility" (cf. II.i.240) 138 **naked** i.e., "without any coat
underneath" (North) 140 **pass** pass over 141 **voices** votes 141
bate deduct

Menenius.   Put them not to't.°
          Pray you, go fit you to the custom, and
          Take to you, as your predecessors have,
          Your honor with your form.°

145 *Coriolanus.*   It is a part
          That I shall blush in acting, and might well
          Be taken from the people.

Brutus. [*To Sicinius*]   Mark you that.

Coriolanus. To brag unto them, "Thus I did, and
               thus!"
          Show them th' unaching scars which I should hide,
150   As if I had received them for the hire
          Of their breath only!

Menenius.   Do not stand upon't.°
          We recommend to you, tribunes of the people,
          Our purpose° to them; and to our noble consul
          Wish we all joy and honor.

155 *Senators.* To Coriolanus come all joy and honor!
                    Flourish cornets. Then exeunt. Manet
                                        Sicinius and Brutus.

Brutus. You see how he intends to use the people.

Sicinius. May they perceive's intent! He will require°
               them,
          As if he did contemn what he requested
          Should be in them to give.

Brutus.   Come, we'll inform them
160   Of our proceedings here. On th' marketplace,
          I know, they do attend us.   [*Exeunt.*]

---

142 **Put them not to't** don't test them (by omitting any part of the
ceremony)   145 **Your honor with your form** the honor with the
ceremony it imposes on you   151 **stand upon't** make an issue of it
153 **purpose** proposal   157 **require** ask

[Scene III. *Rome. The Forum.*]

Enter seven or eight Citizens.

First Citizen. Once if he° do require our voices, we
ought not to deny him.

Second Citizen. We may, sir, if we will.

Third Citizen. We have power in ourselves to do it,
but it is a power that we have no power to do; for
if he show us his wounds and tell us his deeds, we
are to put our tongues into those wounds and speak
for them; so, if he tell us his noble deeds, we must
also tell him our noble acceptance of them. Ingratitude is monstrous; and for the multitude to be
ingrateful, were to make a monster of the multitude; of the which we being members, should bring
ourselves to be monstrous members.

First Citizen. And to make us no better thought of, a
little help will serve; for once we stood up° about
the corn, he himself stuck not to call us the many-
headed multitude.

Third Citizen. We have been called so of many; not
that our heads are some brown, some black, some
abram,° some bald, but that our wits are so di-
versely colored. And truly I think, if all our wits
were to issue out of one skull, they would fly east,
west, north, south, and their consent of° one direct
way should be at once to all the points o' th'
compass.

Second Citizen. Think you so? Which way do you
judge my wit would fly?

II.iii.1 **Once if he** if he once   15 **once we stood up** when we took a
stand   20 **abram** auburn   23 **consent of** agreemei t on

Third Citizen. Nay, your wit will not so soon out as
another man's will; 'tis strongly wedged up in a
30   blockhead; but if it were at liberty, 'twould, sure,
southward.

Second Citizen. Why that way?

Third Citizen. To lose itself in a fog; where being
three parts melted away with rotten° dews, the
35   fourth would return for conscience sake, to help
to get thee a wife.°

Second Citizen. You are never without your tricks.
You may, you may.°

Third Citizen. Are you all resolved to give your
40   voices? But that's no matter, the greater part° carries it. I say, if he would incline to the people, there
was never a worthier man.

> *Enter Coriolanus in a gown of humility,*
> *with Menenius.*

Here he comes, and in the gown of humility. Mark
his behavior. We are not to stay all together, but to
45   come by him where he stands, by ones, by twos,
and by threes. He's to make his requests by particulars;° wherein every one of us has a single
honor, in giving him our own voices with our own
tongues. Therefore follow me, and I'll direct you
50   how you shall go by him.

All. Content, content.   [*Exeunt Citizens.*]

Menenius. O sir, you are not right. Have you not
known
The worthiest men have done't?

Coriolanus.   What must I say?—
"I pray, sir"—Plague upon't! I cannot bring
55   My tongue to such a pace. "Look, sir, my wounds!

34 **rotten** unhealthy   35–36 **for conscience . . . wife** i.e., because
of the bastards he had fathered (?)   38 **You may, you may** cf.
"O.K., O.K."   40 **greater part** majority   46–47 **by particulars** to
each in turn

I got them in my country's service, when
Some certain of your brethren roared and ran
From th' noise of our own drums."

Menenius.   O me, the gods!
You must not speak of that. You must desire them
To think upon° you.

Coriolanus.   Think upon me! Hang 'em!   60
I would they would forget me, like the virtues
Which our divines lose by 'em.°

Menenius.   You'll mar all.
I'll leave you. Pray you, speak to 'em, I pray you,
In wholesome° manner.   *Exit.*

Enter three of the Citizens.

Coriolanus.   Bid them wash their faces,
And keep their teeth clean. So, here comes a
     brace.°   65
You know the cause, sir, of my standing here.

Third Citizen. We do, sir; tell us what hath brought
you to't.

Coriolanus. Mine own desert.

Second Citizen. Your own desert?   70

Coriolanus. Ay, not mine own desire.

Third Citizen. How not your own desire?

Coriolanus. No, sir, 'twas never my desire yet to
trouble the poor with begging.

Third Citizen. You must think, if we give you any-   75
thing, we hope to gain by you.

Coriolanus. Well then, I pray, your price o' th' consulship?

First Citizen. The price is, to ask it kindly.

60 **think upon** think well of   62 **lose by 'em** waste on them in
preaching ("pearls before swine")   64 **wholesome** reasonable   65
brace pair (of dogs)

80 *Coriolanus.* Kindly sir, I pray let me ha't. I have
    wounds to show you, which shall be yours in pri-
    vate. Your good voice, sir; what say you?

    Second Citizen. You shall ha't, worthy sir.

    Coriolanus. A match,° sir. There's in all two worthy
85 voices begged. I have your alms. Adieu.

    Third Citizen. But this is something° odd.

    Second Citizen. And 'twere to give again—but 'tis no
    matter.   *Exeunt.*

                Enter two other Citizens.

    Coriolanus. Pray you now, if it may stand° with the
90 tune of your voices that I may be consul, I have
    here the customary gown.

    First Citizen. You have deserved nobly of your coun-
    try, and you have not deserved nobly.

    Coriolanus. Your enigma?

95 *First Citizen.* You have been a scourge to her enemies,
    you have been a rod to her friends. You have not
    indeed loved the common people.

    Coriolanus. You should account me the more virtuous,
    that I have not been common in my love. I will, sir,
100 flatter my sworn brother, the people, to earn a
    dearer estimation of° them; 'tis a condition° they
    account gentle; and since the wisdom of their choice
    is rather to have my hat than my heart, I will prac-
    tice the insinuating nod, and be off° to them most
105 counterfeitly; that is, sir, I will counterfeit the be-
    witchment of some popular man,° and give it boun-
    tiful to the desirers. Therefore, beseech you I may
    be consul.

    ----

    84. **A match** agreed   86 **something** somewhat   89 **stand** agree
    101 **dearer estimation of** higher valuation from   101 **condition** qual-
    ity   104 **be off** take my hat off   106 **popular man** ("friend of the
    people")

Second Citizen. We hope to find you our friend; and
   therefore give you our voices heartily.   *110*

First Citizen. You have received many wounds for
   your country.

Coriolanus. I will not seal° your knowledge with
   showing them. I will make much of your voices
   and so trouble you no farther.   *115*

Both. The gods give you joy, sir, heartily!   [*Exeunt.*]

Coriolanus. Most sweet voices!
   Better it is to die, better to starve,
   Than crave the hire which first we do deserve.
   Why in this woolvish toge° should I stand here,   *120*
   To beg of Hob° and Dick that does appear°
   Their needless vouches?° Custom calls me to't.
   What custom wills, in all things should we do't,
   The dust on antique time would lie unswept,
   And mountainous error be too highly heaped   *125*
   For truth to o'erpeer.° Rather than fool it so,
   Let the high office and the honor go
   To one that would do thus. I am half through:
   The one part suffered, the other will I do.

              Enter three Citizens more.

   Here come moe° voices.   *130*
   Your voices! For your voices I have fought;
   Watched° for your voices; for your voices bear
   Of wounds two dozen odd; battles thrice six
   I have seen, and heard of; for your voices have
   Done many things, some less, some more. Your
      voices!
                                                       135
   Indeed, I would be consul.

---

113 **seal** make authentic (legal sense)   120 **in this woolvish toge** i.e.,
disguising myself (a backhand reference to "wolf in sheep's clothing"; note that Coriolanus "lives like a lamb," according to II.i.12)
121 **Hob** (nickname of "Robert"; a country fellow)   121 **that does
appear** i.e., as they come, one by one   122 **vouches** confirmations
126 **o'erpeer** rise above   130 **moe** more   132 **Watched** kept watch

First Citizen. He has done nobly, and cannot go without any honest man's voice.

Second Citizen. Therefore let him be consul. The gods
140 give him joy, and make him good friend to the
people!

All. Amen, amen. God save thee, noble consul!
                    [*Exeunt Citizens.*]

Coriolanus. Worthy voices!

  Enter Menenius, with Brutus and Sicinius.

Menenius. You have stood your limitation;° and the
tribunes
145 Endue you with the people's voice. Remains
That in th' official marks° invested you
Anon do meet the Senate.

Coriolanus.   Is this done?

Sicinius. The custom of request you have discharged:
The people do admit you, and are summoned
150 To meet anon upon your approbation.°

Coriolanus. Where? At the Senate House?

Sicinius.   There, Coriolanus.

Coriolanus. May I change these garments?

Sicinius.   You may, sir.

Coriolanus. That I'll straight do, and, knowing myself again,
Repair° to th' Senate House.

155 *Menenius.* I'll keep you company. Will you along?°

Brutus. We stay here for the people.

Sicinius.   Fare you well.
          Exeunt Coriolanus and Menenius.

---

144 **limitation** time set for requesting votes 146 **marks** insignia
150 **anon upon your approbation** at once to confirm your appoint-
ment (as consul) 154 **Repair** return 155 **along** come too

He has it° now; and, by his looks, methinks
'Tis warm at's° heart.

Brutus.   With a proud heart he wore
His humble weeds. Will you dismiss the people?

Enter the Plebeians.

Sicinius. How now, my masters,° have you chose this
   man?   160

First Citizen. He has our voices, sir.

Brutus. We pray the gods he may deserve your loves.

Second Citizen. Amen, sir. To my poor unworthy
   notice,
He mocked us when he begged our voices.

Third Citizen.   Certainly;
He flouted us downright.   165

First Citizen. No, 'tis his kind of speech—he did not
   mock us.

Second Citizen. Not one amongst us, save yourself,
   but says
He used us scornfully. He should have showed us
His marks of merit, wounds received for's country.

Sicinius. Why, so he did, I am sure.   170

All. No, no; no man saw 'em.

Third Citizen. He said he had wounds which he could
   show in private;
And with his hat, thus waving it in scorn,
"I would be consul," says he. "Agèd custom,
But by your voices, will not so permit me;   175
Your voices therefore." When we granted that,
Here was "I thank you for your voices. Thank you,
Your most sweet voices. Now you have left your
   voices,

157 **it** (the emotion that "warms his heart," either the satisfaction
of success, or the irritation of offended pride; cf. "his fire," II.i.263)
158 **at's** at his   160 **my masters** gentlemen

I have no further° with you." Was not this mock-
ery?

180 *Sicinius.* Why either were you ignorant° to see't,
Or, seeing it, of such childish friendliness
To yield° your voices?

Brutus.   Could you not have told him
As you were lessoned:° when he had no power,
But was a petty servant to the state,
185 He was your enemy, ever spake against
Your liberties and the charters° that you bear
I' th' body of the weal;° and now, arriving
A place° of potency and sway o' th' state,°
If he should still malignantly remain
190 Fast foe to th' plebeii,° your voices might
Be curses to yourselves? You should have said
That as his worthy deeds did claim no less
Than what he stood for,° so his gracious nature
Would think upon you° for your voices, and
195 Translate° his malice towards you into love,
Standing your friendly lord.

Sicinius.   Thus to have said,
As you were fore-advised, had touched° his spirit
And tried his inclination; from him plucked
Either his gracious promise, which you might,
200 As cause had called you up,° have held him to;
Or else it would have galled his surly nature,
Which easily endures not article°
Tying him to aught. So, putting him to rage,
You should have ta'en th' advantage of his choler,°
And passed him unelected.

205 *Brutus.*   Did you perceive
He did solicit you in free° contempt

179 **no further** no more to do   180 **ignorant** too dull   182 **yield**
give   183 **lessoned** instructed   186 **charters** privileges   187 **weal**
commonwealth   188 **A place** (direct object of "arriving," i.e.,
"reaching")   188 **potency and sway o' th' state** power in managing
the state   190 **plebeii** (Latin for "plebeians")   193 **what he stood
for** the office he ran for   194 **think upon you** think well of you
195 **Translate** transform   197 **touched** tested   200 **As cause had
called you up** as an occasion (emergency) would have roused you
202 **article** condition   204 **choler** anger   206 **free** open

When he did need your loves; and do you think
That his contempt shall not be bruising to you
When he hath power to crush? Why, had your
    bodies
No heart° among you? Or had you tongues to cry°   210
Against the rectorship° of judgment?

Sicinius.   Have you
Ere now denied the asker, and now again,
Of° him that did not ask but mock, bestow
Your sued-for tongues?

Third Citizen. He's not confirmed; we may deny him
    yet.   215

Second Citizen. And will deny him.
I'll have five hundred voices of that sound.

First Citizen. I twice five hundred, and their friends
    to piece 'em.°

Brutus. Get you hence instantly, and tell those friends
They have chose a consul that will from them take   220
Their liberties, make them of no more voice
Than dogs that are as often beat for barking
As therefor° kept to do so.

Sicinius.   Let them assemble;
And, on a safer° judgment, all revoke
Your ignorant election.° Enforce° his pride   225
And his old hate unto you; besides, forget not
With what contempt he wore the humble weed,
How in his suit he scorned you; but your loves,
Thinking upon his services, took from you
Th' apprehension° of his present portance,°   230
Which most gibingly, ungravely, he did fashion
After the inveterate hate he bears you.

Brutus.   Lay

---

210 **heart** spirit 210 **cry** give your voices 211 **rectorship** rule
213 **Of** on 218 **piece 'em** add to them (cf. "piece out") 223 **there-
for** for that reason 224 **safer** sounder 225 **ignorant election**
choice made in ignorance 225 **Enforce** urge, insist on 230 **apprehension** perception 230 **portance** bearing

A fault on us, your tribunes, that we labored,
No impediment between,° but that you must
Cast your election on him.

235 *Sicinius.*   Say you chose him
More after° our commandment than as guided
By your own true affections;° and that your minds,
Preoccupied with what you rather must do
Than what you should, made you against the grain
240 To voice him consul.° Lay the fault on us.

Brutus. Ay, spare us not. Say we read lectures to you,
How youngly he began to serve his country,
How long continued; and what stock he springs of,
The noble house o' th' Marcians, from whence came
245 That Ancus Marcius, Numa's° daughter's son,
Who after great Hostilius here was king;
Of the same house Publius and Quintus were,
That our best water brought by conduits hither;
[And Censorinus that was so surnamed]°
250 And nobly namèd so, twice being censor,
Was his great ancestor.

Sicinius.   One thus descended,
That hath beside well in his person wrought
To be set high in place, we did commend
To your remembrances: but you have found,
255 Scaling° his present bearing with his past,
That he's your fixèd enemy, and revoke
Your sudden° approbation.

Brutus.   Say you ne'er had done't
(Harp on that still) but by our putting on;°
And presently, when you have drawn your number,°
Repair to th' Capitol.

234 **No impediment between** putting no obstacle in your way (i.e., we have made the way free for you to choose him)   236 **after** following   237 **affections** desires   240 **voice him consul** make him consul by your votes   245 **Numa** (second king of Rome)   249 **And . . . surnamed** (see Textual Note, p. 201)   255 **Scaling** weighing   257 **sudden** hasty   258 **putting on** urging   259 **drawn your number** gathered your crowd (of supporters)

Citizens.   We will so. Almost all   260
  Repent in their election.   *Exeunt Plebeians.*

Brutus.   Let them go on;
  This mutiny were better put in hazard°
  Than stay, past doubt, for greater.
  If, as his nature is, he fall in rage
  With their refusal, both observe and answer   265
  The vantage of his anger.°

Sicinius.   To th' Capitol, come.
  We will be there before the stream o' th' people;
  And this shall seem, as partly 'tis, their own,
  Which we have goaded onward.   *Exeunt.*

---

262 **This . . . hazard** i.e., it would be better to run the risk of this
minor disorder   265–66 **answer/The vantage of his anger** take advantage of the opportunity his anger affords

ACT III

[Scene I. *Rome. A street.*]

Cornets. Enter Coriolanus, Menenius, all the Gentry, Cominius, Titus Lartius, and other Senators.

Coriolanus. Tullus Aufidius then had made new head?°

Lartius. He had, my lord; and that it was which caused Our swifter composition.°

Coriolanus. So then the Volsces stand but as at first;
5   Ready, when time shall prompt them, to make road
Upon's° again.

Cominius.   They are worn,° Lord Consul, so
That we shall hardly in our ages° see
Their banners wave again.

Coriolanus.   Saw you Aufidius?

Lartius. On safeguard° he came to me; and did curse
10   Against the Volsces, for they had so vilely
Yielded the town. He is retired to Antium.

Coriolanus. Spoke he of me?

Lartius.   He did, my lord.

III.i.1 **made new head** raised a new force   3 **swifter composition** coming to terms sooner   5–6 **make road/Upon's** invade us   6 **worn** worn out   7 **ages** lifetime   9 **On safeguard** under safe-conduct

Coriolanus.   How? What?

Lartius. How often he had met you, sword to sword;
    That of all things upon the earth he hated
    Your person most; that he would pawn his fortunes   15
    To hopeless restitution,° so he might
    Be called your vanquisher.

Coriolanus.   At Antium lives he?

Lartius. At Antium.

Coriolanus. I wish I had a cause to seek him there,
    To oppose his hatred fully. Welcome home.   20

> *Enter Sicinius and Brutus.*

    Behold, these are the tribunes of the people,
    The tongues o' th' common mouth. I do despise
        them;
    For they do prank them° in authority,
    Against all noble sufferance.°

Sicinius.   Pass no further.

Coriolanus. Ha? What is that?   25

Brutus. It will be dangerous to go on—no further.

Coriolanus. What makes this change?

Menenius. The matter?

Cominius. Hath he not passed the noble and the
    common?°

Brutus. Cominius, no.

Coriolanus.   Have I had children's voices?   30

First Senator. Tribunes, give way; he shall to th'
    marketplace.

Brutus. The people are incensed against him.

---

16 **To hopeless restitution** without hope of their being redeemed
23 **prank them** dress themselves up   24 **Against all noble sufferance**
so that no noble can endure it   29 **the noble and the common** the
patricians and the plebeians

Sicinius.   Stop,
 Or all will fall in broil.°

Coriolanus.   Are these your herd?
 Must these have voices, that can yield them now,°
 And straight disclaim° their tongues? What are
35 your offices?
 You being their mouths, why rule you not their
  teeth?
 Have you not set them on?

Menenius.   Be calm, be calm.

Coriolanus. It is a purposed thing,° and grows by plot,
 To curb the will of the nobility.
40 Suffer't, and live with such as cannot rule,
 Nor ever will be ruled.

Brutus.   Call't not a plot.
 The people cry you mocked them; and of late,
 When corn was given them gratis, you repined,°
 Scandaled° the suppliants for the people, called
  them
45 Time-pleasers, flatterers, foes to nobleness.

Coriolanus. Why, this was known before.

Brutus.   Not to them all.

Coriolanus. Have you informed° them sithence?°

Brutus.   How! I inform them!

Coriolanus. You are like to do such business.

Brutus.   Not unlike
 Each way to better yours.°

Coriolanus. Why then should I be consul? By yond
50 clouds,

---

33 **in broil** into a riot   34 **now** at one time   35 **disclaim** disown
38 **purposed thing** premeditated affair   43 **repined** regretted it   44
Scandaled slandered   47 **informed** instructed   47 **sithence** since
48-49 **Not unlike/Each way to better yours** likely in every way to
do your business better

    Let me deserve so ill as you, and make me
    Your fellow tribune.

Sicinius.   You show too much of that
    For which the people stir.° If you will pass
    To where you are bound, you must inquire your
        way,
    Which you are out of,° with a gentler spirit,   *55*
    Or never be so noble as a consul,
    Nor yoke with him for° tribune.

Menenius.   Let's be calm.

Cominius. The people are abused;° set on.° This
    palt'ring°
    Becomes not Rome; nor has Coriolanus
    Deserved this so dishonored rub,° laid falsely°   *60*
    I' th' plain way of his merit.

Coriolanus.   Tell me of corn!
    This was my speech, and I will speak't again—

Menenius. Not now, not now.

First Senator.   Not in this heat, sir, now.

Coriolanus. Now, as I live, I will.
    My nobler friends, I crave their pardons.   *65*
    For the mutable, rank-scented meiny, let them
    Regard me as I do not flatter, and
    Therein behold themselves. I say again,
    In soothing them, we nourish 'gainst our Senate
    The cockle of rebellion, insolence, sedition,   *70*
    Which we ourselves have ploughed for, sowed,
        and scattered,
    By mingling them with us, the honored number;
    Who lack not virtue, no, nor power, but that
    Which they have given to beggars.

Menenius.   Well, no more.

---

53 **stir** are rebelling   55 **are out of** are straying from   57 **for** as
58 **abused** deceived   58 **set on** incited   58 **palt'ring** cheating   60
rub hindrance (in bowling on the green, any roughness of ground)
60 **falsely** treacherously   66 **meiny** crowd   70 **cockle** weed

First Senator. No more words, we beseech you.

75 *Coriolanus.*   How! No more!
     As for my country I have shed my blood,
     Not fearing outward force, so shall my lungs
     Coin words till their decay° against those measles,°
     Which we disdain should tetter° us, yet sought
     The very way to catch them.

80 *Brutus.*   You speak o' th' people,
     As if you were a god, to punish, not
     A man of their infirmity.°

Sicinius.   'Twere well
     We let the people know't.

Menenius.   What, what? His choler?

Coriolanus. Choler?
85   Were I as patient as the midnight sleep,
     By Jove, 'twould be my mind!

Sicinius.   It is a mind
     That shall remain a poison where it is,
     Not poison any further.

Coriolanus.   Shall remain!
     Hear you this Triton° of the minnows? Mark you
     His absolute "shall"?

Cominius.   'Twas from the canon.°

90 *Coriolanus.*   "Shall"!
     O good but most unwise patricians! Why,
     You grave but reckless senators, have you thus
     Given Hydra here° to choose an officer,
     That with his peremptory "shall," being but
95   The horn and noise o' th' monster's, wants not spirit
     To say he'll turn your current in° a ditch,

---

78 **decay** death   78 **measles** (the disease; and "foul wretches," from
mesel, "leper")   79 **tetter** infect with leprous eruption   82 **of their
infirmity** having the same weaknesses as they   89 **Triton** sea-god,
trumpeter of Neptune (cf. "horn," line 95)   90 **from the canon**
against the law   93 **Given Hydra here** permitted this many-headed
beast   96 **in** (aside) into

And make your channel his? If he have power,
Then vail your ignorance;° if none, awake
Your dangerous lenity. If you are learned,° *wise*
Be not as common fools; if you are not,   100
Let them have cushions° by you. You are plebeians,
If they be senators; and they are no less,°
When, both your voices blended, the great'st taste
Most palates theirs.° They choose their magistrate;
And such a one as he, who puts his "shall,"   105
His popular "shall," against a graver bench°
Than ever frowned in Greece. By Jove himself,
It makes the consuls base; and my soul aches
To know, when two authorities are up,°
Neither supreme, how soon confusion°   110
May enter 'twixt the gap of both and take
The one by th' other.°

Cominius.   Well, on to th' marketplace.

Coriolanus. Whoever gave that counsel to give forth
The corn o' th' storehouse gratis, as 'twas used
Sometime in Greece—

Menenius.   Well, well, no more of that. 115

Coriolanus. Though there the people had more abso-
      lute pow'r,
I say they nourished disobedience, fed
The ruin of the state.

Brutus.   Why shall the people give
One that speaks thus their voice?

Coriolanus.   I'll give my reasons,
More worthier than their voices. They know the
      corn   120

---

98 **vail your ignorance** let your ignorance (that gave the power) bow
(to him)   99 **learned** wise   101 **cushions** (symbol of senatorial
rank; cf. II.ii.s.d.)   102 **no less** i.e., no less than senators   103–104
the great'st taste/Most palates theirs the dominant flavor tastes most
of them (they have the most votes)   106 **bench** court   109 **up** active
110 **confusion** violent disorder (in a revolution)   111-12 **take/The
one by th' other** seize and overthrow one by means of the other

Was not our recompense,° resting well assured
They ne'er did service for't. Being pressed to° th'
    war,
Even when the navel° of the state was touched,
They would not thread° the gates; this kind of
    service
125   Did not deserve corn gratis. Being i' th' war,
Their mutinies and revolts, wherein they showed
Most valor, spoke not for them. Th' accusation
Which they have often made against the Senate,
All cause unborn,° could never be the native°
130   Of our so frank° donation. Well, what then?
How shall this bosom multiplied° digest°
The Senate's courtesy? Let deeds express
What's like to be their words: "We did request it;
We are the greater poll,° and in true fear
135   They gave us our demands." Thus we debase
The nature of our seats, and make the rabble
Call our cares° fears; which will in time
Break ope the locks o' th' Senate and bring in
The crows to peck the eagles.

Menenius.   Come, enough.

Brutus. Enough, with over measure.

140   *Coriolanus.*   No, take more.
What may be sworn by, both divine and human,
Seal what I end withal!° This double worship,
Where one part does disdain with cause, the other
Insult without° all reason; where gentry,° title,
    wisdom,
145   Cannot conclude° but by the yea and no

---

121 **recompense** reward for past services   122 **pressed to** conscripted
for   123 **navel** center (cf. Menenius' fable, I.i)   124 **thread** pass
through   129 **All cause unborn** with no cause in existence   129 **native** original, parent (i.e., their accusation not the origin of our gift)
130 **frank** unsolicited   131 **bosom multiplied** many-bosomed beast
("Hydra," line 93)   131 **digest** (1) digest (2) understand ("bosom"
can mean both "cavity of the stomach" and "heart," i.e., "mind")
134 **poll** number   137 **cares** (concern for the state)   142 **withal** with
144 **without** beyond   144 **gentry** gentle birth   145 **conclude** decide

Of general ignorance—it must omit°
Real necessities, and give way the while
To unstable slightness.° Purpose so barred,° it
    follows
Nothing is done to purpose. Therefore, beseech
    you—
You that will be less fearful than discreet;°   150
That love the fundamental part of state°
More than you doubt° the change on't; that prefer
A noble life before a long, and wish
To jump° a body with a dangerous physic°
That's sure of death without it—at once pluck out 155
The multitudinous tongue;° let them not lick
The sweet which is their poison. Your dishonor
Mangles true judgment, and bereaves the state
Of that integrity° which should become't;
Not having the power to do the good it would,   160
For th' ill which doth control't.°

Brutus.   'Has said enough.

Sicinius. Has spoken like a traitor and shall answer°
    As traitors do.

Coriolanus.   Thou wretch, despite o'erwhelm thee!
    What should the people do with these bald°
        tribunes,
    On whom depending, their obedience fails   165
    To th' greater bench?° In a rebellion,
    When what's not meet, but what must be, was law,
    Then were they chosen; in a better hour

146 **omit** overlook   148 **unstable slightness** unsteady trifling   148
Purpose so barred when the intention (of charting a policy in advance) is so thwarted   150 **less fearful than discreet** i.e., more prudent than fearful (on lines 150–161, see Introduction, p. xxxviii)
151 **fundamental part of state** basic constitution of the government
152 **doubt** fear   154 **jump** risk harming   154 **physic** medicine,
treatment   156 **multitudinous tongue** (the voice of the "Hydra,"
the tribuneship)   159 **integrity** wholeness   161 **control't** overpower
it   162 **answer** i.e., in court, be brought to trial; cf. lines 176, 323
164 **bald** trivial (pun)   166 **th' greater bench** i.e. the senate

Let what is meet be said it must be meet,°
170   And throw their power i' th' dust.

Brutus. Manifest treason!

Sicinius.   This a consul? No.

Brutus. The aediles,° ho!

Enter an Aedile.

Let him be apprehended.

Sicinius. Go, call the people, [*exit Aedile*] in whose
name myself
Attach° thee as a traitorous innovator,
175   A foe to th' public weal. Obey, I charge thee,
And follow to thine answer.°

Coriolanus.   Hence, old goat!°

All [*Patricians*]. We'll surety° him.

Cominius.   Aged sir, hands off.

Coriolanus. Hence, rotten thing, or I shall shake thy
bones
Out of thy garments.

Sicinius.   Help, ye citizens!

Enter a rabble of Plebeians, with the Aediles.

180   *Menenius.* On both sides more respect.

Sicinius. Here's he that would take from you all your
power.

Brutus. Seize him, aediles!

All [*Citizens*]. Down with him, down with him!

Second Senator. Weapons, weapons, weapons!
                    They all bustle about Coriolanus.

---

169 **it must be meet** that it *must* be fitting   172 **aediles** officers attached to the tribunes   174 **Attach** arrest   176 **answer** (legal term
for "meeting a charge")   176 **goat** (the tribunes are evidently
bearded; cf. II.i.89)   177 **surety** stand surety for

[*All.*] Tribunes! — Patricians! — Citizens! — What,
   ho!—   185
   Sicinius!—Brutus!—Coriolanus!—Citizens!—
   Peace, peace, peace!—Stay! Hold! Peace!

Menenius. What is about to be? I am out of breath.
   Confusion's° near. I cannot speak. You, tribunes
   To th' people! Coriolanus, patience!   190
   Speak, good Sicinius.

Sicinius.   Hear me, people; peace!

All [*Citizens*]. Let's hear our tribune. Peace!—Speak,
   speak, speak.

Sicinius. You are at point to lose° your liberties:
   Marcius would have all from you; Marcius,
   Whom late you have named for consul.

Menenius.   Fie, fie, fie! *195*
   This is the way to kindle, not to quench.

First Senator. To unbuild the city, and to lay all flat.

Sicinius. What is the city but the people?

All [*Citizens*].   True,
   The people are the city.

Brutus. By the consent of all, we were established   200
   The people's magistrates.

All [*Citizens*].   You so remain.

Menenius. And so are like to do.

Cominius. That is the way to lay the city flat,
   To bring the roof to the foundation,
   And bury all which yet distinctly ranges,°   205
   In heaps and piles of ruin.

Sicinius.   This deserves death.

---

189 **Confusion** ruin (resulting from civil disorder, cf. line 110)
193 **at point to lose** on point of losing   205 **distinctly ranges** extends
in separate orderly rows (of buildings)

Brutus. Or° let us stand to° our authority,
Or let us lose it. We do here pronounce,
Upon the part o' th' people, in° whose power
210   We were elected theirs,° Marcius is worthy
Of present death.

Sicinius.   Therefore lay hold of him;
Bear him to th' rock Tarpeian,° and from thence
Into destruction cast him.

Brutus.   Aediles, seize him!

All [Citizens]. Yield, Marcius, yield!

Menenius.   Hear me one word;
215   Beseech you, tribunes, hear me but a word.

Aediles. Peace, peace!

Menenius. [*To Brutus*] Be that you seem, truly your
country's friend,
And temp'rately proceed to what you would
Thus violently redress.

Brutus.   Sir, those cold ways,
220   That seem like prudent helps, are very poisonous
Where the disease is violent. Lay hands upon him,
And bear him to the rock.
                              Coriolanus draws his sword.

Coriolanus.   No, I'll die here.
There's some among you have beheld me fighting;
Come, try upon yourselves what you have seen me.

Menenius. Down with that sword! Tribunes, withdraw
225   awhile.

Brutus. Lay hands upon him.

Menenius.   Help Marcius, help,
You that be noble; help him, young and old!

---

207 **Or** either   207 **stand to** stand by   209 **in** by   210 **theirs** i.e.,
their representatives   212 **rock Tarpeian** (from which criminals
were thrown)

All [*Citizens*]. Down with him, down with him!
    In this mutiny,° *the Tribunes, the Aediles, and*
                           the people are beat in.

Menenius. Go, get you to your house; begone, away!
   All will be naught° else.

Second Senator.   Get you gone.

Coriolanus.   Stand fast;   *230*
   We have as many friends as enemies.

Menenius. Shall it be put to that?°

First Senator.   The gods forbid!
   I prithee, noble friend, home to thy house;
   Leave us to cure this cause.°

Menenius.   For 'tis a sore upon us
   You cannot tent° yourself. Begone, beseech you.   *235*

Cominius. Come, sir, along with us.

Coriolanus. I would they were barbarians, as they are,
   Though in Rome littered; not Romans, as they are
      not,
   Though calved i' th' porch o' th' Capitol.°

Menenius.   Begone.
   Put not your worthy° rage into your tongue: *240*
   One time will owe another.°

Coriolanus.   On fair ground
   I could beat forty of them.

Menenius.   I could myself
   Take up a brace° o' th' best of them; yea, the two
      tribunes.

---

228 s.d. **mutiny** riot   229 **naught** ruined   232 **put to that** driven to
that extremity   234 **cause** dispute   235 **tent** treat (cf. I.ix.31)
239 **porch o' th' Capitol** (portico of the temple of Jupiter on the
Capitoline Hill)   240 **worthy** justifiable (?) noble (?)   241 **One time
will owe another** one time (the present, when the people are in revolt) will be compensated by another (when the people are checked)
243 **Take up a brace** take on a couple ("brace" often of dogs)

Cominius. But now 'tis odds beyond arithmetic;°
245   And manhood is called foolery when it stands
Against a falling fabric.° Will you hence
Before the tag° return? Whose rage doth rend
Like interrupted waters, and o'erbear°
What they are used to bear.

Menenius.   Pray you, begone.
250   I'll try whether my old wit be in request
With those that have but little. This must be
    patched
With cloth of any color.

Cominius.   Nay, come away.
               Exeunt Coriolanus and Cominius.

Patrician. This man has marred his fortune.

Menenius. His nature is too noble for the world:
255   He would not flatter Neptune for his trident,
Or Jove for's power to thunder. His heart's his
    mouth:
What his breast forges, that his tongue must vent;
And, being angry, does forget that ever
He heard the name of death.   *A noise within.*
Here's goodly work!

260 *Patrician.*   I would they were abed!

Menenius. I would they were in Tiber! What the
    vengeance!°
Could he not speak 'em fair?°

Enter Brutus and Sicinius, with the rabble again.

Sicinius.   Where is this viper
That would depopulate the city and
Be every man himself?

Menenius.   You worthy tribunes—

---

244 **beyond arithmetic** beyond number 246 **fabric** building 247
tag riffraff ("tag and rag") 248 **o'erbear** overcome 261 **What the
vengeance** (an emphatic "What!"; cf. "What the devil!") 262 **speak
'em fair** talk civilly to them (and so flatter)

Sicinius. He shall be thrown down the Tarpeian rock 265
  With rigorous hands. He hath resisted law,
  And therefore law shall scorn him further trial
  Than the severity of the public power,°
  Which he so sets at nought.

First Citizen.   He shall well know
  The noble tribunes are the people's mouths,   270
  And we their hands.

All [*Citizens*]. He shall, sure on't.

Menenius.   Sir, sir—

Sicinius. Peace!

Menenius. Do not cry havoc,° where you should but
    hunt
  With modest warrant.°

Sicinius.   Sir, how comes't that you
  Have holp° to make this rescue?

Menenius.   Hear me speak: 275
  As I do know the consul's worthiness,
  So can I name his faults.

Sicinius.   Consul! What consul?

Menenius. The consul Coriolanus.

Brutus.   He consul!

All [*Citizens*]. No, no, no, no, no.

Menenius. If, by the tribunes' leave, and yours, good
    people,   280
  I may be heard, I would crave a word or two;
  The which shall turn you to no further harm
  Than so much loss of time.

Sicinius.   Speak briefly then;
  For we are peremptory° to dispatch

268 **the public power** i.e., the power derived from the people
273 **cry havoc** call for general slaughter ("total war")   274 **With
modest warrant** with moderate justification   275 **holp** helped   284
peremptory resolved

285   This viperous traitor. To eject him hence
       Were but our danger,° and to keep him here
       Our certain death. Therefore it is decreed
       He dies tonight.

Menenius.   Now the good gods forbid
       That our renownèd Rome, whose gratitude
290   Towards her deservèd° children is enrolled
       In Jove's own book, like an unnatural dam
       Should now eat up her own!

Sicinius. He's a disease that must be cut away.

Menenius. O, he's a limb that has but a disease;
295   Mortal,° to cut it off; to cure it, easy.
       What has he done to Rome that's worthy death?
       Killing our enemies, the blood he hath lost—
       Which I dare vouch is more than that he hath
       By many an ounce—he dropped it for his country;
300   And what is left, to lose it by his country
       Were to us all that do't and suffer it
       A brand° to th' end o' th' world.

Sicinius.   This is clean kam.°

Brutus. Merely° awry. When he did love his country,
       It honored him.

Menenius.   The service of the foot
305   Being once gangrened, is not then respected
       For what before it was.

Brutus.   We'll hear no more.
       Pursue him to his house and pluck° him thence,
       Lest his infection, being of catching nature,
       Spread further.

Menenius.   One word more, one word!
310   This tiger-footed rage, when it shall find
       The harm of unscanned° swiftness, will, too late,

---

286 **but our danger** only the risk we now run   290 **deservèd** deserving   295 **Mortal** deadly   302 **brand** mark of disgrace   302 **clean
kam** completely wrong (literally *kam* = crooked)   303 **Merely** absolutely   307 **pluck** take   311 **unscanned** thoughtless

Tie leaden pounds° to's° heels. Proceed by process;°
Lest parties (as he is beloved) break out,
And sack great Rome with Romans.

Brutus.   If it were so—

Sicinius. What° do ye talk?   315
Have we not had a taste of his obedience?
Our aediles smote? Ourselves resisted? Come!

Menenius. Consider this: he has been bred i' th' wars
Since 'a could draw a sword, and is ill schooled
In bolted° language; meal and bran together   320
He throws without distinction. Give me leave,
I'll go to him, and undertake to bring him
Where he shall answer, by a lawful form,°
In peace, to his utmost peril.°

First Senator.   Noble tribunes,
It is the humane way. The other course   325
Will prove too bloody, and the end of it
Unknown to the beginning.

Sicinius.   Noble Menenius,
Be you then as the people's officer.
Masters, lay down your weapons.

Brutus.   Go not home.

Sicinius. Meet on the marketplace. We'll attend you
    there,   330
Where, if you bring not Marcius, we'll proceed
In our first way.

Menenius.   I'll bring him to you.
[*To the Senators*] Let me desire your company. He
    must come,
Or what is worst will follow.

Senators.   Pray you, let's to him.
                              Exeunt omnes.°

312 **pounds** pound-weights   312 **to's** to his   312 **process** due process
of law   315 **What** why   320 **bolted** refined (literally, sifted)   323
answer, by a lawful form meet the charges according to the forms of
law   324 **to his utmost peril** at the risk of the severest penalty
334 s.d. **omnes** all (Latin)

[Scene II. *Rome. The house of Coriolanus.*]

Enter Coriolanus with Nobles.

Coriolanus. Let them pull all about mine ears; present
 me
 Death on the wheel° or at wild horses' heels;
 Or pile ten hills on the Tarpeian rock,
 That the precipitation° might down stretch
5 Below the beam of sight;° yet will I still°
 Be thus to them.

A Noble.   You do the nobler.

Coriolanus. I muse° my mother
 Does not approve me further, who was wont
 To call them woolen vassals,° things created
10 To buy and sell with groats;° to show bare heads
 In congregations, to yawn, be still and wonder,
 When one but of my ordinance° stood up
 To speak of peace or war.

Enter Volumnia.

                    I talk of you:
 Why did you wish me milder- Would you have me
15 False to my nature? Rather say I play
 The man I am.

Volumnia.   O, sir, sir, sir,
 I would have had you put your power well on,
 Before you had worn it out.

III.ii.2 **the wheel** (by being bound to a wheel and beaten to death; an
Elizabethan, not Roman, penalty) **4 precipitation** steepness 5 **Below the beam of sight** i.e., beyond the range of sight (*beam* = a ray
passing from the object to the eye) 7 **muse** wonder 9 **woolen
vassals** i.e., rough-dressed members of the lowest class 10 **groats**
four-penny coins 12 **ordinance** rank

Coriolanus.   Let go.°

Volumnia. You might have been enough the man you
    are,
    With striving less to be so. Lesser had been   20
    The thwartings of your dispositions,° if
    You had not showed them how ye were disposed
    Ere they lacked power to cross you.

Coriolanus.   Let them hang.

Volumnia. Ay, and burn too.

     Enter Menenius with the Senators.

Menenius. Come, come, you have been too rough,
    something° too rough;   25
    You must return and mend it.

Senator.   There's no remedy,
    Unless, by not so doing, our good city
    Cleave in the midst° and perish.

Volumnia.   Pray be counseled;
    I have a heart as little apt° as yours,
    But yet a brain that leads my use of anger   30
    To better vantage.

Menenius.   Well said, noble woman!
    Before he should thus stoop to th' herd, but that
    The violent fit o' th' time craves it as physic°
    For the whole state, I would put mine armor on,
    Which I can scarcely bear.

Coriolanus.   What must I do?   35

Menenius. Return to th' tribunes.

Coriolanus.   Well, what then? What then?

Menenius. Repent what you have spoke.

---

18 **Let go** enough of that   21 **dispositions** inclinations   25 **something** somewhat   26–28 **There's . . . midst** there's no help for it; (you
must compromise;) else, because of your failure to do so, our good
city may be split in two   29 **apt** compliant   33 **physic** medical
treatment

Coriolanus. For them! I cannot do it to the gods;
 Must I then do't to them?

Volumnia.   You are too absolute;
40 Though therein you can never be too noble
 But when extremities speak.° I have heard you say,
 Honor and policy, like unsevered° friends,
 I' th' war do grow together. Grant that, and tell me
 In peace what each of them by th' other lose
 That they combine not there.

Coriolanus.   Tush, tush!

45 *Menenius.*   A good demand.

Volumnia. If it be honor in your wars to seem
 The same you are not, which for your best ends
 You adopt° your policy, how is it less or worse
 That it° shall hold companionship in peace
50 With honor as in war; since that to both
 It stands in like request?°

Coriolanus.   Why force° you this?

Volumnia. Because that now it lies you on° to speak
 To th' people, not by your own instruction,
 Nor by th' matter which your heart prompts you,
55 But with such words that are but roted° in
 Your tongue, though but bastards and syllables
 Of no allowance to your bosom's truth.°
 Now, this no more dishonors you at all
 Than to take in° a town with gentle words,
60 Which else would put you to your fortune° and
 The hazard of much blood.
 I would dissemble with my nature, where
 My fortunes and my friends at stake required

---

41 **when extremities speak** when the most critical situations demand
(see Introduction, pp. xxxix–xl)   42 **unsevered** inseparable   48 **adopt**
adopt as   49 **it** (pretense, "to seem/The same you are not")   51
stands in like request is equally in demand   51 **force** urge   52 **it
lies you on** it is your duty   55 **roted** learned by rote   56–57 **but
. . . truth** only false expressions of your heart's true understanding
wholly unacceptable to it   59 **take in** capture   60 **put you to your
fortune** force you to take your chances (in war)

    I should do so in honor.° I am in this°
    Your wife, your son, these senators, the nobles;   65
    And you will rather show our general° louts
    How you can frown than spend a fawn upon 'em
    For the inheritance° of their loves and safeguard
    Of what that want° might ruin.

Menenius.   Noble lady!
    Come, go with us; speak fair; you may salve so,   70
    Not what is dangerous present, but the loss
    Of what is past.

Volumnia.   I prithee now, my son,
    Go to them with this bonnet in thy hand;
    And thus far having stretched it (here be with
      them),
    Thy knee bussing° the stones (for in such business   75
    Action is eloquence, and the eyes of th' ignorant
    More learnèd than the ears), waving° thy head,
    Which° often thus correcting thy stout° heart,
    Now humble as the ripest mulberry
    That will not hold the handling; or° say to them,   80
    Thou art their soldier, and being bred in broils
    Hast not the soft way which, thou dost confess,
    Were fit for thee to use, as they to claim,
    In asking their good loves; but thou wilt frame
    Thyself, forsooth,° hereafter theirs, so far   85
    As thou hast power and person.

Menenius.   This but done,
    Even as she speaks, why, their hearts were yours;
    For they have pardons, being asked, as free°
    As words to little purpose.

---

64 **in honor** in honor bound (*not* Coriolanus' understanding of
"Honor")   64 **I am in this** I speak in this for (implying also, "I
stand in place of")   66 **general** common   68 **inheritance** possession
69 **that want** (of their loves)   74–80 (the text may be corrupt)
75 **bussing** kissing (touching)   77 **waving** bowing up and down   78
Which (subject of "correcting" in a nominative absolute; the sentence is urgent; the syntax, sketchy)   78 **stout** proud   80 **or** (marks
the turn from "action" to "eloquence," line 76)   85 **forsooth** in
truth   88 **free** liberal (to grant)

Volumnia.   Prithee now,
   Go, and be ruled; although I know thou hadst
90   rather
   Follow thine enemy in a fiery gulf°
   Than flatter him in a bower.°

             Enter Cominius.

                Here is Cominius.
Cominius. I have been i' th' marketplace;° and, sir,
   'tis fit
   You make strong party,° or defend yourself
95   By calmness or by absence. All's in anger.

Menenius. Only fair speech.

Cominius.   I think 'twill serve, if he
   Can thereto frame his spirit.

Volumnia.   He must, and will.
   Prithee now, say you will, and go about it.

Coriolanus. Must I go show them my unbarbed
   head sconce?° Must I
100   With my base tongue give to my noble heart
   A lie that it must bear? Well, I will do't.
   Yet, were there but this single plot° to lose,
   This mold° of Marcius, they to dust should grind it,
   And throw't against the wind. To th' marketplace!
105   You have put me now to such a part° which never
   I shall discharge° to th' life.

Cominius.   Come, come, we'll prompt you.

Volumnia. I prithee now, sweet son, as thou hast said
   My praises made thee first a soldier, so,
   To have my praise for this, perform a part
   Thou hast not done before.

110 *Coriolanus.*   Well, I must do't.

91 **in a fiery gulf** into an abyss of flame   92 **bower** ladies' chamber
93 **marketplace** i.e., Forum of ancient Rome   94 **make strong party**
maintain your side strongly   99 **unbarbed sconce** unarmed head
("sconce" often used in comic contexts)   102 **plot** (of earth)
103 **mold** (both "frame" and "earth"; cf. V.iii.22)   105 **part** (in a
play)   106 **discharge** perform

Away, my disposition, and possess me
Some harlot's° spirit! My throat of war be turned,
Which quired° with my drum, into a pipe° *voice.*
Small as an eunuch or the virgin voice
That babies lulls asleep! The smiles of knaves   115
Tent in my cheeks, and schoolboys' tears take up°
The glasses of my sight!° A beggar's tongue
Make motion through my lips, and my armed
   knees,
Who bowed but in my stirrup, bend like his
That hath received an alms! I will not do't;   120
Lest I surcease° to honor mine own truth, *cease*
And by my body's action teach my mind
A most inherent° baseness.

Volumnia.   At thy choice then.
To beg of thee, it is my more dishonor
Than thou of them. Come all to ruin! Let   125
Thy mother rather feel thy pride than fear
Thy dangerous stoutness,° for I mock at death
With as big heart as thou. Do as thou list.°
Thy valiantness was mine, thou suck'st it from me,
But owe° thy pride thyself. *own*

Coriolanus.   Pray, be content: 130
Mother, I am going to the marketplace;
Chide me no more. I'll mountebank° their loves,
Cog° their hearts from them, and come home be-
   loved
Of all the trades in Rome. Look, I am going.
Commend me to my wife. I'll return consul;   135
Or never trust to what my tongue can do
I' th' way of flattery further.

112 **harlot** rascal (used of both sexes)   113 **quired** sang harmoni-
ously   113 **pipe** i.e., voice   116 **take up** possess   117 **The glasses of
my sight** my eyeballs   121 **surcease** cease   123 **inherent** firmly
settled   126–27 **feel . . . stoutness** suffer the effects of thy pride, but
not fear the danger of it (*stoutness* = obstinacy, as in North, nearly
equal to "pride"; cf. line 78)   127 **thou list** you please   130 **owe**
own, have   132 **mountebank** win their loves by tricky actions (cf. a
"mountebank," a quack doctor, who puts on an act to sell his
wares)   133 **Cog** cheat

Volumnia.   Do your will. *Exit Volumnia.*

Cominius. Away, the tribunes do attend you. Arm
    yourself
To answer mildly; for they are prepared
140 With accusations, as I hear, more strong
Than are upon you yet.

Coriolanus. The word° is "mildly." Pray you, let
    us go.
Let them accuse me by invention,° I
Will answer in° mine honor.

Menenius.   Ay, but mildly.

145 *Coriolanus.* Well, mildly be it then—mildly.   *Exeunt.*

[Scene III. *Rome. The Forum.*]

Enter Sicinius and Brutus.

Brutus. In this point charge him home,° that he
    affects°
Tyrannical power. If he evade us there,
Enforce him° with his envy° to the people,
And that the spoil got on° the Antiates
Was ne'er distributed.

Enter an Aedile.

5   What, will he come?

Aedile. He's coming.

Brutus.   How accompanied?

142 **word** password   143 **accuse me by invention** invent accusations
against me   **144 in** in a way consistent with   III.iii.1 **charge him
home** press your accusations against him to the limit   1 **affects** aims
at   3 **Enforce him** press him hard   3 **envy** ill-will   4 **got on** won
from

Aedile. With old Menenius and those senators
That always favored him.

Sicinius.   Have you a catalog
Of all the voices that we have procured,
Set down by th' poll?°

Aedile.   I have; 'tis ready.   10

Sicinius. Have you collected them by tribes?

Aedile.   I have.

Sicinius. Assemble presently° the people hither:
And when they hear me say "It shall be so
I' th' right and strength o' th' commons," be it
either
For death, for fine, or banishment, then let them,   15
If I say "Fine," cry "Fine!"—if "Death," cry
"Death!"
Insisting on the old prerogative
And power i' th' truth o' th' cause.°

Aedile.   I shall inform them.

Brutus. And when such time° they have begun to
cry,
Let them not cease, but with a din confused   20
Enforce° the present execution
Of what we chance to sentence.

Aedile.   Very well.

Sicinius. Make them be strong, and ready for this
hint,°
When we shall hap to give't them.

Brutus.   *anger*   Go about it. [*Exit Aedile.*]
Put him to° choler straight. He hath been used   25
Ever to conquer and to have his worth°

10 **by th' poll** by counting heads   12 **presently** at once (cf. line 21)
18 **i' th' truth o' th' cause** resting in the justice of the case   19 **when
such time** at such time when   21 **Enforce** press for   23 **hint** opportunity   25 **Put him to** drive him to   26 **his worth** his pennyworth,
i.e., his fill

Of contradiction. Being once chafed, he cannot
Be reined again to temperance; then he speaks
What's in his heart, and that is there which looks
With us° to break his neck:

*Enter Coriolanus, Menenius, and Cominius,
with others.*

30 *Sicinius.*   Well, here he comes.

Menenius. Calmly, I do beseech you.

Coriolanus. Ay, as an ostler, that for th' poorest piece°
Will bear the knave by th' volume.° Th' honored
   gods
Keep Rome in safety, and the chairs of justice
35 Supplied with worthy men! Plant love among's!
Throng our large temples with the shows of peace,
And not our streets with war!

First Senator.   Amen, amen.

Menenius. A noble wish.

Enter the Aedile, with the Plebeians.

Sicinius. Draw near, ye people.

Aedile. List to your tribunes. Audience!° peace, I
40   say!

Coriolanus. First, hear me speak.

Both Tribunes.   Well, say. Peace, ho!

Coriolanus. Shall I be charged no further than this
   present?°
Must all determine° here?

Sicinius.   I do demand,°
If you submit you to the people's voices,
45 Allow° their officers, and are content

29–30 **looks/With us** promises in harmony with our intent   32 **piece**
coin   33 **bear the knave by th' volume** endure being called knave
enough times to fill a book   40 **Audience** give ear   42 **this present**
this immediate occasion   43 **determine** reach a conclusion   43 **demand** ask   45 **Allow** acknowledge

   To suffer lawful censure for such faults
   As shall be proved upon you.

Coriolanus.   I am content.

Menenius. Lo, citizens, he says he is content.
   The warlike service he has done, consider; think
   Upon the wounds his body bears, which show   *50*
   Like graves i' th' holy churchyard.

Coriolanus.   Scratches with briers,
   Scars to move laughter only.

Menenius.   Consider further,-
   That when he speaks not like a citizen,
   You find him like a soldier.° Do not take
   His rougher accents for malicious sounds,   *55*
   But, as I say, such as become a soldier
   Rather than envy° you.

Cominius.   Well, well, no more.

Coriolanus. What is the matter
   That, being passed for consul with full voice,
   I am so dishonored that the very hour   *60*
   You take it off again?

Sicinius.   Answer to us.

Coriolanus. Say, then. 'Tis true, I ought so.

Sicinius. We charge you, that you have contrived to
   take
   From Rome all seasoned° office, and to wind
   Yourself into° a power tyrannical,   *65*
   For which you are a traitor to the people.

Coriolanus. How! Traitor!

Menenius.   Nay, temperately! Your promise.

---

54 **like a soldier** (see Introduction, p. xxiv)   57 **envy** express malice
towards   64 **seasoned** established (or "moderate," "well moder-
ated")   64–65 **wind/Yourself into** make your way by indirect and
crooked means

Coriolanus. The fires i' th' lowest hell fold in the
    people!
    Call me their traitor, thou injurious° tribune!
70   Within° thine eyes sat twenty thousand deaths,
    In thy hands clutched as many millions, in
    Thy lying tongue both numbers, I would say
    "Thou liest" unto thee with a voice as free°
    As I do pray the gods.

Sicinius.   Mark you this, people?

All [Citizens]. To th' rock, to th' rock with him!

75 *Sicinius.*   Peace!
    We need not put new matter to his charge,
    What you have seen him do and heard him speak,
    Beating your officers, cursing yourselves,
    Opposing laws with strokes, and here defying
80   Those whose great power must try him—even this,
    So criminal and in such capital° kind,
    Deserves th' extremest death.

Brutus.   But since he hath
    Served well for Rome—

Coriolanus.   What do you prate of service?

Brutus. I talk of that that know it.

85 *Coriolanus.* You!

Menenius. Is this the promise that you made your
    mother?

Cominius. Know, I pray you—

Coriolanus.   I'll know no further.
    Let them pronounce the steep Tarpeian death,°
    Vagabond exile, flaying, pent° to linger
90   But with a grain a day, I would not buy
    Their mercy at the price of one fair word,

---

69 **injurious** insulting   70 **Within** if within   73 **free** unrestrained
81 **capital** (defined by line 82)   88 **steep Tarpeian death** cf. line 103
89 **pent** i.e., "Let them pronounce" the sentence of being "pent,"
imprisoned

Nor check my courage° for what they can give,
To have't with saying "Good morrow."

Sicinius.   For that he has
(As much as in him lies°) from time to time
Envied against° the people, seeking means   *95*
To pluck away their power, as now° at last
Given hostile strokes, and that not° in the presence
Of dreaded justice, but on the ministers
That do distribute it—in the name o' th' people,
And in the power of us the tribunes, we,   *100*
Even from this instant, banish him our city,
In peril of precipitation
From off the rock Tarpeian, never more
To enter our Rome gates. I' th' people's name,
I say it shall be so.   *105*

All [*Citizens*]. It shall be so, it shall be so! Let him
      away!
He's banished, and it shall be so.

Cominius. Hear me, my masters and my common
      friends—

Sicinius. He's sentenced; no more hearing.

Cominius.   Let me speak.
I have been consul, and can show for Rome   *110*
Her enemies' marks upon me. I do love
My country's good with a respect more tender,
More holy and profound, than mine own life,
My dear wife's estimate,° her womb's increase
And treasure of my loins; then if I would   *115*
Speak that—

Sicinius.   We know your drift. Speak what?

Brutus. There's no more to be said, but he is banished
As enemy to the people and his country.
It shall be so.

92 **courage** spirit   94 **as in him lies** as lies in his power   95 **Envied
against** shown malice towards   96 **as now** with respect to this
occasion (or, "now," "as" being redundant)   97 **not** not only   114
estimate worth

All [*Citizens*]. It shall be so, it shall be so.

Coriolanus. You common cry° of curs, whose breath
120   I hate
       As reek° o' th' rotten fens, whose loves I prize
       As the dead carcasses of unburied men
       That do corrupt my air, I banish you.
       And here remain with your uncertainty!
125   Let every feeble rumor shake your hearts!
       Your enemies, with nodding of their plumes,
       Fan you into despair! Have the power still
       To banish your defenders, till at length
       Your ignorance (which finds not till it feels,°
130   Making but reservation of yourselves,°
       Still° your own foes) deliver you as most
       Abated° captives to some nation
       That won you without blows! Despising
       For you the city, thus I turn my back.
135   There is a world elsewhere.

                Exeunt Coriolanus, Cominius, [*Menenius,*]
                        with the other Senators.

Aedile. The people's enemy is gone, is gone!

All [*Citizens*]. Our enemy is banished, he is gone!
       Hoo—oo!
                They all shout, and throw up their caps.

Sicinius. Go see him out at gates, and follow him,
       As he hath followed you, with all despite;°
140   Give him deserved vexation.° Let a guard
       Attend us through the city.

All [*Citizens*]. Come, come, let's see him out at gates;
       come!
       The gods preserve our noble tribunes! Come.
                                        Exeunt.

---

120 **cry** pack   121 **reek** mist   129 **finds not till it feels** does not understand until it suffers the consequences   130 **Making . . . yourselves** saving only yourselves   131 **Still** ever   132 **Abated** beaten
down   139 **despite** contempt   140 **Give him deserved vexation**
torment him as he deserves

ACT IV

[Scene I. *Rome. Before a gate of the city.*]

*Enter Coriolanus, Volumnia, Virgilia, Menenius,
Cominius, with the young Nobility of Rome.*

Coriolanus. Come, leave your tears; a brief farewell.
    The beast
With many heads butts me away. Nay, mother,
Where is your ancient courage? You were used
To say extremities was° the trier of spirits;
That common chances common men could bear;   5
That when the sea was calm all boats alike
Showed mastership in floating; fortune's blows°
When most struck home, being gentle wounded
    craves
A noble cunning.° You were used to load me
With precepts that would make invincible   10
The heart that conned° them.

Virgilia. O heavens! O heavens!

Coriolanus.   Nay, I prithee, woman—

IV.i.4 **extremities was** (plural subject permissible in Elizabethan
usage)   7 **fortune's blows** (supply introductory "that")   7–9 **fortune's . . . cunning** (when fortune's blows strike hardest, to act the
gentleman though wounded demands a noble use of intelligence)
11 **conned** studied

   Volumnia. Now the red pestilence strike all trades in
      Rome,
     And occupations perish!

   Coriolanus.   What, what, what!
15   I shall be loved when I am lacked. Nay, mother,
    Resume that spirit when you were wont to say,
    If you had been the wife of Hercules,
    Six of his labors you'd have done, and saved
    Your husband so much sweat. Cominius,
20   Droop not; adieu. Farewell, my wife, my mother.
    I'll do well yet. Thou old and true Menenius,
    Thy tears are salter than a younger man's,
    And venomous to thine eyes. My sometime°
      general,
    I have seen thee stern, and thou hast oft beheld
25   Heart-hard'ning spectacles; tell these sad women
    'Tis fond° to wail inevitable strokes,
    As 'tis to laugh at 'em. My mother, you wot° well
    My hazards still have been your solace,° and
    Believe't not lightly—though I go alone,
30   Like to a lonely dragon, that his fen
    Makes feared and talked of more than seen—your
      son
    Will or exceed the common° or be caught
    With cautelous° baits and practice.°

   Volumnia.   My first son,
    Whither wilt thou go? Take good Cominius
35   With thee awhile. Determine on some course
    More than a wild exposture° to each chance
    That starts i' th' way before thee.

   Coriolanus.   O the gods!

   Cominius. I'll follow thee a month, devise with thee
    Where thou shalt rest, that thou mayst hear of us

---

23 **sometime** former   26 **fond** foolish   27 **wot** know   28 **solace** interest   32 **or exceed the common** either surpass the usual achievements of men   33 **cautelous** crafty   33 **practice** treachery   36 **exposture** exposure

And we of thee. So, if the time thrust forth   *40*
A cause for thy repeal,° we shall not send
O'er the vast world to seek a single man,
And lose advantage,° which doth ever cool
I' th' absence of the needer.°

Coriolanus.   Fare ye well!
Thou hast years upon thee; and thou art too full   *45*
Of the wars' surfeits to go rove with one
That's yet unbruised. Bring° me but out at gate.
Come, my sweet wife, my dearest mother, and
My friends of noble touch;° when I am forth,
Bid me farewell, and smile. I pray you, come.   *50*
While I remain above the ground you shall
Hear from me still, and never of me aught
But what is like me formerly.

Menenius.   That's worthily
As any ear can hear. Come, let's not weep.
If I could shake off but one seven years   *55*
From these old arms and legs, by the good gods,
I'd° with thee every foot.

Coriolanus.   Give me thy hand.
Come.   *Exeunt.*

[Scene II. *Rome. Near the gate.*]

*Enter the two Tribunes, Sicinius and Brutus,
with the Aedile.*

Sicinius. Bid them all° home; he's gone, and we'll no
   further.

41 **repeal** recall   43 **advantage** the opportune moment   44 **needer**
(of "advantage")   47 **Bring** conduct   49 **noble touch** tested nobility (cf. "touchstone")   57 **I'd** I would (go)   IV.ii.1 **them all** (the
plebeians)

The nobility are vexed, whom we see have sided
In his behalf.

Brutus.   Now we have shown our power,
Let us seem humbler after it is done
Than when it was a-doing.

5   *Sicinius.*   Bid them home.
Say their great enemy is gone, and they
Stand in their ancient strength.

Brutus.   Dismiss them home. [*Exit Aedile.*]
Here comes his mother.

Enter Volumnia, Virgilia, and Menenius.

Sicinius.   Let's not meet her.

Brutus.   Why?

Sicinius. They say she's mad.

10   *Brutus.* They have ta'en note of us. Keep on your way.

Volumnia. O, y'are well met. Th' hoarded° plague o'
th' gods
Requite your love!

Menenius.   Peace, peace, be not so loud.

Volumnia. If that I could for weeping, you should
hear—
Nay, and you shall hear some. [*To Brutus*] Will
you be gone?

Virgilia. [*To Sicinius*] You shall stay too. I would I
15   had the power
To say so to my husband.

Sicinius.   Are you mankind?°

Volumnia. Ay, fool; is that a shame? Note but this,
fool.
Was not a man my father? Hadst thou foxship°

---

11 **hoarded** stored up (for punishment)   16 **mankind** mad, of man-
like violence (Sicinius' meaning; but Volumnia takes it in the sense
of "human")   18 **foxship** cunning

To banish him that struck more blows for Rome
Than thou hast spoken words?

Sicinius.   O blessed heavens!   20

Volumnia. Moe° noble blows than ever thou wise
    words;
And for Rome's good. I'll tell thee what—yet go!
Nay, but thou shalt stay too. I would my son
Were in Arabia,° and thy tribe before him,
His good sword in his hand.

Sicinius.   What then?

Virgilia.   What then!   25
He'd make an end of thy posterity.

Volumnia. Bastards and all.
Good man, the wounds that he does bear for Rome!

Menenius. Come, come, peace.

Sicinius. I would he had continued to his country   30
As he began, and not unknit himself
The noble knot he made.°

Brutus.   I would he had.

Volumnia. "I would he had!" 'Twas you incensed the
    rabble;
Cats, that can judge as fitly of his worth
As I can of those mysteries which heaven   35
Will not have earth to know.

Brutus.   Pray, let's go.

Volumnia. Now, pray, sir, get you gone;
You have done a brave deed. Ere you go, hear this:
As far as doth the Capitol exceed
The meanest house in Rome, so far my son—   40
This lady's husband here, this, do you see?
Whom you have banished—does exceed you all.

Brutus. Well, well, we'll leave you.

21 Moe more   24 **Arabia** a desert (outside Roman law and order)
32 **noble knot he made** (bond to Rome made by his heroic deeds)

Sicinius.   Why stay we to be baited
With° one that wants her wits?   *Exit Tribunes.*

Volumnia.   Take my prayers with you.
45 I would the gods had nothing else to do
But to confirm my curses! Could I meet 'em
But once a day, it would unclog my heart
Of what lies heavy to't.

Menenius.   You have told them home,°
And by my troth you have cause. You'll sup with
me?

50 *Volumnia.* Anger's my meat; I sup upon myself,
And so shall starve with feeding. Come, let's go.
Leave this faint puling,° and lament as I do,
In anger, Juno-like. Come, come, come.
Exeunt [Volumnia and Virgilia].

Menenius. Fie, fie, fie!   *Exit.*

[Scene III. *Between Rome and Antium.*]

Enter a Roman and a Volsce.

Roman. I know you well, sir, and you know me: your
name, I think, is Adrian.

Volsce. It is so, sir. Truly, I have forgot you.

Roman. I am a Roman; and my services are, as you
5   are, against 'em.° Know you me yet?

Volsce. Nicanor? No!

Roman. The same, sir.

Volsce. You had more beard when I last saw you; but

44 **With** by   48 **told them home** ("hit them where it hurts")   52 **puling** whining   IV.iii.5 **'em** the Romans

your favor° is well appeared° by your tongue.
What's the news in Rome? I have a note° from the   *10*
Volscian state to find you out there. You have well
saved me a day's journey.

Roman. There hath been in Rome strange insurrec-
tions; the people against the senators, patricians,
and nobles.   *15*

Volsce. Hath been! Is it ended then? Our state thinks
not so; they are in a most warlike preparation, and
hope to come upon them in the heat of their
division.

Roman. The main blaze of it is past, but a small thing   *20*
would make it flame again; for the nobles receive°
so to heart the banishment of that worthy Coriolanus, that they are in a ripe aptness to take all
power from the people and to pluck from them
their tribunes forever. This lies glowing, I can tell   *25*
you, and is almost mature for the violent breaking
out.

Volsce. Coriolanus banished!

Roman. Banished, sir.

Volsce. You will be welcome with this intelligence,   *30*
Nicanor.

Roman. The day serves well for them° now. I have
heard it said the fittest time to corrupt a man's wife
is when she's fall'n out with her husband. Your
noble Tullus Aufidius will appear well in these   *35*
wars, his great opposer, Coriolanus, being now in
no request of° his country.

Volsce. He cannot choose.° I am most fortunate thus
accidentally to encounter you. You have ended my
business, and I will merrily accompany you home.   *40*

_____

9 **favor** face   9 **appeared** made to appear   10 **a note** instructions
21 **receive** take   32 **them** (the Volscians)   36–37 **in no request of**
in no demand by   38 **cannot choose** (but appear well)

Roman. I shall, between this° and supper, tell you
most strange things from Rome, all tending to the
good of their adversaries. Have you an army ready,
say you?

45 *Volsce.* A most royal one; the centurions° and their
charges,° distinctly billeted,° already in th' entertainment,° and to be on foot at an hour's warning.

Roman. I am joyful to hear of their readiness, and am
the man, I think, that shall set them in present
50 action. So, sir, heartily well met, and most glad of
your company.

Volsce. You take my part from me, sir. I have the
most cause to be glad of yours.

Roman. Well, let us go together.   *Exeunt.*

[Scene IV. *Antium. Before Aufidius' house.*]

*Enter Coriolanus in mean apparel, disguised
and muffled.*

Coriolanus. A goodly city is this Antium. City,
'Tis I that made thy widows: many an heir
Of these fair edifices 'fore my wars°
Have I heard groan and drop. Then know me not,
5 Lest that thy wives with spits and boys with stones
In puny battle slay me.

Enter a Citizen.

Save you,° sir.

41 **this** this time   45 **centurions** commanders of smallest unit
(century) of a Roman legion   46 **charges** men under them   46 **distinctly billeted** separately enrolled   46–47 **in th' entertainment** in
service (maintained by the army)   IV.iv.3 **'fore my wars** before my
attacks   6 **Save you** God save you

Citizen. And you.

Coriolanus.   Direct me, if it be your will,
  Where great Aufidius lies.° Is he in Antium?

Citizen. He is, and feasts the nobles of the state
  At his house this night.

Coriolanus.   Which is his house, beseech you?   10

Citizen. This here before you.

Coriolanus.   Thank you, sir: farewell.
                                        Exit Citizen.
  O world, thy slippery turns! Friends now fast sworn,
  Whose double bosoms seems° to wear one heart,
  Whose hours, whose bed, whose meal and exercise
  Are still together, who twin, as 'twere, in love   15
  Unseparable, shall within this hour,
  On a dissension of a doit,° break out
  To bitterest enmity. So fellest° foes,
  Whose passions and whose plots have broke their
    sleep
  To take the one the other, by some chance,   20
  Some trick° not worth an egg, shall grow dear
    friends
  And interjoin their issues.° So with me:
  My birthplace hate I, and my love's upon
  This enemy town. I'll enter. If he slay me,
  He does fair justice; if he give me way,   25
  I'll do his country service.   *Exit.*

---

8 **lies** lives   13 **seems** (perhaps an old plural in -s)   17 **of a doit**
worth a doit (coin of little value; cf. I.v.6)   18 **fellest** fiercest   21
trick trifle   22 **interjoin their issues** let their children intermarry;
become close partners in action ("issues" in sense of "deeds"?)

[Scene V. *Antium. A hall in Aufidius' house.*]

Music plays. Enter a Servingman.

First Servingman. Wine, wine, wine! What service is
here! I think our fellows are asleep.   [*Exit.*]

Enter another Servingman.

Second Servingman. Where's Cotus? My master calls
for him. Cotus!   *Exit.*

Enter Coriolanus.

Coriolanus. A goodly house. The feast smells well,
but I
5   Appear not like a guest.

Enter the First Servingman.

First Servingman. What would you have, friend?
Whence are you? Here's no place for you: pray go
to the door!°   *Exit.*

10   *Coriolanus.* I have deserved no better entertainment,
In being Coriolanus.

Enter Second Servingman.

Second Servingman. Whence are you, sir? Has the
porter his eyes in his head that he gives entrance to
such companions?° Pray get you out.

15   *Coriolanus.* Away!

Second Servingman. "Away!" Get you away.

Coriolanus. Now thou'rt troublesome.

IV.v.9 **to the door** out of doors   14 **companions** fellows (in bad
sense)

Second Servingman. Are you so brave?° I'll have you
　talked with anon.°

　　Enter Third Servingman; the first meets him.

Third Servingman. What fellow's this?　　　　　　　20

First Servingman. A strange one as ever I looked on!
　I cannot get him out o' th' house. Prithee call my
　master to him.

Third Servingman. What have you to do here, fellow?
　Pray you avoid° the house.　　　　　　　　　　　25

Coriolanus. Let me but stand; I will not hurt your
　hearth.

Third Servingman. What are you?

Coriolanus. A gentleman.

Third Servingman. A marv'lous° poor one.　　　　30

Coriolanus. True, so I am.

Third Servingman. Pray you, poor gentleman, take up
　some other station; here's no place for you. Pray
　you avoid. Come.

Coriolanus. Follow your function,° go and batten° on　35
　cold bits.
　　　　　　　　　　　Pushes him away from him.

Third Servingman. What, you will not? Prithee, tell
　my master what a strange guest he has here.

Second Servingman. And I shall.
　　　　　　　　　　　Exit Second Servingman.

Third Servingman. Where dwell'st thou?　　　　　40

Coriolanus. Under the canopy.°

Third Servingman. Under the canopy!

Coriolanus. Ay.

---

18 **brave** impudent　19 **anon** soon　25 **avoid** leave　30 **marv'lous**
strangely　35 **Follow your function** do your regular work　35 **bat-
ten** grow fat　41 **canopy** sky (cf. "canopy" over a throne)

Third Servingman. Where's that?

45 *Coriolanus.* I' th' city of kites and crows.

Third Servingman. I' th' city of kites and crows! What
an ass it is! Then thou dwell'st with daws° too?

Coriolanus. No, I serve not thy master.

Third Servingman. How, sir! Do you meddle with my
50 master?

Coriolanus. Ay; 'tis an honester service than to meddle with thy mistress. Thou prat'st, and prat'st;
serve with thy trencher.° Hence!

Beats him away.

Enter Aufidius with the [Second] Servingman.

Aufidius. Where is this fellow?

55 *Second Servingman.* Here, sir. I'd have beaten him
like a dog, but for disturbing the lords within.

Aufidius. Whence com'st thou? What wouldst thou?
Thy name?
Why speak'st not? Speak, man. What's thy name?

Coriolanus. [*Unmuffling*]   If, Tullus,
Not yet thou know'st me, and, seeing me, dost not
60 Think me° for the man I am, necessity
Commands me name myself.

Aufidius.   What is thy name?

Coriolanus. A name unmusical to the Volscians' ears,
And harsh in sound to thine.

Aufidius.   Say, what's thy name?
Thou hast a grim appearance, and thy face
65 Bears a command° in't. Though thy tackle's torn,
Thou show'st° a noble vessel. What's thy name?

47 **daws** (foolish birds)   53 **trencher** wooden plate   60 **Think me**
i.e., take me   65 **a command** i.e., a look of authority   66 **show'st**
appear'st

Coriolanus. Prepare thy brow to frown. Know'st thou
   me yet?

Aufidius. I know thee not. Thy name!

Coriolanus. My name is Caius Marcius, who hath
   done
  To thee particularly, and to all the Volsces,   *70*
  Great hurt and mischief;° thereto witness may
  My surname, Coriolanus. The painful° service,
  The extreme dangers, and the drops of blood
  Shed for my thankless country, are requited
  But with that surname—a good memory°   *75*
  And witness of the malice and displeasure
  Which thou shouldst bear me. Only that name
   remains.
  The cruelty and envy° of the people,
  Permitted by our dastard nobles, who
  Have all forsook me, hath devoured the rest;   *80*
  And suffered me by th' voice of slaves to be
  Whooped out of Rome. Now, this extremity
  Hath brought me to thy hearth; not out of hope
  (Mistake me not) to save my life; for if
  I had feared death, of all the men i' th' world   *85*
  I would have 'voided thee; but in mere spite,
  To be full quit of° those my banishers,
  Stand I before thee here. Then if thou hast
  A heart of wreak° in thee, that wilt revenge
  Thine own particular wrongs and stop those maims   *90*
  Of shame° seen through thy country, speed thee
   straight
  And make my misery serve thy turn. So use it
  That my revengeful services may prove
  As benefits to thee; for I will fight
  Against my cank'red° country with the spleen°   *95*
  Of all the under fiends.° But if so be

71 **mischief** serious harm   72 **painful** laborious   75 **memory** me·
morial   78 **envy** ill-will   87 **full quit of** fully revenged on (cf. "quits
with")   89 **heart of wreak** vengeful heart   90–91 **maims/Of shame**
shameful wounds (e.g., the Roman occupation of Corioli)   95
cank'red corrupted (by ingratitude and envy)   95 **spleen** rage
96 **under fiends** devils in hell

Thou dar'st not this and that to prove more for-
   tunes°
Thou'rt tired, then, in a word, I also am
Longer to live most weary, and present
100 My throat to thee and to thy ancient malice;
Which not to cut would show thee but a fool,
Since I have ever followed thee with hate,
Drawn tuns° of blood out of thy country's breast,
And cannot live but to thy shame, unless
It be to do thee service.

105 *Aufidius.*   O Marcius, Marcius!
Each word thou hast spoke hath weeded from my
   heart
A root of ancient envy. If Jupiter
Should from yond cloud speak divine things,
And say " 'Tis true," I'd not believe them more
110 Than thee, all noble Marcius. Let me twine
Mine arms about that body, where against
My grainèd ash° an hundred times hath broke
And scarred the moon with splinters. Here I clip°
The anvil of my sword, and do contest
115 As hotly and as nobly with thy love
As ever in ambitious strength I did
Contend against thy valor. Know thou first,
I loved the maid I married; never man
Sighed truer breath. But that° I see thee here,
120 Thou noble thing, more dances my rapt° heart
Than when I first my wedded mistress saw
Bestride my threshold. Why, thou Mars, I tell thee,
We have a power on foot,° and I had purpose
Once more to hew thy target° from thy brawn,°
125 Or lose mine arm for't. Thou hast beat me out°
Twelve several times, and I have nightly since
Dreamt of encounters 'twixt thyself and me.
We have been down together in my sleep,

---

97 **prove more fortunes** try the chances of fortune further   103 **tuns**
casks   112 **grainèd ash** spear of ash, the grain showing   113 **clip**
embrace   119 **that** because   120 **rapt** enraptured   123 **power on
foot** force in the field   124 **target** shield   124 **brawn** brawny arm
125 **out** completely

Unbuckling helms, fisting each other's throat,
And waked° half dead with nothing. Worthy
    Marcius,   *130*
Had we no other quarrel else to Rome but that
Thou art thence banished, we would muster all
From twelve to seventy, and pouring war
Into the bowels of ungrateful Rome,
Like a bold flood o'erbeat.° O, come, go in,   *135*
And take our friendly senators by th' hands,
Who now are here, taking their leaves of me
Who am prepared against your territories,
Though not for Rome itself.

Coriolanus.   You bless me, gods!

Aufidius. Therefore, most absolute° sir, if thou wilt
    have   *140*
The leading of thine own revenges, take
Th' one half of my commission,° and set down°—
As best thou art experienced, since thou know'st
Thy country's strength and weakness—thine own
    ways,
Whether to knock against the gates of Rome,   *145*
Or rudely visit them in parts remote
To fright them ere destroy. But come in.
Let me commend thee first to those that shall
Say yea to thy desires. A thousand welcomes!
And more a friend than e'er an enemy;   *150*
Yet, Marcius, that was much. Your hand:
    most welcome!   *Exeunt.*

        Enter° two of the Servingmen.

First Servingman. Here's a strange alteration!

Second Servingman. By my hand, I had thought to
    have strucken him with a cudgel; and yet my mind
    gave me° his clothes made a false report of him.   *155*

___

130 **waked** (I have) awakened   135 **o'erbeat** surge over (the land)
140 **absolute** perfect   142 **my commission** the forces under me
142 **set down** determine   151s.d. **Enter** (perhaps they come forward
from backstage, since neither has been assigned an *"Exit"*)   154–55
my mind gave me I had an idea

First Servingman. What an arm he has! He turned me
about with his finger and his thumb, as one would
set up a top.

Second Servingman. Nay, I knew by his face that there
160   was something in him; he had, sir, a kind of face,
methought—I cannot tell how to term it.

First Servingman. He had so, looking as it were—
would I were hanged, but I thought there was more
in him than I could think.

165 *Second Servingman.* So did I, I'll be sworn. He is
simply the rarest man i' th' world.

First Servingman. I think he is; but a greater soldier
than he, you wot° one.

Second Servingman. Who, my master?

170 *First Servingman.* Nay, it's no matter for that.

Second Servingman. Worth six on him.

First Servingman. Nay, not so neither. But I take him
to be the greater soldier.

Second Servingman. Faith, look you, one cannot tell
175   how to say that. For the defense of a town our
general is excellent.

First Servingman. Ay, and for an assault too.

           Enter the Third Servingman.

Third Servingman. O slaves, I can tell you news—
news, you rascals!

180 *Both* [*First and Second Servingmen*]. What, what,
what? Let's partake.

Third Servingman. I would not be a Roman, of all
nations; I had as lief° be a condemned man.

Both. Wherefore? Wherefore?

168–77 (the *First Servingman* is cautiously and cunningly vague in
his references to the "greater soldier")   168 **wot** know   183 **lief**
willingly

Third Servingman. Why here's he that was wont to 185
thwack our general—Caius Marcius.

First Servingman. Why do you say "thwack our
general"?

Third Servingman. I do not say "thwack our general,"
but he was always good enough for him. 190

Second Servingman. Come, we are fellows° and
friends. He was ever too hard for him; I have heard
him say so himself.

First Servingman. He was too hard for him directly,°
to say the troth on't. Before Corioles he scotched° 195
him and notched him like a carbonado.°

Second Serviceman. And he had been cannibally
given, he might have boiled and eaten him too.

First Servingman. But more of thy news?

Third Servingman. Why, he is so made on° here 200
within as if he were son and heir to Mars; set at
upper end o' th' table; no question asked him by
any of the senators but they stand bald° before
him. Our general himself makes a mistress of him;
sanctifies himself with's hand,° and turns up the 205
white o' th' eye° to his discourse. But the bottom°
of the news is, our general is cut i' th' middle
and but one half of what he was yesterday, for the
other has half by the entreaty and grant of the
whole table.° He'll go, he says, and sowl° the 210
porter of Rome gates by th' ears. He will mow all
down before him, and leave his passage polled.°

---

191 fellows comrades **194 directly** plainly **195 scotched** slashed
196 carbonado meat scored with knife, for broiling **200 so made
on** made so much of **203 bald** bareheaded **205 sanctifies himself
with's hand** touches his hand as if it were a holy relic **205–06 turns
up the white o' th' eye** (in pious wonder) **206 bottom** last (jokingly
for "the climax") **209–10 has . . . table** i.e., has half because all at
the table beg him to take it, and give it to him **210 sowl** drag
212 polled cleared (used of cutting hair)

Second Servingman. And he's as like to do't as any
man I can imagine.

215 *Third Servingman.* Do't! He will do't; for look you,
sir, he has as many friends as enemies; which
friends, sir, as it were, durst not (look you, sir)
show themselves (as we term it) his friends whilst
he's in directitude.°

220 *First Servingman.* Directitude! What's that?

Third Servingman. But when they shall see, sir, his
crest up° again and the man in blood,° they will
out of their burrows (like conies° after rain) and
revel all with him.

225 *First Servingman.* But when goes this forward?

Third Servingman. Tomorrow, today, presently.° You
shall have the drum struck up this afternoon. 'Tis
as it were a parcel° of their feast, and to be executed ere they wipe their lips.

230 *Second Servingman.* Why, then we shall have a stirring
world again. This peace is nothing but to rust iron,
increase tailors, and breed ballad-makers.

First Servingman. Let me have war, say I; it exceeds
peace as far as day does night; it's sprightly walk-
235 ing, audible,° and full of vent.° Peace is a very
apoplexy, lethargy; mulled,° deaf, sleepy, insensi-
ble; a getter of more bastard children than war's a
destroyer of men.

Second Servingman. 'Tis so; and as wars in some sort
240 may be said to be a ravisher, so it cannot be denied
but peace is a great maker of cuckolds.

First Servingman. Ay, and it makes men hate one
another.

---

219 **directitude** (comic mistake for "discredit"?)   222 **crest up** (like
an animal aroused)   222 **in blood** in top condition   22.. **conies** rabbits   226 **presently** now   228 **parcel** part   235 **audible** of good
hearing   235 **full of vent** with plenty of outlets for energy (?: cf.
I.i.226)   236 **mulled** dulled (like wine sweetened and heated)

Third Servingman. Reason: because they then less
need one another. The wars for my money. I hope   245
to see Romans as cheap as Volscians. They are
rising,° they are rising.

Both [First and Second Servingmen]. In, in, in, in!
                                            Exeunt.

[Scene VI. *Rome. A public place.*]

Enter the two Tribunes, Sicinius and Brutus.

Sicinius. We hear not of him, neither need we fear
    him;
  His remedies are tame.° The present peace
  And quietness of the people, which before
  Were in wild hurry,° here do make his friends
  Blush that the world goes well; who rather had,   5
  Though they themselves did suffer by't, behold
  Dissentious numbers pest'ring° streets than see
  Our tradesmen singing in their shops, and going
  About their functions friendly.

Brutus. We stood to't° in good time.   10

                Enter Menenius.

                                Is this Menenius?

Sicinius. 'Tis he, 'tis he. O, he is grown most kind
  Of late. Hail, sir!

Menenius.   Hail to you both!

Sicinius. Your Coriolanus is not much missed

---

247 **rising** getting up from table IV.vi.2 **His remedies are tame** his
attempts to "cure" the state are (now) harmless (cf. "dangerous
physic," III.i.154)   4 **hurry** commotion   7 **pest'ring** filling with
disturbance   10 **stood to't** made an issue of it

But with his friends. The commonwealth doth stand,
15 And so would do, were he more angry at it.

Menenius. All's well; and might have been much better, if
He could have temporized.

Sicinius.   Where is he, hear you?

Menenius. Nay, I hear nothing. His mother and his wife
Hear nothing from him.

Enter three or four Citizens.

All [*Citizens*]. The gods preserve you both!

20 *Sicinius.*   Good-e'en,° our neighbors.

Brutus. Good-e'en to you all, good-e'en to you all.

First Citizen. Ourselves, our wives, and children, on our knees,
Are bound to pray for you both.

Sicinius.   Live, and thrive!

Brutus. Farewell, kind neighbors. We wished Coriolanus
Had loved you as we did.

25 *All* [*Citizens*].   Now the gods keep you!

Both Tribunes. Farewell, farewell.

Exeunt Citizens.

Sicinius. This is a happier and more comely° time
Than when these fellows ran about the streets
Crying confusion.°

Brutus.   Caius Marcius was
30 A worthy officer i' th' war, but insolent,
O'ercome with pride, ambitious past all thinking,
Self-loving—

20 **Good-e'en** good evening   27 **comely** respectable   29 **Crying confusion** calling for disorder

Sicinius.   And affecting° one sole throne,
Without assistance.°

Menenius.   I think not so.

Sicinius. We should by this, to all our lamentation,
If he had gone forth consul, found° it so.   *35*

Brutus. The gods have well prevented it, and Rome
Sits safe and still without him.

Enter an Aedile.

Aedile.   Worthy tribunes,
There is a slave, whom we have put in prison,
Reports the Volsces with two several powers°
Are ent'red in the Roman territories,   *40*
And with the deepest malice of the war
Destroy what lies before 'em.

Menenius.   'Tis Aufidius,
Who, hearing of our Marcius' banishment,
Thrusts forth his horns° again into the world,
Which were inshelled when Marcius stood for
    Rome,   *45*
And durst not once peep out.

Sicinius.   Come, what talk you
Of Marcius?

Brutus. Go see this rumorer whipped. It cannot be
The Volsces dare break with us.

Menenius.   Cannot be!
We have record that very well it can;   *50*
And three examples of the like hath been
Within my age. But reason with° the fellow,
Before you punish him, where he heard this,
Lest you shall chance to whip your information
And beat the messenger who bids beware   *55*
Of what is to be dreaded.

---

32 **affecting** aiming at   33 **Without assistance** not sharing his powers
with others   35 **found** have found   39 **several powers** separate
forces   44 **horns** (like a snail)   52 **reason with** talk with

Sicinius.   Tell not me:
  I know this cannot be.

Brutus.   Not possible.

                    Enter a Messenger.

Messenger. The nobles in great earnestness are going
  All to the Senate House. Some news is coming
60 That turns° their countenances.

Sicinius.   'Tis this slave—
  Go whip him 'fore the people's eyes—his raising,°
  Nothing but his report.

Messenger.   Yes, worthy sir,
  The slave's report is seconded;° and more,
  More fearful, is delivered.

Sicinius.   What more fearful?

65 *Messenger.* It is spoke freely out of many mouths,
  How probable I do not know, that Marcius,
  Joined with Aufidius, leads a power 'gainst Rome,
  And vows revenge as spacious as between
  The young'st and oldest thing.°

Sicinius.   This is most likely!

70 *Brutus.* Raised only that the weaker sort may wish
  Good Marcius home again.

Sicinius.   The very trick on't.

Menenius. This is unlikely:
  He and Aufidius can no more atone°
  Than violent'st contrariety.

                Enter [a second] Messenger.

75 *Second Messenger.* You are sent for to the Senate.
  A fearful army, led by Caius Marcius

60 **turns** changes   61 **his raising** his starting (i.e., the rumor; note
comma and the following explanatory phrase)   63 **seconded** confirmed (by further reports)   68–69 **as spacious . . . thing** covering
the span between youngest and oldest, i.e., the whole population
73 **atone** be reconciled

Associated with Aufidius, rages
Upon our territories, and have already
O'erborne their way,° consumed with fire, and took
What lay before them.   80

Enter Cominius.

Cominius. O, you have made good work!

Menenius.   What news? What news?

Cominius. You have holp to ravish your own daugh-
ters and
To melt the city leads° upon your pates,
To see your wives dishonored to° your noses—

Menenius. What's the news? What's the news?   85

Cominius. Your temples burnèd in their cement, and
Your franchises, whereon you stood,° confined
Into an auger's bore.

Menenius.   Pray now, your news?—
You have made fair work, I fear me.—Pray, your
news?—
If Marcius should be joined wi' th' Volscians—

Cominius.   If!   90
He is their god; he leads them like a thing
Made by some other deity than Nature,
That shapes man better; and they follow him
Against us brats with no less confidence
Than boys pursuing summer butterflies,   95
Or butchers killing flies.

Menenius.   You have made good work,
You and your apron-men;° you that stood so much
Upon the voice of occupation° and
The breath of garlic-eaters!

Cominius.   He'll shake
Your Rome about your ears.

79 **O'erborne their way** (like a stream) overflowed everything in their
way   83 **leads** roofs   84 **to** before   87 **franchises, whereon you
stood** rights on which you insisted   97 **apron-men** artisans   98 **occupation** manual workers

100 *Menenius.*   As Hercules
     Did shake down mellow fruit. You have made fair
       work!

Brutus. But is this true, sir?

Cominius.   Ay; and you'll look pale
     Before you find it other. All the regions
     Do smilingly revolt, and who resists
105   Are mocked for valiant ignorance,
     And perish constant° fools. Who is't can blame
       him?
     Your enemies and his find something in him.

Menenius. We are all undone, unless
     The noble man have mercy.

Cominius.   Who shall ask it?
110   The tribunes cannot do't for shame; the people
     Deserve such pity of him as the wolf
     Does of the shepherds. For his best friends, if they
     Should say "Be good to Rome," they charged° him
       even
     As those should do that had deserved his hate,
     And therein showed° like enemies.

115 *Menenius.*   'Tis true:
     If he were putting to my house the brand
     That should consume it, I have not the face
     To say "Beseech you, cease." You have made fair
       hands,°
     You and your crafts! You have crafted fair!°

Cominius.   You have brought
120   A trembling upon Rome, such as was never
     S' incapable° of help.

Tribunes.   Say not we brought it.

---

106 **constant** loyal   113 **charged** would attack, urge (both senses relevant)   115 **showed** would show   118 **made fair hands** handled matters finely   119 **crafted fair** plied your trade (of cunning) beautifully   121 **S' incapable** so unsusceptible

Menenius. How! Was't we? We loved him, but, like
  beasts
  And cowardly nobles, gave way unto your clusters,°
  Who did hoot him out o' th' city.

Cominius.   But I fear
  They'll roar him in again. Tullus Aufidius,   *123*
  The second name of men,° obeys his points°
  As if he were his officer. Desperation
  Is all the policy, strength, and defense,
  That Rome can make against them.

        Enter a troop of Citizens.

Menenius.   Here come the clusters.
  And is Aufidius with him? You are they   *130*
  That made the air unwholesome when you cast
  Your stinking greasy caps in hooting at
  Coriolanus' exile. Now he's coming,
  And not a hair upon a soldier's head
  Which will not prove a whip. As many coxcombs°   *135*
  As you threw caps up will he tumble down,
  And pay you for your voices.° 'Tis no matter;
  If he could burn us all into one coal,°
  We have deserved it.

Omnes. Faith, we hear fearful news.

First Citizen.   For mine own part,   *140*
  When I said banish him, I said 'twas pity.

Second Citizen. And so did I.

Third Citizen. And so did I; and, to say the truth, so
  did very many of us. That we did, we did for the
  best; and though we willingly consented to his ban- *145*
  ishment, yet it was against our will.

Cominius. Y'are goodly things, you voices!

Menenius.   You have made

123 **clusters** crowds   126 **second name of men** second in renown
(to Coriolanus)   126 **points** directions (?)   135 **coxcombs** fools'
heads (cf. costume of a fool)   137 **voices** votes   138 **coal** piece of
burned fuel (cf. charcoal)

Good work, you and your cry!° Shall's° to the
Capitol?

Cominius. O, ay, what else?   *Exeunt both.*

150 *Sicinius.* Go masters, get you home; be not dismayed;
These are a side° that would be glad to have
This true which they so seem to fear. Go home,
And show no sign of fear.

First Citizen. The gods be good to us! Come, masters,
155 let's home. I ever said we were i' th' wrong when we
banished him.

Second Citizen. So did we all. But come, let's home.
                              Exit Citizens.

Brutus. I do not like this news.

Sicinius. Nor I.

160 *Brutus.* Let's to the Capitol. Would half my wealth
Would buy this for a lie!

Sicinius.   Pray, let's go.
                              Exeunt Tribunes.

[Scene VII. *A camp not far from Rome.*]

Enter Aufidius with his Lieutenant.

Aufidius. Do they still fly to th' Roman?

Lieutenant. I do not know what witchcraft's in him,
but
Your soldiers use him as the grace 'fore meat,
Their talk at table and their thanks at end;
5 And you are dark'ned° in this action sir,
Even by your own.°

148 **cry** pack   148 **Shall's** shall us (we)   151 **side** faction   IV.vii.5
dark'ned put in the shade   6 **your own** your own men

Aufidius.   I cannot help it now,
Unless by using means° I lame the foot
Of our design. He bears himself more proudlier,
Even to my person, than I thought he would
When first I did embrace him; yet his nature   *10*
In that's no changeling,° and I must excuse
What cannot be amended.

Lieutenant.   Yet I wish, sir—
I mean for your particular°—you had not
Joined in commission° with him, but either
Have borne the action of yourself, or else   *15*
To him had left it solely.

Aufidius. I understand thee well; and be thou sure,
When he shall come to his account, he knows not
What I can urge against him. Although it seems,
And so he thinks, and is no less apparent   *20*
To th' vulgar eye, that he bears all things fairly,
And shows good husbandry° for the Volscian state,
Fights dragon-like, and does achieve as soon
As draw his sword. Yet he hath left undone
That which shall break his neck or hazard mine,   *25*
Whene'er we come to our account.

Lieutenant. Sir, I beseech you, think you he'll carry
    Rome?

Aufidius. All places yields to him ere he sits down,°
And the nobility of Rome are his;
The senators and patricians love him too.   *30*
The tribunes are no soldiers, and their people
Will be as rash in the repeal, as hasty
To expel him thence. I think he'll be to Rome
As is the osprey° to the fish, who takes it
By sovereignty of nature.° First he was   *35*
A noble servant to them, but he could not

7 **using means** taking steps   11 **no changeling** i.e., he is the self-same
man   13 **your particular** your own sake   14 **Joined in commission**
shared the command   22 **husbandry** management   28 **sits down**
lays siege   34 **osprey** fish hawk   35 **By sovereignty of nature** (refers to the osprey's supposed power of subduing its prey before
touching it)

Carry his honors even.° Whether 'twas pride,
Which out of daily fortune ever taints°
The happy° man; whether defect of judgment,
40 To fail in the disposing of those chances
Which he was lord of; or whether nature,
Not to be other than one thing, not moving
From th' casque° to th' cushion,° but commanding
     peace
Even with the same austerity and garb
45 As he controlled the war; but one of these—
As he hath spices° of them all—not all,
For I dare so far free him—made him feared,
So hated, and so banished. But he has a merit
To choke it in the utt'rance.° So our virtues
50 Lie in th' interpretation of the time;°
And power, unto itself most commendable,
Hath not a tomb so evident as a chair°
T' extol what it hath done.
One fire drives out one fire; one nail, one nail;
Rights by rights founder, strengths by strengths do
55   fail.°
Come, let's away. When, Caius, Rome is thine,
Thou art poor'st of all; then shortly art thou mine.

                                        Exeunt.

---

37 **even** (and keep his balance)   38 **daily fortune ever taints** success
coming day after day always infects   39 **happy** lucky   43 **casque**
helmet, i.e., military life   43 **cushion** i.e., position of authority in
civil life; cf. III.i.101   46 **spices** flavors, i.e., traces   48–49 **a merit/
To choke it in the utt'rance** a merit that is nullified in the very act
of being expressed (because of faults inseparable from the particular
virtues being praised)   50 **the time** the age (our contemporaries)
52 **chair** (of the speaker who praises the achievements made possible
by "power," line 51; probably with reference to the Roman rostrum,
or speakers' platform)   54–55 **One fire . . . fail** (examples of the
self-destructive process described in lines 48–53)

ACT V

[Scene I. *Rome. A public place.*]

*Enter Menenius, Cominius, Sicinius, Brutus,
the two Tribunes, with others.*

Menenius. No, I'll not go. You hear what he hath
    said
Which was sometime° his general, who loved him
In a most dear particular.° He called me father;
But what o' that? Go you that banished him,
A mile before his tent fall down, and knee   *5*
The way° into his mercy. Nay, if he coyed°
To hear Cominius speak, I'll keep at home.

Cominius. He would not seem to know me.

Menenius.   Do you hear?

Cominius. Yet one time he did call me by my name.
I urged our old acquaintance, and the drops   *10*
That we have bled together. Coriolanus
He would not answer to; forbad all names;
He was a kind of nothing, titleless,
Till he had forged himself a name o' th' fire
Of burning Rome.

V.i.2 **sometime** formerly   3 **a most dear particular** a most precious
intimacy   5–6 **knee/The way** make your way on your knees   6 **coyed**
showed reluctance

15 *Menenius.*   Why, so! You have made good work!
  A pair of tribunes that have wracked° fair Rome
  To make coals° cheap! A noble memory!

  Cominius. I minded° him how royal 'twas to pardon
  When it was less expected; he replied,
20 It was a bare° petition of a state
  To one whom they had punished.

  Menenius.   Very well.
  Could he say less?

  Cominius. I offered° to awaken his regard
  For's private friends. His answer to me was,
25 He could not stay to pick them in a pile
  Of noisome musty chaff. He said 'twas folly,
  For one poor grain or two, to leave unburnt
  And still to nose th' offense.°

  Menenius.   For one poor grain or two!
  I am one of those; his mother, wife, his child,
30 And this brave fellow too, we are the grains;
  You are the musty chaff, and you are smelt
  Above the moon. We must be burnt for you.

  Sicinius. Nay, pray, be patient; if you refuse your aid
  In this so never-needed° help, yet do not
35 Upbraid's with our distress. But, sure, if you
  Would be your country's pleader, your good tongue,
  More than the instant army we can make,°
  Might stop our countryman.

  Menenius.   No, I'll not meddle.

  Sicinius. Pray you, go to him.

  Menenius.   What should I do?

40 *Brutus.* Only make trial what your love can do
  For Rome, towards° Marcius.

---

16 **wracked** ruined 17 **coals** charcoal 18 **minded** reminded 20 **bare**
mere 23 **offered** tried 28 **nose th' offense** smell the offensive stuff
34 **so never-needed** never so needed (as now) 37 **the instant army
we can make** the army we can raise at this time 41 **towards** in relation to

Menenius.   Well, and say that Marcius
    Return me, as Cominius is returned,
    Unheard—what then?
    But as a discontented friend, grief-shot°
    With his unkindness? Say't be so?

Sicinius.   Yet your good will   45
    Must have that thanks from Rome after the measure
    As you intended well.°

Menenius.   I'll undertake't:
    I think he'll hear me. Yet to bite his lip
    And hum at good Cominius much unhearts° me.
    He was not taken well;° he had not dined.   50
    The veins unfilled, our blood is cold, and then
    We pout upon the morning, are unapt
    To give or to forgive; but when we have stuffed
    These pipes and these conveyances° of our blood
    With wine and feeding, we have suppler souls   55
    Than in our priestlike fasts. Therefore I'll watch
       him
    Till he be dieted to° my request,
    And then I'll set upon him.

Brutus. You know the very road into his kindness,
    And cannot lose your way.

Menenius.   Good faith, I'll prove° him,   60
    Speed° how it will. I shall ere long have knowledge
    Of my success.   *Exit.*

Cominius.   He'll never hear him.

Sicinius.   Not?

Cominius. I tell you he does sit in gold, his eye
    Red as 'twould burn Rome, and his injury°
    The jailer to his pity. I kneeled before him;   65

44 **grief-shot** struck by grief   46–47 **after the measure/As you intended well** in proportion to your good intentions   49 **unhearts** dis-
courages   50 **taken well** approached at a good time   54 **convey-
ances** channels   57 **dieted to** prepared for by feeding   60 **prove**
make trial of   61 **Speed** turn out   64 **injury** sense of the wrong
done to him

'Twas very faintly he said "Rise"; dismissed me
Thus with his speechless hand. What he would do
He sent in writing after me, what he would not,
Bound with an oath to yield° to his conditions;
70   So that all hope is vain,°
Unless° his noble mother and his wife,
Who (as I hear) mean to solicit him
For mercy to his country. Therefore, let's hence,
And with our fair entreaties haste them on.

                                        Exeunt.

[Scene II. *Entrance of the Volscian camp
before Rome.*]

Enter Menenius to the Watch on Guard.

First Watch. Stay. Whence are you?

Second Watch.   Stand, and go back.

Menenius. You guard like men, 'tis well; but, by your
     leave,
I am an officer of state, and come
To speak with Coriolanus.

First Watch.   From whence?

Menenius.   From Rome.

First Watch. You may not pass, you must return: our
5   general
     Will no more hear from thence.

_____

67–69 **What . . . yield** i.e., he sent a written message saying what he
would do and what he would not, all this (the statement of terms)
being bound with an oath that we should yield (text probably corrupt)   70 **vain** (because the conditions are ruinous)   71 **Unless** except for (or perhaps "solicit him," line 72, is to be understood:
"unless his noble mother and his wife solicit him")

Second Watch. You'll see your Rome embraced with
     fire, before
   You'll speak with Coriolanus.

Menenius.   Good my friends,
   If you have heard your general talk of Rome
   And of his friends there, it is lots to blanks°   *10*
   My name hath touched your ears: it is Menenius.

First Watch. Be it so; go back. The virtue of your
     name
   Is not here passable.°

Menenius.   I tell thee, fellow,
   Thy general is my lover. I have been
   The book of his good acts whence men have read   *15*
   His fame unparalleled—haply amplified;
   For I have ever verified° my friends
   (Of whom he's chief) with all the size that verity
   Would without lapsing° suffer. Nay, sometimes,
   Like to a bowl upon a subtle° ground,   *20*
   I have tumbled past the throw,° and in his praise
   Have almost stamped° the leasing.° Therefore,
     fellow,
   I must have leave to pass.

First Watch. Faith, sir, if you had told as many lies
   in his behalf as you have uttered words in your   *25*
   own, you should not pass here; no, though it were
   as virtuous to lie as to live chastely. Therefore go
   back.

Menenius. Prithee, fellow, remember my name is
   Menenius, always factionary° on the party of your   *30*
   general.

V.ii.10 **lots to blanks** (more than an even chance; "lots" refers to
tickets in a lottery taking prizes; "blanks," to those not taking
prizes)   13 **passable** current (of money, but with a pun on "password")   17 **verified** testified to the merit of   19 **lapsing** slipping
(into error)   20 **subtle** deceptive   21 **tumbled past the throw** rolled
beyond the proper distance   22 **stamped** given currency to (cf.
"stamp" a coin)   22 **leasing** falsehood   30 **factionary** an active
worker

Second Watch. Howsoever you have been his liar, as
you say you have, I am one that, telling true under
him, must say you cannot pass. Therefore go back.

35 *Menenius.* Has he dined, canst thou tell? For I would
not speak with him till after dinner.

First Watch. You are a Roman, are you?

Menenius. I am, as thy general is.

First Watch. Then you should hate Rome, as he does.
40 Can you, when you have pushed out your gates the
very defender of them, and in a violent popular
ignorance given your enemy your shield, think to
front° his revenges with the easy groans of old
women, the virginal palms of your daughters, or
45 with the palsied intercession of such a decayed
dotant° as you seem to be? Can you think to blow
out the intended fire your city is ready to flame in,
with such weak breath as this? No, you are deceived; therefore, back to Rome, and prepare for
50 your execution. You are condemned; our general
has sworn you out of reprieve and pardon.

Menenius. Sirrah, if thy captain knew I were here, he
would use me with estimation.°

First Watch. Come, my captain knows you not.

55 *Menenius.* I mean, thy general.

First Watch. My general cares not for you. Back, I
say; go, lest I let forth your half-pint of blood.
Back—that's the utmost of your having.° Back.

Menenius. Nay, but, fellow, fellow—

Enter Coriolanus with Aufidius.

60 *Coriolanus.* What's the matter?

Menenius. Now, you companion,° I'll say an errand°

43 **front** face   46 **dotant** dotard   53 **estimation** esteem   58 **of your
having** you can get   61 **companion** fellow   61 **say an errand** give
a message

for you; you shall know now that I am in estimation; you shall perceive that a Jack guardant° cannot office me° from my son Coriolanus. Guess but
by my entertainment° with him if thou stand'st not   65
i' th' state of hanging, or of some death more long
in spectatorship and crueller in suffering; behold
now presently, and swoon for what's to come upon
thee. [*To Coriolanus*] The glorious gods sit in
hourly synod about thy particular prosperity, and   70
love thee no worse than thy old father Menenius
does! O my son, my son! Thou art preparing fire
for us; look thee, here's water to quench it. I was
hardly° moved to come to thee; but being assured
none but myself could move thee, I have been   75
blown out of your° gates with sighs; and conjure
thee to pardon Rome and thy petitionary° countrymen. The good gods assuage thy wrath, and turn
the dregs of it upon this varlet here; this, who, like
a block,° hath denied my access to thee.   80

Coriolanus. Away!

Menenius. How! Away!

Coriolanus. Wife, mother, child, I know not. My
      affairs
Are servanted° to others. Though I owe
My revenge properly,°·my remission° lies   85
In Volscian breasts. That we have been familiar,°
Ingrate forgetfulness° shall poison rather
Than pity note how much.° Therefore be gone.
Mine ears against your suits are stronger than
Your gates against my force. Yet, for° I loved thee,   90
Take this along; I writ it for thy sake,

---

63 **Jack guardant** wretch of a sentry   64 **office me** use his office to
keep me   65 **entertainment** reception   74 **hardly** with difficulty
76 **your** (of Rome)   77 **petitionary** who are asking for mercy
80 **block** blockhead   84 **servanted** subject (servant-like)   84–85 **I
owe/My revenge properly** my revenge belongs to me alone   85 **re-
mission** power to pardon   86 **That we have been familiar** our
intimacy in the past   87 **Ingrate forgetfulness** my ungrateful forgetfulness   88 **how much** (how much "we have been familiar," how
great the intimacy was)   90 **for** because

And would have sent it. Another word, Menenius,
I will not hear thee speak. This man, Aufidius,
Was my beloved in Rome; yet thou behold'st.

95 *Aufidius.* You keep a constant° temper.

Exeunt [Coriolanus and Aufidius].
Manet the Guard and Menenius.

First Watch. Now, sir, is your name Menenius?

Second Watch. 'Tis a spell, you see, of much power.
You know the way home again.

First Watch. Do you hear how we are shent° for
100 keeping your greatness back?

Second Watch. What cause, do you think, I have to
swoon?

Menenius. I neither care for th' world nor your general. For such things as you, I can scarce think
105 there's any, y'are so slight. He that hath a will to
die by himself° fears it not from another. Let your
general do his worst. For you, be that you are,
long; and your misery increase with your age! I
say to you, as I was said to, Away!   *Exit.*

110 *First Watch.* A noble fellow, I warrant him.

Second Watch. The worthy fellow is our general. He's
the rock, the oak not to be wind-shaken.

Exit Watch.

---

95 **constant** loyal, true   99 **shent** scolded   106 **by himself** by his
own hand

[Scene III. *The tent of Coriolanus.*]

Enter Coriolanus and Aufidius [with others].

Coriolanus. We will before the walls of Rome to-
    morrow
  Set down° our host. My partner in this action,
  You must report to th' Volscian lords how plainly°
  I have borne° this business.

Aufidius.   Only their ends
  You have respected; stopped your ears against   5
  The general suit of Rome; never admitted
  A private whisper—no, not with such friends
  That thought them sure of you.

Coriolanus.   This last old man,
  Whom with a cracked heart I have sent to Rome,
  Loved me above the measure of a father,
  Nay, godded me° indeed. Their latest refuge   10
  Was to send him; for whose old love I have
  (Though I showed° sourly to him) once more
    offered
  The first conditions, which they did refuse
  And cannot now accept; to grace° him only   15
  That thought he could do more, a very little
  I have yielded to. Fresh embassies and suits,
  Nor° from the state nor private friends, hereafter
  Will I lend ear to. (*Shout within.*) Ha! What shout
    is this?
  Shall I be tempted to infringe my vow   20
  In the same time 'tis made? I will not.

V.iii.2 **Set down** i.e., in a siege   3 **plainly** openly   4 **borne** conducted
11 **godded me** made me a god   11 **latest refuge** last resource
13 **showed** appeared   15 **grace** honor   18 **Nor** neither

Enter Virgilia, Volumnia, Valeria, young Marcius,
with Attendants.

My wife comes foremost; then the honored mold°
Wherein this trunk° was framed, and in her hand
The grandchild to her blood. But out, affection!
25   All bond and privilege of nature, break!
Let it be virtuous to be obstinate.
What is that curtsy worth? Or those doves' eyes,
Which can make gods forsworn? I melt, and am not
Of stronger earth° than others. My mother bows,
30   As if Olympus° to a molehill should
In supplication nod; and my young boy
Hath an aspect of intercession which
Great Nature cries "Deny not." Let the Volsces
Plough Rome, and harrow Italy! I'll never
35   Be such a gosling to obey instinct, but stand
As if a man were author of himself
And knew no other kin.

Virgilia.   My lord and husband!

Coriolanus. These eyes are not the same I wore in
    Rome.

Virgilia. The sorrow that delivers° us thus changed
    Makes you think so.

40   *Coriolanus.*   Like a dull actor now,
I have forgot my part and I am out,
Even to a full disgrace.—Best of my flesh,
Forgive my tyranny;° but do not say,
For that, "Forgive our Romans." O, a kiss
45   Long as my exile, sweet as my revenge!
Now, by the jealous queen of heaven,° that kiss
I carried from thee, dear, and my true lip
Hath virgined it e'er since. You gods! I prate,°
And the most noble mother of the world

22–37 (see Introduction p. xlii)   22 **mold** form (also "earth")
23 **trunk** body   28–29 **not/Of stronger earth** cf. "our common
clay"   30 **Olympus** a mountain, home of the Greek gods   35 **to**
as to   39 **delivers** presents   41 **out** speechless ("stuck")   43 **tyranny** cruelty   46 **queen of heaven** Juno, guardian of marriage
48 **prate** babble

Leave unsaluted. Sink, my knee, i' th' earth; *Kneels.*   50
Of thy deep duty° more impression° show
Than that of common sons.

Volumnia.   O, stand up blest!
Whilst with no softer cushion than the flint
I kneel before thee, and unproperly°
Show duty, as mistaken all this while   55
Between the child and parent.   [*Kneels.*]

Coriolanus.   What's this?
Your knees to me? To your corrected° son?
Then let the pebbles on the hungry° beach
Fillip° the stars! Then let the mutinous winds
Strike the proud cedars 'gainst the fiery sun,   60
Murd'ring impossibility, to make
What cannot be, slight work.

Volumnia.   Thou art my warrior;
I holp to frame thee. Do you know this lady?

Coriolanus. The noble sister of Publicola,
The moon of Rome, chaste as the icicle   65
That's curdied° by the frost from purest snow
And hangs on Dian's temple—dear Valeria!

Volumnia. This is a poor epitome° of yours,°
Which by th' interpretation of full time°
May show° like all yourself.

Coriolanus.   The god of soldiers,°   70
With the consent of supreme Jove, inform°
Thy thoughts with nobleness, that thou mayst
    prove
To shame unvulnerable, and stick° i' th' wars

---

51 **duty** reverence   51 **impression** i.e., "i' th' earth"   54 **unproperly**
(defined by lines 55–56: in a way that does not belong to me, as
though I had always misunderstood the relation between child and
parent)   57 **corrected** who is corrected (by your kneeling)   58 **hungry**
barren   59 **Fillip** strike   66 **curdied** congealed   68 **epitome** brief
but comprehensive version of a larger work   68 **of yours** belonging
to you, of you   69 **time** ("time" is compared to a commentator on
a text)   70 **show** appear   70 **god of soldiers** Mars, Coriolanus' special divinity   71 **inform** imbue (give an inner form or character to)
73 **stick** stand out

Like a great sea-mark,° standing every flaw,°
And saving those that eye thee!

75 *Volumnia.*   Your knee, sirrah.°

Coriolanus. That's my brave boy!

Volumnia. Even he, your wife, this lady, and myself
Are suitors to you.

Coriolanus.   I beseech you, peace!
Or, if you'd ask, remember this before:
80 The thing I have forsworn° to grant may never
Be held by you denials.° Do not bid me
Dismiss my soldiers, or capitulate°
Again with Rome's mechanics.° Tell me not
Wherein I seem unnatural. Desire not
85 T' allay my rages and revenges with
Your colder reasons.

Volumnia.   O, no more, no more!
You have said you will not grant us anything;
For we have nothing else to ask but that
Which you deny already. Yet we will ask,
90 That, if you fail in° our request, the blame
May hang upon your hardness. Therefore hear us.

Coriolanus. Aufidius, and you Volsces, mark; for
we'll
Hear nought from Rome in private. Your request?

Volumnia. Should we be silent and not speak, our
raiment
95 And state of bodies would bewray° what life
We have led since thy exile. Think with thyself
How more unfortunate than all living women
Are we come hither; since that thy sight, which
should

---

74 **a great sea-mark** some prominent object that guides mariners
(cf. "landmark," the common modern term)   74 **flaw** gust of wind
75 **sirrah** sir (affectionately)   80 **forsworn** sworn not to   81 **denials**
i.e., refusals to all of you (therefore, plural)   82 **capitulate** arrange
terms   83 **mechanics** manual laborers   90 **fail in** fail to grant
95 **bewray** reveal

Make our eyes flow with joy, hearts dance with
   comforts,
Constrains them weep and shake with fear and
   sorrow,   100
Making the mother, wife, and child, to see
The son, the husband, and the father, tearing
His country's bowels out. And to poor we°
Thine enmity's most capital:° thou barr'st us
Our prayers to the gods, which is a comfort   105
That all but we enjoy. For how can we,
Alas, how can we for our country pray,
Whereto we are bound, together with thy victory,
Whereto we are bound? Alack, or° we must lose
The country, our dear nurse, or else thy person,   110
Our comfort in the country. We must find
An evident° calamity, though we had
Our wish, which side should win; for either thou
Must as a foreign recreant° be led
With manacles through our streets, or else   115
Triumphantly tread on thy country's ruin,
And bear the palm for having bravely shed
Thy wife and children's blood. For myself, son,
I purpose not to wait on fortune till
These wars determine.° If I can not persuade thee   120
Rather to show a noble grace° to both parts°
Than seek the end of one, thou shalt no sooner
March to assault thy country than to tread
(Trust to't, thou shalt not) on thy mother's womb
That brought thee to this world.

Virgilia.   Ay, and mine,   125
That brought you forth this boy, to keep your name
Living to time.°

Boy.   'A° shall not tread on me;
I'll run away till I am bigger, but then I'll fight.

---

103 **we** (for "us") 104 **capital** deadly 109 **or** either 112 **evident**
certain 114 **recreant** traitor 120 **determine** come to an end
121 **grace** consideration, favor 121 **parts** sides (parties) 126–127 **keep**
your name/Living to time perpetuate your name (keep living as long
as time lasts) 127 **'A** he

Coriolanus. Not of a woman's tenderness to be,
130   Requires nor child nor woman's face to see.
  I have sat too long.

Volumnia.   Nay, go not from us thus.
                           [*Rises.*]
  If it were so that our request did tend
  To save the Romans, thereby to destroy
  The Volsces whom you serve, you might condemn
    us,
135   As poisonous of your honor. No, our suit
  Is that you reconcile them; while the Volsces
  May say "This mercy we have showed," the
    Romans,
  "This we received"; and each in either side
  Give the all-hail to thee, and cry "Be blest
  For making up this peace!" Thou know'st, great
140   son,
  The end of war's uncertain; but this certain,
  That, if thou conquer Rome, the benefit
  Which thou shalt thereby reap is such a name
  Whose repetition will be dogged with curses,
145   Whose chronicle thus writ,° "The man was noble,
  But with his last attempt° he wiped it° out,
  Destroyed his country, and his name remains
  To th' ensuing age abhorred." Speak to me, son.
  Thou hast affected the fine strains° of honor,
150   To imitate the graces of the gods,°
  To tear with thunder the wide cheeks o' th' air,
  And yet to charge° thy sulphur° with a bolt
  That should but rive an oak. Why dost not speak?
  Think'st thou it honorable for a noble man
155   Still to remember wrongs? Daughter, speak you:
  He cares not for your weeping. Speak thou, boy:
  Perhaps thy childishness will move him more

145 **writ** will be written   146 **attempt** undertaking   146 **it** (his nobility)   149 **affected the fine strains** aimed at the refinements   150 **graces of the gods** (qualities that give the gods splendor and power; illustrated with irony, lines 151–53)   152 **charge** load (make heavy, or "load," as of a gun)   152 **sulphur** lightning (see Introduction p. xliv)

Than can our reasons. There's no man in the world
More bound to's mother, yet here he lets me prate
Like one i' th' stocks. Thou hast never in thy life   *160*
Showed thy dear mother any courtesy,
When she (poor hen) fond of° no second brood,
Has clocked° thee to the wars, and safely home
Loaden° with honor. Say my request's unjust,
And spurn me back. But if it be not so,   *165*
Thou art not honest,° and the gods will plague thee,
That thou restrain'st from me the duty which
To a mother's part belongs. He turns away.
Down, ladies! Let us shame him with our knees.
To his surname Coriolanus 'longs more pride   *170*
Than pity to our prayers. Down! An end;
This is the last. So we will home to Rome,
And die among our neighbors. Nay, behold's!°
This boy, that cannot tell what he would have,
But kneels and holds up hands for fellowship,   *175*
Does reason° our petition with more strength
Than thou hast to deny't. Come, let us go.
This fellow had a Volscian to his mother;
His wife is in Corioles, and his child
Like him by chance. Yet give us our dispatch.°   *180*
I am hushed until our city be a-fire,
And then I'll speak a little.

                                        Holds her by the hand, silent.

Coriolanus.   O mother, mother!
What have you done? Behold, the heavens do ope,
The gods look down, and this unnatural scene
They laugh at. O my mother, mother! O!   *185*
You have won a happy victory to Rome;
But, for your son—believe it, O, believe it!—
Most dangerously you have with him prevailed,
If not most mortal to° him. But let it come.
Aufidius, though I cannot make true wars,   *190*
I'll frame convenient° peace. Now, good Aufidius,

162 **fond of** eager for   163 **clocked** clucked   164 **Loaden** laden
166 **honest** honorable   173 **behold's** behold us   176 **reason** plead
for   180 **dispatch** dismissal   189 **mortal to** with deadly results for
191 **convenient** fitting

Were you in my stead, would you have heard
A mother less? Or granted less, Aufidius?

Aufidius. I was moved withal.° by it

Coriolanus.   I dare be sworn you were!
195 And, sir, it is no little thing to make
Mine eyes to sweat compassion. But, good sir,
What peace you'll make, advise me. For my part,
I'll not to Rome, I'll back with you; and pray you
Stand to° me in this cause. O mother! Wife!
By

Aufidius. [*Aside*] I am glad thou hast set thy mercy
200   and thy honor
At difference in thee. Out of that I'll work
Myself a former fortune.° Regain his power & Position

Coriolanus. [*To Volumnia and Virgilia*] Ay, by and
by;
But we will drink together; and you shall bear
A better witness back than words, which° we
205 On like conditions will have countersealed.
Come, enter with us. Ladies, you deserve
To have a temple° built you. All the swords
In Italy, and her confederate arms,°
Could not have made this peace.   *Exeunt.*

[Scene IV. *Rome. A public place.*]

Enter Menenius and Sicinius.
                    corner
Menenius. See you yond coign° o' th' Capitol, yond
cornerstone?

194 **withal** by it (thereby)   199 **Stand to** stand by   201–202 **work/
Myself a former fortune** regain my former position and power
204 **which** i.e., the written document   207 **temple** (of the Fortune
of Women; see Plutarch, p. 246)   208 **confederate arms** allied
powers   V.iv.1 **coign** corner

Sicinius. Why, what of that?

Menenius. If it be possible for you to displace it with
your little finger, there is some hope the ladies of   5
Rome, especially his mother, may prevail with him.
But I say there is no hope in't; our throats are sentenced, and stay upon° execution.

Sicinius. Is't possible that so short a time can alter the
condition of a man?   10

Menenius. There is difference between a grub and a
butterfly; yet your butterfly was a grub. This Marcius is grown from man to dragon: he has wings;
he's more than a creeping thing.

Sicinius. He loved his mother dearly.   15

Menenius. So did he me; and he no more remembers
his mother now than an eight-year-old horse. The
tartness of his face sours ripe grapes. When he
walks, he moves like an engine° and the ground
shrinks before his treading. He is able to pierce a   20
corslet° with his eye, talks like a knell, and his
hum° is a battery.° He sits in his state° as a thing
made for Alexander.° What he bids be done is finished with his bidding. He wants nothing of a god
but eternity and a heaven to throne in.   25

Sicinius. Yes, mercy, if you report him truly.

Menenius. I paint him in the character. Mark what
mercy his mother shall bring from him. There is no
more mercy in him than there is milk in a male
tiger; that shall our poor city find. And all this is   30
'long of° you.

Sicinius. The gods be good unto us!

Menenius. No, in such a case the gods will not be

8 **stay upon** wait for   19 **engine** machine of war   21 **corslet** body
armor   21–22 **his hum** i.e., his saying "Hum!"   22 **battery** beating
of drums for an attack   22 **state** chair of state   22–23 **thing made
for Alexander** image of Alexander the Great   31 **'long of** along of,
because of

good unto us. When we banished him, we respected
35 not them; and, he returning to break our necks,
they respect not us.

Enter a Messenger.

Messenger. Sir, if you'd save your life, fly to your
house.
The plebeians have got your fellow-tribune,
And hale° him up and down; all swearing if
40 The Roman ladies bring not comfort home
They'll give him death by inches.

Enter another Messenger.

Sicinius.   What's the news?

Second Messenger. Good news, good news! The ladies
have prevailed,
The Volscians are dislodged,° and Marcius gone.
A merrier day did never yet greet Rome,
No, not th' expulsion of the Tarquins.

45 *Sicinius.*   Friend,
Art thou certain this is true? Is't most certain?

Second Messenger. As certain as I know the sun is
fire.
Where have you lurked,° that you make doubt
of it?
Ne'er through an arch so hurried the blown° tide,
As the recomforted through th' gates. Why, hark
50   you!

Trumpets, hautboys;° drums beat; all together.
The trumpets, sackbuts,° psalteries,° and fifes,
Tabors° and cymbals, and the shouting Romans,
Make the sun dance. Hark you! (*A shout within.*)

Menenius.   This is good news.
I will go meet the ladies. This Volumnia

39 hale haul   43 are dislodged have broken up camp   48 lurked
been hiding   49 blown swollen (by wind)   50 s.d. hautboy (original
of the modern oboe)   51 sackbuts trombones   51 psalteries harp-
like stringed instruments   52 Tabors small drums

Is worth of consuls, senators, patricians,   55
A city full; of tribunes such as you,
A sea and land full. You have prayed well today.
This morning for ten thousand of your throats
I'd not have given a doit. Hark, how they joy!

               Sound still with the shouts.

Sicinius. First, the gods bless you for your tidings;
    next,   60
Accept my thankfulness.

Second Messenger.   Sir, we have all
    Great cause to give great thanks.

Sicinius.   They are near the city!

Second Messenger. Almost at point to enter.

Sicinius.   We'll meet them,
    And help the joy.   *Exeunt.*

[Scene V. *Rome. Near the gate.*]

*Enter two Senators, with Ladies, passing over the
Stage, with other Lords.*

First Senator. Behold our patroness, the life of Rome!
Call all your tribes together, praise the gods,
And make triumphant fires; strew flowers before
    them.
Unshout the noise that banished Marcius,
Repeal° him with the welcome of his mother.   5
Cry "Welcome, ladies, welcome!"

All.   Welcome, ladies,
    Welcome!

          A flourish with drums and trumpets.

V.v.5 **Repeal** recall

[Scene VI. *Corioli. A public place.*]

Enter Tullus Aufidius, with Attendants.

Aufidius. Go tell the lords o' th' city I am here.
  Deliver them this paper. Having read it,
  Bid them repair to th' marketplace, where I,
  Even in theirs and in the commons' ears,
5 Will vouch the truth of it. Him° I accuse
  The city ports° by this hath entered, and
  Intends t' appear before the people, hoping
  To purge himself with words. Dispatch.
                          [*Exeunt Attendants.*]

Enter three or four Conspirators of Aufidius' faction.

  Most welcome!

First Conspirator. How is it with our general?

10 *Aufidius.*   Even so
  As with a man by his own alms empoisoned,°
  And with° his charity slain.

Second Conspirator.   Most noble sir,
  If you do hold the same intent wherein
  You wished us parties,° we'll deliver you
  Of your great danger.

15 *Aufidius.*   Sir, I cannot tell;
  We must proceed as we do find the people.

Third Conspirator. The people will remain uncertain
      whilst
  'Twixt you there's difference; but the fall of either
  Makes the survivor heir of all.

V.vi.5 **Him** he whom 6 **ports** gates 11 **empoisoned** destroyed
12 **with** by 14 **parties** partisans

Aufidius.   I know it,
   And my pretext to strike at him admits   *staked* 20
   A good construction. I raised him, and I pawned°
   Mine honor for his truth;° who being so heightened,
   He watered his new plants with dews of flattery,
   Seducing so my friends; and, to this end,
   He bowed his nature, never known before   25
   But to be rough, unswayable, and free.

Third Conspirator. Sir, his stoutness°   *proud obstinacy*
   When he did stand for consul, which he lost
   By lack of stooping—

Aufidius.   That I would have spoke of.
   Being banished for't, he came unto my hearth,   30
   Presented to my knife his throat. I took him,
   Made him joint-servant with me;° gave him way°
   In all his own desires; nay, let him choose
   Out of my files,° his projects to accomplish,
   My best and freshest men; served his designments°   *designs* 35
   In mine own person; holp to reap the fame
   Which he did end° all his; and took some pride
   To do myself this wrong; till at the last
   I seemed his follower, not partner; and
   He waged me with his countenance,° as if   40
   I had been mercenary.°

First Conspirator.   So he did, my lord.
   The army marveled at it; and, in the last,°   *finally*
   When he had carried° Rome and that we looked
   For no less spoil than glory—

Aufidius.   *strength*   There was it:°
   For which my sinews° shall be stretched upon° him.   *against* 45
   At° a few drops of women's rheum,° which are
                                       tears

21 **pawned** staked   22 **truth** loyalty   27 **stoutness** proud obstinacy
32 **joint-servant with me** sharer of my service (to the state)   32 **gave
him** way humored him   34 **files** ranks   35 **designments** designs
37 **end** get in (of crops)   40 **waged me with his countenance** for
wages gave me patronizing looks   41 **mercenary** serving for pay
42 **in the last** in the last place, finally   43 **carried** won   44 **There
was it** that was the crucial thing   45 **sinews** i.e., strength   45 **upon**
against   46 **At** at the price of   46 **rheum** tears

As cheap as lies, he sold the blood and labor
Of our great action. Therefore shall he die,
And I'll renew me in his fall. But hark!

    Drums and trumpets sounds, with great shouts
                  of the people.

First Conspirator. Your native town you entered like
50   a post,°
    And had no welcomes home; but he returns,
    Splitting the air with noise.

Second Conspirator.   And patient fools,
    Whose children he hath slain, their base throats
    tear
    With giving him glory.

Third Conspirator.   Therefore, at your vantage,°
55   Ere he express himself or move the people
    With what he would say, let him feel your sword,
    Which we will second.° When he lies along,°
    After your way his tale pronounced° shall bury
    His reasons with his body.

Aufidius.   Say no more:
60   Here come the lords.

        Enter the Lords of the city.

All Lords. You are most welcome home.

Aufidius.   I have not deserved it.
    But, worthy lords, have you with heed perused
    What I have written to you?

All [*Lords*].   We have.

First Lord.   And grieve to hear't.
    What faults he made before the last, I think
65   Might have found easy fines;° but there to end
    Where he was to begin, and give away

---

50 **post** messenger   54 **at your vantage** at a moment opportune for
you   57 **second** support (with our swords)   57 **along** stretched at
full length   58 **After your way his tale pronounced** his story told
in your version   65 **fines** penalties

    The benefit of our levies,° answering us
    With our own charge,° making a treaty where
    There was a yielding—this admits no excuse.

Aufidius. He approaches. You shall hear him.   *70*

    Enter Coriolanus, marching with drum and colors,
    the commoners being with him.

Coriolanus. Hail, lords! I am returned your soldier;
    No more infected° with my country's love
    Than when I parted° hence, but still subsisting°
    Under your great command. You are to know
    That prosperously I have attempted, and   *75*
    With bloody passage° led your wars even to
    The gates of Rome. Our spoils we have brought
       home
    Doth more than counterpoise a full third part
    The charges° of the action. We have made peace
    With no less honor to the Antiates   *80*
    Than shame to th' Romans; and we here deliver,
    Subscribed° by th' consuls and patricians,
    Together with the seal o' th' senate, what
    We have compounded° on.

Aufidius.   Read it not, noble lords;
    But tell the traitor in the highest degree   *85*
    He hath abused your powers.

Coriolanus. Traitor! How now!

Aufidius.   Ay, traitor, Marcius!

Coriolanus.   Marcius!

Aufidius. Ay, Marcius, Caius Marcius! Dost thou
    think
    I'll grace° thee with that robbery, thy stol'n name
    Coriolanus, in Corioles?   *90*

67 **our levies** the armies we raised   67–68 **answering us/With our own charge** paying us (only) with our own expenditure   72 **infected** (see Introduction, p. xlv)   73 **parted** departed   73 **subsisting** remaining   76 **passage** action   78–79 **more . . . charges** exceed the costs by a whole third (cf. line 68)   82 **Subscribed** signed   84 **compounded** agreed   89 **grace** honor

You lords and heads o' th' state, perfidiously
He has betrayed your business and given up,
For certain drops of salt, your city Rome,
I say "your city," to his wife and mother;
95   Breaking his oath and resolution, like
A twist° of rotten silk; never admitting
Counsel o' th' war; but at his nurse's tears
He whined and roared away your victory;
That° pages blushed at him, and men of heart°
Looked wond'ring each at others.

100 *Coriolanus.*   Hear'st thou, Mars?

Aufidius. Name not the god, thou boy of tears!

Coriolanus.   Ha!

Aufidius. No more.

Coriolanus. Measureless liar, thou hast made my
       heart
Too great for what contains it. "Boy"! O slave!
105   Pardon me, lords, 'tis the first time that ever
I was forced to scold. Your judgments, my grave
       lords,
Must give this cur the lie; and his own notion°—
Who wears my stripes impressed upon him, that
Must bear my beating to his grave—shall join
110 To thrust the lie unto him.

First Lord. Peace, both, and hear me speak.

Coriolanus. Cut me to pieces, Volsces, men and lads,
Stain all your edges on me. "Boy"! False hound!
If you have writ your annals true, 'tis there,°
115   That, like an eagle in a dovecote, I
Fluttered your Volscians in Corioles.
Alone I did it. "Boy"?

Aufidius.   Why, noble lords,

96 **twist** thread (made of more than one strand)   99 **That** so that
99 **of heart** of spirit   107 **notion** understanding   114 **there** (written)
there

Will you be put in mind of his blind fortune,°
Which was your shame, by this unholy braggart,
'Fore your own eyes and ears?

All Conspirators.   Let him die for't.   *120*

All People. Tear him to pieces!—Do it presently!°—
He killed my son!—My daughter!—He killed my
cousin Marcius!—He killed my father!

Second Lord. Peace, ho! no outrage, peace!
The man is noble, and his fame folds in° embraced   *125*
This orb o' th' earth. His last offenses to us
Shall have judicious° hearing. Stand,° Aufidius,
And trouble not the peace.   *stop*

Coriolanus.   O that I had him,
With six Aufidiuses or more—his tribe,
To use my lawful sword!

Aufidius.   Insolent villain!   *130*

All Conspirators. Kill, kill, kill, kill, kill him!
  Draw the Conspirators and kills Marcius, who falls.
                              Aufidius stands on him.

Lords.   Hold, hold, hold, hold!

Aufidius. My noble masters, hear me speak.

First Lord.   O Tullus!

Second Lord. Thou hast done a deed whereat valor
  will weep.

Third Lord. Tread not upon him. Masters all, be
  quiet;
  Put up your swords.   *135*

Aufidius. My lords, when you shall know—as in this
  rage
  Provoked by him, you cannot—the great danger
  Which this man's life did owe you,° you'll rejoice

---

118 **blind fortune** mere good luck (Fortune is a blind goddess)
121 **presently** at once   125 **folds in** embraces   127 **judicious** judi-
cial   127 **Stand** stop   138 **did owe you** held in payment for you

That he is thus cut off. Please it your honors
140 To call me to your senate, I'll deliver° *prove*
Myself your loyal servant, or endure
Your heaviest censure.° *sentence*

First Lord.   Bear from hence his body,
And mourn you for him. Let him be regarded
As the most noble corse° that ever herald
Did follow to his urn.

145 Second Lord.   His own impatience
Takes from Aufidius a great part of blame.
Let's make the best of it.

Aufidius.   My rage is gone,
And I am struck with sorrow. Take him up.
Help, three o' th' chiefest soldiers; I'll be one.
150 Beat thou the drum, that it speak mournfully;
Trail your steel pikes. Though in this city he
Hath widowed and unchilded many a one,
Which to this hour bewail the injury,
Yet he shall have a noble memory.°
155 Assist.

                              Exeunt bearing the body of Marcius.
                              A dead march sounded.

                              FINIS

140 **deliver** prove   142 **censure** sentence   144 **corse** corpse   154 **memory** memorial

Textual Note

The text of *Coriolanus* has survived only in the First Folio (1623), on which the present edition is based. There are no records of performances earlier than 1623, but there is a mocking imitation of the curious phrase, "lurched all swords of the garland" (II.ii.102), in Ben Jonson's *Epicoene, or The Silent Woman* (1609). It is therefore almost certain that the play was written and performed not later than 1609. The use in Menenius' fable of the body and its members of expressions from William Camden's *Remains* of 1605 and the probable allusion to the Midlands revolt of 1607, point to a date of 1607 or later. (See "The Source of *Coriolanus*," p. 204.) There is also the possible reference to the Great Frost of 1607–08 in the phrase "the coal of fire upon the ice" (I.i.174). It seems safe to assume that *Coriolanus* was written after *Antony and Cleopatra,* somewhere between 1607 and 1609.

The Folio text of *Coriolanus* might be described, like that of *The Tempest,* as a distinguished one; it was prepared with great care and is especially remarkable for its elaborate stage directions. W. W. Greg's assertion that the text was printed from the author's manuscript is now widely accepted. The stage directions, presumably Shakespeare's own, are those of a man of the theater who has his eye on the stage and the actors. For example: *"Enter Marcius and Aufidius, at several doors"* (I.viii); *"They all bustle about Coriolanus"* (III.i.184); and the most telling gesture of the play, *"Holds her by the hand, silent"* (V.iii.182).

But though the text brings us so close to the practicing hand of the poet-playwright, it was edited and printed by mortal men. It has a fairly high number of errors, and emendations have been found necessary in at least twenty to twenty-five places. One line has been omitted (II.iii. 249), and in two passages the style is so cryptic as to seem almost surely corrupt (III.ii.74–80; V.i.67–69). The most disturbing defect of the Folio text of *Coriolanus* is the widespread mislineation. There are many lines that are either too short or too long, as measured by the usual blank-verse norm, and it is often very hard to determine where the line division should occur. Most of these abnormalities, it has been pointed out, come in short speeches, or at the end or beginning of speeches in rapid dialogue. There are a relatively few instances in which speeches are assigned to seemingly inappropriate speakers. There are also variations in the names of speakers, most of them of little significance, and usually in names of minor persons. The town that gives the hero his honorific title is usually called "Corioles," though "Coriolus" and "Corialus" also occur. There is considerable uncertainty as to how both "Corioles" and "Coriolanus" are to be accented. The common reader, like the learned editor, is free to follow his rhythmic sense in particular lines: "Coríoles" or "Coriôles"? "Coriolânus" (the usual pronunciation) or "Coríolanus"?

The present edition follows the Folio text closely, but spelling and punctuation are modernized, abbreviations are amplified, names of speakers regularized, and some stage directions are moved slightly. The act divisions (translated from Latin) are those of the Folio; no scenes, except the first, are indicated in the Folio text. All other scene divisions printed here (in square brackets) are those of the Globe edition. The list of readings given in the following table includes only those words in the Folio that have been omitted or emended. The reading adopted in this edition is printed in italics, followed by the original reading in roman.

I.i.7 *Marcius* Martius (throughout the play) 16 *on* one 28 *First Citizen* All 35 *Second Citizen* All 58 *First Citizen* 2 Cit. (throughout the rest of Scene i) 93 *stale't* scale't 111 *tauntingly* taintingly 215 *Shouting* Shooting 219 *unroofed* vnroo'st 227 s.d. *Junius* Annius 240 *Lartius* Lucius

I.ii.s.d. *Corioles* Coriolus 4 *on* one 30 *They've* Th'haue

I.iii.39 *that's* that 46 *sword, contemning. Tell* sword. Contenning, tell 85 *Virgilia* Vlug. 87 *yarn* yearne 88 *Ithaca* Athica 102 *whom* who

I.iv.s.d., 12 s.d. *Corioles* Corialus 31 *herd of—boils* Heard of Byles 42 *trenches. Follow's* Trenches followes 45 s.d. *Enters the gates* Enter the Gati 57 *Were* Weare 58 *Cato's* Calues

I.vi.21 *Who's* Whose 22 *flayed* Flead 53 *Antiates* Antients 70 *Lesser* Lessen

I.viii.7 *Holloa* hollow

I.ix.46 *coverture* Ouerture 50 *shout* shoot 65 *Caius Marcius* Marcus Caius (in this order throughout)

I.x.30 *cypress* Cyprus

II.i.24 *how are* ho ware 58 *cannot* can 63 *you* you you 66 *bisson* beesome 171 *Coriolanus* Martius Caius Coriolanus 184 *wear* were 186 *Coriolanus* Com. 192 *you* yon 210 s.d. *Brutus* Enter Brutus 219 *flamens* Plamins 240 *napless* Naples 261 *touch* teach

II.ii.26 *ascent* assent 51 *state's* states 82 *one on's* on ones 92 *chin* Shinne 93 *bristled* brizled

II.iii.29 *wedged* wadg'd 44 *all together* altogether 71 *Ay, not* I, but 119 *hire* higher 120 *toge* tongue 249 *And Censorinus that was so surnamed* [F omits. This line, invented by N. Delius in his edition of 1872, is indebted to Plutarch. See below, p. 209] 260 *Citizens* All

III.i.33 *herd* Heard 48 *Coriolanus* Com. 91 *good* God! 92 *reckless* wreaklesse 126 *Their* There 143 *Where one* Whereon 185 *All* [F has no speech prefix here, but gives "All" before line 187] 214 *All* [Citizens] All Ple. 228 *him!* him. Exeunt. 229 *your* our 230 *Coriolanus* Com. 236 *Cominius* Corio. 237 *Coriolanus* Mene. [speech assigned to Menenius through line 241] 239 *Menenius* [see preceding note] 286 *our* one 322 *bring him* bring him in peace

III.ii.21 *thwartings* things 32 *herd* heard 55 *roted* roated 115 *lulls* lull

III.iii.32 *for th'* fourth   36 *Throng* Through   55 *accents* Actions
89 *flaying* Fleaing   99 *do* doth   110 *for* from   135 s.d. *The other
Senators* Cumalijs

IV.i.24 *thee* the   34 *Whither wilt* Whether will

IV.iii.35 *will* well

IV.iv.23 *hate* haue

IV.v.3 *master* M.   82 *Whooped* Hoop'd   98 *Thou'rt* Th'art   113 *clip*
cleep   183 *lief* liue   236 *sleepy* sleepe

IV.vi.4 *do* do we   34 *lamentation* Lamention   90 *wi' th'* with
138 *one* oue

IV.vii.34 *osprey* Aspray   37 *'twas* 'was   39 *defect* detect   49 *virtues*
Vertue   55 *founder* fouler

V.i.16 *wracked fair* wrack'd for

V.ii.s.d. *on* or   16 *haply* happely   61 *errand* arrant   64–65 *but by
my* but my   102 *swoon* swoond

V.iii.48 *prate* pray   63 *holp* hope   104 *enmity's* enmities   141 *war's*
Warres   149 *fine* fiue   152 *charge* change   169 *him with* him with
him with   192 *stead* steed

V.iv.50 s.d. *all together* altogether

V.v.4 *Unshout* Vnshoot

V.vi.116 *Fluttered* Flatter'd   131 s.d. *the Conspirators* both the
Conspirators

The Source of
Coriolanus

The main source used by Shakespeare in writing *Coriolanus* is the *Life of Coriolanus* in Sir Thomas North's translation of Plutarch's *Lives of the Noble Grecians and Romans* (first published in 1579). Comparison of the play with the *Life* will remind us that both "source" and "use" are misleading terms for describing what happens when a writer of the first rank makes a new work out of an old one. In writing *Coriolanus,* Shakespeare was not merely borrowing discrete items from Plutarch; he was engaged in a total imaginative act, seeking to satisfy his inner measure of what was right for his own sensibility, for his sense of the hero's character, and for his complex "feel" of the dramatic world that was coming into being as he wrote. Our certainty that the play is one of Shakespeare's "most assured artistic successes," as T. S. Eliot has said, is strengthened when we discover what he accepted and what he rejected, and particularly when we see how he adapted his borrowings to his vision of Coriolanus and the tragedy as a whole.

Shakespeare's vision—though for all time—was not timeless in origin, but shaped in part by the social and literary culture in which he lived and by the audience for which he produced his plays. We have seen in the Introduction (pp. xxvii–xxxiv) how the Greco-Roman heroic ideal in its Renaissance form had an effect on *Coriolanus* and on its meaning for contemporary and succeeding audiences. Shakespeare's treatment of civil disorders in Republican Rome was almost certainly affected also by popular protests and uprisings in England during the early 1600's, disturbances brought on by the enclosure of farm lands and by the lack of grain and the consequent "dearth." That Shakespeare takes the famine as the principal cause for the plebeians' complaints, rather than as in Plutarch "the sore oppression of usurers," is almost certainly traceable to the unrest in England, and, more especially, to the Midlands revolt of 1607. The extensive emphasis in the play—as compared with the *Life*—on the body-state metaphor is probably to be explained in part by the contemporary concern with the dangers of insurrection. Shakespeare also elaborated on Plutarch's brief tale of the body and its members by drawing on Sidney's *Apology for Poetry,* Livy's *Roman History,* both in the original and in the translation of Philemon Holland (1600), and William Camden's *Remains of a Greater Work Concerning Britain* (1605).

The main events of Shakespeare's play, including the important scenes of Coriolanus' attack on the tribuneship (III.i), his banishment and his joining Aufidius (IV.i,v), and the climactic scene with his mother (V.iii), are all based on Plutarch. The principal features that Shakespeare stresses in his portrayal of Coriolanus have their origin, at least in an elementary form, in the pages of the *Life.* But Shakespeare has given even greater importance than Plutarch to Coriolanus' pride and uncontrollable temper and especially to the close emotional bond to his mother. (See also Introduction, pp. xxxv–vii.) Some critics have seen in the prominent role of Menenius, of which there is only the slightest hint in Plutarch (pp. 214–15), Shakespeare's intention of minimizing the social isolation that Plutarch ascribes to his hero, his unfitness for association with other men. But Menenius spends much of his time warning Coriolanus of these deficiencies, and of the likely consequences of his heroically simple and inept behavior. It also should be noted that in spite of his temperamental aloneness, Plutarch's hero, like Shakespeare's, has strong political supporters among the patricians. Where Shakespeare departs, and significantly, is in eliminating all references to political maneuvering by Coriolanus, of which there are fairly many instances in the *Life*. Other critics have noted that Plutarch attributes a reputation for eloquence to Coriolanus, whereas Shakespeare seems to stress his lack of ability as a speaker and debater. But the point surely is that Shakespeare, as Menenius explains, endows Coriolanus with the eloquence of a soldier—violent and powerful, though often tactless, utterance. He has but one style, and hence his calls for the defense of the state sound strangely like his calls to battle. (Compare III.i.149–57 and I.vi.67–75.)

A survey of the principal scenes that are wholly or largely invented by Shakespeare will give some idea of how thoroughly he adapted Plutarch's moral history to fit his peculiar dramatic subject of the Achillean hero exposed to the complexities and necessary compromises of the Roman-Jacobean political world. First, there are all the episodes in which Menenius figures prominently, with the exception of that part of the first scene in which he tells his fable. The occasion for this moral lesson, the retreat to the Sacred Mount, is passed over by Shakespeare, though Plutarch's narrative of it contains his sole mention of Menenius (pp. 214–15). In Livy's *History*, Menenius dies soon after this event takes place. All the other scenes in which Menenius does so much to defend Coriolanus against his enemies, or enhance his noble exploits, or to temper his wrath, are entirely of Shakespeare's making. In II.i, there is the bitterly comic telling-off of the tribunes, followed by the joyous welcome of the returning hero; in II.iii, the dialogue with Coriolanus and with the tribunes during the election scene; and the further exchanges with the tribunes in III.i, after Coriolanus has been accused of being a traitor. Although in some of these earlier scenes Shakespeare is using Menenius to voice arguments advanced by the more politic patricians of the *Life*, he had little basis in Plutarch for the prominent part taken by Menenius in a number of the scenes that follow Coriolanus' banishment. As often in this play, Shakespeare telescopes two or three Plutarchan scenes into one, centering the action on one of his more important characters. The scene in which Menenius begs Coriolanus to spare

Rome is—like Cominius' report of his own attempt—a substitution for one of several embassies from Rome described in Plutarch's narrative.

Shakespeare has invented all of the scenes in which Volumnia figures, with the exception of the women's embassy of V.iii. The scene that introduces Volumnia, Virgilia, and Valeria (I.iii), in which Volumnia shows that she had indeed made Coriolanus after her own image of "valiantness," grows from a single remark in the *Life* about the "joy his mother did take of him." The later scene in which she and Menenius urge Coriolanus to act "mildly" in answering the tribunes (III.ii) is a brilliant piece of dramatic foreshadowing, preparing for the final submisson of son to mother in Act V. (One characteristic of the play is the number of scenes that have close parallels, in which Coriolanus goes through the same routines but under changed circumstances, which he alone seems not to notice. Hence the odd *déjà vu,* almost nightmarish quality of much of the action in the latter part of the play.) Shakespeare also introduces a number of other scenes or episodes in which Volumnia has an important part, such as her rejoicing over her son's return from war (II.i), her farewell at the gate and her railing afterward (IV.i,ii), and her triumphant return from the final embassy (V.v). The speeches and scenes in which Shakespeare builds up the ambiguous hate-love relationship between Aufidius and Coriolanus in anticipation of their meeting in IV.v. grow from a single reference to their rivalry in the *Life* (p. 232).

But no listing of inventions or parallels between *Coriolanus* and Plutarch's narrative can give a true impression of how wonderfully Shakespeare has transformed the Plutarchan original, even when seeming to follow it closely. The most obvious example, Volumnia's great appeal (Act V.iii.19–209), offers the most telling proof of the art with which Shakespeare adapted North's language to suit the immediate context while keeping in view the larger dramatic and poetic design of the play. A few instances may suggest what can be learned by comparing the scene with the original in North's translation (pp. 242–45). Where Plutarch's Coriolanus is "overcome with natural affection" even before his mother speaks, Shakespeare's hero is caught in a violently shifting debate between the claims of nature, great and small, a conflict expressed in direct speech wholly invented by Shakespeare (lines 22–37). As we have seen (Introduction, pp. xxxv–vi), the debate is not limited to this speech but runs deeply through the play. In the play, in which the bond with the mother is so central to the hero's character, the son kneels first to the mother, and in the wholly new passages between Coriolanus and his son, we are reminded of the parallel to Hector (in a domestic and "natural" moment Coriolanus becomes less Achillean); we are reminded too of the early scene in which the boy-killer of butterflies is Coriolanus in miniature. The image he invokes of "a great sea-mark" is rooted in the imagery of natural forces and "things" so characteristic of Shakespeare's awesome and nonhuman hero. An example of where the verbal parallels are closest will indicate the remarkable depth and consistency of Shakespeare's dramatic and poetic art:

> *Volumnia.*   thou shalt no sooner
> March to assault thy country than to tread
> (Trust to't, thou shalt not) on thy mother's womb
> That brought thee to this world.
>
> (V.iii.122–25)

> ... thou shalt see, my son, and trust unto it, thou shalt no sooner march forward to assault thy country, but thy foot shall tread upon thy mother's womb that brought thee first into this world.
>
> (Plutarch's *Life of Coriolanus,* p. 244)

Shakespeare has closely imitated in his verse the climactic form of North's sentence, with its skillful suspension through well-placed pauses and the repeated "thou shalt"; but by building the whole speech to end at this point, he has exploited the emotional climax much more fully than North, who has Volumnia go straight on with "And I may not defer to see the day. . . ." More important, Shakespeare anticipates the image earlier in the speech in a way to make inescapable the identification of the mother's physical self with "mother Rome." North has Volumnia say earlier, "making myself to see my son, and my daughter here her husband, besieging the walls of his native country. . . ." Shakespeare brings this triple allegiance home and focuses it in a metaphor of such violence that even Coriolanus must feel the unnaturalness of his behavior and recognize in advance the implication of the final image:

> Making the mother, wife, and child, to see
> The son, the husband, and the father, tearing
> His country's bowels out.
>
> (V.iii.101–103)

The identity of "mothers," human and national, is quietly underlined a moment later in Volumnia's passing reference to "The country, our dear nurse. . . ." Compare with this North's relatively aloof and cold "the nurse of their native country." But the full impact of the appeal would be lost if we did not feel back of these physical mother-and-country images the recurring metaphors of the body politic and the large dramatic and philosophic premise they express. The personal and the patriotic appeals, which Shakespeare found in Plutarch, have been fused with a local intensity of feeling and with a far-reaching reference to Shakespeare's view, both of his individual characters and of the society in which they act. Dryden once spoke of Shakespeare as having "all the images of Nature . . . present to him" as he wrote. In comparing Volumnia's speech with its "source," we see Shakespeare writing *Coriolanus* with one eye on North, to be sure, but with all the images of the play and all their dramatic values present to his plastic imagination.

from

The Lives of the Noble Grecians and Romans

The Life of Caius Martius Coriolanus

The house of the Martians at Rome was of the number of the patricians, out of the which have sprung many noble personages, whereof Ancus Martius was one, King Numa's daughter's son, who was King of Rome after Tullus Hostilius. Of the same house were Publius and Quintus, who brought to Rome their best water they had, by conduits. Censorinus also came of that family, that was so surnamed because the people had chosen him Censor twice. Through whose persuasion they made a law, that no man from thenceforth might require or enjoy the Censorship twice.

In printing the following selections from North's version of the *Life of Coriolanus,* most passages have been omitted that have no observable relation to Shakespeare's play. The text reprinted here is that of W. W. Skeat: *Shakespeare's Plutarch* (1895), with some further modernization of spelling and punctuation; and further division of the text into paragraphs. North's translation was first published in a folio of 1579. New editions also appeared in 1595 and in 1603. Variations among the three editions in the text of the *Life of Coriolanus* are slight, though minor misprints of the 1579 text have often been corrected in the text of 1595 (and some new errors have been introduced). There are occasional improvements in the text of 1603. Skeat used an edition of 1612, which is a reproduction of the edition of 1603. Which of the three earlier editions Shakespeare used in writing *Coriolanus* has not been determined.

Caius Martius, whose life we intend now to write, being left an orphan by his father, was brought up under his mother a widow; who taught us by experience, that orphanage bringeth many discommodities to a child, but doth not hinder him to become an honest man, and to excel in virtue above the common sort; as they that are meanly born wrongfully do complain, that it is the occasion of their casting away, for that no man in their youth taketh any care of them to see them well brought up and taught that were meet. This man also is a good proof to confirm some men's opinions, that a rare and excellent wit, untaught, doth bring forth many good and evil things together; as a fat soil that lieth unmanured bringeth forth both herbs and weeds. For this Martius' natural wit and great heart did marvelously stir up his courage to do and attempt notable acts. But on the other side, for lack of education, he was so choleric and impatient, that he would yield to no living creature, which made him churlish, uncivil, and altogether unfit for any man's conversation. Yet men marveling much at his constancy, that he was never overcome with pleasure nor money and how he would endure easily all manner of pains and travails, thereupon they well liked and commended his stoutness and temperancy. But for all that, they could not be acquainted with him, as one citizen useth to be with another in the city. His behavior was so unpleasant to them by reason of a certain insolent and stern manner he had, which, because he was too lordly, was disliked. And to say truly, the greatest benefit that learning bringeth unto men is this: that it teacheth men that be rude and rough of nature, by compass and rule of reason, to be civil and courteous, and to like better the mean state than the higher. Now in those days, valiantness was honored in Rome above all other virtues, which they call *virtus,* by the name of virtue itself, as including in that general name all other special virtues besides. So that *virtus* in the Latin was as much as valiantness.

But Martius, being more inclined to the wars than any other gentleman of his time, began from his childhood to give himself to handle weapons, and daily did exercise himself therein; and he esteemed outward armor to no purpose, unless one were naturally armed within. Moreover he did so exercise his body to hardness and all kind of activity, that he was very swift in running, strong in wrestling, and mighty in griping, so that no man could ever cast him. Insomuch as those that would try masteries with him for strength and nimbleness would say when they were overcome, that all was by reason of his natural strength and hardness of ward, that never yielded to any pain or toil he took upon him.

The first time he went to the wars, being but a stripling, was when Tarquin, surnamed the proud (that had been King of Rome and was driven out for his pride, after many attempts made by sundry battles to come in again, wherein he was ever overcome), did come to Rome with all the aid of the Latins, and many other people of Italy; even as it were to set up his whole rest upon a battle by them, who with a great and mighty army had undertaken to put him into his kingdom again, not so much to pleasure him, as to overthrow the power of the Romans, whose greatness they both feared and envied. In this battle, wherein were many hot and sharp encounters of either party, Martius valiantly fought in the sight of the Dictator; and a Roman soldier being thrown to the ground even hard by him, Martius straight bestrid him and slew the enemy with his own hands, that had before overthrown the Roman. Hereupon, after the battle was won, the Dictator did not forget so noble an act, and therefore first of all he crowned Martius with a garland of oaken boughs. For whosoever saveth the life of a Roman, it is a manner among them, to honor him with such a garland.

Moreover, it is daily seen that honor and reputation lighting on young men before their time, and before they have any great courage by nature, the desire to win more dieth straight in them, which easily happeneth, the same having no deep root in them before. Where contrariwise, the first honor that valiant minds do come unto doth quicken up their appetite, hasting them forward, as with force of wind, to enterprise things of high-deserving praise. For they esteem not to receive reward for service done, but rather take it for a remembrance and encouragement, to make them do better in time to come, and be ashamed also to cast their honor at their heels, not seeking to increase it still by like desert of worthy valiant deeds. This desire being bred in Martius, he strained still to pass himself in manliness; and being desirous to show a daily increase of his valiantness, his noble service did still advance his fame, bringing in spoils upon spoils from the enemies. Whereupon, the captains that came afterwards (for envy of them that went before) did contend who should most honor him, and who should bear most honorable testimony of his valiantness. Insomuch as the Romans having many wars and battles in those days, Coriolanus was at them all; and there was not a battle fought from whence he returned not with some reward of honor.

And as for other, the only respect that made them valiant was that they hoped to have honor; but touching Martius, the only thing that made him to love honor was the joy he saw his mother did take of him. For he thought nothing made him so happy and honorable, as that his mother might hear everybody praise and commend him, that she might always see him return with a crown upon his head, and that she might still embrace him with tears running down her cheeks for joy. Which desire they say Epaminondas did avow and confess to have been in him, as to think himself a most happy and blessed man, that his father and mother in their lifetime had seen the victory he won in the plain of Leuctres. Now as for Epaminondas, he had this good hap, to have his father and mother living, to be partakers of his joy and prosperity. But Martius, thinking all due to his mother that had been also due to his father if he had lived, did not only content himself to rejoice and honor her, but at her desire took a wife also, by whom he had two young children, and yet never left his mother's house therefore.

Now he being grown to great credit and authority in Rome for his valiantness, it fortuned there grew sedition in the city, because the Senate did favor the rich against the people, who did complain of the sore oppression of usurers, of whom they borrowed money. For those that had little were yet spoiled of that little they had by their creditors, for lack of ability to pay the usury, who offered their goods to be sold to them that would give most. And such as had nothing left, their bodies were laid hold on, and they were made their bondmen, notwithstanding all the wounds and cuts they showed, which they had received in many battles, fighting for defense of their country and commonwealth. Of the which, the last war they made was against the Sabines, wherein they fought upon the promise the rich men had made them, that from thenceforth they would intreat them more gently, and also upon the word of Marcus Valerius, chief of the Senate, who, by authority of the council, and in the behalf of the rich, said they should perform that they had promised. But after that they had faithfully served in this last battle of all, where they overcame their enemies, seeing they were never a whit the better, nor more gently intreated, and that the Senate would give no ear to them but made as though they had forgotten the former promise, and suffered them to be made slaves and bondmen to their creditors, and besides, to be turned out of all that ever they had, they fell then even to flat rebellion and mutiny, and to stir up dangerous tumults within the city.

The Romans' enemies, hearing of this rebellion, did straight enter the territories of Rome with a marvelous great power, spoiling and burning all as they came. Whereupon the Senate immediately made open proclamation, by sound of trumpet, that all those that were of lawful age to carry weapon should come and enter their names into the muster-master's book, to go to the wars; but no man obeyed their commandment. Whereupon their chief magistrates and many of the Senate began to be of divers opinions among themselves. For some thought it was reason they should somewhat yield to the poor people's request, and that they should a little qualify the severity of the law. Other held hard against that opinion, and that was Martius for one. For he alleged that the creditors' losing their money they had lent was not the worst thing that was herein, but that the lenity that was favored was a beginning of disobedience, and that the proud attempt of the communalty was to abolish law and to bring all to confusion. Therefore, he said, if the Senate were wise, they should betimes prevent and quench this ill-favored and worse-meant beginning. The Senate met many days in consultation about it; but in the end they concluded nothing.

The poor common people, seeing no redress, gathered themselves one day together; and one encouraging another, they all forsook the city and encamped themselves upon a hill, called at that day the Holy Hill, along the river of Tiber, offering no creature any hurt or violence, or making any show of actual rebellion, saving that they cried as they went up and down that the rich men had driven them out of the city, and that throughout all Italy they might find air, water, and ground to bury them in. Moreover, they said, to dwell at Rome was nothing else but to be slain, or hurt with continual wars and fighting for defense of the rich men's goods.

The Senate, being afraid of their departure, did send unto them certain of the pleasantest old men, and the most acceptable to the people among them. Of those Menenius Agrippa was he who was sent for chief man of the message from the Senate. He, after many good persuasions and gentle requests made to the people on the behalf of the Senate, knit up his oration in the end with a notable tale, in this manner: that on a time all the members of man's body did rebel against the belly, complaining of it that it only remained in the midst of the body without doing anything, neither did bear any labor to the maintenance of the rest; whereas all other parts and members did labor painfully, and were very careful to satisfy the appetites and desires of the body. And so the belly, all this notwithstanding, laughed at their folly and said, "It is true, I first receive all meats that nourish man's body; but afterwards I send it again to the nourishment of other parts of the same." "Even so," quoth he, "O you, my masters, and citizens of Rome, the reason is alike between the Senate and you. For matters being well digested, and their counsels thoroughly examined, touching the benefit of the commonwealth, the senators are cause of the common commodity that cometh unto every one of you."

These persuasions pacified the people conditionally, that the Senate would grant there should be yearly chosen five magistrates, which they now call *Tribuni plebis,* whose office should be to defend the poor people from violence and oppression. So Junius Brutus and Sicinius Vellutus were the first tribunes of the people that were chosen, who had only been the causers and procurers of this sedition. Hereupon, the city being grown again to good quiet and unity, the people immediately went to the wars, showing that they had a good will to do better than ever they did, and to be very willing to obey the magistrates in that they would command concerning the wars.

Martius also, though it liked him nothing to see the greatness of the people thus increased, considering it was to the prejudice and imbasing of the nobility, and also saw that other noble patricians were troubled as well as himself, he did persuade the patricians to show themselves no less forward and willing to fight for their country than the common people were, and to let them know by their deeds and acts, that they did not so much pass the people in power and riches as they did exceed them in true nobility and valiantness.

In the country of the Volsces, against whom the Romans made war at that time, there was a principal city and of most fame, that was called Corioles, before the which the consul Cominius did lay siege. Wherefore all the other Volsces, fearing lest that city should be taken by assault, they came from all parts of the country to save it, intending to give the Romans battle before the city, and to give an onset on them in two several places. The consul Cominius understanding this, divided his army also into two parts; and taking the one part with himself, he marched towards them that were drawing to the city out of the country; and the other part of his army he left in the camp with Titus Lartius (one of the valiantest men the Romans had at that time) to resist those that would make any sally out of the city upon them.

So the Coriolans, making small account of them that lay in camp before the city, made a sally out upon them, in the which at the first the Coriolans had the better, and drave the Romans back again into the trenches of their camp. But Martius being there at that time, running out of the camp with a few men with him, he slew the first enemies he met withal, and made the rest of them stay upon the sudden, crying out to the Romans that had turned their backs, and calling them again to fight with a loud voice. For he was even such another, as Cato would have a soldier and a captain to be, not only terrible and fierce to lay about him, but to make the enemy afeared with the sound of his voice and grimness of his countenance. Then there flocked about him immediately a great number of Romans; whereat the enemies were so afeared that they gave back presently. But Martius, not staying so, did chase and follow them to their own gates that fled for life. And there perceiving that the Romans retired back, for the great number of darts and arrows which flew about their ears from the walls of the city, and that there was not one man amongst them that durst venture himself to follow the flying enemies into their city, for that it was full of men of war very well armed and appointed, he did encourage his fellows with words and deeds, crying out to them that fortune had opened the gates of the city, more for the followers than the fliers. But all this notwithstanding, few had the hearts to follow him.

Howbeit Martius, being in the throng amongst the enemies, thrust himself into the gates of the city and entered the same among them that fled, without that any one of them durst at the first turn their face upon him or offer to stay him. But he, looking about him, and seeing he was entered the city with very few men to help him, and perceiving he was environed by his enemies that gathered round about to set upon him, did things, as it is written, wonderful and incredible, as well for the force of his hand, as also for the agility of his body. And with a wonderful courage and valiantness he made a lane through the midst of them and overthrew also those he laid at; that some he made run to the furthest part of the city, and other for fear he made yield themselves, and to let fall their weapons before him. By this means Martius, that was gotten out, had some leisure to bring the Romans with more safety into the city.

The city being taken in this sort, the most part of the soldiers began incontinently to spoil, to carry away, and to look up the booty they had won. But Martius was marvelous angry with them, and cried out on them that it was no time now to look after spoil and to run straggling here and there to enrich themselves, whilst the other consul and their fellow-citizens peradventure were fighting with their enemies, and how that, leaving the spoil, they should seek to wind themselves out of danger and peril. Howbeit, cry and say to them what he could, very few of them would hearken to him. Wherefore taking those that willingly offered themselves to follow him, he went out of the city and took his way toward that part where he understood the rest of the army was, exhorting and entreating them by the way that followed him not to be fainthearted; and oft holding up his hands to heaven, he besought the gods to be gracious and favorable unto him, that he might come in time to the battle, and in a good hour to hazard his life in defense of his countrymen. . . .

When they saw him at his first coming, all bloody and in a sweat, and but with a few men following him, some thereupon began to be afeared. But soon after, when they saw him run with a lively cheer to the Consul and to take him by the hand, declaring how he had taken the city of Corioles, and that they saw the consul Cominius also kiss and embrace him, then there was not a man but took heart again to him and began to be of good courage; some hearing him report, from point to point, the happy success of this exploit, and other also conjecturing it by seeing their gestures afar off. Then they all began to call upon the Consul to march forward and to delay no longer, but to give charge upon the enemy. Martius asked him how the order of their enemy's battle was and on which side they had placed their best fighting men. The Consul made him answer that he thought the bands which were in the vaward of their battle were those of the Antiates, whom they esteemed to be the warlikest men, and which, for valiant courage, would give no place to any of the host of their enemies. Then prayed Martius to be set directly against them. The Consul granted him, greatly praising his courage.

Then Martius, when both armies came almost to join, advanced himself a good space before his company and went so fiercely to give charge on the vaward that came right against him, that they could stand no longer in his hands: he made such a lane through them, and opened a passage into the battle of the enemies. But the two wings of either side turned one to the other, to compass him in between them; which the consul Cominius perceiving, he sent thither straight of the best soldiers he had about him. So the battle was marvelous bloody about Martius, and in a very short space many were slain in the place. But in the end the Romans were so strong that they distressed the enemies and brake their array, and scattering them, made them fly. Then they prayed Martius that he would retire to the camp, because they saw he was able to do no more, he was already so wearied with the great pain he had taken and so faint with the great wounds he had upon him. But Martius answered them, that it was not for conquerors to yield, nor to be fainthearted; and thereupon began afresh to chase those that fled, until such time as the army of the enemies was utterly overthrown, and numbers of them slain and taken prisoners.

The next morning betimes Martius went to the Consul and the other Romans with him. There the consul Cominius, going up to his chair of state in the presence of the whole army, gave thanks to the gods for so great, glorious, and prosperous a victory. Then he spake to Martius, whose valiantness he commended beyond the moon, both for that he himself saw him do with his eyes, as also for that Martius had reported unto him. So in the end he willed Martius that he should choose out of all the horses they had taken of their enemies, and of all their goods they had won (whereof there was great store) ten of every sort which he liked best, before any distribution should be made to other. Besides this great honorable offer he had made him, he gave him, in testimony that he had won that day the price of prowess above all other, a goodly horse with a caparison, and all furniture to him; which the whole army beholding, did marvelously praise and commend. But Martius, stepping forth, told the Consul he most thankfully accepted the gift of his horse, and was a glad man besides that his service had deserved his general's commendation. And as for his other offer, which was rather a mercenary reward than a honorable recompense, he would have none of it, but was contented to have his equal part with the other soldiers. "Only, this grace," said he, "I crave and beseech you to grant me. Among the Volsces there is an old friend and host of mine, an honest wealthy man, and now a prisoner; who, living before in great wealth in his own country, liveth now a poor prisoner in the hands of his enemies. And yet notwithstanding all this his misery and misfortune, it would do me great pleasure if I could save him from this one danger, to keep him from being sold as a slave."

The soldiers, hearing Martius' words, made a marvelous great shout among them, and there were more that wondered at his great contentation and abstinence when they saw so little covetousness in him, than they were that highly praised and extolled his valiantness. For even they themselves that did somewhat malice and envy his glory, to see him thus honored and passingly praised, did think him so much the more worthy of an honorable recompense for his valiant service, as the more carelessly he refused the great offer made unto him for his profit; and they esteemed more the virtue that was in him that made him refuse such rewards, than that which made them to be offered to him, as unto a worthy person. For it is far more commendable to use riches well than to be valiant; and yet it is better not to desire them than to use them well.

After this shout and noise of the assembly was somewhat appeased, the consul Cominius began to speak in this sort: "We cannot compel Martius to take these gifts we offer him if he will not receive them, but we will give him such a reward for the noble service he hath done as he cannot refuse. Therefore we do order and decree that henceforth he be called Coriolanus, unless his valiant acts have won him that name before our nomination." And so ever since, he still bare the third name of Coriolanus. And thereby it appeareth that the first name the Romans have, as Caius, was as our Christian name now. The second, as Martius, was the name of the house and family they came of. The third was some addition given, either for some act or notable service, or for some mark on their face, or of some shape of their body, or else for some special virtue they had. Even so did the Grecians in old time give additions to princes by reason of some notable act worthy memory. As when they have called some "Soter" and "Callinicos," as much to say as "savior" and "conqueror." . . .

Now when this war was ended, the flatterers of the people began to stir up sedition again, without any new occasion or just matter offered of complaint. For they did ground this second insurrection against the nobility and patricians upon the people's misery and misfortune that could not but fall out, by reason of the former discord and sedition between them and the nobility. Because the most part of the arable land within the territory of Rome was become heathy and barren for lack of plowing, for that they had no time nor mean to cause corn to be brought them out of other countries to sow, by reason of their wars; which made the extreme dearth they had among them. Now those busy prattlers that sought the people's goodwill by such flattering words, perceiving great scarcity of corn to be within the city—and though there had been plenty enough, yet the common people had no money to buy it— they spread abroad false tales and rumors against the nobility, that they, in revenge of the people, had practiced and procured the extreme dearth among them.

Furthermore, in the midst of this stir, there came ambassadors to Rome from the city of Velitres, that offered up their city to the Romans and prayed them they would send new inhabitants to replenish the same, because the plague had been so extreme among them and had killed such a number of them, as there was not left alive the tenth person of the people that had been there before. So the wise men of Rome began to think that the necessity of the Velitrians fell out in a most happy hour; and how, by this occasion, it was very meet, in so great a scarcity of victuals, to disburden Rome of a great number of citizens; and by this means as well to take away this new sedition and utterly to rid it out of the city, as also to clear the same of many mutinous and seditious persons, being the superfluous ill humors that grievously fed this disease. Hereupon the Consuls pricked out all those by a bill, whom they intended to send to Velitres, to go dwell there as in form of a colony. And they levied out all the rest that remained in the city of Rome a great number to go against the Volsces, hoping, by the mean of foreign war, to pacify their sedition at home. Moreover, they imagined, when the poor with the rich, and the mean sort with the nobility, should by this device be abroad in the wars and in one camp, and in one service, and in one like danger, that then they would be more quiet and loving together.

But Sicinius and Brutus, two seditious tribunes, spake against either of these devices and cried out upon the noblemen that under the gentle name of a colony they would cloak and color the most cruel and unnatural fact as might be: because they sent their poor citizens into a sore infected city and pestilent air, full of dead bodies unburied, and there also to dwell under the tuition of a strange god that had so cruelly persecuted his people. "This were," said they, "even as much as if the Senate should headlong cast down the people into a most bottomless pit; and are not yet contented to have famished some of the poor citizens heretofore to death, and to put other of them even to the mercy of the plague; but afresh they have procured a voluntary war, to the end they would leave behind no kind of misery and ill wherewith the poor silly people should not be plagued, and only because they are weary to serve the rich." The common people, being set on a broil and bravery with these words, would not appear when the Consuls called their names by a bill, to prest them for the wars, neither would they be sent out to this new colony; insomuch as the Senate knew not well what to say or to do in the matter.

Martius then, who was now grown to great credit, and

a stout man besides, and of great reputation with the noblest men of Rome, rose up and openly spake against these flattering Tribunes. And for the replenishing of the city of Velitres, he did compel those that were chosen to go thither and to depart the city, upon great penalties to him that should disobey. But to the wars the people by no means would be brought or constrained. So Martius, taking his friends and followers with him, and such as he could by fair words entreat to go with him, did run certain forays into the dominion of the Antiates, where he met with great plenty of corn and had a marvelous great spoil, as well of cattle as of men he had taken prisoners, whom he brought away with him, and reserved nothing for himself. Afterwards, having brought back again all his men that went out with him, safe and sound to Rome, and every man rich and loaden with spoil, then the home-tarriers and house-doves that kept Rome still began to repent them that it was not their hap to go with him, and so envied both them that had sped so well in this journey. And also, of malice to Martius, they spited to see his credit and estimation increase still more and more, because they accounted him to be a great hinderer of the people.

Shortly after this, Martius stood for the consulship; and the common people favored his suit, thinking it would be a shame to them to deny and refuse the chiefest noble-man of blood, and most worthy person of Rome, and specially him that had done so great service and good to the commonwealth. For the custom of Rome was at that time that such as did sue for any office should for certain days before be in the marketplace, only with a poor gown on their backs, and without any coat underneath, to pray the citizens to remember them at the day of election. Which was thus devised, either to move the people the more, by requesting them in such mean apparel, or else because they might show them their wounds they had gotten in the wars in the service of the commonwealth, as manifest marks and testimonies of their valiantness. . . .

Now Martius, following this custom, showed many wounds and cuts upon his body, which he had received in seventeen years' service at the wars, and in many sundry battles, being ever the foremost man that did set out feet to fight. So that there was not a man among the people but was ashamed of himself, to refuse so valiant a man: and one of them said to another, "We must needs choose him consul, there is no remedy." But when the day of election was come, and that Martius came to the market-place with great pomp, accompanied with all the Senate and the whole nobility of the city about him, who sought to make him consul with the greatest instance and entreaty they could, or ever attempted for any man or matter, then the love and goodwill of the common people turned straight to an hate and envy toward him, fearing to put this office of sovereign authority into his hands, being a man somewhat partial towards the nobility, and of great credit and authority amongst the patricians, and as one they might doubt would take away altogether the liberty from the people. Whereupon, for these considerations, they refused Martius in the end, and made two other that were suitors, consuls.

The Senate, being marvelously offended with the people, did account the shame of this refusal rather to redound to themselves than to Martius; but Martius took it in far worse part than the Senate, and was out of all patience. For he was a man too full of passion and choler, and too much given over to self-will and opinion, as one of a high mind and great courage that lacked the gravity and affability that is gotten with judgment of learning and reason, which only is to be looked for in a governor of state; and that remembered not how willfulness is the thing of the world, which a governor of a commonwealth, for pleasing should shun, being that which Plato called "solitariness," as in the end, all men that are willfully given to a self-opinion and obstinate mind, and who will never yield to others' reason but to their own, remain without company and forsaken of all men. For a man that will live in the world must needs have patience, which lusty bloods make but a mock at. So Martius, being a stout man of nature, that never yielded in any respect, as one thinking that to overcome always and to have the upper hand in all matters, was a token of magnanimity and of no base and faint courage—which spitteth out anger from the most weak and passioned part of the heart, much like the matter of an impostume—went home to his house, full freighted with spite and malice against the people, being accompanied with all the lustiest young gentlemen, whose minds were nobly bent, as those that came of noble race, and commonly used for to follow and honor him. But then specially they flocked about him, and kept him company to his much harm, for they did but kindle and inflame his choler more and more, being sorry with him for the injury the people offered him; because he was their captain and leader to the wars, that taught them all martial discipline and stirred up in them a noble emulation of honor and valiantness, and yet, without envy praising them that deserved best.

In the mean season there came great plenty of corn to Rome that had been bought, part in Italy, and part was sent out of Sicily, as given by Gelon the tyrant of Syracusa; so that many stood in great hope that the dearth of victuals being holpen, the civil dissension would also cease. The Senate sat in council upon it immediately; the common people stood also about the palace where the council was kept, gaping what resolution would fall out; persuading themselves that the corn they had bought should be sold good cheap, and that which was given should be divided by the poll, without paying any penny; and the rather, because certain of the senators amongst them did so wish and persuade the same.

But Martius, standing upon his feet, did somewhat sharply take up those who went about to gratify the people therein, and called them people-pleasers and traitors to the nobility. "Moreover," he said, "they nourished against themselves the naughty seed and cockle of insolence and sedition, which had been sowed and scattered abroad amongst the people, which they should have cut off, if they had been wise, in their growth; and not (to their own destruction) have suffered the people to establish a magistrate for themselves of so great power and authority as that man had to whom they had granted it.

Who was also to be feared, because he obtained what he would and did nothing but what he listed, neither passed for any obedience to the consuls but lived in all liberty, acknowledging no superior to command him, saving the only heads and authors of their faction, whom he called his magistrates. Therefore," said he, "they that gave counsel and persuaded that the corn should be given out to the common people *gratis,* as they used to do in the cities of Greece, where the people had more absolute power, did but only nourish their disobedience, which would break out in the end to the utter ruin and overthrow of the whole state. For they will not think it is done in recompense of their service past, sithence they know well enough they have so oft refused to go to the wars when they were commanded; neither for their mutinies when they went with us, whereby they have rebelled and forsaken their country; neither for their accusations which their flatterers have preferred unto them, and they have received, and made good against the Senate. But they will rather judge, we give and grant them this as abasing ourselves and standing in fear of them, and glad to flatter them every way. By this means their disobedience will still grow worse and worse; and they will never leave to practice new sedition and uproars. Therefore it were a great folly for us, methinks, to do it. Yea, shall I say more? We should, if we were wise, take from them their tribuneship, which most manifestly is the embasing of the consulship, and the cause of the division of the city. The state whereof, as it standeth, is not now as it was wont to be, but becometh dismembered in two factions, which maintains always civil dissension and discord between us, and will never suffer us again to be united into one body."

Martius, dilating the matter with many such like reasons, won all the young men and almost all the rich men to his opinion; insomuch, as they rang it out, that he was the only man and alone in the city who stood out against the people and never flattered them. There were only a few old men that spake against him, fearing lest some mischief might fall out upon it, as indeed there followed no great good afterward. For the tribunes of the people, being present at this consultation of the Senate, when they saw that the opinion of Martius was confirmed with the more voices, they left the Senate and went down to the people, crying out for help, and that they would assemble to save their tribunes.

Hereupon the people ran on head in tumult together, before whom the words that Martius spake in the Senate were openly reported; which the people so stomached that even in that fury they were ready to fly upon the whole Senate. But the tribunes laid all the fault and burthen wholly upon Martius, and sent their sergeants forthwith to arrest him, presently to appear in person before the people to answer the words he had spoken in the Senate. Martius stoutly withstood these officers that came to arrest him. Then the tribunes in their own persons, accompanied with the aediles, went to fetch him by force, and so laid violent hands upon him. Howbeit, the noble patricians, gathering together about him, made the tribunes give back, and laid sore upon the aediles; so for that time the night parted them, and the tumult appeased.

The next morning betimes, the Consuls, seeing the people in an uproar, running to the marketplace out of all parts of the city, they were afraid lest all the city would together by the ears. Wherefore assembling the Senate in all haste, they declared how it stood them upon to appease the fury of the people with some gentle words or grateful decrees in their favor; and moreover, like wise men, they should consider it was now no time to stand at defense and in contention, nor yet to fight for honor against the commonalty, they being fallen to so great an extremity and offering such imminent danger. Wherefore they were to consider temperately of things, and to deliver some present and gentle pacification. The most part of the senators that were present at this council thought this opinion best, and gave their consents unto it.

Whereupon the Consuls, rising out of council, went to speak unto the people as gently as they could, and they did pacify their fury and anger, purging the Senate of all the unjust accusations laid upon them, and used great modesty in persuading them and also in reproving the faults they had committed. And as for the rest, that touched the sale of corn, they promised there should be no disliking offered them in the price. So the most part of the people being pacified, and appearing so plainly, by the great silence that was among them, as yielding to the Consuls and liking well of their words, the tribunes then of the people rose out of their seats, and said: "Forasmuch as the Senate yielded unto reason, the people also for their part, as became them, did likewise give place unto them; but notwithstanding, they would that Martius should come in person to answer to the articles they had devised. First, whether he had not solicited and procured the Senate to change the present state of the commonweal, and to take the sovereign authority out of the people's hands? Next, when he was sent for by authority of their officers, why he did contemptuously resist and disobey? Lastly, seeing he had driven and beaten the aediles into the marketplace before all the world, if, in doing this, he had not done as much as in him lay to raise civil wars and to set one citizen against another?"

All this was spoken to one of these two ends: either that Martius, against his nature, should be constrained to humble himself and to abase his haughty and fierce mind; or else, if he continued still in his stoutness, he should incur the people's displeasure and ill will so far that he should never possibly win them again. Which they hoped would rather fall out so than otherwise; as indeed, they guessed unhappily, considering Martius' nature and disposition.

So Martius came and presented himself to answer their accusations against him, and the people held their peace and gave attentive ear to hear what he would say. But where they thought to have heard very humble and lowly words come from him, he began not only to use his wonted boldness of speaking (which of itself was very rough and unpleasant, and did more aggravate his accusation than purge his innocency) but also gave himself in his words to thunder, and look therewithal so grimly, as though he made no reckoning of the matter. This stirred coals among the people, who were in wonderful fury at it, and their hate and malice grew so toward him that they could hold no longer, bear, nor endure his bravery and careless boldness. Whereupon Sicinius, the cruelest and stoutest of the tribunes, after he had whispered a little with his companions, did openly pronounce, in the face of all the people, Martius as condemned by the tribunes to die. Then presently he commanded the aediles to apprehend him and carry him straight to the rock Tarpeian and to cast him headlong down the same.

When the aediles came to lay hands upon Martius to do that they were commanded, divers of the people themselves thought it too cruel and violent a deed. The noblemen, being much troubled to see so much force and rigor used, began to cry aloud, "Help Martius." So those that laid hands on him being repulsed, they compassed him in round among themselves, and some of them, holding up their hands to the people, besought them not to handle him thus cruelly. But neither their words nor crying out could aught prevail; the tumult and hurly-burly was so great, until such time as the tribunes' own friends and kinsmen, weighing with themselves the impossibleness to convey Martius to execution without great slaughter and murder of the nobility, did persuade and advise not to proceed in so violent and extraordinary a sort as to put such a man to death without lawful process in law, but that they should refer the sentence of his death to the free voice of the people.

Then Sicinius, bethinking himself a little, did ask the patricians for what cause they took Martius out of the officers' hands that went to do execution? The patricians asked him again why they would of themselves so cruelly and wickedly put to death so noble and valiant a Roman as Martius was, and that without law and justice? "Well then," said Sicinius, "if that be the matter, let there be no quarrel or dissension against the people; for they do grant your demand, that his cause shall be heard according to the law. Therefore," said he to Martius, "we do will and charge you to appear before the people, the third day of our next sitting and assembly here, to make your purgation for such articles as shall be objected against you, that by free voice the people may give sentence upon you as shall please them." The noblemen were glad then of the adjournment, and were much pleased they had gotten Martius out of this danger.

In the mean space before the third day of their next session came about, the same being kept every ninth day continually at Rome (whereupon they call it now in Latin *Nundinae*), there fell out war against the Antiates, which gave some hope to the nobility that this adjournment would come to little effect, thinking that this war would hold them so long, as that the fury of the people against him would be well suaged or utterly forgotten, by reason of the trouble of the wars. But contrary to expectation, the peace was concluded presently with the Antiates, and the people returned again to Rome.

Then the patricians assembled oftentimes together, to consult how they might stand to Martius and keep the tribunes from occasion to cause the people to mutine again and rise against the nobility. And there Appius Claudius (one that was taken ever as an heavy enemy to the people) did avow and protest that they would utterly abase the authority of the Senate and destroy the commonweal if they would suffer the common people to have authority by voices to give judgment against the nobility. On the other side again, the most ancient senators, and such as were given to favor the common people, said that when the people should see they had authority of life and death in their hands, they would not be so cruel and fierce, but gentle and civil. More also, that it was not for contempt of nobility or the Senate that they sought to have the authority of justice in their hands, as a preeminence and prerogative of honor, but because they feared that themselves should be contemned and hated of the nobility. So as they were persuaded, that so soon as they gave them authority to judge by voices, they would leave all envy and malice to condemn any.

Martius, seeing the Senate in great doubt how to resolve, partly for the love and goodwill the nobility did bear him, and partly for the fear they stood in of the people, asked aloud of the tribunes what matter they would burden him

with? The tribunes answered him that they would show
how he did aspire to be king, and would prove that all
his actions tended to usurp tyrannical power over Rome.
Martius, with that, rising upon his feet, said that thereupon he did willingly offer himself to the people, to be
tried upon that accusation; and that if it were proved by
him he had so much as once thought of any such matter,
that he would then refuse no kind of punishment they
would offer him—"Conditionally," quoth he, "that you
charge me with nothing else beside, and that ye do not
also abuse the Senate." They promised they would not.
Under these conditions the judgment was agreed upon,
and the people assembled.

And first of all the tribunes would in any case (whatsoever became of it) that the people should proceed to
give their voices by tribes, and not by hundreds. For by
this means the multitude of the poor needy people (and
all such rabble as had nothing to lose, and had less regard
of honesty before their eyes) came to be of greater force
(because their voices were numbered by the poll) than
the noble honest citizens, whose persons and purse did
dutifully serve the commonwealth in their wars. And then,
when the tribunes saw they could not prove he went about
to make himself king, they began to broach afresh the
former words that Martius had spoken in the Senate in
hindering the distribution of the corn at mean price unto
the common people and persuading also to take the office
of tribuneship from them. And for the third, they charged
him anew that he had not made the common distribution
of the spoil he had gotten in the invading the territories
of the Antiates, but had of his own authority divided it
among them who were with him in that journey.

But this matter was most strange of all to Martius,
looking least to have been burdened with that as with any
matter of offense. Whereupon being burdened on the sudden, and having no ready excuse to make even at that
instant, he began to fall a praising of the soldiers that
had served with him in that journey. But those that were
not with him, being the greater number, cried out so loud
and made such a noise that he could not be heard. To

conclude, when they came to tell the voices of the tribes, there were three voices odd, which condemned him to be banished for ever. After declaration of the sentence, the people made such joy as they never rejoiced more for any battle they had won upon their enemies, they were so brave and lively and went home so jocundly from the assembly, for triumph of this sentence.

The Senate again, in contrary manner, were as sad and heavy, repenting themselves beyond measure that they had not rather determined to have done and suffered anything whatsoever before the common people should so arrogantly and outrageously have abused their authority. There needed no difference of garments, I warrant you, nor outward shows, to know a plebeian from a patrician, for they were easily discerned by their looks. For he that was on the people's side looked cheerfully on the matter. But he that was sad and hung down his head, he was sure of the noblemen's side, saving Martius alone, who neither in his countenance nor in his gait did ever show himself abashed, or once let fall his great courage. But he only, of all other gentlemen that were angry at his fortune, did outwardly show no manner of passion, nor care at all of himself. Not that he did patiently bear and temper his evil hap in respect of any reason he had, or by his quiet condition; but because he was so carried away with the vehemency of anger and desire of revenge, that he had no sense nor feeling of the hard state he was in; which the common people judge not to be sorrow, although indeed it be the very same. For when sorrow (as you would say) is set on fire, then it is converted into spite and malice, and driveth away for that time all faintness of heart and natural fear. And this is the cause why the choleric man is so altered and mad in his actions, as a man set on fire with a burning ague; for when a man's heart is troubled within, his pulse will beat marvelous strongly.

Now that Martius was even in that taking, it appeared true soon after by his doings. For when he was come home to his house again, and had taken his leave of his mother and wife, finding them weeping and shrieking out for sorrow, and had also comforted and persuaded them to be content with his chance, he went immediately to the gate of the city, accompanied with a great number of patricians that brought him thither. From whence he went on his way with three or four of his friends only, taking nothing with him nor requesting anything of any man. So he remained a few days in the country at his houses, turmoiled with sundry sorts and kinds of thoughts such as the fire of his choler did stir up.

In the end, seeing he could resolve no way to take a profitable or honorable course, but only was pricked forward still to be revenged of the Romans, he thought to raise up some great wars against them, by their nearest neighbors. Whereupon he thought it his best way first to stir up the Volsces against them, knowing they were yet able enough in strength and riches to encounter them, notwithstanding their former losses they had received not long before, and that their power was not so much impaired as their malice and desire was increased to be revenged of the Romans. Now in the city of Antium there was one called Tullus Aufidius, who, for his riches as also for his nobility and valiantness, was honored among the Volsces as a king. Martius knew very well that Tullus did more malice and envy him than he did all the Romans besides, because that many times, in battles where they met, they were ever at the encounter one against another, like lusty courageous youths striving in all emulation of honor, and had encountered many times together. Insomuch as, besides the common quarrel between them, there was bred a marvelous private hate, one against another.

Yet notwithstanding, considering that Tullus Aufidius was a man of a great mind, and that he above all other of the Volsces most desired revenge of the Romans for the injuries they had done unto them, he did an act that confirmed the words of an ancient poet to be true, who said:

It is a thing full hard, man's anger to withstand,
If it be stiffly bent to take an enterprise in hand.
For then most men will have the thing that they desire,

Although it cost their lives therefore, such force hath
wicked ire.

And so did he. For he disguised himself in such array and
attire, as he thought no man could ever have known him
for the person he was, seeing him in that apparel he had
upon his back; and as Homer said of Ulysses:

So did he enter into the enemies' town.

It was even twilight when he entered the city of Antium,
and many people met him in the streets, but no man
knew him. So he went directly to Tullus Aufidius' house,
and when he came thither, he got him up straight to the
chimney hearth and sat him down, and spake not a word
to any man, his face all muffled over. They of the house
spying him wondered what he should be, and yet they
durst not bid him rise. For ill-favoredly muffled and disguised as he was, yet there appeared a certain majesty in
his countenance and in his silence. Whereupon they went
to Tullus, who was at supper, to tell him of the strange
disguising of this man.

Tullus rose presently from the board, and coming towards him, asked him what he was and wherefore he
came. Then Martius unmuffled himself, and after he had
paused awhile, making no answer, he said unto him: "If
thou knowest me not yet, Tullus, and, seeing me, dost not
perhaps believe me to be the man I am indeed, I must
of necessity bewray myself to be that I am. I am Caius
Martius, who hath done to thyself particularly, and to all
the Volsces generally, great hurt and mischief, which I
cannot deny for my surname of Coriolanus that I bear.
For I never had other benefit nor recompense of the true
and painful service I have done, and the extreme dangers
I have been in, but this only surname—a good memory
and witness of the malice and displeasure thou shouldest
bear me. Indeed the name only remaineth with me; for
the rest the envy and cruelty of the people of Rome have
taken from me, by the sufferance of the dastardly nobility
and magistrates, who have forsaken me, and let me be

banished by the people. This extremity hath now driven me to come as a poor suitor to take thy chimney hearth, not of any hope I have to save my life thereby. For if I had feared death, I would not have come hither to have put myself in hazard, but pricked forward with desire to be revenged of them that thus have banished me; which now I do begin, in putting my person into the hands of their enemies. Wherefore, if thou hast any heart to be wrecked of the injuries thy enemies have done thee, speed thee now, and let my misery serve thy turn, and so use it as my service may be a benefit to the Volsces; promising thee that I will fight with better goodwill for all you than I did when I was against you, knowing that they fight more valiantly who know the force of the enemy than such as have never proved it. And if it be so that thou dare not and that thou art weary to prove fortune any more, then am I also weary to live any longer. And it were no wisdom in thee, to save the life of him who hath been heretofore thy mortal enemy, and whose service now can nothing help nor pleasure thee."

Tullus, hearing what he said, was a marvelous glad man, and taking him by the hand, he said unto him: "Stand up, O Martius, and be of good cheer, for in proffering thyself unto us thou doest us great honor; and by this means thou mayest hope also of greater things at all the Volsces' hands." So he feasted him for that time and entertained him in the honorablest manner he could, talking with him of no other matter at that present. But within few days after, they fell to consultation together in what sort they should begin their wars.

Now on the other side, the city of Rome was in marvelous uproar and discord, the nobility against the commonalty, and chiefly for Martius' condemnation and banishment. Moreover, the priests, the soothsayers, and private men also came and declared to the Senate certain sights and wonders in the air, which they had seen and were to be considered of. . . .

Tullus and Martius had secret conference with the greatest personages of the city of Antium, declaring unto them that now they had good time offered them to make war with the Romans, while they were in dissension one with another. They answered them, they were ashamed to break the league, considering that they were sworn to keep peace for two years. Howbeit, shortly after, the Romans gave them great occasion to make war with them. For on a holy day, common plays being kept in Rome, upon some suspicion or false report, they made proclamation by sound of trumpet that all the Volsces should avoid out of Rome before sunset. Some think this was a craft and deceit of Martius, who sent one to Rome to the Consuls to accuse the Volsces falsely, advertising them how they had made a conspiracy to set upon them while they were busy in seeing these games, and also to set their city on fire.

This open proclamation made all the Volsces more offended with the Romans than ever they were before. And Tullus, aggravating the matter, did so inflame the Volsces against them that in the end they sent their ambassadors to Rome, to summon them to deliver their lands and towns again, which they had taken from them in times past, or to look for present wars. The Romans, hearing this, were marvelously nettled and made no other answer but this: "If the Volsces be the first that begin war, the Romans will be the last that will end it." Incontinently upon return of the Volsces' ambassadors and delivery of the Romans' answer, Tullus caused an assembly general to be made of the Volsces, and concluded to make war upon the Romans. This done, Tullus did counsel them to take Martius into their service, and not to mistrust him for the remembrance of anything past, but boldly to trust him in any matter to come; for he would do them more service in fighting for them than ever he did them displeasure in fighting against them. So Martius was called forth, who spake so excellently in the presence of them all that he was thought no less eloquent in tongue than warlike in show, and declared himself both expert in wars and wise with valiantness.

Thus he was joined in commission with Tullus as general of the Volsces, having absolute authority between them to follow and pursue the wars. But Martius, fearing

lest tract of time to bring this army together with all the
munition and furniture of the Volsces would rob him of
the mean he had to execute his purpose and intent, left
order with the rulers and chief of the city to assemble the
rest of their power and to prepare all necessary provision
for the camp. Then he, with the lightest soldiers he had
and that were willing to follow him, stole away upon the
sudden, and marched with all speed, and entered the territories of Rome before the Romans heard any news of
his coming. Insomuch as the Volsces found such spoil
in the fields, as they had more than they could spend in
their camp and were weary to drive and carry away that
they had.

Howbeit, the gain of the spoil and the hurt they did
to the Romans in this invasion was the least part of his
intent. For his chiefest purpose was to increase still the
malice and dissension between the nobility and the commonalty. And to draw that on, he was very careful to
keep the noblemen's lands and goods safe from harm and
burning, but spoiled all the whole country besides, and
would suffer no man to take or hurt anything of the noblemen's. This made greater stir and broil between the nobility and the people than was before. For the noblemen
fell out with the people because they had so unjustly
banished a man of so great valor and power. The people,
on the other side, accused the nobility; how they had
procured Martius to make these wars to be revenged of
them—because it pleased them to see their goods burnt
and spoiled before their eyes, whilst themselves were well
at ease and did behold the people's losses and misfortunes,
knowing their own goods safe and out of danger—and
how the war was not made against the noblemen, that had
the enemy abroad to keep that they had in safety. Now
Martius, having done his first exploit (which made the
Volsces bolder and less fearful of the Romans), brought
home all the army again without loss of any man.

After their whole army (which was marvelous great
and very forward to service) was assembled in one camp,
they agreed to leave part of it for garrison in the country
about, and the other part should go on and make the war

upon the Romans. So Martius bade Tullus choose and take which of the two charges he liked best. Tullus made him answer; he knew by experience that Martius was no less valiant than himself, and how he ever had better fortune and good hap in all battles than himself had. Therefore he thought it best for him to have the leading of those that would make the wars abroad, and himself would keep home, to provide for the safety of the cities of his country and to furnish the camp also of all necessary provision abroad. . . .

In this while, all went still to wrack at Rome. For, to come into the field to fight with the enemy, they could not abide to hear of it, they were one so much against another, and full of seditious words, the nobility against the people, and the people against the nobility. Until they had intelligence at the length that the enemies had laid siege to the city of Lavinium, in the which were all the temples and images of their gods their protectors, and from whence came first their ancient original, for that Aeneas at his first arrival into Italy did build that city. Then fell there out a marvelous sudden change of mind among the people, and far more strange and contrary in the nobility. For the people thought it good to repeal the condemnation and exile of Martius. The Senate, assembled upon it, would in no case yield to that—who either did it of a self-will to be contrary to the people's desire, or because Martius should not return through the grace and favor of the people. Or else, because they were thoroughly angry and offended with him that he would set upon the whole, being offended but by a few, and in his doings would show himself an open enemy besides unto his country. Notwithstanding, the most part of them took the wrong they had done him in marvelous ill part, and as if the injury had been done unto themselves. Report being made of the Senate's resolution, the people found themselves in a straight; for they could authorize and confirm nothing by their voices, unless it had been first propounded and ordained by the Senate.

But Martius, hearing this stir about him, was in a greater rage with them than before; inasmuch as he raised his siege incontinently before the city of Lavinium, and going towards Rome, lodged his camp within forty furlong of the city, at the ditches called Cluiliae. His encamping so near Rome did put all the whole city in a wonderful fear. Howbeit, for the present time it appeased the sedition and dissension betwixt the nobility and the people. For there was no consul, senator, nor magistrate that durst once contrary the opinion of the people for the calling home again of Martius.

When they saw the women in a marvelous fear, running up and down the city, the temples of the gods full of old people weeping bitterly in their prayers to the gods, and finally, not a man either wise or hardy to provide for their safety, then they were all of opinion that the people had reason to call home Martius again to reconcile themselves to him, and that the Senate, on the contrary part, were in marvelous great fault to be angry and in choler with him, when it stood them upon rather to have gone out and entreated him. So they all agreed together to send ambassadors unto him, to let him understand how his countrymen did call him home again, and restored him to all his goods, and besought him to deliver them from this war.

The ambassadors that were sent were Martius' familiar friends and acquaintance, who looked at the least for a courteous welcome of him, as of their familiar friend and kinsman. Howbeit they found nothing less; for at their coming they were brought through the camp to the place where he was set in his chair of state, with a marvelous and an unspeakable majesty, having the chiefest men of the Volsces about him. So he commanded them to declare openly the cause of their coming. Which they delivered in the most humble and lowly words they possibly could devise, and with all modest countenance and behavior agreeable to the same. When they had done their message for the injury they had done him, he answered them very hotly and in great choler. But as general of the Volsces he willed them to restore unto the Volsces all their lands and cities they had taken from them in former wars, and moreover, that they should give them the like honor and freedom of Rome as they had before given to the Latins.

For otherwise they had no other mean to end this war, if they did not grant these honest and just conditions of peace. Thereupon he gave them thirty days respite to make him answer.

So the ambassadors returned straight to Rome, and Martius forthwith departed with his army out of the territories of the Romans. This was the first matter wherewith the Volsces (that most envied Martius' glory and authority) did charge Martius with. Among those, Tullus was chief, who though he had received no private injury or displeasure of Martius, yet the common fault and imperfection of man's nature wrought in him, and it grieved him to see his own reputation blemished through Martius' great fame and honor, and so himself to be less esteemed of the Volsces than he was before. This fell out the more, because every man honored Martius, and thought he only could do all, and that all other governors and captains must be content with such credit and authority as he would please to countenance them with. From hence they derived all their first accusations and secret murmurings against Martius. For private captains, conspiring against him, were very angry with him and gave it out that the removing of the camp was a manifest treason, not of the towns, nor forts, nor of arms, but of time and occasion, which was a loss of great importance, because it was that which in reason might both loose and bind all, and preserve the whole. . . .

Now all the city was full of tumult, fear, and marvelous doubt what would happen, until at the length there fell out such a like matter, as Homer oftimes said they would least have thought of. For in great matters that happen seldom, Homer saith, and crieth out in this sort:

> The goddess Pallas she, with her fair glistering eyes,
> Did put into his mind such thoughts, and made him so
>   devise.

And in another place:

> But sure some god hath tane out of the people's mind

Both wit and understanding eke, and have therewith
assigned
Some other simple spirit, instead thereof to bide,
That so they might their doings all, for lack of wit,
misguide.

And in another place:

The people of themselves did either it consider,
Or else some god instructed them, and so they join'd
together.

Many reckon not of Homer, as referring matters unpossible and fables of no likelihood or troth unto man's
reason, free will, or judgment, which indeed is not his
meaning. But things true and likely he maketh to depend
of our own free will and reason. For he oft speaketh
these words:

I have thought it in my noble heart.

And in another place:

Achilles angry was, and sorry for to hear
Him so to say, his heavy breast was fraught with pensive
fear.

And in another place:

Bellerophon (she) could not move with her fair tongue,
So honest and so virtuous he was, the rest among.

But in wondrous and extraordinary things, which are done
by secret inspirations and motions, he doth not say that
God taketh away from man his choice and freedom of
will, but that he doth move it; neither that he doth work
desire in us, but objecteth to our minds certain imaginations whereby we are led to desire, and thereby doth not
make this our action forced, but openeth the way to our
will and addeth thereto courage and hope of success.
For either we must say that the gods meddle not with the

causes and beginnings of our actions; or else what other means have they to help and further men? It is apparent that they handle not our bodies nor move not our feet and hands when there is occasion to use them, but that part of our mind from which these motions proceed is induced thereto, or carried away by such objects and reasons, as God offereth unto it.

Now the Roman ladies and gentlewomen did visit all the temples and gods of the same, to make their prayers unto them. But the greatest ladies (and more part of them) were continually about the altar of Jupiter Capitolin, among which troup by name was Valeria, Publicola's own sister—the self-same Publicola who did such notable service to the Romans, both in peace and wars, and was dead also certain years before, as we have declared in his life. His sister Valeria was greatly honored and reverenced among all the Romans, and did so modestly and wisely behave herself that she did not shame nor dishonor the house she came of. So she suddenly fell into such a fancy as we have rehearsed before, and had (by some god, as I think) taken hold of a noble device.

Whereupon she rose and the other ladies with her, and they all together went straight to the house of Volumnia, Martius' mother, and coming in to her, found her and Martius' wife, her daughter-in-law, set together and having her husband Martius' young children in her lap. Now all the train of these ladies sitting in a ring round about her, Valeria first began to speak in this sort unto her: "We ladies are come to visit you ladies (my lady Volumnia and Virgilia) by no direction from the Senate, nor commandment of other magistrate, but through the inspiration (as I take it) of some god above; who, having taken compassion and pity of our prayers, hath moved us to come unto you, to entreat you in a matter as well beneficial for us as also for the whole citizens in general, but to yourselves in special (if it please you to credit me), and shall redound to your more fame and glory than the daughters of the Sabines obtained in former age, when they procured loving peace instead of hateful war between their fathers and their husbands. Come on, good ladies, and let us go all together unto Martius, to entreat him to take pity upon us, and also to report the truth unto him, how much you are bound unto the citizens; who notwithstanding they have sustained great hurt and losses by him, yet they have not hitherto sought revenge upon your persons by any discourteous usage, neither ever conceived any such thought or intent against you, but to deliver you safe into his hands, though thereby they look for no better grace or clemency from him." When Valeria had spoken this unto them, all the other ladies together, with one voice, confirmed that she had said.

Then Volumnia in this sort did answer her: "My good ladies, we are partakers with you of the common misery and calamity of our country, and yet our grief exceedeth yours the more, by reason of our particular misfortune, to feel the loss of my son Martius' former valiancy and glory, and to see his person environed now with our enemies in arms, rather to see him forthcoming and safe kept than of any love to defend his person. But yet the greatest grief of our heaped mishaps is to see our poor country brought to such extremity that all the hope of the safety and preservation thereof is now unfortunately cast upon us simple women; because we know not what account he will make of us, since he hath cast from him all care of his natural country and commonweal, which heretofore he hath holden more dear and precious than either his mother, wife, or children. Notwithstanding, if ye think we can do good, we will willingly do what you will have us; bring us to him, I pray you. For if we cannot prevail, we may yet die at his feet, as humble suitors for the safety of our country."

Her answer ended, she took her daughter-in-law and Martius' children with her, and being accompanied with all the other Roman ladies, they went in troup together unto the Volsces' camp; whom when they saw, they of themselves did both pity and reverence her, and there was not a man among them that once durst say a word unto her. Now was Martius set then in his chair of state, with all the honors of a general, and when he had spied the women coming afar off, he marveled what the matter meant. But afterwards knowing his wife, which came foremost, he determined at the first to persist in his obstinate and inflexible rancor. But overcome in the end with natural affection and being altogether altered to see them, his heart would not serve him to tarry their coming to his chair, but coming down in haste he went to meet them, and first he kissed his mother and embraced her a pretty while, then his wife and little children. And nature so wrought with him that the tears fell from his eyes, and he could not keep himself from making much of them but yielded to the affection of his blood, as if he had been violently carried with the fury of a most swift running stream.

After he had thus lovingly received them, and perceiving that his mother Volumnia would begin to speak to him, he called the chiefest of the council of the Volsces to hear what she would say. Then she spake in this sort: "If we held our peace, my son, and determined not to speak, the state of our poor bodies, and present sight of our raiment, would easily bewray to thee what life we have led at home since thy exile and abode abroad. But think now with thyself, how much more unfortunate than all the women living we are come hither, considering that the sight which should be most pleasant to all other to behold, spiteful fortune had made most fearful to us, making myself to see my son, and my daughter here her husband, besieging the walls of his native country; so as that which is the only comfort to all other in their adversity and misery, to pray unto the gods and to call to them for aid, is the only thing which plungeth us into most deep perplexity. For we cannot, alas, together pray both for victory to our country and for safety of thy life also: but a world of grievous curses, yea, more than any mortal enemy can heap upon us, are forcibly wrapt up in our prayers. For the bitter sop of most hard choice is offered thy wife and children, to forgo one of the two: either to lose the person of thyself or the nurse of their native country.

"For myself, my son, I am determined not to tarry till fortune, in my lifetime, do make an end of this war. For if I cannot persuade thee rather to do good unto both parties than to overthrow and destroy the one, preferring love and nature before the malice and calamity of wars, thou shalt see, my son, and trust unto it, thou shalt no sooner march forward to assault thy country, but thy foot shall tread upon thy mother's womb that brought thee first into this world. And I may not defer to see the day, either that my son be led prisoner in triumph by his natural countrymen, or that he himself do triumph of them, and of his natural country.

"For if it were so, that my request tended to save thy country, in destroying the Volsces, I must confess, thou wouldest hardly and doubtfully resolve on that. For as to destroy thy natural country, it is altogether unmeet and unlawful, so were it not just and less honorable to betray those that put their trust in thee. But my only demand consisteth to make a jail-delivery of all evils, which delivereth equal benefit and safety both to the one and the other, but most honorable for the Volsces. For it shall appear that, having victory in their hands, they have of special favor granted us singular graces, peace, and amity, albeit themselves have no less part of both than we. Of which good, if so it came to pass, thyself is the only author, and so hast thou the only honor. But if it fail and fall out contrary, thyself alone deservedly shalt carry the shameful reproach and burthen of either party.

"So, though the end of war be uncertain, yet this notwithstanding is most certain: that, if it be thy chance to conquer, this benefit shalt thou reap of thy goodly conquest, to be chronicled the plague and destroyer of thy country. And if fortune overthrow thee, then the world will say that through desire to revenge thy private injuries, thou hast forever undone thy good friends, who did most lovingly and courteously receive thee."

Martius gave good ear unto his mother's words, without interrupting her speech at all, and after she had said what she would, he held his peace a pretty while and answered not a word. Hereupon she began again to speak unto him, and said: "My son, why dost thou not answer me? Dost thou think it good altogether to give place unto thy choler and desire of revenge, and thinkest thou it not honesty for thee to grant thy mother's request in so weighty a cause? Dost thou take it honorable for a noble man to remember the wrongs and injuries done him, and dost not in like case think it an honest noble man's part, to be thankful for the goodness that parents do show to their children, acknowledging the duty and reverence they ought to bear unto them? No man living is more bound to show himself thankful in all parts and respects than thyself; who so unnaturally showest all ingratitude. Moreover (my son) thou hast sorely taken of thy country, exacting grievous payments upon them, in revenge of the injuries offered thee; besides, thou hast not hitherto showed thy poor mother any courtesy. And therefore it is not only honest, but due unto me, that without compulsion I should obtain my so just and reasonable request of thee. But since by reason I cannot persuade thee to it, to what purpose do I defer my last hope?" And with these words, herself, his wife and children fell down upon their knees before him.

Martius, seeing that, could refrain no longer, but went straight and lift her up, crying out, "Oh, Mother, what have you done to me?" And holding her hard by the right hand, "Oh, Mother," said he, "you have won a happy victory for your country, but mortal and unhappy for your son; for I see myself vanquished by you alone." These words being spoken openly, he spake a little apart with his mother and wife, and then let them return again to Rome, for so they did request him.

And so remaining in camp that night, the next morning he dislodged and marched homeward into the Volsces' country again, who were not all of one mind nor all alike contented. For some misliked him and that he had done; other, being well pleased that peace should be made, said that neither the one nor the other deserved blame nor reproach. Other, though they misliked that was done, did not think him an ill man for that he did, but said he was not to be blamed, though he yielded to such a forcible extremity. Howbeit, no man contraried his departure, but all obeyed his commandment, more for respect of his worthiness and valiancy than for fear of his authority.

Now the citizens of Rome plainly showed in what fear and danger their city stood of this war, when they were delivered. For so soon as the watch upon the walls of the city perceived the Volsces' camp to remove, there was not a temple in the city but was presently set open and full of men wearing garlands of flowers upon their heads, sacrificing to the gods, as they were wont to do upon the news of some great obtained victory. And this common joy was yet more manifestly showed by the honorable courtesies the whole Senate and people did bestow on their ladies. For they were all thoroughly persuaded and did certainly believe that the ladies only were cause of the saving of the city and delivering themselves from the instant danger of the war.

Whereupon the Senate ordained that the magistrates, to gratify and honor these ladies, should grant them all that they would require. And they only requested that they would build a temple of Fortune for the women, unto the building whereof they offered, themselves, to defray the whole charge of the sacrifices and other ceremonies belonging to the service of the gods. Nevertheless, the Senate, commending their goodwill and forwardness, ordained that the temple and image should be made at the common charge of the city. Notwithstanding that, the ladies gathered money among them and made with the same a second image of Fortune, which the Romans say did speak as they offered her up in the temple and did set her in her place; and they affirm that she spake these words: "Ladies, ye have devoutly offered me up." Moreover, that she spake that twice together, making us to believe things that never were and are not to be credited. . . .

Now when Martius was returned again into the city of Antium from his voyage, Tullus, that hated and could no longer abide him for the fear he had of his authority, sought diverse means to make him away, thinking if he let slip that present time, he should never recover the like and fit occasion again. Wherefore Tullus, having procured many other of his confederacy, required Martius might be deposed from his estate to render up account to the Volsces of his charge and government. Martius, fearing to become a private man again under Tullus being general (whose authority was greater otherwise than any other among all the Volsces), answered; he was willing to give up his charge and would resign it into the hands of the lords of the Volsces, if they did all command him, as by all their commandment he received it. And moreover, that he would not refuse even at that present to give up an account unto the people, if they would tarry the hearing of it.

The people hereupon called a common council, in which assembly there were certain orators appointed that stirred up the common people against him; and when they had told their tales, Martius rose up to make them answer. Now, notwithstanding the mutinous people made a marvelous great noise, yet when they saw him, for the reverence they bare unto his valiantness, they quieted themselves and gave him audience to allege with leisure what he could for his purgation. Moreover, the honestest men of the Antiates, and who most rejoiced in peace, showed by their countenance that they would hear him willingly and judge also according to their conscience.

Whereupon Tullus, fearing that if he did let him speak, he would prove his innocency to the people, because amongst other things he had an eloquent tongue; besides that the first good service he had done to the people of the Volsces did win him more favor than these last accusations could purchase him displeasure; and furthermore, the offense they laid to his charge was a testimony of the goodwill they ought him; for they would never have thought he had done them wrong for that they took not the city of Rome, if they had not been very near taking of it by means of his approach and conduction. For these causes Tullus thought he might no longer delay his pretense and enterprise, neither to tarry for the mutining and rising of the common people against him. Wherefore those that were of the conspiracy began to cry out that he was not to be heard, and that they would not suffer a traitor to usurp tyrannical power over the tribe of the Volsces, who would not yield up his state and authority. And in saying these words, they all fell upon him and killed him in the marketplace, none of the people once offering to rescue him.

Howbeit, it is a clear case that this murder was not generally consented unto of the most part of the Volsces. For men came out of all parts to honor his body, and did honorably bury him, setting out his tomb with great store of armor and spoils, as the tomb of a worthy person and great captain. The Romans, understanding of his death, showed no other honor or malice, saving that they granted the ladies their request they made, that they might mourn ten months for him. And that was the full time they used to wear blacks for the death of their fathers, brethren, or husbands, according to Numa Pompilius' order who established the same, as we have enlarged more amply in the description of his life.

Now Martius being dead, the whole state of the Volsces heartily wished him alive again. For, first of all, they fell out with the Aeques (who were their friends and confederates) touching preeminence and place; and this quarrel grew on so far between them that frays and murders fell out upon it, one with another. After that, the Romans overcame them in battle, in which Tullus was slain in the field, and the flower of all their force was put to the sword; so that they were compelled to accept most shameful conditions of peace, in yielding themselves subject unto the conquerors and promising to be obedient at their commandment.

Commentaries

A. C. BRADLEY

Coriolanus

BRITISH ACADEMY SHAKESPEARE
LECTURE, 1912

Coriolanus[1] is beyond doubt among the latest of Shakespeare's tragedies: there is some reason for thinking it the last. Like all those that succeeded *Hamlet,* it is a tragedy of vehement passion; and in none of them are more striking revolutions of fortune displayed. It is full of power, and almost every one feels it to be a noble work. We may say of it, as of its hero, that, if not one of Shakespeare's greatest creations, it is certainly one of his biggest.

Nevertheless, it is scarcely popular. It is seldom acted, and perhaps no reader ever called it his favorite play. Indeed, except for educational purposes, it is probably, after *Timon,* the least generally read of the tragedies.

[1] Shakespeare's treatment of his subject is often best understood through comparison with his authority, Plutarch's *Life of Coriolanus* in North's translation, a translation most conveniently read in the volume edited by Prof. Skeat and entitled *Shakespeare's Plutarch.* For a full development of the comparison, and, generally, for a discussion of the play much more complete than mine could be, see Prof. MacCallum's book, *Shakespeare's Roman Plays and their Background* (1910), which is admirable both for its thoroughness and for the insight and justice of its criticism. I should perhaps add that, though I read the greater part of Prof. MacCallum's book when it appeared, I was prevented from going on to the chapters on *Coriolanus,* and did so only after writing my lecture. I left untouched in the lecture the many observations which this reading confirmed, but on one or two doubtful points I have added a Postscript.

From *A Miscellany* by A. C. Bradley. London: Macmillan and Co. Ltd., 1929. Reprinted by permission of Macmillan & Co. Ltd.

Even the critic who feels bound to rank it above *Romeo and Juliet*, and even above *Julius Caesar*, may add that he prefers those dramas all the same; and if he ignores his personal preferences, still we do not find him asking whether it is not the equal of the four great tragedies. He may feel this doubt as to *Antony and Cleopatra*, but not as to *Coriolanus*.

The question why this should be so will at once tell us something about the drama. We cannot say that it shows any decline in Shakespeare's powers, though in parts it may show slackness in their use. It has defects, some of which are due to the historical material; but all the tragedies have defects, and the material of *Antony and Cleopatra* was even more troublesome. There is no love-story; but then there is none in *Macbeth,* and next to none in *King Lear*. Thanks in part to the badness of the Folio text, the reader is impeded by obscurities of language and irritated by the mangling of Shakespeare's meter; yet these annoyances would not much diminish the effect of *Othello*. It may seem a more serious obstacle that the hero's faults are repellent and chill our sympathy; but Macbeth, to say nothing of his murders, is a much less noble being than Coriolanus. All this doubtless goes for something; yet there must be some further reason why this drama stands apart from the four great tragedies and *Antony and Cleopatra*. And one main reason seems to be this. Shakespeare could construe the story he found only by conceiving the hero's character in a certain way; and he had to set the whole drama in tune with that conception. In this he was, no doubt, perfectly right; but he closed the door on certain effects, in the absence of which his whole power in tragedy could not be displayed. He had to be content with something less, or rather with something else; and so have we.

Most of the great tragedies leave a certain imaginative impression of the highest value, which I describe in terms intended merely to recall it. What we witness is not the passion and doom of mere individuals. The forces that meet in the tragedy stretch far beyond the little group of figures and the tiny tract of space and time in which they appear. The darkness that covers the scene, and the light that strikes across it, are more than our common night and day. The hero's fate is, in one sense, intelligible, for it follows from his character and the conditions in which he is placed; and yet everything, character, conditions, and issue, is mystery. Now of this effect there is very little in *Coriolanus*. No doubt the story has a universal meaning, since the contending forces are permanent constituents of human nature; but that peculiar *imaginative* effect or atmosphere is hardly felt. And, thinking of the play, we notice that the means by which it is produced elsewhere are almost absent here. One of these means is the use of the supernatural; another a treatment of nature which makes her appear not merely as a background, nor even merely as a conscious witness of human feelings, sufferings, and deeds, but as a vaster fellow-actor and fellow-sufferer. Remove in fancy from *Hamlet, Lear,* and *Macbeth* all that appeals to imagination through these means, and you find them utterly changed, but brought nearer to *Coriolanus*. Here Shakespeare has deliberately withdrawn his hand from those engines. He found, of course, in Plutarch allusions to the gods, and some of these he used; but he does not make us feel that the gods take part in the story. He found also wonders in the firmament, portents, a strange vision seen by a slave, a statue that spoke. He found that the Romans in their extremity sent the priests, augurs, and soothsayers to plead with Coriolanus; and that the embassy of the women which saved Rome was due to a thought which came suddenly to Valeria, which she herself regarded as a divine inspiration, and on the nature of which Plutarch speculates. But the whole of this Shakespeare ignored. Nor would he use that other instrument I spoke of. Coriolanus was not the man to be terrified by twilight, or to feel that the stars or the wind took part against or with him. If Lear's thunderstorm had beat upon his head, he would merely have set his teeth. And not only is the mystery of nature absent; she is scarcely present even as a background. The hero's grim description of his abode in exile as "the city of kites and crows" (it is not in Plutarch) is almost all we have. In short, *Coriolanus* has scarcely more atmosphere, either supernatural or natural, than the average serious prose drama of today.

In Shakespeare's greatest tragedies there is a second source—in one or two the chief source—of supreme imaginative appeal, the exhibition of inward conflict, or of the outburst of one or another passion, terrible, heart-rending, or glorious to witness. At these moments the speaker becomes the greatest of poets; and yet, the dramatic convention admitted, he speaks in character. The hero in *Coriolanus* is never thus the greatest of poets, and he could not be so without a breach of more than dramatic convention. His nature is large, simple, passionate; but (except in one point, to which I will return, as it is irrelevant here) his nature is not, in any marked degree, imaginative. He feels all the rapture, but not, like Othello, all the poetry, of war. He covets honor no less than Hotspur, but he has not Hotspur's vision of honor. He meets with ingratitude, like Timon, but it does not transfigure all mankind for him. He is very eloquent, but his only free eloquence is that of vituperation and scorn. It is sometimes more than eloquence, it is splendid poetry; but it is never such magical poetry as we hear in the four greatest tragedies. Then, too, it lies in his nature that his deepest and most sacred feeling, that for his mother, is almost dumb. It governs his life and leads him uncomplaining towards death, but it cannot speak. And, finally, his inward conflicts are veiled from us. The change that came when he found himself alone and homeless in exile is not exhibited. The result is partly seen in the one soliloquy of this drama, but the process is hidden. Of the passion that possesses him when his triumph seems at hand we get a far more vivid idea from the words of Cominius than from any words of his own:

> I tell you he does sit in gold, his eye
> Red as 'twould burn Rome.

In the most famous scene, when his fate is being decided, only one short sentence reveals the gradual loosening of his purpose during his mother's speech. The actor's face and hands and bearing must show it, not the hero's voice; and his submission is announced in a few quiet words, deeply moving and impressive, but destitute of the effect we know elsewhere of a lightning flash that rends the darkness and discloses every cranny of the speaker's soul. All this we can see to be as it should be, but it does set limits to the flight of Shakespeare's imagination.

I have spoken of something that we miss in *Coriolanus*. Unfortunately there is something which a good many readers find, or think they find, and which makes it distasteful to them. A political conflict is never the center of interest in Shakespeare's plays, but in the historical plays it is an element more or less essential, and in this one it is very prominent. Here, too, since it may be plausibly described as a conflict between people and nobles, or democracy and aristocracy, the issue is felt to be still alive. And Shakespeare, it is thought, shows an animus, and sides against the people. A hundred years ago Hazlitt, dealing with this tragedy, wrote: "Shakespeare himself seems to have had a leaning to the arbitrary side of the question, perhaps from some feeling of contempt for his own origin; and to have spared no occasion of baiting the rabble. What he says of them is very true; what he says of their betters is also very true, though he dwells less upon it." This language is very tentative and mild compared with that of some later writers. According to one, Shakespeare "loathed the common Englishman." He was a neuropath who could not endure the greasy aprons and noisome breath of mechanics, and "a snob of the purest English water." According to another, he was probably afflicted for some years with an "enormous self-esteem." A hero similarly afflicted, and a nauseous mob—behold the play!

I do not propose to join this dance, or even to ask whether any reasonable conjecture as to Shakespeare's political views and feelings could be formed from the study of this play and of others. But it may be worthwhile to mention certain questions which should be weighed by

anyone who makes the adventure. Are not the chief weaknesses and vices shown by the populace, or attributed to
it by speakers, in these plays, those with which it had
been habitually charged in antiquity and the Middle Ages;
and did not Shakespeare find this common form, if nowhere else, in Plutarch? Again, if these traits and charges
are heightened in his dramas, what else do we expect in
drama, and especially in that of the Elizabethans?
Granted, next, that in Shakespeare the people play a
sorry political part, is that played by English nobles and
Roman patricians much more glorious or beneficent? And
if, in Hazlitt's phrase, Shakespeare says more of the faults
of the people than of those of their betters, would we have
him give to humble unlettered persons the powers of invective of lordly orators? Further, is abuse of the people
ever dramatically inappropriate in Shakespeare; and is
it given to Henry the Fifth, or Brutus (who had some
cause for it), or, in short, to any of the most attractive
characters? Is there not, besides, a great difference between his picture of the people taken as individuals, even
when they talk politics, and his picture of them as a
crowd or mob? Is not the former, however humorously
critical, always kindly; and is a personal bias really
needed to account for the latter? And, to end a cata-
logue easy to prolong, might not that talk, which is
scarcely peculiar to Shakespeare, about greasy caps and
offensive odors, have some other origin than his artistic
nerves? He had, after all, some little gift of observation,
and, when first he mixed with a class above his own, might
he not resemble a son of the people now who, coming
among his betters, observes with amusement the place
held in their decalogue by the morning bath? I do not
for a moment suggest that, by weighing such questions as
these, we should be led to imagine Shakespeare as any
more inclined to champion the populace than Spenser or
Hooker or Bacon; but I think we should feel it extremely
hazardous to ascribe to him any political feelings at all,
and ridiculous to pretend to certainty on the subject.

   Let us turn to the play. The representation of the people, whatever else it may be, is part of a dramatic design.

This design is based on the main facts of the story, and these imply a certain character in the people and the hero. Since the issue is tragic, the conflict between them must be felt to be unavoidable and well-nigh hopeless. The necessity for dramatic sympathy with both sides demands that on both there should be some right and some wrong, both virtues and failings; and if the hero's monstrous purpose of destroying his native city is not to extinguish our sympathy, the provocation he receives must be great. This being so, the picture of the people is, surely, no darker than it had to be; the desired result would have been more easily secured by making it darker still. And one must go further. As regards the political situation, the total effect of the drama, it appears to me, is this. The conflict of hero and people is hopeless; but it is he alone who makes the conflict of patricians and plebeians, I do not say hopeless, but in any high degree dangerous. The people have bad faults, but no such faults as, in his absence, would prevent a constitutional development in their favor.

I will not try to describe their character, but I will illustrate this statement by comparing two accusations of their opponents with the facts shown; for these we must accept, but the accusations we must judge for ourselves. In the first scene the people are called cowards, both by the hero and by their friendly critic, Menenius. Now there is no sign that they possess the kind of courage expected of gentlemen, or feel the corresponding shame if their courage fails. But if they were cowards, how could Rome be standing where we see it stand? They are the common soldiers of Rome. And when we see them in war, what do we find? One division, under Cominius, meets the Volscians in the field; the other, under Coriolanus, assaults Corioli. Both are beaten back. This is what Cominius says to his men:

> Breathe you, my friends: well fought: we are come off
> Like Romans, neither foolish in our stands,
> Nor cowardly in retire.

Nothing hints that the other division has not fought well

or was cowardly in retire; but it was encouraged before-
hand with threats, and, on its failure, with a torrent of
curses and abuse. Nevertheless it advances again and
forces the enemy to the gates, which Coriolanus enters,
calling on his men to follow him.

> *First Sol.* Foolhardiness; not I.
> *Second Sol.* Nor I.
> *First Sol.* See, they have shut him in.
> *All.* To the pot, I warrant him.

Disgusting, no doubt; but the answer to threats and curses.
They would not have served Cominius so; and indeed,
when Lartius comes up and merely suggests to them to
"fetch off" the reappearing hero, they respond at once
and take the city. These men are not cowards; but their
conduct depends on their leaders. The same thing is seen
when Coriolanus himself appeals to the other division for
volunteers to serve in the van. For once he appeals nobly,
and the whole division volunteers.

Another charge he brings against the people is that they
can neither rule nor be ruled. On this his policy of
"thorough" is based. Now, judging from the drama, one
would certainly say that they could not rule alone—that
a pure democracy would lead to anarchy, and perhaps to
foreign subjection. And one would say also that they probably could not be ruled by the patricians if all political
rights were denied them. But to rule them, while granting
them a place in the constitution, would seem quite fea-
sible. They are, in fact, only too easy to guide. No doubt,
collected into a mob, led by demagogues, and maddened
by resentment and fear, they become wild and cruel. It
is true, also, that, when their acts bear bitter fruit, they
disclaim responsibility and turn on their leaders: "that
we did, we did for the best; and though we willingly consented to his banishment, yet it was against our will." But
they not only follow their tribunes like sheep; they receive abuse and direction submissively from anyone who
shows goodwill. They are fundamentally good-natured,
like the Englishmen they are, and have a humorous con-

sciousness of their own weaknesses. They are, beyond doubt, mutable, and in that sense untrustworthy; but they are not by nature ungrateful, or slow to admire their bitterest enemy. False charges and mean imputations come from their leaders, not from them. If one of them blames Coriolanus for being proud, another says he cannot help his pride. They insist on the bare form of their right to name him consul, but all they want is the form, and not the whole even of that. When he asks one of them, "Well then, I pray, your price of the consulship?" the answer, "The price is to ask it kindly," ought to have melted him at once; yet when he asks it contemptuously it is still granted. Even later, when the arts of the tribunes have provoked him to such a storm of defiant and revolutionary speech that both the consulship and his life are in danger, one feels that another man might save both with no great trouble. Menenius tells him that the people

> have pardons, being ask'd, as free
> As words to little purpose.

His mother and friends urge him to deceive the people with false promises. But neither false promises nor apologies are needed; only a little humanity and some acknowledgment that the people are part of the state. He is capable of neither, and so the conflict is hopeless. But it is so not because the people, or even the tribunes, are what they are, but because he is what we call an "impossible" person.

The result is that all the force and nobility of Rome's greatest man have to be thrown away and wasted. That is tragic; and it is doubly so because it is not only his faults that make him impossible. There is bound up with them a nobleness of nature in which he surpasses everyone around him.

We see this if we consider, what is not always clear to the reader, his political position. It is not shared by any of the other patricians who appear in the drama. Critics have called him a Tory or an ultra-Tory; but the tribune who calls him a "traitorous innovator" is quite as near the mark. The people have been granted tribunes. The tribunate is a part of the constitution, and it is accepted, with whatever reluctance, by the other patricians. But Coriolanus would abolish it, and that not by law but by the sword. Nor would this content him. The right of the people to control the election of the consul is no new thing; it is an old traditional right; but it, too, he says, might well be taken away. The only constitution tolerable in his eyes is one where the patricians are the state, and the people a mere instrument to feed it and fight for it. It is this conviction that makes it so dangerous to appoint him consul, and also makes it impossible for him to give way. Even if he could ask pardon for his abuse of the people, he could not honestly promise to acknowledge their political rights.

Now the nobleness of his nature is at work here. He is not tyrannical; the charge brought against him of aiming at a tyranny is silly. He is an aristocrat. And Shakespeare has put decisively aside the statement of Plutarch that he was "churlish, uncivil, and altogether unfit for any man's conversation." Shakespeare's hero, though he feels his superiority to his fellow-patricians, always treats them as equals. He is never rude or overbearing. He speaks to them with the simple directness or the bluff familiarity of a comrade. He does not resent their advice, criticism, or reproof. He shows no trace of envy or jealousy, or even of satisfaction at having surpassed them. The suggestion of the tribunes that he is willing to serve under Cominius because failure in war will be credited to Cominius, and success in war to himself, shows only the littleness of their own minds. The patricians are his fellows in a community of virtue—of a courage, fidelity, and honor, which cannot fail them because they are "true-bred," though the bright ideal of such virtue become perfect still urges them on. But the plebeians, in his eyes, are destitute of this virtue, and therefore have no place in this community. All they care for is food in peace, looting in war, flattery from their demagogues; and they will not even clean their teeth. To ask anything of them is to insult not merely himself but the virtues that he worships. To give them a real share in citizenship is treason to Rome; for Rome means these virtues. They are not Romans, they are the rats of Rome.

He is very unjust to them, and his ideal, though high, is also narrow. But he is magnificently true to it, and even when he most repels us we feel this and glory in him. He is never more true to it than when he tries to be false; and this is the scene where his superiority in nobleness is most apparent. He, who had said of his enemy, "I hate him worse than a promise-breaker," is urged to save himself and his friends by promises that he means to break. To his mother's argument that he ought no more to mind deceiving the people than out-witting an enemy in war, he cannot give the obvious answer, for he does not really count the people his fellow-countrymen; but the proposal that *he* should descend to lying or flattering astounds him. He feels that if he does so he will never be himself again; that his mind will have taken on an inherent baseness and no mere simulated one. And he is sure, as we are, that he simply cannot do what is required of him. When at last he consents to try, it is solely because his mother bids him and he cannot resist her chiding. Often he reminds us of a huge boy; and here he acts like a boy whose sense of honor is finer than his mother's, but who is too simple and too noble to frame the thought.

Unfortunately he is altogether too simple and too ig-norant of himself. Though he is the proudest man in Shakespeare, he seems to be unaware of his pride, and is hurt when his mother mentions it. It does not prevent him from being genuinely modest, for he never dreams that he has attained the ideal he worships; yet the sense of his own greatness is twisted round every strand of this worship. In almost all his words and deeds we are con-scious of the tangle. I take a single illustration. He cannot endure to be praised. Even his mother, who has a charter to extol her blood, grieves him when she praises him. As for others,

> I had rather have one scratch my head i' the sun
> When the alarum were struck, than idly sit
> To hear my nothings monster'd.

His answer to the roar of the army hailing him "Coriolanus" is, "I will go wash." His wounds are "scratches with briars." In Plutarch he shows them to the people without demur; in Shakespeare he would rather lose the consulship. There is a greatness in all this that makes us exult. But who can assign the proportions of the elements that compose this impatience of praise: the feeling (which we are surprised to hear him express) that he, like hundreds more, has simply done what he could; the sense that it is nothing to what might be done; the want of human sympathy (for has not Shelley truly said that fame is love disguised?); the pride which makes him feel that he needs no recognition, that after all he himself could do ten times as much, and that to praise his achievement implies a limit to his power? If any one could solve this problem, Coriolanus certainly could not. To adapt a phrase in the play, he has no more introspection in him than a tiger. So he thinks that his loathing of the people is all disgust at worthlessness, and his resentment in exile all a just indignation. So too he fancies that he can stand

> As if a man were author of himself
> And knew no other kin,

while in fact public honor and home affections are the breath of his nostrils, and there is not a drop of stoic blood in his veins.

What follows on his exile depends on this self-ignorance. When he bids farewell to his mother and wife and friends he is still excited and exalted by conflict. He comforts them; he will take no companion; he will be loved when he is lacked, or at least he will be feared; while he remains alive, they shall always hear from him, and never aught but what is like him formerly. But the days go by, and no one, not even his mother, hears a word. When we see him next, he is entering Antium to offer his services against his country. If they are accepted, he knows what he will do; he will burn Rome.

As I have already remarked, Shakespeare does not exhibit to us the change of mind which issues in this frightful purpose; but from what we see and hear later we can tell how he imagined it; and the key lies in that idea of *burning* Rome. As time passes, and no suggestion of recall reaches Coriolanus, and he learns what it is to be a solitary homeless exile, his heart hardens, his pride swells to a mountainous bulk, and the wound in it becomes a fire. The fellow-patricians from whom he parted lovingly now appear to him ingrates and dastards, scarcely better than the loathsome mob. Somehow, he knows not how, even his mother and wife have deserted him. He has become nothing to Rome, and Rome shall hear nothing from him. Here in solitude he can find no relief in a storm of words; but gradually the blind intolerable chaos of resentment conceives and gives birth to a vision, not merely of battle and indiscriminate slaughter, but of the whole city one tower of flame. To see that with his bodily eyes would satisfy his soul; and the way to the sight is through the Volscians. If he is killed the moment they recognize him, he cares little: better a dead nothing than the living nothing Rome thinks him. But if he lives, she shall know what he is. He bears himself among the Volscians with something that resembles self-control; but what controls him is the vision that never leaves him and never changes, and his eye is red with its glare when he sits in his state before the doomed city.[2]

This is Shakespeare's idea, not Plutarch's. In Plutarch there is not a syllable about the burning of Rome. Coriolanus (to simplify a complicated story) intends to humiliate his country by forcing on it disgraceful terms of peace. And this, apart from its moral quality, is a reasonable design. The Romans, rather than yield to fear, decline to treat unless peace is first restored; and therefore it will be necessary to assault the city. In the play we find a single vague allusion to some unnamed conditions which, Coriolanus knows, cannot now be accepted; but everywhere, among both Romans and Volscians, we hear of the burning of Rome, and in the city there is no hope of successful resistance. What Shakespeare wanted was a simpler and more appalling situation than he found in

[2] See Postscript, p. 270.

Plutarch, and a hero enslaved by his passion and driven blindly forward. How blindly, we may judge, if we ask the questions: what will happen to the hero if he disappoints the expectation he has raised among the Volscians, when their leader is preparing to accuse him even if he fulfills it: and, if the hero executes his purpose, what will happen to his mother, wife, and child: and how can it be executed by a man whom we know in his home as the most human of men, a husband who is still the lover of his wife, and a son who regards his mother not merely with devoted affection but with something like religious awe? Very likely the audience in the theatre was not expected to ask these questions, but it *was* expected to see in the hero a man totally ignorant of himself, and stumbling to the destruction either of his life or of his soul.

In speaking of the famous scene where he is confronted with Volumnia and Valeria, Virgilia and her boy, and the issue is decided, I am obliged to repeat what I have said elsewhere in print;[3] and I must speak in the first person because I do not know how far others share my view. To me the scene is one in which the tragic feelings of fear and pity have little place. Such anxiety as I feel is not for the fate of the hero or of anyone else: it is, to use religious language, for the safety of his soul. And when he yields, though I know, as he divines, that his life is lost, the emotion I feel is not pity: he is above pity and above life. And the anxiety itself is but slight: it bears no resemblance to the hopes and fears that agitate us as we approach the end in *Othello* or *King Lear*. The whole scene affects me, to exaggerate a little, more as a majestic picture of stationary figures than as the fateful climax of an action speeding to its close. And the structure of the drama seems to confirm this view. Almost throughout the first three acts—that is, up to the banishment—we have incessant motion, excited and resounding speech, a violent oscillation of fortunes. But, after this, the dramatic tension is suddenly relaxed, and, though it increases again, it is never allowed to approach its pre-

[3] *Shakespearean Tragedy*, p. 84.

vious height. If Shakespeare had wished it to do so in this scene, he had only to make us wait in dread of some interposition from Aufidius, at which the hero's passion might have burst into a fury fatal even to the influence of Volumnia. But our minds are crossed by no shadow of such dread. From the moment when he catches sight of the advancing figures, and the voice of nature—what he himself calls "great nature"—begins to speak in his heart long before it speaks aloud to his ear, we know the end. And all this is in harmony with that characteristic of the drama which we noticed at first—we feel but faintly, if at all, the presence of any mysterious or fateful agency. We are witnessing only the conquest of passion by simple human feelings, and *Coriolanus* is as much a drama of reconciliation as a tragedy. That is no defect in it, but it is a reason why it cannot leave the same impression as the supreme tragedies, and should be judged by its own standard.

A tragedy it is, for the passion is gigantic, and it leads to the hero's death. But the catastrophe scarcely diminishes the influence of the great scene. Since we know that his nature, though the good in it has conquered, remains unchanged, and since his rival's plan is concerted before our eyes, we wait with little suspense, almost indeed with tranquility, the certain end. As it approaches it is felt to be the more inevitable because the steps which lead to it are made to repeat as exactly as possible the steps which lead to his exile. His task, as then, is to excuse himself, a task the most repugnant to his pride. Aufidius, like the tribunes then, knows how to render its fulfillment impossible. He hears a word of insult, the same that he heard then—"traitor." It is followed by a sneer at the most sacred tears he ever shed, and a lying description of their effect on the bystanders; and his pride, and his loathing of falsehood and meanness, explode, as before, in furious speech. For a moment he tries to check himself and appeals to the senators; but the effort seems only to treble his rage. Though no man, since Aufidius spoke, has said a word against him, he defies the whole nation, recalling the day of its shame and his own triumph, when

alone, like an eagle, he fluttered the dovecotes in Corioli.
The people, who had accompanied him to the marketplace, splitting the air with the noise of their enthusiasm,
remember their kinsfolk whom he slaughtered, change
sides, and clamor for his death. As he turns on Aufidius,
the conspirators rush upon him, and in a moment, before
the vision of his glory has faded from his brain, he lies
dead. The instantaneous cessation of enormous energy
(which is like nothing else in Shakespeare) strikes us
with awe, but not with pity. As I said, the effect of the
preceding scene, where he conquered something stronger
than all the Volscians and escaped something worse
than death, is not reversed; it is only heightened by a renewed joy in his greatness. Roman and Volscian will have
peace now, and in his native city patrician and plebeian
will move along the way he barred. And they are in life,
and he is not. But life has suddenly shrunk and dwindled,
and become a home for pygmies and not for him.[4]

Dr. Johnson observed that "the tragedy of *Coriolanus*
is one of the most amusing of our author's performances."
By "amusing" he did not mean "mirth-provoking"; he
meant that in *Coriolanus* a lively interest is excited and
sustained by the variety of the events and characters; and
this is true. But we may add that the play contains a good
deal that is amusing in the current sense of the word—
more of this, it has been observed, than do the other
Roman tragedies. When the people appear as individuals
they are frequently more or less comical. Shakespeare
always enjoyed the inconsequence of the uneducated

---

[4] I have tried to indicate the effect at which Shakespeare's imagination
seems to have aimed. I do not say that the execution is altogether adequate.
And some readers, I know, would like Coriolanus to die fighting. Shakespeare's idea is probably to be gathered from the hero's appeal to the
senators to judge between Aufidius and him, and from the word "lawful"
in the last speech:

> O that I had him,
> With six Aufidiuses, or more, his tribe,
> To use my lawful sword!

He is not before the people only, but before the senators, his fellow-
patricians, though of another city. Besides—if I may so put it—if Coriolanus were allowed to fight at all, he would have to annihilate the whole
assembly.

mind, and its tendency to express a sound meaning in an absurd form. Again, the talk of the servants with one another and with the muffled hero, and the conversation of the sentinels with Menenius, are amusing. There is a touch of comedy in the contrast between Volumnia and Virgilia when we see them on occasions not too serious. And then, not only at the beginning, as in Plutarch, but throughout the story, we meet with that pleasant and wise old gentleman, Menenius, whose humor tells him how to keep the peace while he gains his point, and to say without offense what the hero cannot say without raising a storm. Perhaps no one else in the play is regarded from beginning to end with such unmingled approval, and this is not lessened when the failure of his embassy to Coriolanus makes him the subject as well as the author of mirth. If we regard the drama from this point of view we find that it differs from almost all the tragedies, though it has a certain likeness to *Antony and Cleopatra*. What is amusing in it is, for the most part, simply amusing, and has no tragic tinge. It is not like the gibes of Hamlet at Polonius, or the jokes of the clown who, we remember, is digging Ophelia's grave, or that humor of Iago which for us is full of menace; and who could dream of comparing it with the jesting of Lear's fool? Even that Shakespearean audacity, the interruption of Volumnia's speech by the hero's little son, makes one laugh almost without reserve. And all this helps to produce the characteristic tone of this tragedy.

The drawing of the character of Aufidius seems to me by far the weakest spot in the drama. At one place, where Aufidius moralizes on the banishment of the hero, Shakespeare, it appears to some critics, is himself delivering a speech which tells the audience nothing essential and ends in desperate obscurity.[5] Two other speeches have been criticized. In the first, Aufidius, after his defeat in the field, declares that, since he cannot overcome his rival in fair fight, he will do it in any way open to him, however dishonorable. The other is his lyrical cry of rapture when Coriolanus discloses himself in the house at

[5] But Prof. MacCallum's defense of this passage is perhaps successful

Antium. The intention in both cases is clear. Aufidius is contrasted with the hero as a man of much slighter and less noble nature, whose lively impulses, good and bad, quickly give way before a new influence, and whose action is in the end determined by the permanent pressure of ambition and rivalry. But he is a man of straw. He was wanted merely for the plot, and in reading some passages in his talk, we seem to see Shakespeare yawning as he wrote. Besides, the unspeakable baseness of his sneer at the hero's tears is an injury to the final effect. Such an emotion as mere disgust is out of place in a tragic close; but I confess I feel nothing but disgust as Aufidius speaks the last words, except some indignation with the poet who allowed him to speak them, and an unregenerate desire to see the head and body of the speaker lying on opposite sides of the stage.

Though this play is by no means a drama of destiny, we might almost say that Volumnia is responsible for the hero's life and death. She trained him from the first to aim at honor in arms, to despise pain, and to

> forget that ever
> He heard the name of death;

to strive constantly to surpass himself, and to regard the populace with inhuman disdain as

> things created
> To buy and sell with groats.

Thus she led him to glory and to banishment. And it was she who, in the hour of trial, brought him to sacrifice his pride and his life.

Her sense of personal honor, we saw, was less keen than his; but she was much more patriotic. We feel this superiority even in the scene that reveals the defect; in her last scene we feel it alone. She has idolized her son; but, whatever motive she may appeal to in her effort to move him, it is not of him she thinks; her eyes look past him and are set on Rome. When, in yielding, he tells her that she has won a happy victory for her country, but a victory most dangerous, if not most mortal, to her son, she answers nothing. And her silence is sublime.

These last words would be true of Plutarch's Volumnia. But in Plutarch, though we hear of the son's devotion, and how he did great deeds to delight his mother, neither his early passion for war nor his attitude to the people is attributed to her influence, and she has no place in the action until she goes to plead with him. Hence she appears only in majesty, while Shakespeare's Volumnia has a more varied part to play. She cannot be majestic when we see her hurrying through the streets in wild exultation at the news of his triumph; and where, angrily conquering her tears, she rails at the authors of his banishment, she can hardly be called even dignified. What Shakespeare gains by her animation and vehemence in these scenes is not confined to them. He prepares for the final scene a sense of contrast which makes it doubly moving and impressive.

In Volumnia's great speech he is much indebted to Plutarch, and it is, on the whole, in the majestic parts that he keeps most close to his authority. The open appeal to affection is his own; and so are the touches of familiar language. It is his Volumnia who exclaims, "here he lets me prate like one i' the stocks," and who compares herself, as she once was, to a hen that clucks her chicken home. But then the conclusion, too, is pure Shakespeare; and if it has not majesty, it has something dramatically even more potent. Volumnia, abandoning or feigning to abandon hope, turns to her companions with the words:

> Come, let us go:
> This fellow had a Volscian to his mother;
> His wife is in Corioli, and his child
> Like him by chance. Yet give us our dispatch:
> I am hush'd until our city be a-fire,
> And then I'll speak a little.[6]

Her son's resolution has long been tottering, but now it falls at once. Throughout, it is not the substance of her appeals that moves him, but the bare fact that she ap-

---

[6] What she will utter, I imagine, is a mother's dying curse.

peals. And the culmination is that she ceases to appeal, and defies him. This has been observed by more than one critic. I do not know if it has been noticed[7] that on a lower level exactly the same thing happens when she tries to persuade him to go and deceive the people. The moment she stops, and says, in effect, "Well, then, follow your own will," his will gives way. Deliberately to set it against hers is beyond his power.

Ruskin, whose terms of praise and blame were never overcautious, wrote of Virgilia as "perhaps the loveliest of Shakespeare's female characters." Others have described her as a shrinking submissive being, afraid of the very name of a wound, and much given to tears. This description is true; and, I may remark in passing, it is pleasant to remember that the hero's letter to his mother contained a full account of his wounds, while his letter to his wife did not mention them at all. But the description of these critics can hardly be the whole truth about a woman who inflexibly rejects the repeated invitations of her formidable mother-in-law and her charming friend to leave her house; who later does what she can to rival Volumnia in rating the tribunes; and who at last quietly seconds Volumnia's assurance that Coriolanus shall only enter Rome over her body. Still these added traits do not account for the indefinable impression which Ruskin received (if he did not rightly interpret it), and which thousands of readers share. It comes in part from that kind of muteness in which Virgilia resembles Cordelia, and which is made to suggest a world of feeling in reserve. And in part it comes from the words of her husband. His greeting when he returns from the war, and she stands speechless before him:

> My gracious silence, hail!
> Wouldst thou have laugh'd had I come coffin'd home,
> That weep'st to see me triumph? Ah, my dear,
> Such eyes the widows in Corioli wear,
> And mothers that lack sons:

his exclamation when he sees her approaching at their last meeting and speaks first of her and not of Volumnia:

⁷ Yes, it is noticed by Prof. MacCallum.

What is that curtsy worth, or those doves' eyes
Which can make gods forsworn? I melt, and am not
Of stronger earth than others;

these words envelop Virgilia in a radiance which is reflected back upon himself. And this is true also of his
praise of Valeria in the lines perhaps most often quoted
from this drama:

> The noble sister of Publicola,
> The moon of Rome, chaste as the icicle
> That's curdied by the frost from purest snow,
> And hangs on Dian's temple: dear Valeria!

I said that at one point the hero's nature *was* in a high
degree imaginative; and it is here. In his huge violent
heart there was a store, not only of tender affection, but
of delicate and chivalrous poetry. And though Virgilia
and Valeria evoke its expression we cannot limit its range.
It extends to the widows and mothers in Corioli; and we
feel that, however he might loathe and execrate the people, he was no more capable of injury or insult to a
daughter of the people than Othello, or Chaucer's Knight,
or Don Quixote himself.

POSTSCRIPT

Professor Case, in the Introduction to his admirable
Arden edition of *Coriolanus,* while approving the interpretation suggested in this paragraph of the change in the
hero's mind, withholds his assent to the stress laid in the
paragraph on the particular idea of the *burning* of Rome.
Instead of arguing the question I will simply describe the
way in which the emphasis on that particular idea came
to impress me.

When I was studying the play afresh with a view to
this lecture, I noticed that, as the action approached its
climax, the image of fire, not present to me before, became increasingly present, persistent and vivid; and at
last, when Cominius, reporting his futile embassy to the
hero, exclaims,

> I tell you he does sit in gold, his eye
> Red as 'twould burn Rome,

I said to myself, "Yes, *that* image of vengeance is what came to him in the solitude of his exile and has now become a possession." And, if I could have doubted this, doubt would have vanished when I reached Volumnia's speech (v.iii.131), and read the words, its *final* words,

> Yet give us our dispatch:
> I am hushed until our city be a-fire,
> And then I'll speak a little.

The "possession" is shattered, and the catastrophe sure— and welcome.

Dismissing imagination, I have now made a research, and some readers may be interested in the result.

Throughout the greater part of the play, though there is plenty of fighting and Corioles is taken, we hear, I think, nothing of any burning of towns or cities. There is a mention of fire at II.1.263–65, but it is the fire of contention between the hero and the people; and the "burning" and "fires" of III.ii.24 and III.iii.68 are those of hell; and even at IV.iii.20–25, where the image of fire is decidedly more vivid, this fire is that of the anger of the two parties in Rome. But in IV.vi.79, 83, 86, 116, 138, we have crowded and vivid references to the burning of the Roman territory by the army of Coriolanus, and to the prospect of his burning the city. And then, after a short scene, comes, at V.i.14, 17, 27, 32 (where Cominius makes the report of his interview and repeats the words of Coriolanus) fire-image after fire-image, the series culminating at 64 in that of the "eye red as 'twould burn Rome." In the next scene (7, 47, 72) the series, naturally, continues; but in V.iii. where Volumnia is to appear, it ceases (for the hero is inwardly beginning to yield), until it reappears in her final words. And, after that, we have only the reference (V.v.3) to the "triumphant fires" in the saved city.

WYNDHAM LEWIS

from *The Lion and the Fox*

Troilus and Cressida, Professor Schelling says, is "the only play in which we feel that his [Shakespeare's] charity and equanimity for the moment failed him and turned to bitterness and cynicism." That is a statement that appears to me typically sentimentalist and untrue. For is it not possible to match out of *Lear, Timon, Hamlet, Macbeth,* the "bitterest" that can be found in *Troilus*? The *cynical railer, altofronto* type, is one to which Shakespeare, far from being averse, seems particularly partial. Hamlet or Jaques provide incessant and deeply "bitter" examples. It seems beyond all contradiction that, however that statement affects your opinion of this gigantic poet, the *altofronto* mood was a permanent and characteristic one with him. That (accepting it, as best you can) you have to reconcile it with the "heroism" of his Antonys, Hectors and Othellos. No more than you can get a unity of time and place with Shakespeare can you get a unity of soul.

Before going further into this I will repeat the judgments at which I have arrived. In a sense, perhaps, Falstaff was Shakespeare's knight, as Don Quixote was the knight of Cervantes. For in the sphere of comedy, of tragicomedy, that is the natural parallel. And Sir John is the antithesis of Don Quixote. But Shakespeare had another, and almost a separate, department; and that was full of quixotic shapes. Timon, Coriolanus, Brutus, Hamlet, *are all Quixotes.* Only he sees them all, except perhaps Othello, more coldly than Cervantes saw his *hijo seco,*

From *The Lion and the Fox* by Wyndham Lewis. London: Methuen & Co. Ltd., 1951; New York: Hillary House, Inc., 1955. Reprinted by permission of Methuen & Co. Ltd.

save when something like a sexual excitement seems to take possession of him, and he begins caressing and adoring his hero as though he were a woman—like another Antonio in front of a Sebastian, in *Twelfth Night*.

To take only one of these—and I will choose the one that introduces naturally the next point that we shall have to take up—Coriolanus. That is the great creation that establishes Shakespeare—for those who want to see him as such—as "the feudal poet." Coriolanus is the demented "aristocrat," the incarnation of violent snobbery. In that, as in most Elizabethan plays, you get the invective against the "multitude." The spirit of Marston is found in it in full force; though there is nowhere in it as convinced an "aristocratism" as terminates the following lines from *Antonio and Mellida*:

> O rotten props of the craz'd multitude,
> How you still double, falter, under the lightest chance
> That strains your veins! Alas, one battle lost,
> Your whorish love, your drunken healths—your houts
>   and shouts,
> Your smooth God save's, and all your devil's last
> That tempts our quiet to your hell of throngs!

But Coriolanus, as a figure, is of course the super-snob. Of all Shakespeare's heroes he is the coldest, and the one that Shakespeare himself seems to have felt most coldly towards. He was the child of Volumnia, not of Shakespeare, and one that never became anything but a schoolboy, crazed with notions of privilege and social distinction, incapable of thinking (not differing in that from the rest of Shakespeare's nursery of colossi), but also congealed into a kind of machine of unintelligent pride. He is like a Nietzschean, artificial "aristocrat," with little nobility in the sense that Don Quixote caricaturally embodied the noble, but possessing only a maniacal intolerance and stiffness.

There is a hollowness in the "heroics" in Coriolanus. But no hero could ever expect to be quite safe with the author of *Troilus and Cressida*. The following description, for instance, of the behavior of the little son of Coriolanus by a friend of the family is "true to life," but too true not to have been observed with a mind detached from any infatuation with the speakers. It is impossible that this picture of a little Coriolanus growing up "just like his father" is not meant to illuminate Coriolanus for us:

> *Valeria.* O' my word, the father's son; I'll swear, 'tis a very pretty boy. O' my troth, I looked upon him o' Wednesday half an hour together; has such a confirmed countenance. I saw him run after a gilded butterfly; and when he caught it, he let it go again; and after it again; and over and over he comes, and up again; catched it again: or whether his fall enraged him, or how 'twas, he did so set his teeth; and tear it. O, I warrant, how he mammocked it!
> *Volumnia.* One on's father's moods.
> *Valeria.* Indeed, la, 'tis a noble child.
> *Virgilia.* A crack, madam.

"*Indeed, la, 'tis a noble child*" is a remark that would certainly not pass the censorship in a despotic super-feudal state, or recommend its author to a Nietzschean. And had Shakespeare wished to engage the sympathy of almost any audience with this fine little fellow, he certainly would not have chosen such a pretty and also flimsy thing as a butterfly to show him wracking one of his "father's moods" on.

It would appear that Shakespeare means at this point to show us the true Coriolanus, a cruel and stupid child, and to show him to us through the eyes of what he conceived to be a typical member of this early Roman society, Valeria, "dear Valeria"—"as chaste as an icicle," of the same composition as Volumnia. So it would appear, and why should we not accept that as Shakespeare's intention? But there are, of course, many reasons why such things should be bowdlerized, as it were, by the critic. But Shakespeare is full of scandalous matter that has to be hushed up. When the critic arrives at certain passages in *Lear* or *Macbeth* (as regards *Troilus and Cressida* he ignores the whole thing as far as possible) he will refer in a sober voice to this little "lapse from sanity" of Shake-

speare, and then hurry on. Edgar's remark about his
father's blindness in the fifth act of *King Lear* is one of
these:

> The gods are just, and of our pleasant vices
> Make instruments to plague us:
> The dark and vicious place where thee he got,
> Cost him his eyes.

That is one of Shakespeare's more notorious "lapses."
Troilus and Cressida is one vast "lapse," and *Timon* is almost another. But, in spite of these disturbing phenomena,
the improper nature of much that is spread everywhere
through all the plays is denied or ignored. And so in
process of time whole plays, like *Coriolanus,* have received
an interpretation that is contradicted everywhere in the
play itself. Sir James Robertson, for instance, in writing
of *Coriolanus,* treats Valeria and the chip-of-the-old-block
episode as follows:

"It was probably a circumstantial accident that gave
us, in addition to those incomparable portraits of women,
yet a third, that of Valeria, who . . . has strictly nothing
to do with the action of the play save to suggest anew,
by her account of the boy Marcius, how even admirable
women may miseducate children. Shakespeare is careful
to insist on her nobility and charm by putting a warm
eulogium of her in the mouth of Coriolanus; but had
before introduced her as enjoying the episode of the child
rending a butterfly in pieces."

He had indeed "before introduced her" in the act of
enjoying the spectacle of this promising young chief engaged in a characteristic Roman sport, and preparing
himself for the martial preoccupations of the life that
awaited him. But we are not to suppose that Shakespeare
meant her to be anything less than noble, and possessed
of the greatest charm. Indeed, has he not been "careful
to insist on" this in a "warm eulogium of her in the mouth
of Coriolanus"? (The "warm eulogium" referred to is, of
course, when Coriolanus later describes her as "an icicle.")

Now this in manner and in matter is very typical of

English Shakespearian criticism. If the play is read with any interest and attention, this version of Sir James Robertson's of a charming "lady of great nobility," in the case of Valeria, will be seen as what it is—the deferential euphuism of a highly respectable upper-servant of the old English school. That large class of able middle-class men, domiciled in universities, of the type of the correct and snobbish family solicitor, usually ending life with a few irrelevant honors, is responsible as a rule for Shakespeare criticism. Sir James Robertson is better than that, but still is of that genus of critics. Shakespeare, both in the circumstances of a rough and bitter life, and in the vigor and recklessness of his mind, will not fit that social framework. So, as we have said, most Shakespeare criticism comes to be a mild adaptation and bowdlerization, the sort of meaningless respectability of the English professional man smeared over everything that looks too stark, or that would seem to make it difficult to describe Shakespeare subsequently as "with a kindly twinkle in his eye," or as "a gentleman": "gentle" alone ("gentle Shakespeare") would not be regarded as possessing any particular relevance.

So the Valeria episode is explained by Sir James Robertson as showing how "even admirable women may miseducate children." And there is an end of it: it means nothing more than that: it is an unfortunate episode, undoubtedly—it leaves an unfortunate impression: but it is introduced by the poet after one of those incessant readings of Montaigne (in which he seems to have spent most of his time), and is a little burst of educationalist enthusiasm—nothing more! The picture is paradoxically put into the mouth of *a most charming and well-bred woman*; which again may have been intended by this most ingenious of poets to show how strong *custom* is, and how it may induce even the most gracious of gentlewomen to let slip a few remarks that might be misunderstood by someone not familiar—ahem!—with the *natural kindliness* that is such a characteristic of the nobility and gentry—ahem—of any land or period of history!

This episode of the little budding Coriolanus is, how-

ever, with the utmost consistency, typical of the play and
Shakespeare's treatment of Coriolanus from beginning to
end. It is an astonishingly close picture of a particularly
cheerless and unattractive snob, such as must have pullu-
lated in the court of Elizabeth, and such as the English
public-school and university system has produced ever
since. He is a fearless and efficient leader in war, with
every opportunity of training, and the stimulus of self-
interest, to be such—and nothing else. In every other
respect he is a glum, vain and extremely peevish dog, always abusing a crowd of supers for not incessantly flattering him, and furthering his interests and those of
Volumnia; with exhortations to deeds of matchless heroism, for which, if they performed them, they would receive
nothing but further abuse, bearing largely on the respective diet of the carefully kept dog in the fine marble kennel
and the ill-kept dog in the mud one. Both these species
have their faults, and Coriolanus is allowed to hit off those
of the rabble with sufficient force; as when he chides them:

> He that depends
> Upon your favors swims with fins of lead
> And hews down oaks with rushes. Trust ye? Hang ye!
> With every minute ye do change your mind,
> And call him noble that was now your hate,
> Him vile that was your garland.

But since his own small senatorial crowd prove themselves equally undependable, and are separated by almost
as wide a trench from his demented ideal of authority,
this abuse remains a Timon-like outpouring of unreason
from the point of view of life's realities. Menenius
Agrippa, Cominius or Titus Lartius are the real workaday
"aristocrats," and are as much strangers to an ideal of
inflexible authority as are the people themselves: and
naturally veer to the popular side when this quixotic doc-
trinaire pushes them to uphold the letter of their superiority.

In war the "thunder-like percussion" of his "sounds"
is a martial rhetoric Shakespeare was very capable of

measuring. And therewith Aufidius sounds the Machiavellian note—which caused Coleridge so much embarrassment: when the Volscian leader says that as he is unable to beat him fairly, as "man to man," he must "potch at him some way," a Volscian soldier remarks, "He's the devil!" referring to Coriolanus; and Aufidius replies:

> Bolder, though not so subtle. My valor's poison'd
> With only suffering stain by him,

and we then get the Achilles-Hector situation, with the same frantic and luscious sensuality of strife that is reproduced in the battlefield rivalries of the Greek and Trojan captains, and in the case of Hotspur and Prince Hal.

The confrontation of Coriolanus and his mother, Volumnia, in Act III, scene 2, is the most characteristic of the piece, and gives the true interpretation of Coriolanus. He is shown there as the child, drilled into a second nature which goes on mechanically obeying. His mother —whose ultra-Roman despotism has been shown in other scenes—has coached and formed him into the madman he is. Then, when he comes fresh from acting on her teaching, to his own undoing, he is suddenly, with a naïve confusion, confronted with his mother's disapproval. And the obedient schoolboy, rebuked for doing what he has been taught to do, turns with baffled reproach on his teacher:

> *Coriolanus.* I muse my mother
> Does not approve me further, who was wont
> To call them woolen vassals; things created
> To buy and sell with groats, to show bare heads
> In congregations, to yawn, be still, and wonder,
> When one but of my ordinance stood up
> To speak of peace or war.
>   [*Enter* VOLUMNIA]
>   I talk of you:
> Why did you wish me milder? Would you have me
> False to my nature? Rather say I play
> The man I am.

Volumnia. O, sir, sir, sir,
I would have had you put your power well on,
Before you had worn it out.
    Cor. Let go.
    Vol. You might have been enough the man you are,
With striving less to be so.

This scene between Coriolanus and his mother is the key to the play: it shows Coriolanus as the rigid and hyp-notized schoolboy influenced in his most susceptible years by a snobbish and violent parent, and urged into a course of destruction, which, the machine of an idea, he mes-merically pursues: it is now too late even for the master-mind to pull him up.

The scene to which this critical confrontation of the mother and son should be compared is the last scene of all, when he is killed by Aufidius and his followers. The word with which he is dismissed from the scene of this world is "Boy," and he is shown as resenting it very much indeed.

    Aufidius. He has betray'd your business, and given up,
For certain drops of salt, your city Rome
(I say "your city") to his wife and mother;
Breaking his oath and resolution, like
A twist of rotten silk; never admitting
Counsel o' the war; but, at his nurse's tears,
He whin'd and roar'd away your victory;
That pages blush'd at him, and men of heart
Look'd wondering at each other.
    Cor. Hear'st thou, Mars?
    Auf. Name not the god, thou boy of tears!
    Cor. Ha!
    Auf. No more.
    Cor. Measureless liar, thou hast made my heart
Too great for what contains it. Boy! O slave!—
Pardon me, lords, 'tis the first time that ever
I was forc'd to scold.

But during the ensuing lines he goes on repeating "Boy!"—which epithet appears to have entirely over-powered him:

Cor. Cut me to pieces, Volsces; men and lads,
Stain all your edges on me.—Boy! false hound!
If you have writ your annals true, 'tis there,
That, like an eagle in a dovecote, I
Flutter'd your Volscians in Corioli:
Alone I did it.—Boy!

"Boy" is almost the last word of Coriolanus. The action of his little son as described by Valeria is one of the things that anyone would chiefly remember in the play, and is the thing in it to which the critics naturally turn, and which they have to explain away to fit their substituted picture. And the child-parent situation is the mechanism of the piece in any case. Since we possess a great deal of evidence as to what Shakespeare thought of military glory and martial events, we have no reason to suppose that the military heroics in *Coriolanus* are of a different order to what they are elsewhere. There is the curious demented sensuality that he is fond of attributing to military rivals, but which is not an element calculated to increase the atmosphere of respect at their feats of daring: it even makes them—the Hotspurs, Achilles, Hals and so forth—a little ridiculous. As to this feudal poet's courtly leanings, I do not think they are proved. He is quite ready to support his characters when the moment arrives for them to abuse the "many-headed multitude" (which was the usual term—"we have been called so of many," the Citizen in Act II, scene 3, says). Shakespeare no doubt agreed with all the abuse his puppet Coriolanus was called upon to hurl at the Roman crowd. It would very nearly describe what Shakespeare probably felt about the London crowd of his time, and especially as he came in contact with it at the theatre. But from this to supposing that he had discriminated between this crowd and that other smaller crowd to which Coriolanus belonged —the crowd that thronged the more expensive seats of the Bankside theatres—is a long step of snobbish unreason and self-deception that we have no right to assume Shakespeare at all likely to have taken. For him *l'un vaudrait l'autre,* I expect. For it was human nature about

which Shakespeare wrote, and he did not write on a tone
of morals, nor on one of class prejudice or class illusion.

Coriolanus is no more a play to exhibit the virtues and
destinies of the aristocrat (with a strong propaganda for a
severe oligarchical form of government, and a strong snobbish illusion about the graceful advantages of the aristocratic life) than it is a play of educationist propaganda,
whether for or against a certain type of training. It is a
play about a conventional military hero, existing as the
characteristic ornament of a strong aristocratic system.
Shakespeare was neither for or against him, on propa-
gandist, feudal or nonfeudal grounds. He was quite ready
to curse the crowd with him: and he was equally ready
to examine with as little pleasure the child of a harsh
practical system, abusing his many advantages, and showing to perfection how the top, as likewise the under, dog
is unsatisfactory and foolish, the one very nearly worthy
of the other—the violent, dull, conceited leader, and the
resentful but cowardly slave. Meantime the play is charged
with a magnificent rhetoric, as wherever any character
utters Shakespeare's blank verse. Coriolanus speaks frequently like a god; also the *altofronto* tone is adopted by
him from time to time, as by most Shakespeare heroes—
his banter and bitterness being often just the same as that
of Hamlet, Timon or Lear. But that is Shakespeare's own
voice and manner that you hear, the central surge, that,
wherever the music he is making excites him, comes out
and is heard. What belongs properly to Coriolanus is not
meant by Shakespeare to be attractive: he shows none of
the sympathy for him that he does for Othello, Antony
or Timon. Yet he is cast for the lion part; and Shakespeare
gives him, as remarked above, his portion of magnificent
music. Also he has to the full one of the great requisites
of the Shakespearian *lion;* he is completely helpless, child-
like, truthful and unfortunate. So it is the rôle, rather
than the figure filling it, that would set the tragic organ
playing.

The *fox* is there too; the tribunes Sicinius and Brutus
supply the Iago element very adequately, except that no
unpopularity is concentrated on them.

D. A. TRAVERSI

from *An Approach to Shakespeare*

Coriolanus has rarely satisfied the critics. Most of them have found it frigid and have even suggested that Shakespeare's interest flagged in the writing of it; on the other hand, an important minority—including T. S. Eliot and J. Middleton Murry—have been considerably attracted by the play, and have even found an important place for it in the development of their own experience.[1] The only point upon which there seems to be agreement is that *Coriolanus* is difficult and that its artistic quality is peculiar. Even sympathetic critics must account for the fact that the figure of the hero is harsh and at times grotesque, while Aufidius' behavior is puzzling and inconsistent. It is the task of a critical interpretation of the play to decide whether these contradictions are part of the stuff of the author's experience, or whether they are only the odds and ends left over by imperfect assimilation.

The mastery displayed in the verse of *Coriolanus* does not suggest declining powers or lack of interest. There is an interesting example of this in the very first verse speech of the play, when Menenius rebukes the citizens for their mutterings:

> For your wants,
> Your suffering in this dearth, you may as well
> Strike at the heaven with your staves as lift them
> Against the Roman state; whose course will on

[1] See J. Middleton Murry's essay on "A Neglected Heroine of Shakespeare," *Countries of the Mind* (London, 1922) and, for T. S. Eliot, the essay on *Hamlet* (*Selected Essays*) and the two poems entitled "Coriolan."

From *An Approach to Shakespeare* by D. A. Traversi. London: Sands & Co. (Publishers) Ltd., 1938. Reprinted by permission of Sands & Co. (Publishers) Ltd.

> The way it takes, cracking ten thousand curbs
> Of more strong link asunder than can ever
> Appear in your impediment. For the dearth,
> The gods, not the patricians, make it, and
> Your knees to them, not arms, must help.   (I,i)

It is impossible not to feel that this is an example of the unique, free mastery of Shakespeare's later verse. We should be aware of the conciseness of the last sentence, of the way in which the "not arms" parenthesis enables us to grasp the essential contrast without the distraction that would result from a full statement of the alternatives; it is a telescoping of language that follows the movement of living thought. More important is the way in which the rhythm of the earlier lines serves to develop a nervous power in the words, expressing the irresistible motion of tremendous and unfeeling force. Once more, the force is not only stated but given concrete embodiment in the movement of the verse. The division of "cracking" and "asunder," both words which carry with them strong feelings of physical separation, bear the reader over the intervening words so that this experience partakes of the irresistible movement of the Roman state. The emotional impetus thus created is then brought to a sudden curb by the ending of the sentence in the middle of the familiar blank verse unit of the line, an ending prepared for and emphasized by the decisive Latin word "impediment." The movement of the verse, in fact, is that of a poet who is in complete mastery of his medium, which has become a pliant instrument to express the subtle movement of his consciousness. It is sufficient to suggest that *Coriolanus* is a great play.

I have quoted the passage, however, less to establish Shakespeare's powers of versification than to introduce the issues with which the play deals. The central feeling of the speech is clearly that suggested by the phrase "strike at the heaven with your staves," and emphasized in the nervous strength of the passage as a whole. To be certain of this, we may reinforce the impression of "staves" by referring to Menenius' talk of the citizens' "bats and clubs" just above, echoed once more by "stiff bats and clubs" in the course of the same argument. Professor Wilson Knight, in *The Imperial Theme*,[2] acutely pointed out that these phrases, and others of the same kind, give a peculiar sensation of hardness and ruthless impenetrability to the play. In other words, the sense of social stiffness and utter incompatibility is woven by Shakespeare into the emotional texture of his work, and gives a peculiar tone to the political and social study which underlies it. The "bats and clubs" of the contending parties strike at one another in a closed universe; the "heavens," with all their associations of light and "grace," remain rigid and impenetrable, so that we can almost hear the "stiff" weapons clang when raised against them. This sense of hard hostility is essential to *Coriolanus,* and is repeated, as we shall see, in the play's attitude toward war and in the character of the hero himself. For the present, we shall merely note the vividness of Shakespeare's political study of Roman conditions, the sense of a social order hardened into insensibility on the one hand and unworthiness on the other, the patricians and the people utterly out of contact with one another, hard, hostile, exclusive in their attitude. The patricians have no contact with the people; Menenius' speech stresses their merciless lack of feeling and responsibility, and Coriolanus himself caricatures his warlike valor in the following speech:

> Would the nobility lay aside their ruth,
> And let me use my sword, I'd make a quarry,
> With thousands of these quartered slaves, as high
> As I could pick my lance. (I,i)

This perversion of the traditional speech of warlike heroes is a masterpiece of irony. On the other hand, the people are weak, worthless, and brutal, easily led astray by the scheming tribunes, and quite incapable of seeing beyond the selfish ends of the moment.

All this is more or less apparent. Much more important is the image under which Shakespeare develops this

[2] London, 1932.

discord and gives it significance. The theme is a variation of that of "degree," so prominent in *Troilus and Cressida,* but here less "metaphysically" and more socially conceived. The verse of *Troilus,* however, even that given to Ulysses, is not equal to that of *Coriolanus* in the precision which denotes mastery of experience; the comparative lack of organization which accompanies the extraordinary complexity of the language in the earlier play indicates, as we have seen, a mind overwhelmed by a superabundance of new conceptions—conceptions which will need to be worked out in the developing pattern of the tragedies. As in *Troilus,* however, the essential image which Shakespeare chose to give point to his study is that of the functioning of the human body. As usual, it appears almost at once in order to set clearly the tone of the play. Menenius develops it fully in his fable to the citizens:

> There was a time when all the body's members
> Rebell'd against the belly; thus accused it:
> That only like a gulf it did remain
> I' the midst of the body, idle and unactive,
> Still cupboarding the viand, never bearing
> Like labor with the rest; where the other instruments
> Did see and hear, devise, instruct, walk, feel,
> And, mutually participate, did minister
> Unto the appetite and affection common
> Of the whole body. (I,i)

Now this speech and the discussion which follows are based on North's Plutarch, but are there stated in the abstract manner of the moralist, occupying only a few lines and in no way suggesting the individuality of Shakespeare's version. Upon this basis the poet created a fundamental criticism of Roman society—fundamental precisely because it was not merely political, but based upon a sensation of fine living developed through the whole pattern of the tragedies. The speech has been so worded, in short, as to invest a political commonplace with Shakespeare's own sense of poetic significance.

The first point to notice concerns the quality of feeling

conveyed by the verse. The prevailing tone is one of idleness, of stagnation, of a general obstruction of everything that suggests life and activity. We note before everything the unhealthy heaviness of "idle and unactive," and the direct coarseness implied by the vernacular of "cupboarding." Then we find this contrasted with the very noticeable livening of the verse when Menenius comes to speak of "the other instruments," the senses and active parts of the body. This balance of two contrasted elements, the keenness of the senses carrying with it a related feeling of sluggishness and physical repulsion, is already evident in the earlier plays. Here, too, this intensity of feeling is connected with the contrasted baseness and satiation of lust. The feeling of the speech is given another subtle turn by the reference to "the appetite and affection common." "Appetite" has behind it associations with the "universal wolf" of Ulysses' great speech, as well as with frequent Elizabethan references to incontinence; the latter are further strengthened by the word "common," so often used by Shakespeare's contemporaries to indicate promiscuity. The fable conveys then a feeling, very like that of *Troilus,* of a social organism in disorder and decay, an impression further strengthened by the prominence given to the idea of food and the process of digestion. Greed and satiety are the main images by which we are prepared for the tragedy of *Coriolanus.*

So far, in substance if not in detail, we have most of the critics with us. It is generally recognized that there are elements of disorder and decadence in the Rome presented in this play. But there is also a feeling that the author's sympathies were with the patricians. This view, however, immediately lands us in the perplexities already indicated, on the strength of which this tragedy has so often been condemned as a failure. If Coriolanus is really the "hero," and the patricians on the whole an admirable class, why is his behavior so inconsistent, not to say degrading? A moment's consideration of this same speech will show us that the scope of Shakespeare's political analysis is much more ample than many of his critics would have us believe. For the patricians are presented to us in the likeness of the "belly," with the result that there is an essential contrast between their stagnation and their indispensability. Menenius criticizes justly the failure of the populace to play a proper part in the social organism; but the figure he chooses to elaborate his point turns the argument equally against his own position. Though the belly was indispensable to the proper working of the body, it was also "idle and unactive," self-satisfied in the security of its position; in this connection we should note that brilliant stroke:

> With a kind of smile,
> Which ne'er came from the lungs, but even thus . . .
>
> (I,i)

with its fine balance between the comic and the complacent. Shakespeare goes even further. He gives to the First Citizen some of the most bitter and penetrating words in the whole discussion. There is no hiding the force with which the "cormorant belly" and "the sink o' the body" cut through the complacent assumption of superiority recorded by Menenius. Lastly, we should not pass over Shakespeare's ambiguous attitude toward the belly as distributor of food to the whole body; if it gives life to the rest of the body, it is also the receptacle of the worthless bran.

The result of this speech then is a very acute apprehension of the condition of a social organism, as revealed through the power of a living and penetrating sensibility. We are shown a populace incapable of discerning its own good, vicious and vulgar, and needing the leadership of a class superior to itself. On the other hand, we are also shown a patrician class who have forfeited their right to superiority by showing a complete selfishness and lack of responsibility. They are, in fact, merely subsisting on a position gained in the more or less distant past. Both these factions are set in an iron social framework which permits no contact, no community of interests, nothing but repression on one side and animal discontent on the other. That is the full intention of the inflexible quality of Menenius' first speech.

Having provided as a background such a many-sided social study, Shakespeare was not likely to place in the foreground a hero whom he regarded as a simple and romantic warrior struck down by the worthless and ungrateful people. Even those who have tended to this view have always been baffled by the way in which the play stresses both Coriolanus' proud obstinacy and his unnatural lack of feeling for the whole setting of his past life. It is more hopeful to approach him through the feeling expressed in the war poetry of the play, and more particularly by Cominius in his eulogy at the Capitol:

> His pupil age
> Man-enter'd thus, he waxed like a sea;
> And, in the brunt of seventeen battles since,
> He lurch'd all swords of the garland. . . .
> . . . as weeds before
> A vessel under sail, so men obey'd,
> And fell below his stern: his sword, death's stamp,
> Where it did mark, it took; from face to foot
> He was a thing of blood, whose every motion
> Was timed with dying cries: alone he enter'd
> The mortal gate of the city, which he painted
> With shunless destiny; aidless came off,
> And with a sudden reinforcement struck
> Corioli like a planet: now all's his:
> When, by and by, the din of war 'gan pierce
> His ready sense; then straight his doubled spirit
> Requicken'd what in flesh was fatigate,
> And to the battle came he; where he did
> Run reeking o'er the lives of men, as if
> 'Twere a perpetual spoil; and till we call'd
> Both field and city ours, he never stood
> To ease his breast with panting.   (II,ii)

It is impossible not to feel at once that this is Shakespeare at his mature best; who else would have used that bold comparison "man-enter'd," in which explicitness is waived in favor of speed and immediacy of expression? The verse moves with the utmost ease and freedom, a perfectly plastic medium for catching shifts of feeling;

such a shift is recorded in the emphasized contrast between the splendor of "he waxed like a sea" and the leaden reality of "lurch'd" and "brunt." These things are conveyed easily to a reader who is prepared for them; the voice is carried irresistibly by rhythms which are always based on living speech to the proper emphasis, the delicately felt pause by which Shakespeare so often converts the statement of a fact into its apprehension by a completely sensitive response. The line

> And with a sudden reinforcement struck
> Corioli . . . ,

with its telling isolation of "struck" at the end of the line, is an outstanding example; it produces the sense of weighty and fatal pressure which is so essential to the impression aimed at.

So we come to the feeling of the speech. In it Shakespeare is using his unique capacity for compressing the feelings that underlie his exploration of a situation into the unity of a single utterance, whose central images are conversely radiated out into the surrounding matter, of which they serve at once as a concentration and a point of departure. It is in this sense that the mature plays could be described, from the point of view of their poetic structure, as organic, the product of a sensibility whose life was not only diffused through a play but concentrated into every part of it. The speech gives us a peculiar impression of Coriolanus as a warrior. It stresses at once his energy, his splendid and superabundant life, and his heaviness, his cruelty, almost his fantastic absurdity; and the two are part of the same man. The first of these qualities is expressed not only in the rich, splendid image we have already noted—"he waxed like a sea"—but it is also given a definite living quality, a fine nervous delicacy in:

> . . . the din of war 'gan pierce
> His ready sense; then straight his doubled spirit
> Requickened what in flesh was fatigate . . .

This superb sensitive response to "the din of war" is not new in *Coriolanus*. We are carried back to Othello's reaction to "the spirit-stirring drum, the ear-piercing fife," which gives the same impression of the senses at work at the confines of their intensity. War gives rise here to a fine keenness of feeling that is only paralleled by Shakespeare's reaction to love in certain scenes of *Antony and Cleopatra*. It is, indeed, worth remembering that the two plays were written at the same period, for we shall see that there is some association between their respective treatment of love and war.

All this does not mean, of course, that Shakespeare was a crude and ignorant enthusiast for war. He had already, in his earlier period, made a thorough study of the political implications of patriotism in *Henry V* and, if certain aspects of the character of Coriolanus recall Othello, they also suggest how the related strength and weakness of the tragic hero is here used to add mature depth to the treatment of a political theme. The greatness of this speech depends, indeed, upon the manner in which there is intertwined with the sense of superb vitality a dead heaviness, which culminates in an almost grotesque insensibility. That is the reason why the munificence of "he waxed like a sea" is immediately qualified by the ponderous impact of "brunt" and "lurch'd." It should be seen, further, that these lines deal with Coriolanus' growth into manhood. They suggest perfectly the double process which Shakespeare saw and conveyed in his verse in the history of the great soldier. On the one hand, Coriolanus grew into the full development of his powers, the complete expression of his maturity. On the other, his new power converted itself more and more, with success, into heaviness and indifference to life, into an exclusion of the very qualities of sensitivity which maturity should have crowned. So we pass through the splendid and ruthless image of the "vessel under sail" to the description of the sword as "death's stamp," a description which gives it the destructive weight and inflexibility of a battering ram. These things prepare us for the entry of a mechanical warrior, a man turned into an instrument of war, grotesquely indifferent to the suffering he has caused:

> ... from face to foot
> He was a thing of blood, whose every motion
> Was timed with dying cries.   (II,ii)

This impression is further reinforced by the suggestion of
an irresistible impact behind "planet," which helps to
make him no longer a mere warrior, but an "instrument"
(the word is significant in view of what we have already
said about the battering ram) "of shunless destiny"
against "the mortal gates of the city." In the word "mortal"
is contained not only an expression of helplessness but a
protest on the part of downtrodden life against this in-
sentient minister of fate. Then, to balance the argument,
comes that remarkable quickening of the machine which
we have already noted, a quickening followed, however,
by the renewed grotesque callousness of:

> ... he did
> Run reeking o'er the lives of men, as if
> 'Twere a perpetual spoil,   (II,ii)

and we are left with Coriolanus "panting" like a hot-
blooded bull after his orgy of destruction. In this way,
right through Cominius' eulogy, a balance is held which
is essential to a proper reading of the play.

In case it should be thought that too much stress has
been laid on a single passage, it can easily be shown how
this balance is preserved throughout the play and is,
indeed, an integral part of its structure. There is the
feeling of the iron mechanical warrior in the earliest
scenes, as when Titus Lartius speaks of:

> ... thy grim looks and
> The thunder-like percussion of thy sounds;   (I,iv)

and, at the end, when Coriolanus seems to be on the
point of taking his revenge on Rome, we have a very
remarkable prose passage from Menenius:

MENENIUS: The tartness of his face sours ripe grapes:

when he walks, he moves like an engine, and the
ground shrinks before his treading: he is able to pierce
a corslet with his eye; talks like a knell, and his hum
is a battery. He sits in his state, as a thing made for
Alexander. What he bids to be done is finished with
his bidding. He wants nothing of a god but eternity
and a heaven to throne in.

SICINIUS: Yes, mercy, if you report him truly.

MENENIUS: I paint him in the character. Mark what
mercy his mother shall bring from him; there is no
more mercy in him than there is milk in a male tiger.

(V,iv)

This is a fine example of the prose of Shakespeare's late
period, prose which is not content to develop the facts
of a situation, but is informed with the same continual
consciousness of the emotional unity of the play as that
which is reflected in the verse. Passing by that fine enlist-
ment of the palate in the opening image, we come once
more to a description of the human war-machine, this
time absolutely explicit. The later part of the speech suggests not only the grotesque lack of human feeling in this
machine but also the futility of this artificial insensibility.
This comparison of Coriolanus' pretensions with a state of
divinity was clearly Shakespeare's expression of a fundamental criticism, for he had already put it once into the
mouth of the tribunes. Brutus had said:

> You speak of the people,
> As if you were a god to punish, not
> A man of their infirmity.   (III,i)

On a great many accounts of the play it would be very
hard to explain the wisdom of these utterances given to
the otherwise detestable tribunes. But, as we have suggested, Shakespeare's insight was keener than that of his
critics, and so the tribunes are allowed to throw the
clearest light of all upon the futility which is undeniably
part of Coriolanus' character. This vanity, moreover, is
brought home to us by a further stroke of irony, for we
know, as Menenius does not, that this supposedly in-

flexible warrior has not only self-consciously paraded his firmness before Aufidius—

> Shall I be tempted to infringe my vow,
> In the same time 'tis made? I will not . . .

> Aufidius, and you Volsces, mark; for we'll
> Hear naught from Rome in private. Your request?—
>   (V,iii)

but has capitulated at the very moment of his posing. As Aufidius says, with a bitter cynicism which is part of the spirit of this play:

> At a few drops of women's rheum, which are
> As cheap as lies, he sold the blood and labor
> Of our great action . . .   (V,vi)

That, at least, is one aspect of Coriolanus' career as a warrior.

The other aspect, however, as we have already suggested in discussing Cominius' speech, is equally present. There is no question that this play connects the action of war with a sense of splendid and living ecstasy. The most obvious example is to be found in the scene where Coriolanus first meets Aufidius, after his exile, and the Volscian general addresses him in the following terms:

>   Let me twine
> Mine arms about that body, where against
> My grained ash an hundred times hath broke,
> And scarr'd the moon with splinters: here I clip
> The anvil of my sword, and do contest
> As hotly and as nobly with thy love
> As ever in ambitious strength I did
> Contend against thy valor. Know thou first,
> I loved the maid I married; never man
> Sigh'd truer breath; but that I see thee here,
> Thou noble thing! more dances my rapt heart
> Than when I first my wedded mistress saw
> Bestride my threshold.   (IV,v)

The note of exaltation reminds us once more of *Antony and Cleopatra*. Here too the life that expresses itself in war is communicated in terms of love. From Aufidius' behavior in this play, we should not have expected him to express ecstasy (if, indeed, such a word were within the compass of his experience) in terms of his own emotions in love. But the justification, of course, is less in character than in the emotional makeup of the play. In character the discrepancy between poetry and behavior helps to emphasize the dual nature of Aufidius, poised strangely between heroism and treachery prompted by jealous selfishness, just as Coriolanus, in Cominius' speech, is poised between divinity and insensibility. But these divergences of personal principle are only products of the disharmony to be found in the social analysis of the play, and this analysis is in turn a projection of the original poetic mood. The martial exaltation of Coriolanus and Aufidius is counterbalanced by their respective brutality and treachery, in the same way that the superior keenness and vividness of the senses in Menenius' opening parable is necessarily attached to the grossness of the "cormorant belly" from which they try in vain to free themselves.

A type of poetry identical in quality with that which we have just discussed in Aufidius is also to be found in Coriolanus himself, as we shall see if we consider some of the speeches, which are among his finest, made when he returns to his family after his triumph at Corioli. Outstanding among them, perhaps, is:

> My gracious silence, hail!
> Would'st thou have laugh'd had I come coffin'd home,
> That weep'st to see me triumph?[3]   (II,i)

The experience with which the critic of *Coriolanus* has to establish contact is one that, while forming a single emotional whole, has to include the divergence between this and the warrior who "moves like an engine" over the corpses he has battered to death. That is the central contradiction, to which those in Aufidius' behavior are

[3] This passage and others like it in the play have been admirably discussed by J. Middleton Murry in his essay above mentioned [i.e., in "A Neglected Heroine of Shakespeare," *Countries of the Mind*].

merely subsidiary. There is a split at the heart of Shakespeare's experience which introduces a division into the fabric of his play, both at Rome and Corioli. That split, already to be observed in the dramatist's presentation of the related strength and weakness of his tragic heroes and in the attitude which these heroes adopt towards themselves, is related to a political study of the type originally presented in the English historical plays and here taken up in the light of the intervening tragic development. The sensation of life expressed in terms of passion, worked out so triumphantly at certain moments in Antony, is here studied, at the same period, in its relationship to war; and war is seen as a product of the same life, but one which tends to the death which is its opposite. *Coriolanus,* in fact, is at once the complement of *Antony and Cleopatra* and its reversal. In the latter play defeat in war becomes, in some sense and for the duration of certain scenes, the prelude to a triumph in the vitality of love; in *Coriolanus* victory in war is accompanied by a callous hardening of feeling, which only reasserts itself to give an ironic note to the hero's fate.

It is worthwhile, at this point, to refer a little more fully to the irony of the play, which gives it a note not easily squared with its usual definition as a tragedy; this fact helps, perhaps more than any other, to account for the prevalent critical uneasiness. This irony is, as in all Shakespeare's political plays, a critical irony; that is, it springs out of a vigilant hostility to unsustained pretensions and unexamined enthusiasms. Perhaps its most successful expression is that exposure of the characters of Volumnia and Valeria (I,iii), which shows the lack of human feeling in Coriolanus to be rooted in the outlook of his family, and so, in turn, in the general social maladjustments we have already discussed. In this way the scene has an important structural position, for it serves to connect the personal tragedy of Coriolanus with the wider social study. The scene is an invention of Shakespeare's; one cannot imagine that Plutarch would have thought of Valeria speaking of Coriolanus' son in this way:

O' my word, the father's son; I'll swear, 'tis a very pretty
boy. O' my troth, I looked upon him o' Wednesday half
an hour together; he has such a confirmed countenance.
I saw him run after a gilded butterfly; and when he caught
it, he let it go again; and after it again; and over and over
he comes, and up again; catched it again: or whether his
fall enraged him, or how 'twas, he did so set his teeth and
tear it; O, I warrant, how he mammocked it!   (I,iii)

The whole passage is a sufficient exposure of the deadly
lack of feeling which surrounds Coriolanus, and of which
he partakes; indeed, it is emphasized that the boy is
"the father's son." To complete the impression, we need
only the crushing irony implicit in Valeria's comment:
"Indeed, la, 'tis a noble child." The author of this scene
was the same who had once written Falstaff's penetrating
remarks on "honor" in the assured balance of a spirit
that was not less artistic for being truly critical. Instead
of Sir Walter Blunt's "grinning honor" we have Volumnia's ideal:

. . . had I a dozen sons . . . I had rather eleven die nobly
for their country than one voluptuously surfeit out of
action.

But in *Coriolanus* the clear-sighted outlook of *Henry IV*
is reinforced by the experience gained in the whole body
of the tragedies, so that it becomes part of an emotional
whole more complex than itself. A good deal in the study
of the hero was taken from traditional sources; Plutarch,
according to North, had already suggested that Coriolanus
was "so cholericke and impacient, that he would yeeld
to no liuing creature: which made him churlishe, unciuill,
and altogether unfit for any man's conuersation." It is
also true that there was a substantial precedent in traditional farce for the refusal to accept a great classical warrior at the most heroic estimate; Shakespeare had done
this himself in *Troilus and Cressida*. When the Roman
soldiers refuse to follow Coriolanus into the gates of the
besieged city (I,iv), and when he scolds them with most

unheroic vituperation in the same scene, his behavior was
not strange to an Elizabethan mind. Only the scholars
might be shocked.

When all this has been conceded, however, there remains the essence of Shakespeare's achievement to be
accounted for. As we have suggested, the greatness and
uniqueness of this play are due to the fact that Shakespeare judged the political situation in Rome in the light
of his own experience developed in the tragedies. The
failure of Coriolanus is a failure in sensitivity, a failure
in living; and it represents a failure on the part of a whole
society. The hero is shown always in relation to that
society, and conditioned by it; it explains him, and his
tragedy illuminates it. Perhaps the fundamental quality of
the verse reflects the sense of a continual clash between
a certain fineness of sensibility and an iron rigidity which
accompanies and contrasts with it. Some of these contrasts are expressed by incidental comparisons that have
a magnificent tactual immediacy; such are:

> When steel grows soft as the parasite's silk,   (I,ix)

and:

> . . . nature,
> Not to be other than one thing, not moving
> From the casque to the cushion, but commanding peace
> Even with the same austerity and garb
> As he controll'd the war . . .   (IV,vii)

where the first gives an immediate impression of different
and opposed textures in the closest contact, and where
the second emphasizes the contrast between the casques
and the cushion by the rigid strength given in "austerity
and garb." Such passages indicate the quality of this play.
In it we find a sensation of life expressed in terms of a
transcendent passion, but continually chafing against the
iron of an unnatural rigidity, which is reflected in a stiffness in family relations and in a hardened social order.
Coriolanus' great lyric passages are not continual and

spontaneous, like those of Antony at his best moments. They seem rather to burst out against a perpetual restraint, to be produced by a continual friction against the iron insensibility which he has inherited. Coriolanus is hopelessly divided between his unnatural discipline of "honor" and his natural, but incompletely mature, humanity. That is the real source of the play's irony, and the reason why he never carries any course of action to its complete fulfillment. His "honor" is turned by his class and family into a willingness, if only temporary, to gain power at any price. There are few things in Shakespeare more ironic than the way Coriolanus has to use his wounds to gain election to the consulship; but, having debased himself, his natural pride intervenes, and he falls. But, precisely because he is divided, his reaction does not reinstate him as a heroic character, but expresses itself in petulant and ridiculous curses against "the common cry of curs," "the reek o' the rotten fens," the people whom he has just courted to gain power. The same contradiction is seen in his last exploits. Egoism has always prompted him to his wars; we are told in the opening dialogue that his prowess was due to his desire "to please his mother, and to be partly proud." It drives him to neglect all natural feeling and to return at the head of his former enemies to sack Rome. Such a change, after his sworn hatred of Aufidius, is in itself ironic. But this inhuman project cannot overcome the other part of his nature—what should have been in a harmonious personality normal feeling but is in his divided state weakness—so that he gives up his idea in the very moment of success. Such division and paralysis can only end in his rather absurd and ironic death. Shakespeare makes him die indignant at being called "Boy!" by those whom he had once beaten, in a mixture of "scolding" (by his own confession) and an attempt to justify himself in the light of his past exploits. This justification is felt to be the final proof of the tragic futility of his career.

Suggested References

The number of possible references is vast and grows alarmingly. (The *Shakespeare Quarterly* devotes a substantial part of one issue each year to a list of the previous year's work, and *Shakespeare Survey*—an annual publication—includes a substantial review of recent scholarship, as well as an occasional essay surveying a few decades of scholarship on a chosen topic.) Though no works are indispensable, those listed below have been found helpful.

1. Shakespeare's Times

Byrne, M. St. Clare. *Elizabethan Life in Town and Country*. Rev. ed. New York: Barnes & Noble, Inc., 1961. Chapters on manners, beliefs, education, etc., with illustrations.

Craig, Hardin. *The Enchanted Glass: the Elizabethan Mind in Literature*. New York and London: Oxford University Press, 1936. The Elizabethan intellectual climate.

Joseph, B. L. *Shakespeare's Eden: The Commonwealth of England 1558–1629*. New York: Barnes & Noble, Inc., 1971. An account of the social, political, economic, and cultural life of England.

Nicoll, Allardyce (ed.). *The Elizabethans*. London: Cambridge University Press, 1957. An anthology of Elizabethan writings, especially valuable for its illustrations from paintings, title pages, etc.

Shakespeare's England. 2 vols. Oxford: The Clarendon Press, 1916. A large collection of scholarly essays on a wide variety of topics (e.g., astrology, costume, gardening, horsemanship), with special attention to Shakespeare's references to these topics.

Tillyard, E. M. W. *The Elizabethan World Picture*. London: Chatto & Windus, 1943; New York: The Macmillan Company, 1944. A brief account of some Elizabethan ideas of the universe.

Wilson, John Dover (ed.). *Life in Shakespeare's England*. 2nd ed. New York: The Macmillan company, 1913. An anthology of Elizabethan writings on the countryside, superstitions, education, the court, etc.

2. Shakespeare

Barnet, Sylvan. *A Short Guide to Shakespeare*. New York: Harcourt Brace Jovanovich, Inc., 1974. An introduction to all of the works and to the traditions behind them.

Bentley, Gerald E. *Shakespeare: A Biographical Handbook*. New Haven, Conn.: Yale University Press, 1961. The facts about Shakespeare, with virtually no conjecture intermingled.

Bradby, Anne (ed.). *Shakespeare Criticism, 1919–1935*. London: Oxford University Press, 1936. A small anthology of excellent essays on the plays.

Bush, Geoffrey Douglas. *Shakespeare and the Natural Condition*. Cambridge, Mass.: Harvard University Press; London: Oxford University Press, 1956. A short, sensitive account of Shakespeare's view of "Nature," touching most of the works.

Chambers, E. K. *William Shakespeare: A Study of Facts and Problems*. 2 vols. London: Oxford University Press, 1930. An invaluable, detailed reference work; not for the casual reader.

Chute, Marchette. *Shakespeare of London*. New York: E. P. Dutton & Co., Inc., 1949. A readable biography fused with portraits of Stratford and London life.

Clemen, Wolfgang H. *The Development of Shakespeare's Imagery*. Cambridge, Mass.: Harvard University Press, 1951. (Originally published in German, 1936.) A temperate account of a subject often abused.

Craig, Hardin, *An Interpretation of Shakespeare*. Columbia, Missouri: Lucas Brothers, 1948. A scholar's book designed for the layman. Comments on all the works.

Dean, Leonard F. (ed.). *Shakespeare: Modern Essays in Criticism*. New York: Oxford University Press, 1957. Mostly mid-twentieth-century critical studies, covering Shakespeare's artistry.

Granville-Barker, Harley. *Prefaces to Shakespeare*. 2 vols. Princeton, N.J.: Princeton University Press, 1946–47. Essays on ten plays by a scholarly man of the theater.

Harbage, Alfred. *As They Liked It*. New York: The Macmillan Company, 1947. A sensitive, long essay on Shakespeare, morality, and the audience's expectations.

————. *William Shakespeare: A Reader's Guide*. New York: Farrar, Straus, 1963. Extensive comments, scene by scene, on fourteen plays.

Ridler, Anne Bradby (ed.). *Shakespeare Criticism, 1935–1960*. New York and London: Oxford University Press, 1963. An excellent continuation of the anthology edited earlier by Miss Bradby (see above).

Schoenbaum, S. *Shakespeare's Lives*. Oxford: Clarendon Press, 1970. A review of the evidence, and an examination of many biographies, including those by Baconians and other heretics.

————. *William Shakespeare: A Compact Documentary Life*. New York: Oxford University Press. 1977. A readable presentation of all that the documents tell us about Shakespeare.

Smith, D. Nichol (ed.). *Shakespeare Criticism*. New York: Oxford University Press, 1916. A selection of criticism from 1623 to 1840, ranging from Ben Jonson to Thomas Carlyle.

Spencer, Theodore. *Shakespeare and the Nature of Man*. New York: The Macmillan Company, 1942. Shakespeare's plays in relation to Elizabethan thought.

Stoll, Elmer Edgar. *Shakespeare and Other Masters*. Cambridge, Mass.: Harvard University Press; London: Oxford University Press, 1940. Essays on tragedy, comedy, and aspects of dramaturgy, with special reference to some of Shakespeare's plays.

Traversi, D. A. *An Approach to Shakespeare*. Rev. ed. New York: Doubleday & Co., Inc., 1956. An analysis of the plays, beginning with words, images, and themes, rather than with characters.

Van Doren, Mark. *Shakespeare*. New York: Henry Holt & Company, Inc., 1939. Brief, perceptive readings of all of the plays.

Whitaker, Virgil K. *Shakespeare's Use of Learning*. San Marino, Calif.: Huntington Library, 1953. A study of the relation of Shakespeare's reading to his development as a dramatist.

3. Shakespeare's Theater

Adams, John Cranford. *The Globe Playhouse*. Rev. ed. New York: Barnes & Noble, Inc., 1961. A detailed conjecture about the physical characteristics of the theater Shakespeare often wrote for.

Beckerman, Bernard. *Shakespeare at the Globe, 1599–1609*. New York: The Macmillan Company, 1962. On the playhouse and on Elizabethan dramaturgy, acting, and staging.

Chambers, E. K. *The Elizabethan Stage*. 4 vols. New York: Oxford University Press, 1923. Reprinted with corrections, 1945. An indispensable reference work on theaters, theatrical companies, and staging at court.

Gurr, Andrew. *The Shakespearean Stage 1574–1642*. Cambridge: Cambridge University Press, 1970. On the acting companies, the actors, the playhouses, the stages, and the audiences.

Harbage, Alfred. *Shakespeare's Audience*. New York: Columbia University Press; London: Oxford University Press, 1941. A study of the size and nature of the theatrical public.

Hodges, C. Walter. *The Globe Restored*. London: Ernest Benn, Ltd., 1953; New York: Coward-McCann, Inc., 1954. A well-illustrated and readable attempt to reconstruct the Globe Theatre.

Kernodle, George R. *From Art to Theatre: Form and Convention in the Renaissance*. Chicago: University of Chicago Press, 1944. Pioneering and stimulating work on the symbolic and cultural meanings of theater construction.

Nagler, A. M. *Shakespeare's Stage*. Tr. by Ralph Manheim. New Haven, Conn.: Yale University Press, 1958. An excellent brief introduction to the physical aspect of the playhouse.

Smith, Irwin. *Shakespeare's Globe Playhouse*. New York: Charles Scribner's Sons, 1957. Chiefly indebted to J. C. Adams' controversial book, with additional material and scale drawings for model-builders.

Venezky, Alice S. *Pageantry on the Shakespearean Stage*. New York: Twayne Publishers, Inc., 1951. An examination of spectacle in Elizabethan drama.

4. Miscellaneous Reference Works

Abbott, E. A. *A Shakespearean Grammar*. New edition. New York: The Macmillan Company, 1877. An examination of differences between Elizabethan and modern grammar.

Berman, Ronald. *A Reader's Guide to Shakespeare's Plays,*
rev. ed. Glenview, Ill.: Scott, Foresman and Company,
1973. A short bibliography of the chief articles and books
on each play.

Bullough, Geoffrey. *Narrative and Dramatic Sources of
Shakespeare.* 5 vols. Vols. 6 and 7 in preparation. New
York: Columbia University Press; London: Routledge &
Kegan Paul, Ltd., 1957–. A collection of many of the
books Shakespeare drew upon.

Campbell, Oscar James, and Edward G. Quinn. *The Reader's
Encyclopedia of Shakespeare.* New York: Thomas Y.
Crowell Co., 1966. More than 2,700 entries, from a few
sentences to a few pages on everything related to Shakespeare.

Greg, W. W. *The Shakespeare First Folio.* New York and
London: Oxford University Press, 1955. A detailed yet
readable history of the first collection (1623) of Shakespeare's plays.

Kökeritz, Helge. *Shakespeare's Names.* New Haven, Conn.:
Yale University Press, 1959; London: Oxford University
Press, 1960. A guide to the pronunciation of some 1,800
names appearing in Shakespeare.

———. *Shakespeare's Pronunciation.* New Haven, Conn.:
Yale University Press; London: Oxford University Press,
1953. Contains much information about puns and rhymes.

Linthicum, Marie C. *Costume in the Drama of Shakespeare
and His Contemporaries.* New York and London: Oxford
University Press, 1936. On the fabrics and dress of the age,
and references to them in the plays.

Muir, Kenneth. *Shakespeare's Sources.* London: Methuen &
Co., Ltd., 1957. Vol. 2 in preparation. The first volume, on
the comedies and tragedies, attempts to ascertain what
books were Shakespeare's sources, and what use he made
of them.

Onions, C. T. *A Shakespeare Glossary.* London: Oxford University Press, 1911; 2nd ed., rev., with enlarged addenda,
1953. Definitions of words (or senses of words) now obso-
lete.

Partridge, Eric. *Shakespeare's Bawdy.* Rev. ed. New York:
E. P. Dutton & Co., Inc.; London: Routledge & Kegan
Paul, Ltd., 1955. A glossary of bawdy words and phrases.

Shakespeare Quarterly. See headnote to Suggested References.

Shakespeare Survey. See headnote to Suggested References.

Smith, Gordon Ross. *A Classified Shakespeare Bibliography*

1936–1958. University Park, Pa.: Pennsylvania State University Press, 1963. A list of some 20,000 items on Shakespeare.

5. *Coriolanus*

Brockbank, Philip, ed. *The Arden Edition of the Works of William Shakespeare: Coriolanus*. London: Methuen & Co., Ltd., 1976.

Browning, I. R. "Coriolanus—'Boy of Tears,'" *Essays in Criticism*, 5 (1955), 18–31.

Charney, Maurice (ed.). *Discussions of Shakespeare's Roman Plays*. Boston: D. C. Heath & Company, 1964. (Selections by Samuel Johnson, Paul A. Jorgensen, Willard Farnham, and D. J. Enright).

Ellis-Fermor, Una. *Shakespeare the Dramatist*. London: Methuen & Co., Ltd., 1961.

Frye, Dean. "Commentary in Shakespeare: The Case of Coriolanus," *Shakespeare Studies*, *1*, ed. J. Leeds Barroll. Cincinnati: University of Cincinnati, 1965, pp. 105–17.

Farnham, Willard. *Shakespeare's Tragic Frontier*. Berkeley, Calif.: University of California Press; London: Cambridge University Press, 1950.

Heuer, Herman. "From Plutarch to Shakespeare: A Study of Coriolanus," *Shakespeare Survey 10*, ed. Allardyce Nicoll. New York and London: Cambridge University Press, 1957, pp. 50–59.

Holloway, John. *The Story of the Night*. London: Routledge & Kegan Paul, Ltd., 1961.

Kitto, H. D. F. *Poiesis: Structure and Thought*. Cambridge: Cambridge University Press, 1966.

Knight, G. Wilson. *The Imperial Theme. Further Interpretations of Shakespeare's Tragedies Including the Roman Plays*. New York and London: Oxford University Press, 1931; 3rd ed., London: Methuen & Co. Ltd., 1951.

Knights, L. C. *Some Shakespearean Themes*. Stanford, Calif.: Stanford University Press, 1959; London: Chatto & Windus, 1959.

MacCallum, M. W. *Shakespeare's Roman Plays and their Background*. London: Macmillan and Co. Ltd., 1910.

MacLure, Millar. "Shakespeare and the Lonely Dragon," *University of Toronto Quarterly*, 24 (1955), 109–20.

Maxwell, J. C. "Animal Imagery in *Coriolanus*," *Modern Language Review*, 42 (1947), 417–21.

Murry, John Middleton. *John Clare and Other Studies.* New York and London: Peter Nevill Ltd., 1950.

Oliver, H. J. "Coriolanus as Tragic Hero," *Shakespeare Quarterly,* 10 (1959), 53–60.

Palmer, John. *Political Characters of Shakespeare.* London: Macmillan and Co. Ltd., 1945.

Rabkin, Norman. "*Coriolanus:* The Tragedy of Politics," *Shakespeare Quarterly,* 17 (1966), 195–212.

Sicherman, Carol. "Coriolanus: the Failure of Words," *ELH,* 39 (1972), 189–207.

Spencer, T. J. B. *Shakespeare: The Roman Plays.* New York: British Book Centre, Inc.; London: Longmans, Green & Co. Ltd., 1963.

Traversi, D. A. *Shakespeare: The Roman Plays.* Stanford, Calif.: Stanford University Press; London: Hollis & Carter, 1963.

Van Dyke, Joyce, "Making a Scene: Language and Gesture in *Coriolanus,*" *Shakespeare Survey 30,* ed. Kenneth Muir. London: Cambridge university Press, 1977, pp. 135–46.

Waith, Eugene. *The Herculean Hero.* New York: Columbia University Press; London: Chatto & Windus, 1962.